BEGINNER'S LUCK

BY LAURA PEDERSEN

Fiction
Beginner's Luck
Going Away Party

Nonfiction
Play Money

BEGINNER'S LUCK

Laura Pedersen

Ballantine Books • New York

Beginner's Luck is a work of fiction. Names, characters, places, and incidents are the products of the author's imagination or are used fictitiously. Any resemblance to actual events, locales, or persons, living or dead, is entirely coincidental.

A Ballantine Book
Published by The Random House Publishing Group

Published in the United States by Ballantine Books, an imprint of The Random House Publishing Group, a division of Random House, Inc., New York, and simultaneously in Canada by Random House of Canada Limited, Toronto.

This book contains an excerpt from the forthcoming book *The Big Shuffle* by Laura Pedersen. This excerpt has been set for this edition only and may not reflect the final content of the forthcoming edition.

www.thereaderscircle.com

ISBN 978-0-345-45830-8

Cover illustration by Paul Hess
Cover design by Monica Benalcazar
Text design by Nancy Singer

Manufactured in the United States of America

First Edition: January 2003

9 8 7 6

For all the teachers . . .

How does one reach for the stars without
a strong set of shoulders to stand upon?

It is inevitable when one has a
great need of something one finds it.

—*Gertrude Stein*

ACKNOWLEDGMENTS

♠

Special thanks to Carolyn Fireside for her passion and creativity and to Maureen O'Neal at Ballantine Books for her steadfast support. With everlasting gratitude to my literary agent, Judith Ehrlich, for her enthusiasm, continuous stream of ideas, love of stories, and most of all, her kindness and friendship. Ongoing appreciation for everyone back at the kibbutz—Willie, Julie, Aimee, Michael, Elliott, Cecilia, Lucy, and all the critters.

PROLOGUE

♠

Was there ever a single moment about which you later wondered, "What would my life be like now if *that* hadn't happened?" Would the present be the same or completely different? And do we really make choices about what will happen to us, or is it all in the hands of fate?

Some people like to say that things happen for a reason, while others insist that life is random. I'm not so sure I believe either one. Because anyone who has ever played poker knows that most wins involve a certain amount of skill and probability. On the other hand, you still need the cards. And you need them at the right moment.

My "moment" occurred in a grocery store, of all places, and my ace was a sign on a bulletin board. Whether it was fate, luck, or probability, I guess I'll never know. But as you'll soon see, it led to an incredibly bizarre chain of events that completely altered the direction of my life.

Of course now it's difficult to imagine what my world would be like had I *not* happened upon that sign at the exact second I did. But I'm sure of one thing, that I wouldn't be here telling you this story. In fact, I don't know if I'd still be here at all. And I definitely know that I wouldn't be me—a person who has come to understand that just as the words and the notes form the music, so do the people and places in our lives make us who we are.

1

Down and Out in Cosgrove County

♦

It's only midafternoon and already the whole day is a bust. I may only be a sixteen-year-old girl, but I'm an experienced gambler and so I believe in probability, not luck. However on days like this, you really have to wonder.

The air is hot and still and feels like a weight up against my chest. I push down hard on the pedals of my bike because I'm so aggravated. Who does that cheapskate Mr. Exner think he is, trying to give me fifty cents apiece for Titleist golf balls that were hit twice at most? Balls I can clearly see he's repackaging as *new* and hawking for twelve bucks a dozen. Meantime *I'm* the one with leeches all over my ass after dredging the swamp otherwise known as the Municipal Golf Course. Grown-ups love to chisel teenagers because they figure we don't really need the money, that we're only going to blow it on concerts and incense. And then they wonder why we start packing automatic weapons in our lunch boxes.

However, I decide to conserve my anger for this afternoon's soccer game. Our opponents, the Timpany Tigers, are a ferocious team—tall, mean, yellow-eyed, and all elbows. They live atop one of Ohio's thirty-eight hazardous waste sites, and obviously more than a few drums of toxic chemicals have seeped into their drinking water.

It's almost two o'clock when the school parking lot comes into view. Only thoughts are churning in my head like an out-of-control slot machine, so I forget to look before hanging a Louie and therefore don't notice the handicapped school bus creeping along behind me. Fade to blacktop.

I regain muscle movement in a hailstorm. The hard white golf balls clunking against my skull have acquired the velocity of flying soup cans. Bloody gravel-flecked road pizza now decorates my palms. And though my wrists are only bruised, it feels as if I've just arm-wrestled a security guard. Both elbows of my sweater are torn, and even though this outfit can't exactly be classified as women's better sportswear, Mom will be mad that it's headed for the trash instead of her beloved hand-me-down bin.

The driver of the bus, a middle-aged man in full Mr. Rogers cardigan and khakis regalia, dashes over with a look of awestruck terror—fearful of a lawsuit, yet secretly thrilled by the job security of another rider for his specially ramp-equipped vehicle.

"Are you all right?" His radio is poised, ready to call 911.

"I'm okay. My fault." Gradually I rise and check to ascertain whether all my limbs are still attached and look around to make sure I'm not seeing double. Only I'm seeing spots. Eighty-two white spots bouncing across the blacktop and into the gully, almost fifty bucks' worth of golf balls. Do I chase after them? No. I'll miss the last class and won't be allowed to play in the soccer game.

After adjusting the handlebars I remount my bike. The bus driver slowly follows me into the school parking lot. Part of me wishes he would just gun it and finish me off like a lame horse. The sunny September afternoon only serves to make the dark gray cinder-block building appear even more flat and gruesome than usual, if that's possible.

Aside from this particular architectural monstrosity the town is okay looking—stately old buildings like the courthouse and the public library with pitched roofs, a couple of white pillars out front, and stone carvings of people in togas with some leaves stuck in their hair. But Patrick Henry High School was built much later. Before that the district wasn't big enough to have its own public school. And when the Town Council finally did get around to building one they apparently hired an escaped mental patient who thought it would be a terrific idea to combine the steel and glass construction of a smelting plant with the concrete block design of a maximum-security prison. Walking through the metal doors, you basically expect someone in a warden's uniform to throw a pile of license plates, a brush, and a can of black paint your way and bark *start stenciling*. The institution certainly brings to mind the three R's—ropes, revolvers, and razor blades.

When I enter the building a bell alerts me that the next period starts in exactly two minutes. There's barely enough time to stop at my locker. As I grab my social studies notebook another bell heralds the start of the final class of the day.

It's not as if social studies is any great party I don't want to miss out on. But Mr. Graves, my teacher, also happens to be the soccer coach. And if he discovers that I wasn't in the brig all day he won't let me play. The other slow self-starters are busy trying to blend into the laminated Mercator projection world map covering most of the back wall. There's one chair left in the last row in front of New Zealand.

On his pudgy round face Mr. Graves wears square-shaped glasses with black plastic frames that double as bulletproof shields. They make his pupils appear to be contracting and expanding as he shifts his eyeballs from left to right, and so behind his back the kids call him Old Fish Eyes. He's chalked a list of the original thirteen colonies on the blackboard along with the names of the companies or individuals that founded them, in what year, when they received a charter, and their status in 1775. He could have distributed photo-copies of this list. But no, he's worried that life is too cushy for us, what with EraserMate pens and word processors. Back when he was in school kids probably had to hunt pterodactyls in order to make ink out of the blood.

With all the best intentions I carefully scribe *Hallie Palmer, Grade 11 S.S.* at the top of a clean white page with delicate aquamarine lines horizontally traversing it. However, the paper presents an opportunity to perform a few calculations of my own. With approximately twenty-one hundred dollars in the bank and the birthday money from my folks, if everything goes exactly according to plan, a used car should be within reach in two more weeks. Though if I'd taken Cheap Old Mr. Exner's offer of forty-one bucks for the stupid golf balls rather than insisted on waiting to shop them to Mr. Burke down at the hardware store, I wouldn't have wasted an entire morning's work.

Leaning my head back against the Tasman Sea on the smooth vinyl map, I nod off. The school may teach a lot about history, but somehow they missed the advent of the window shade. It must be a hundred degrees near the out-side wall. And I'd been up most of the night before handicapping tomorrow's horse races. A couple other kids are also slowly losing consciousness, as if fairy dust has been sprinkled, and eyelids simultaneously droop to Mr. Graves's hypnotic buzz: *Pine-forested Georgia, with the harbor of Savannah nourishing its chief settlement, was formally founded in 1733.*

When the ten-minute bell clangs like a fire alarm from out of the speaker above the round Seth Thomas wall clock, all the covert dozers, myself included, are jarred awake. The gaze of the entire class automatically drifts upward in the direction of the clock, which briefly shivers from the vibration, the second hand practically moving backward until the clattering subsides. Mr. Graves continues like an icebreaker crushing through the North Atlantic, but to no avail. It's Friday afternoon of homecoming weekend and the room is whirring with the sound of closing notebooks, giggling girls, crumpling papers, and the rasps of metal chairs scraping across the floor. For Mr. Graves to go on is like trying to halt sailors heading down the gangplank for a long-awaited shore leave. A boy in the second row hurls a softball-sized rubber band ball directly above Mr. Graves's head. It goes *thwack* just inches away from the top of his skull and bounces back into the fast hands of another student. Mr. Graves turns quickly (at least quickly for him) in an attempt to catch the perpetrator in the act. As he scans the classroom we all work hard at looking angelically innocent.

The end-of-class bell finally rings. As I follow the chattering crowd toward the hallway and freedom, I hear Mr. Graves intone "Hallie Palmer" as if he's about to begin the Reading of the Will. Pausing in front of his nicked-up wooden desk, I automatically scan the work surface to determine if he's in possession of any incriminating documents—referrals, bad test papers, unsigned permission slips. But there's nothing. Maybe I'm just getting busted for the catnap. Mr. Graves is so affectless that he never gives himself away. In fact, he'd make an excellent draw-poker player. You wouldn't be able to tell if he was bluffing, had a royal flush, or if he'd passed away from acute angina at some point during the hand. However, my own heart sinks when he opens with "I didn't see you at the pep rally this morning."

"Oh, yeah," I say, "I went to the library to catch up on—"

"The office sends me a copy of the absentee list every afternoon," he interrupts. "Do you think you can fool me by showing up for the last class of the day with torn clothes, fresh scrapes on your hands, and a sunburn?" he says as passionately as if he's reading aloud from a VCR manual. "You're off the team."

There's no point arguing. In his three centuries of teaching, Old Fish Eyes has heard it all—alien abductions, teen amnesia, seeing the Virgin Mary in your Bunsen burner during a chemistry lab and having her tell you to rush to the mall.

I nod my head and walk toward the door. I'm a firm believer in the convicts' code: Don't do the crime if you can't do the time.

"I'm sorry," he adds, with not a hint of remorse. "You're a good halfback. But if you're hurt on the field your parents' lawyer will sue the school district. And if you're not here for at least half the day, then the insurance company won't accept the liability."

And that's when I make my decision. They can't throw me off the team. Because I quit! And not only do I quit soccer, but I quit school, too. I'm outta here!

2

Count Me Out

♣

The first benefit of being a dropout is more satisfying than holding a trio of deuces in a game of low-ball poker. I'll no longer have to navigate the porn auditions in the hallways after school—couples leaning against institutional green lockers making out as if they might die over the weekend while playing Quake III on their computers and never cop another feel again as long as they live. Aside from the sex-starved, the only other kids left are those staying for sports, band, student government, or detention.

The bell rings to announce that if your butt is assigned to detention then that's where it had better be or else you've just upgraded yourself to in-school suspension. I automatically glance up at the aluminum framed clock bolted to the ceiling in the middle of the hallway. The entire student body is robotic in that we all involuntarily search for the nearest timepiece as soon as we hear a bell, even if it's just an oven timer at home.

Out of the corner of my eye I catch someone peering around the corner at the far end of the hallway. For a split second I think it might be Craig Larkin and my stomach does an involuntary flip. Another look, however, reveals a skinny ferretlike boy who is the complete opposite of Craig.

Creeping in my direction is fifteen-year-old Brandt Shaeffer. He skipped first grade after a teacher discovered him doing long division during the shoe-tying part of the program and so now he's in eleventh grade even though he's a year younger than everyone else. It makes a person wonder how such a stupid older sister like Sheryl could possibly have a smart younger brother like Brandt. I guess genes are a lot like poker and sometimes it's just the luck of the draw.

I walk in the opposite direction so as to dump all my notebooks into the oversized garbage pail by the stairwell, only Brandt darts in front of me, hunched over his enormous pile of books like a nervous chipmunk sneaking off with an overly large nut that he fears will be expropriated by a flying squirrel.

"Hi, Hallie," he croaks in that ever-shifting contralto voice which sounds as if permanent orange juice mucus is lodged in his throat.

"Hi, Branch," I reply. This is what everyone calls him since he's tall and reed thin and runs on the cross-country team when the wind isn't strong enough to blow him over.

"What's new in your galaxy?" he asks.

"I've been kicked off the soccer team and I'm dropping out of school," I reply.

Obviously he thinks I'm joking or the comment doesn't even register. Most likely the latter, since it appears as if something heavy is on his mind, like he's just discovered that Einstein may have taken a wrong turn somewhere with that relativity stuff.

It's worth noting that Branch is drawn to me because I am also good in math. Only while he was the darling of the elementary school for his problem-solving prowess I was simultaneously being accused of cheating for getting the answers without showing my work. Brandt used his innate ability with numbers to analyze the universe, like with his science project on the Big Bang Theory that blew up half the classroom. I, on the other hand, became an enthusiast of probability theory, starting with crazy eights in kindergarten and working my way up to seven-card stud by the end of sixth grade. This was with the help of a private tutorial from Mr. Simmons, the elementary school janitor, who harbored no ethical dilemma when it came to taking lunch money off an eight-year-old.

Anyway, Brandt's always had this twisted notion that because we're both freaks we should stick together, or worse, that there exists a cosmic force in the universe that has destined us for each other.

"Ahem." He rearranges the phlegm in his throat. "I was wondering if you wanted to go to the homecoming dance."

Perfect opportunity for total high school cruelty. I think, *Yeah, Branch, I'd love to go to the homecoming dance. Only not with you. Ha ha!*

"Thanks, Branch, but I have to baby-sit my little brothers and sisters."

"Oh, okay, well then maybe—"

I'm rescued by the sight of Jane coming down the stairs. "Oh, there she is!" I say as if I've been eagerly waiting for Jane and fly over to my best friend, who is rushing toward the front door, outfitted in her customary running shorts, T-shirt, and softball spikes.

"I didn't want to intrude," Jane says sarcastically as I follow her outside. The Branch Crush has become a running joke. "You two make such a cute couple."

"Cut it out," I say and playfully push her on the shoulder.

She eyes the bacon rasher scrapes on my hands and knees and says, "Looks like social studies was interactive today."

We walk to the curb where my other friend Gwen is busy unloading a box of crepe paper and a big heap of pastel-colored tissues folded and then tied with green twist-ties to look like flowers.

"Oh, Hallie!" exclaims the clothing-conscious Gwen upon seeing my torn and bloodstained attire.

"What are you doing with all this junk?" I change the subject.

"Decorating the junior class float for the homecoming parade," says Jane. "Why don't you help us? We'll be in the parking lot right next to the football players." She gives me a knowing nudge, since my heartthrob Craig Larkin will of course be practicing with the team.

"I'd love to, but I have this incredible allergy to crepe paper."

"Then meet us at the pizza parlor later," says Gwen. "We'll save you some ribbons for your hair." She starts wrapping my head mummy-style with a bright pink streamer and I quickly ride off.

3

Loaded Dice

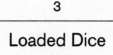

Saturday morning I awaken to the aroma of frying bacon and my fourteen-year-old sister Louise's annoying red and black pom-poms scraping against my face. It's definitely a game day.

"The superintendent called and Hallie's going to end up in R-E-F-O-R-M S-C-H-O-O-L." Louise spells out the final words in cheerleader style as if it's the name of the home team.

"Umm," I say sleepily and turn over.

At that moment the twins, Darlene and Davy, still in their flannel footsy pajamas with the trap doors, come twirling helter-skelter into our bedroom like uncontainable wildfire—six years old and a blur of bright red hair with orange freckles in flame-red pajamas.

"Mom and Dad want everyone downstairs right now," Davy exclaims breathlessly.

"They have thomething important to tell uth," Darlene lisps with excitement.

"I'll bet we're getting a puppy," concludes Davy.

A puppy. Yeah, right. Dream on. With nine people in this house there isn't room for a frigging fishbowl. "I wouldn't get too excited," I say. "Last time they called a meeting it was to announce that showers were being limited to three minutes and that if we didn't stop using the telephone so much Dad would install a pay phone."

In the kitchen we all take our places around the long wooden table, Dad sitting at one end, underneath the black metal plaque with GRACE etched onto it in gold letters, just in case anyone needs a prompter, and Mom at the opposite end, next to Francie, the baby, who is perched in her high chair with a fresh rope of snot dangling from her nose. Francie is almost three and so technically she's no longer a baby. But that's all anyone ever calls her, The Baby. If you have six older brothers and sisters I suppose that's all you'll ever be, even when you're fifty-five. Personally, I like my position as number two, since it's easy to vanish. Dad is working all of that jock stuff out of his system with firstborn Eric, and Mom is always busy propelling a youngster through potty training.

On the weekends breakfast is usually okay—scrambled eggs and bacon or pancakes. During the week it's crappy generic cereal with milk or instant oatmeal. Only by Wednesday the milk has usually run out and so we drink powdered cow, which tastes like watered-down baking soda. Usually I just skip breakfast at home and buy chocolate donuts on the way to school.

When we all finish eating—total chewing time about two minutes—Dad clears his throat and yells at Teddy to either eat his bacon strips or leave them on the plate, but to stop pretending they're worms and twisting them around the rungs of his fork.

Then Dad swipes at his mouth with a crumpled napkin and cheerily announces, "Your mother and I have some exciting news." I can deduce by my mom's nervous laughter that this is not "exciting" in the sense that we're all going to Disneyland or moving into a desperately needed larger house. "You're going to have a new little brother or sister," he says as if we can now begin the applause.

Davy and Darlene screech with delight and enthusiastically wriggle in their seats. And why not? It's someone brand-new for them to torture, the same way Eric and Louise and I used to hold their heads over the toilet bowl and flush it again and again while Mom and Dad were out bowling. Teddy looks blankly from Mom to Dad as if to say, *If you want to go to the store and buy another baby, what's that got to do with my baseball cards?* Teddy is ten, towheaded, skinny as a straw, and his only concern in life is to meet a Cleveland Indians baseball player and become the team water boy. I've helpfully suggested that he concentrate more on the mascot end of things.

Across the table square-shouldered Eric is hunched over his plate and certainly doesn't appear to be overly "excited." In fact, I know he's running the numbers to determine if there's any chance he'll have to triple up on a room. There isn't. But Eric has never been what one would call the Human Abacus, even when it comes to one-digit equations. We'd all better pray nothing happens to his right arm that would prevent him from making those long accurate passes out on the football field. When Eric finally does succeed in combining the birthrate with the existing architecture a look of great relief washes over his face like the sun emerging from behind the clouds, followed by a smile. "Congratulations," he says. "That's terrific, Mom." He kisses her on the cheek and excuses himself in order to get to the Astroturf. What a suck-up.

Eric truly has nothing to worry about. The baby probably arrives next April or May. By then he'll have a football scholarship to Indiana University and by the middle of August be out of here for good in order to start practice. The Hoosier coach has been covering his every move like an old lady playing ten bingo cards. Eric's got it made in the shade of the stadium and the electronic scoreboard.

Louise and I lock eyes across the table. If this is anything like Francie's arrival then we're going to get stuck making lunches, doing laundry, cleaning the house, and baby-sitting the twin terrors. And if it's a girl they'll move Darlene in with us. Sixteen is too old to be sleeping in Furby-infested bunk beds. Thank God I'll be long gone to Nevada by then. Dad catches our exchanged glances of horror and says in a gruff manner indicating that it would not be a good idea to be anything *but* very, very pleased, "Aren't you girls thrilled for your mother?"

"Of course," Louise manages to say with forced cheer.

Not able to make myself play the game, I bob my head while gulping down some watery orange juice made from concentrate. Mom purposely waters down all our juice to "stretch it." Likewise she mixes crushed oats into the ground chuck to make that go further. At this rate, make that *birthrate*, she's going to be mixing vats of wood pulp into our food after the new baby is born.

"Okay, everyone get ready for the big game." Dad claps his hands as if he's already applauding one of Eric's miraculous passes. Mom scrapes Francie's face with a spoon and then shoves the twice-eaten gruel back into her mush.

"Hallie, remain at the table, please," Dad says and then clears his throat, which he automatically does before ripping into any of us kids.

The twins instantly and simultaneously begin to chant, "Hallie's a turnip!"

"Shut up, you little twerps!" I swat Davy on the backside with my spoon as he escapes by climbing underneath the table and between the chair legs.

"It's not turnip, dear, it's truant," Mom patiently corrects as they exit.

"Mr. Collier from your school came over to the house yesterday," Dad sternly informs me.

"Honey, what's the matter?" Mom interrupts him. "Why won't you attend school? Why won't you tell us what's wrong? They've tested you for dyslexia, attention deficit disorder, and even hearing loss."

"What?" I ask, unable to help myself. But the joke flies right over her head.

"For *hearing loss*," she repeats in a louder and more modulated voice. "They've tested you for everything and the bottom line is that you're not a stupid girl, Hallie. Do you think you need glasses? Is something at school bothering you?"

Yeah, something there is bothering me all right. Basically everything.

"Listen, I was in school all day," I lie. "I just missed homeroom and was accidentally marked absent." It's a pathetic story. Last year I concocted phenomenal excuses involving microtwisters and even saving the entire town from an attack by killer bees. Life has reached an all-time low. I've lost my will to con.

"Don't lie to me, young lady!" Dad's face turns dark red as he pushes back his chair from the head of the table and says the word *lady* as if he means anything but. Ever since Francie was born he no longer has the stamina to smack us, thank God. Younger brothers and sisters have no idea the shit their older siblings endure while wearing down youthful energetic parents. By the time this new baby is a teenager it can just yank out Dad's oxygen tube or hide his hearing aid whenever he gets annoying.

But now Dad just shakes his head and paces the kitchen floor, occasionally striking the countertop with the palm of his hand in order to make me jump. To remind me that he *can* whack kids, that it's in his contract. And as soon as he gets a decent night's sleep, he just might do it, too. Dad is tall, clean-shaven, and broad-shouldered and you can tell that he played ball in high school and college. Whatever kind of ball—he played it. He's even got the bad knees to prove it. In the springtime he walks as if leaning into a strong wind. And you never want to ask him for money when it rains.

"First, you're grounded until I receive a report card that demonstrates to me that you've caught up on your schoolwork."

So much for the final three weeks of the racetrack.

"And second, your mother and I aren't giving you the money to put toward a car. If your school reports are good, then we'll revisit the finances this summer." *Revisit the finances* is Dad's favorite expression after *Who's going to pay for that?*

"What?" The money toward the car was my birthday present. It didn't have to do with good grades or bad behavior. "But Dad! The summer is nine months away! The *summer* just *ended*! And what about Eric? He got a car when he turned sixteen!"

"Your brother Eric goes to school, plays three sports a year, and works part-time at the Star-Mart." Dad ticks these items off on his right hand as if I might need a visual aid. "Eric is using that car to make something of himself, to get ahead in this world."

The translation here is of course that I would use a car to drive to the racetrack, pool hall, and Indian casino, and thus it would only serve as a motorized accessory to my inevitable downfall. My face quivers with approaching tears, but I refuse to give my parents the satisfaction. Last year I'd read this book *The Light in the Forest* about a white boy raised by Leni-Lenape Indians from the time he was four years old and I'd decided to also stand pain stoically like an Indian, and a good poker player, and to never show my emotions.

"What if I pay for the car myself?" I ask to gauge exactly how bad the situation is.

Dad looks at Mom, who is loading breakfast plates into the dishwasher, but she only gives the *I agree with whatever you decide* maternal shrug. Mom is fortunate that with her perfect complexion, wavy light brown hair, and hazel eyes she looks attractive without any makeup, because I don't know that she's going to find time to put any on ever again. As it is she's doing four barrels of wash and two truckloads of dishes per day. Once when I saw her wedding photos it was like, *Who is that?*

"Pay for it yourself? I suppose that's fine," Dad says. "So long as you can cover the running costs. And earning the money better not interfere with your schoolwork."

Obviously it upsets Mom that at least one of her children isn't going to attend college. Just wait until she discovers she's given birth to a high school dropout. In her maternal playbook truancy is just one pearl away from shoplifting on the add-a-bead necklace of life. From there it's off to mend fences at the women's prison farm outside of Lima, Ohio. I wish I *were* at the women's prison farm. Anywhere would be better than this house. In fact, solitary confinement would be a *treat.*

4

Going for Broke

★

Monday morning I turn out of the driveway and pedal in the direction of school, just in case anyone is watching, but as soon as it's safe I veer off in the direction of the bank and my new life as a full-time gambler.

My balance is $2,110.35. Another fifteen hundred is needed to buy even the worst junker. Eric had mentioned a cashier's job at the Star-Mart paying $6.25 an hour. Great, I'd have to work 240 hours blathering "cash or debit card" and the politically charged "paper or plastic?" while wrapped in a smelly brown apron. Forget it.

When I ask to close my account the teller becomes suspicious. The manager wants to see some ID and inquires if the service has been disappointing. I explain that the drive-through window is somewhat difficult to operate from a bicycle but that once I buy a car I'll start saving again. He says that if I leave five dollars he'll give my account student status and it will remain open for another four weeks without any penalties. Foolishly I agree. There's no one quite so blinded by hope as a gambler betting her life savings.

That accomplished, I dodge the seven-dollar admission fee at the race-track by sneaking in through the laundry entrance where the uniforms for the grill operators and the smocks for the employees who man the betting windows are delivered.

The weather has been warm and dry and as a result the track is fast and the handicapping is straightforward. Several hundred seagulls stand fanned out across the neatly manicured grounds, all pointing their yellow-orange beaks in exactly the same direction, letting the wind smooth their white and pale gray feathers. Looking at their robotic conformity reminds me of school.

After ticking off my picks in the *The Daily Racing Form* I browse for cars in the Auto Swap Sheet. Soon a familiar voice singing his favorite folk song and paean to hookydom in a pleasant bass drifts across the stands: *Run children run, the patteroller catch you, Run children run, it's almost day. That child ran and that child flew, That child lost her Sunday shoe.* Approaching is a cheerful and dapper fellow dressed in green-and-white checkered pants, a navy cardigan, and polished white leather shoes, wearing a boating cap carefully arranged at a jaunty angle. The entire getup is his idea of a *GQ* magazine profile of the prosperous midwestern bookie.

"What's new at the Rialto?" Cappy casually tosses off his standard greeting while extending a pack of Doublemint gum in my direction with one piece sticking out the top like a forced ace in a card trick. Whenever he's shuffling gum it means he's trying to quit the cancer sticks.

"Thanks." The gum goes in my pocket for later. I'm like a squirrel hoarding any and all tidbits for the cold winter months ahead.

Cappy sits down next to me on the bleachers, only we both face forward to keep track of any revisions flashed on the electronic tote board.

"You look like a guy who's just beaten the odds," I say with a touch of envy.

"Indeed I am. Cleaned up on a baseball game last night. Usually I don't stick my neck out, but it's been a good season and the boss is allowed to have some fun once in a while. That's the whole point of being self-employed, isn't it?"

" 'Gratulations," I say. "Maybe some of your luck will wear off on me."

"A good gambler—"

We finish his maxim in unison, "never trades on luck. Luck is for losers."

"You show me a winner or a war hero who believes in luck and I'll show you a racetrack for unicorns," adds Cappy.

"I know, I know," I say. "It's the percentages."

"Speaking of which, when are you going to come and work for me? This is penny-ante shit, Hallie. Just like Vegas roulette, where the hold is around twelve and a half percent no matter what schmucky tourist in a sequined sweat suit wins or loses. There's a reason they call it *Lost Wages*. And the only one who consistently makes money in *this* quadruped boiler room is the house, skimming their five percent no matter what nags run and no matter how you bet them."

Of course, he's right. The owners of the racetracks and pool halls and OTB parlors and even the stockbrokers stay in business year in and year out. It's only the customers and the suckers who are washed away.

"Thanks, but getting hit in the head with cue sticks while working the phones in the back room of your gin joint and inhaling secondhand smoke all night isn't exactly the career I had in mind for myself."

"For you I'd be willing to tart the place up a bit—you know, put in a soda machine, buy some toilet paper, maybe even a spider plant."

"Cappy, do the words *house of correction* mean anything to you?"

"House of correction." Cappy poses with palm to chin and pretends to muse. "Let me see . . . House of Blues, House of Pancakes, houseboat, *House & Garden, House at Pooh Corner* . . . house of correction, you say?"

Eventually he hits his head like in a V-8 commercial. "Oh. House of *correction.* Of course. The clink. Sure, it makes me think of *Pomp & Circumstance.* The Crossbar Campus is where I got my high school diploma. And my best clients are in a minimum-security lockup outside of Akron brushing up on their tennis. Show me a man with time and money and phone privileges and no access to pretty girls and I'll show you a profit."

"Thanks for the offer, Caps. I'll think about it."

"Okay, Calculator Kid, cogitate upon it. But remember, you don't earn a living in this business by *playing* the slot machines. You hafta *own* them. And I'd be willing to start you at thirty G's a year. Tax-free."

The horses begin to high-step out onto the track and trot skittishly over to the starting line. The jockey on the giddy four-horse, Merrily We Roll Along, has to make a circle and reapproach the electronic starting gate.

"Good luck, kiddo." He gives me a friendly clunk on the shoulder with his rolled-up racing form. "Stop by the office for a game of eight-ball sometime this week. I've got a new shot to show you. And in the meantime—"

"Don't take any wooden nickels," we finish his well-known warning together.

5

A Sucker's Diary

♠

Finally the bugler in his formal purple jacket raises his silver horn to summon the thoroughbreds for the first race. It's post time. "They're at the gate," bellows the announcer's megaphoned voice, followed by the familiar whoop "They're *off*!" and then the thunder of hooves.

I don't have any money on the first race. And I avoid the daily double after what happened last week. The fourth and eighth races are two-year-old fillies, total unknowns, and so there's no point in bothering with those either. You may as well spend your time with a Bible and a calendar trying to determine the Second Coming. To win big it's necessary to find the race where the horse has better odds than everyone thinks it has—not so much a long shot as a perceived long shot.

Anyway, I know that what I'm doing today isn't smart. You never try to make a huge hit out of desperation, particularly when lacking a good-sized bankroll to back you up. The mark of a skilled gambler is to grind it out slow and regular-like, and every once in a while, when the sun and the moon and the stars all line up and the odds are in your favor big time, then you lay down the wad and clean out the house.

The third race doesn't pan out. My horse, Little Dorrit, goes off the board with six-to-one odds, which I'm pleased with, but then she comes in third place. Shit. Who ever thought that Mary Is Contrary could run so fast on a firm course. And on the *outside*. That old glue pot usually only comes to life when galloping in mud up to her forelocks.

So then I turn all chickenshit and bet only eighty bucks on Beelzebub's Boy in the fifth and of course he ends up winning. Just goes to show you, the less you bet the more you lose when you win. But at least I have my confidence back. Only now that it appears as if my luck is changing, who do I see but my *un*beloved Brandt.

"Hey, Hallie!" Brandt's lips and tongue are all tangerine-stained from an orange slushee that he's clutching in his right hand, looking just like my little brother Davy after he eats a Popsicle. In his other mitt is a half-inch-thick stack of racing tickets. What did he do, I wonder, go and bet on every horse?

"Hi, Branch," I say.

"Can I buy you a slushee?"

"Uh, no thanks." Just looking at his puffy orange lips is enough to make me want a vodka straight up. "Since when did you become a track junkie?"

"I've been working on a system based on mathematical fluctuations," he announces proudly and holds up the fistful of tickets. "By entering all the past performances and workout records into my computer and then programming it to simulate a race as if they are running against one another, and presto!"

It sounds to me that the sooner the whole Shaeffer family gets into Gamblers Anonymous the better. First I see his old lady out at the casino playing blackjack and now Branch has his own "system." I can't help but wonder what game of chance his sister Sheryl, and my competitor for Craig Larkin's affection, is into. Hopefully it's Russian roulette.

Branch follows me down to Shed Row, the area behind the stables where the clockers, grooms, and trainers are walking and bathing some of the horses that have already run and the track employees are preparing the winner's circle for a big deal cup in the twelfth race that I don't give a shit about. I used to hang around the stalls trying to pick up tips but eventually decided it's a huge waste of time since everyone, even the teenagers who mix the fly spray, talk big, as if they know more than they do.

It's then that I glance up at the tote board and practically keel over. Buffalo Gal has been scratched in the eleventh race. This is not my horse but in fact the only horse I was worried would beat my horse, Madame Horsefly. I can't believe my luck! The race is mine. I quickly calculate that I have about $360 left and if Madame Horsefly wins, and I know she will, I'll clear almost $2,000. But if I can only bet $500 dollars, I'll make enough for the car.

"Hey, Branch," I yell. He's standing under the tote board and translating some last-minute statistics into reverse polar notation and punching them into his handheld Hewlett-Packard scientific calculator. He comes tripping over like a baby giraffe just getting the hang of its legs.

"How's your system doing? Would you be able to float me a hundred and forty dollars for an hour? Better yet, I'll cut you in for five percent if Madame Horsefly wins, in addition to repaying the stake."

Branch appears crushed, like most guys when they realize that cash can often go further than charm, especially in the dating game. "Gee, I'm sorry, Hallie. These are all two-dollar tickets." Woefully he looks down at the peach and white stack. "I spent all my money at a *Star Trek* convention in Cleveland last weekend."

I truly wish he hadn't told me that last part. There is such a thing as *too* much information, even at the racetrack.

Damn. Where can I get that kind of a loan in an hour? Eric! Last November he'd banked at least $500 from the grandparents on his birthday. It's a quarter after four. He'll be at football practice. I grab my bike from behind the ambulance that always waits near the edge of the turf track. The sky darkens slightly as clouds roll in, making it appear as if it might start to pour at any moment. From the west comes a rumble of thunder that sounds as if God is clearing his throat prior to making a big announcement.

Just as I arrive at the high school practice field the cold raindrops begin to fall, like a swift intake of breath. Eric is a red and black smudge in a crowd of guys busy hurling themselves at big padded coatracks and simultaneously shouting "Unh!"

We huddle on the twenty-yard line.

"I need to borrow a hundred and forty dollars," I say. "It's an emergency."

"Okay, but what's it for?"

"Never mind. I'll pay it back tomorrow."

"Well, all right," he agrees. "I'll give it to you tonight."

"It *can't* wait until tonight," I plead.

"Hallie, are you in some sort of trouble?" he asks seriously.

"No, of course not. I just have a tremendous opportunity. One that's going to evaporate in about"—I look down at my watch—"in about twenty minutes."

"Listen, Hallie, whatever it is, it doesn't sound like a good idea. It sounds to me as if you're dealing drugs."

"Christ, Eric. It's nothing illegal. It's a bet. It's Madame Horsefly in the tenth."

"I don't care if you usually make money at the track, you shouldn't be gambling all the time. It's not . . . it's not normal. Where's it going to get you?"

Sometimes Eric can be really cool. But today, of all days, he has to decide to be the Reverend Billy Pigskin.

"How many times do I have to explain it to you?" I'm begging him now. "It's *not* gambling. I handicap the horses—according to how they've run in previous races. It's a formula—"

But Eric is already clomping back to his buddies, a big hulking lump of unformed clay with all that bulky padding stuffed underneath his practice clothes.

Apparently Craig Larkin has been observing our little scene on the sidelines and now he's heading over. Only Eric intercepts him about fifteen feet away from me. It's impossible to hear what's being said, but by the way Eric shakes his head and raises and drops his arms I can pretty much guess. However, instead of walking back to practice with Eric he continues in my direction. The black and red mesh practice jersey stretches across his expansive shoulders to make the bulldog on the front appear slant-eyed. The rain continues to pelt the field and miles away lightning zigzags across the sky.

"Anything I can help with?" His eyes point to somewhere above my head, as if he's expecting a through pass at any moment.

Desperation overtakes embarrassment by three to one. "Not unless you have a hundred and forty dollars I can borrow," I say, half kidding.

"I do," he says.

"You'd really give me the money?" I say excitedly.

"Sure." He actually looks me in the eyes. "I mean, I don't have it with me. It's at home. And I can't leave practice until quarter past five. Can you wait until then?"

"No," I say. "But thanks all the same."

He looks perplexed. "I have sixty dollars in my wallet. It's in the locker room."

There always comes a defining moment when a gambler must weigh fear against greed, the fear of losing an opportunity against the greed of wanting to win big. Fortunately this only takes a second and the outcome is always the same. "Okay. I really appreciate it."

His cleats chuck little tufts of grass back in my direction. And now the sky opens up and begins teeming. There's no way I'm going to make it back to the track on time.

After Craig gives me the money against my promise to pay him back the next day, I ride to the local Off Track Betting hole, which is always a pain in the ass because you're supposed to be eighteen to place a bet. At the actual racetrack they don't give a damn. The sourpuss woman behind the window at OTB immediately demands ID and continues chipping away at her turquoise nail polish with a plastic pen cap.

Resorting to Plan B, I search for some seedy old coot to place my bet. Blue Nails sees me working the room, but she doesn't give a shit. She just can't sell me the bet. She probably doesn't give a good goddamn if I offer to gang-bang all the guys in order to get someone to place my action. And they are *all* guys. A bunch of worn-out, ashen-faced men who look as if they were thrown out of their jobs *and* their families ten years ago only hadn't yet noticed. And nobody has bothered to tell them, either.

A guy about my grandpa's age leans against the far wall chewing a cigar stub and concentrates on one of the several large monitors suspended from the ceiling, looking very much as if he was recently embalmed but it's starting to wear off.

"Listen, mister, do me a favor and bet four hundred and twenty dollars on Madame Horsefly to come in second for me, wouldja, please?"

His gaze is firmly fixed on the screen overhead, where the horses are being led out of the paddock. The race is going to start in exactly four minutes and ten seconds. Betting at OTB will close in just two minutes. When Gramps eventually glances over at me, an amused look crosses his face. This happens to me a lot, even at the track. *Oh, how cute,* they think, *a little girl betting on the ponies.* As if I'm picking horses because I like what colors the jockeys are flying.

"You know why I'm going to take your action, honey?" A cloud of rancid smoke hits me full in the face every time he pronounces the letter *H.*

Under normal circumstances I'd inform him that all the men who have ever called me "honey" have died facedown in the gutter. And that's only after declaring personal bankruptcy. "Why, mister?" I say all sweet, like the little girl in *Miracle on 34th Street.*

" 'Cause that's my horse and she's gonna win. I had to take a blood pressure pill with a chaser when they scratched Buffalo Gal."

Thank God. He might stink like a week's worth of Havanas soaked in Thunderbird, but at least this codger knows something about the ponies.

"Great." I eagerly press my wet, wrinkled money into his hand.

"Only why to come in second, girlie? She's going to hit pay dirt this race."

The guy is obviously a speed handicapper and not a trip handicapper. "I was going to bet to win before the rain. But now the track is getting all gumbo. She's not a mudder and I've got to play it safe. I really need to get back some cash."

From the permanent squint of his eyes it is obvious that he understands *really need cash* a lot more than *got to play it safe*. A glance up at the monitor shows one minute left to bet. The course is getting sloppier by the second.

"You'd better go to the window," I say.

Gramps points a tobacco-edged fingernail at the tote board. "There's no odds left on second place. You gotta bet her to win."

He's actually right. Dammit, if only I was out there and could see it with my own eyes. But on the monitor it just looks like six furlongs of furrowed shit.

The window whore makes her "last call" announcement.

"Okay." I panic. "Bet it all to win."

He comes back and hands me my tickets. The compressed air horn screeches, the announcer bellows, "They're *off!*" and then immediately starts narrating the race, one impassioned run-on sentence. But I don't need to listen. On the big color screen above us Madame Horsefly makes her way around the first bend and into the lead. The betting parlor comes alive and several of the corpses actually remove the cigarettes that were up until this time surgically attached to their liver lips. It's doubtful any of their wives would believe they could actually get this excited about something.

The colors are a blur as the horses take the fence all smooth in a cluster. They glide into the homestretch and seconds later two horses gallop across the white line side by side. It's a photo finish. Madame Horsefly loses to Heaven's Gait by a nose. There is one gleeful shout, several muttered curses, and then the place becomes a morgue again, as if someone removed all of the stiffs' batteries.

And clobbered by Heaven's Gait of all horses. Jesus, rumor had it that she'd been ticketed twice for loitering during her last workout. Why did I listen to this asshole? That's the second rule of gambling: Never follow anyone you're technically playing against—touts, tipsters, hucksters, suckers, and especially broken-down old geezers. The first rule is of course never to bet more than you can afford to lose. Not only am I now broke and into Craig for sixty bucks, but there's no trust fund or line of credit in sight.

6

Tapped Out

◆

The rain has stopped and the wind is dying down by the time I exit the den of inequality, but it's still a long slow ride to the Star-Mart. This last race was definitely a sign from God. Maybe the old man in the betting parlor *was* God. Imagine if the tobacco companies could get a picture of God smoking a stogie. Anyway, it's time to go straight. At least until I earn back some scratch.

A school bus sprays my entire left side with brown rain as it noisily passes and leaves me wondering if Mr. Attendance Fuckhead has called the house today and turncoated me again. Actually, I feel sorry for the little weasel. I mean, that's his life—trying to rustle up kids who are cutting school. How the hell does he drag himself out of bed in the morning and look in the mirror? What does he say at parties—Yeah, I went to school for twenty years to learn how to scour the local video arcade for teenagers playing hooky. Just Call Me Dick reminds me of those moron businessmen I see playing poker down at the Indian casino who are constantly confusing brains with good luck and are so stuck on their own superiority that they'll break up a full house to try and draw four of a kind.

When the violent orange-and-purple Star-Mart sign comes into view it causes me to take a sharp breath, my last as a free agent, or at least one without a brown smock. Upon entering I duck my head down as far as possible to avoid being recognized and speed-walk directly to the customer service desk to fill out the application for a checkout job. They want a list of previous work experience and also for me to write down "any special knowledge" I possess. "Always split aces and eights when you're playing blackjack, but never tens," I print, using the eraserless pencil nub that they have so generously supplied.

It's only as I'm slinking out of the store that I see Eric waving me over to his bagging station. He must have just arrived from practice. Here comes the big brother "I told you so." Better go and take my medicine, since I just listed him as a reference on my application.

But instead of giving me a hard time he tells me there's a help wanted sign on the bulletin board that he thinks might interest me. The notice is easy to find among all the pictures of lost pets and ads for baby-sitting and word processing services. The letters are in big India ink calligraphy on cream-colored parchment paper. In fact, it looks more like my wealthy cousin Lillian's wedding invitation than a want ad.

SCRUPULOUS YARD PERSON SOUGHT FOR STEADY EMPLOY-MENT AT PRIVATE RESIDENCE WITH SURROUNDING GAR-DENS. $12.00 HOURLY. REFERENCES REQUIRED. INQUIRE IN PERSON AT 48 NUTHATCH LANE.

Twelve bucks an hour! Wow. Working twenty hours a week would net me $1,920 in just two months. Only since it's private I could probably work more than that. Look out Harrah's, here I come!

But what's scrupulous? I'd actually heard my mother say it just a week or so ago, but I'm pretty sure she placed an "un" before the word. Maybe it means strong or outdoorsy. I ask some blue-haired old lady leaving the store. Only I'm not entirely sure how to pronounce it. "Excuse me, ma'am, but do you know what scrupu-loose means?"

"Well, *scru*-pu-lus," she emphasizes the pronunciation, "means trustworthy. It means reliable and dependable." She smiles and carefully sets down her grocery bag on a nearby bank of gumball machines. "*Scruple* is a noun which means an uneasy feeling arising from conscience or principle that tends to hinder action. It's from the Latin *scrupulus*, which is a small unit of measurement."

Oh shit, I think, *she's a retired teacher.*

"It's lucky for you that I'm a retired teacher," she dutifully reports as if this fact is supposed to make me extremely happy.

Instead it makes me realize that she probably gets a pension check. My eyes land on the pyramid of motor oil stacked inside the door. "What a coincidence!" I say. "I'm having a special today and changing the oil of retired teachers for just ten dollars."

She goes for it and twenty minutes later I have a tenner in my pocket. Then it's back to "Yard Person." What kind of references are they looking for? I can operate a lawn mower and pull weeds right up there with the best broke teenager. And I can run an eight-minute mile no problem. That's it! Maybe I can show them my varsity letter. Only I don't want to risk stopping by my house. Being grounded means I'm supposed to go home right after school, and it's already close to six o'clock.

7

The Hard Way

♣

I know approximately where the house in the ad is located. The locals refer to the neighborhood as Birdland because the streets are all named after birds—Warbler Road, Bobwhite Drive, Towhee Point, Swallow Court, Nuthatch Lane, and so forth. But of course they developed it so much that none of those birds are left, just the green-and-white street signs as memorial plaques.

Nuthatch Lane turns out to be a small connector street with only six houses and plenty of land between them. Number forty-eight is set back at the end of a long circular grass driveway with two gravel strips down the middle, lined with tall birch trees planted close together. The silvery-white trunks shimmer in the slanted early-evening light and make a cross-hatching of shade upon the driveway. And though the grounds are entirely landscaped and appear to be well looked after, closer inspection reveals a house in need of a makeover. Peeling paint and rusting gutters conflict with the highly ornamental architecture.

There are two cars parked to the side of the driveway and the front door is open. Tapping lightly on the screen door, it's possible to make out an older woman sitting in a rocker and reading a book. She carefully lays the volume on a side table and threads her way around a lot of fancy wooden chairs and end tables in order to answer the door. I can't recall seeing her around town, but if older people don't have kids or play poker then I usually don't know them. However, she smiles brightly and appears friendly, as if we might know each other from church.

"Hello, dear. Are you here to pick up the chaise longue?" She opens the door and indicates that I should enter. The screen door wheezes loudly and then slams behind me.

"Uh, no. I'm, uh—I saw an ad. I'm here about the yard person position."

An amused smile appears to play across her mouth. "Of course. Then you'll want to speak to Bernard. Oh, where are my manners? My name is Olivia. What is yours?"

"Hallie. Hallie Palmer."

"Oh, Hallie! What a *wonderful* name." She clasps her hands delightedly in front of her chest. "Just like the comet!"

Uh-oh. She could be senile. These big old houses are exactly the kind of places where rich people hide their demented relatives on the third floor so they're free to hurl themselves against dormer windows without attracting too much attention. I'd read *Jane Eyre* freshman year in high school.

Before I have a chance to say anything, she trots off toward the back of the house. She moves really fast for an old lady. "Bernard! Someone is here to inquire about the yard person position." She can also holler pretty good for an old lady.

Upon returning to the front hall she lightly smooths her soft halo of hair with her fingertips, even though there aren't any loose strands since it's pulled into a neat bun at the nape of her neck. A hint of pale blond is still visible on the sides, though it's mostly the color of milkweed. "You must come in and have a cup of Ceylon tea," she says cheerily. "Or perhaps some pink lemonade."

I've never been on a real job interview, so I don't know if it's appropriate to accept. When I went for the job at the service station they just stuck the gas pump nozzle in my one hand and a window scrubber in the other. But here I feel more like I'm at my grandma's house and so I say okay.

We enter a spacious, sunny room that overlooks the backyard. There appear to be three separate gardens, one for vegetables and two for flowers, along with a birdbath, two intricately designed wrought-iron benches painted a glossy white, and lots of birdhouses stuck up in the trees like robins' nests. In the far corner of the yard, just before the woods begin, is a little house that looks as if they cut a chunk off the big house and dropped it back there. It resembles something Beatrix Potter might have rented for Jemima Puddle-Duck and Benjamin Bunny.

Inside I'm afraid to sit down because the chairs are so expensive-looking.

They're old-fashioned and have embroidered seats that are the kind of seats that people under the age of twenty are not even allowed to go near. And so I check the back of my pants before making any sudden sitting moves.

The space around me is overflowing with stuff. Old stuff. There's a gold trunk with ivory bits and pieces stuck into the top that form an intricate Chinese-looking design of gondolas, starbursts, and flowers. The bookshelves hold porcelain vases and blue and white china plates propped up on little brass stands with curlicue feet. On every table, and there are lots of small tables, is a lamp with a fancy stained-glass shade. And sitting only an inch from my lemonade glass is a two-inch-high pink enamel bunny rabbit with a tape measure coming right out of its ass. Where a regular house has one picture on the wall these people have pounded in upwards of a dozen. Mirrors, too. And where a regular house has one rug in the middle of the room, they have twelve. In some spots there's even a small rug on top of a big rug and then long narrow rugs squeezed in between the larger ones. Who ever heard of putting one rug on top of another? Maybe when the top one wears out they just pick it up and throw it away and the next one is all ready to go, like pop-up tissues.

However, the room doesn't appear to be dirty. But then, my mother always says you can't really tell about people until you inspect the kitchen and the bathrooms.

In the doorway appears a tall, elegant man with a wonderful mane of salt-and-pepper hair that makes him look distinguished, but also probably older than he actually is. I can tell by his unlined face that he's probably only about thirty-five. And he doesn't just walk into the room, either. He sweeps into it.

"Bernard, this is Hallie Palmer," says the old lady. "Isn't Hallie a wonderful name? We simply must have someone named Hallie around the house. Among the Viking warriors it meant hero."

Mr. Bernard smiles warmly, just like the woman did when I arrived. And just like a polite person would if a friendly but senile person entered into a conversation. I decide he must be her son. They have similar blue eyes that happen to match the color of the blue in the china plates propped up in the display case behind them. And their cheekbones are both high, though the mother's jawline is softer and makes a shape like the bottom of a heart while his is more square.

"Hallie would like to discuss the opening for a yard person," Ms. Olivia says with formality in her voice but a twinkle in her porcelain eyes.

It makes me wonder if they're just pretending to do the interview to be nice.

"That's splendid!" Mr. Bernard declares. "We are equal opportunity employers."

"Great," I say. "I'm an equal opportunity employee."

"Well done!" says Mr. Bernard, obviously pleased by my response. "Now, Ms. Palmer, I know I'm not supposed to ask this, but do you harbor a drinking problem?"

It's funny the way he addresses me as Ms. Palmer. I almost look over my shoulder to check for my mother before realizing that he's talking to me. "I drink a lot of chocolate Yoo-Hoo, but it's not what I would call a problem. The most I ever have is three in one day."

"Excellent. Lars, the last yard boy, or rather, yard *person*, was in possession of a constitution that had extreme difficulty processing ethanol, and I daresay his work suffered as a result of this deficiency in body chemistry. Those Danes are stupendous craftspeople and they always show up on time, but they can become horrendously depressive when self-medicating."

"Oh," I say.

"No matter, how are you in the garden? Do you know the difference between sweet corn and crabgrass?"

"Sure, we have a vegetable garden at home."

"That's glorious. So when might you commence?"

"You mean start the job?"

He apparently registers the astonished look on my face. "Of course, you'll want a tour of the grounds first, and undoubtedly you have some questions of your own." He hesitates. "And perhaps you wish to sleep on the matter."

"Yes. I mean no. I mean, could you just review the pay?"

"Certainly. The monetary compensation. The pay is—" He turns to the old lady. "Mother, whatever is the pay?"

"Twelve dollars an hour," she answers.

"Oh yes. That's right. Mother does all the household accounts."

I decide that's how it must be in most families—the least reasonable person is in charge of all the money. At least that's how it is at my house.

"I can start tomorrow at eight o'clock or whatever time you want," I say with enthusiasm.

"How is half past eight? That has always appealed to me as a civilized time to begin outdoor work."

I think for sure they're going to ask about school. But maybe not. These folks seem a bit odd. They're hard to read, like two down cards in a game of seven-card stud.

We all stand up, and Mr. Bernard extends his hand as if to seal our employment contract. On the third finger of his left hand is a shiny gold signet ring with a *G* engraved on the front of it. This reminds me that I don't even know their family name. "Excuse me, but what's your last name?"

"We are the Stocktons." He says this proudly, as if confident that anyone with this last name could easily pass a lie-detector test.

"Okay. Then thanks, Mr. and Mrs. Stockton. I'll see you both tomorrow."

"Please call us Olivia and Bernard," the mother chimes in.

I glance at Mr. Stockton to make sure he isn't staring at her as if she forgot to take her pills, but he just nods in agreement.

I'm not sure what to say. "Then please call me Hallie."

"As you wish," he says in this way that's not mocking, but as if we're all in a play. Mr. Bernard glances down at his watch. "Half past six. Perhaps you'd like a quick tour of the premises."

When I nod my head okay, he actually makes a little bow and gallantly ushers me through the doors into the garden and says, "Then without further fondue . . ."

Fondue?

8

Gardeners Anonymous

♥

I follow Mr. Bernard down a cobblestone path of faded pink and gray stones that wends its way around the different gardens. Even though it's early fall, there are still a number of flowers in the first bed. These I mostly recognize—yellow and white irises, impatiens, lilies of all different colors, and red and purple azaleas. At least I think they're azaleas. Closer inspection reveals most of the remaining blooms appear rather tired. But I imagine they were quite beautiful up until a few weeks ago.

"Dahlias, china asters," he points to different plants as if he's taking attendance. "Mauve dwarf asters, heliotrope, violet petunias, tall scabiosas, pink snapdragons, autumn crocuses."

He pauses in front of the second garden. Before us sways an odd assortment of flowers—all different heights, shapes, and colors, though mostly taller and ganglier than what was in the previous bed. I can't identify one stalk or blossom, but they all seem pretty much past it, drooping like flags on a windless day.

"This will all have to come out over the next two weeks," Mr. Bernard says despondently. "And the soil must be turned. Then the other bed has to be pulled up, and there are some bulbs to plant in that one for next year." He points back toward the first garden. "It's a big job." He sighs.

But I notice he doesn't say this in an *Are you sure you're up to it?* tone of voice. It's more like he's saddened that it's all over.

"What kind of flowers are these?" I ask, though mostly to take his mind off the impending bloom doom.

"Wildflowers." He sounds grateful that I've inquired and with his left hand gracefully motions toward the different clusters as if he's the maestro cueing his musicians. "Purple loosestrife, swamp rose mallow, trumpet honeysuckle."

"Pretty names."

His gold ring flashes in the sloped light of the setting sun and reminds me of how Eric and I used to sit in our garden and torch bugs with a magnifying glass.

"Yes, wildflowers are the most exquisite of all, I do believe."

"What's this?" I ask, walking toward a vine of trumpet-shaped purple, pink, and pale blue flowers sprawled across a row of white wooden trellises that border the south side of the garden. This plant doesn't appear to have any intention of folding its cards for the winter.

"Common morning glory," Mr. Bernard replies. "Gorgeous, isn't it? Last summer I attempted to cultivate beach morning glory, but unfortunately it prefers the West Coast."

We stroll past the vegetable patch where there are still pumpkins, watermelons, a few scattered heads of lettuce, some radishes, and stalks of green peppers.

"Do you enjoy pumpkin bread?" he inquires.

"I don't think I've ever had it," I say. "And if Wonder bread doesn't make it, then I know I've never had it."

"Goodness gracious. I'll bake a batch this week."

I'm hoping he's like my great-aunt Vi in that she's always saying that she's going to "whip up" this or that but never actually does. Pumpkin bread sounds totally yucky.

"This is the summerhouse," Mr. Bernard announces as we approach the outbuilding with the large windows and dainty gingerbread trim that I first spotted from the sunporch. Through the glass windows it appears that the interior is a lighter-colored version of the room in which I'd just had my interview. There's an overstuffed couch, two chairs, an array of end tables, five or six lamps with fancy bases, and knickknacks covering every inch of surface space.

A few feet in front of the summerhouse is another flower garden that I hadn't been able to see from the main house. Only two plants are still in bloom, both with enormous ivory-colored flowers. Red Monarch butterflies with black trim dance and mingle among the dried stalks.

Mr. Bernard pauses. "Mother's rose garden," he says. "She'll tell you not to bother tending it, but don't listen to her. Poor things would have perished ages ago if I didn't water, weed, fertilize, and prune. These days the only roses that Mother remembers to water is her Four Roses bourbon every afternoon. In fact, she's currently lobbying to adopt a goat as an environmentally friendly organic lawn mower and fertilizing system. What she doesn't comprehend is that grazing animals, when in the process of fortifying themselves, do *not* differentiate between dandelions and dendrobium, or crabgrass and coriander."

The place is beginning to remind me of a Disney cartoon. Way back here, with the fading sunlight streaking through the trees and the clouds stacked so the ones on top appear to be squashing the ones beneath, a person wouldn't be surprised to run into the Blue Fairy. There's something interesting or attractive or both everywhere you turn. The bird feeders hanging from the lower branches of the ash and maple trees are constructed in various architectural styles—southern plantations, gothic cathedrals, an A-frame log cabin, a palace, and even a riverboat. Mr. Bernard leads me around to the side of the summerhouse and stops in front of a finely cultivated ten-by-twenty-foot bed that looks as if it nurtures nothing but tall sticklike weeds.

"This is my herb garden—chives, rosemary, thyme, sorrel, and so forth—mostly for cooking. It's hidden back here, as I've not yet found a way to make it aesthetically pulchritudinous enough for display, but it's de rigueur if one cooks."

I assume that "de rigueur" means required by law, like a fence around a swimming pool. As for *pulchritudinous*, I can't even hazard a guess. "Is that basil?" I point to the one plant I think I recognize from the pizza parlor.

"Yes." He bends over, gingerly removes a few leaves and places them up to his nose, inhales deeply, closes his eyes for a few seconds, and looks satisfied. Then he hands them to me, as if we're passing a joint in the bleachers at the high school.

"Mmmm," I say agreeably. "I can smell mint, too."

"It's next to your foot. You'll have to sample it in iced tea while taking your break. That reminds me, please don't smoke in the house. It's not good for Father."

"I don't smoke," I reply. But I can't help thinking how funny it is that he's already spoken to me about drinking and smoking when I'm not old enough to do either. I mean, he says all this as if I'm twenty-five or a member of a motorcycle gang.

"We'll have to take in a supply of Yoo-Hoo now, won't we? Hmm . . ." He glances quizzically at the herb garden. "I wonder what nicely accents Yoo-Hoo?"

Again at first I think he must be joking, like about the cigarettes, but he's not.

"Ice cream," I respond, trying to be of assistance.

"Of course. Mother and Father adore ice cream, so that's not a problem." He guides me around to the back of the summerhouse. "And here's the orchard."

Well, it's not *exactly* an orchard. There are about eight gnarly apple trees, five cherry trees, and a scraggly, mostly dead peach tree. But hey, if they want to think they have an orchard, what the hell, I'm just the yard person. And I'm sure the blossoms are lovely in the springtime.

"What's this?" I walk over to a big semicircle composed of ten square-shaped granite slabs about the size of encyclopedias. Next to it sits a weathered rocking chair.

"That's Mother's Druid Circle." Enacting a broad, dismissive wave toward the house, he says this as if Ms. Olivia is indeed a little out of it but for the most part harmless. "She'll have to explain it to you."

"It looks like a mini-Stonehenge."

"I believe that's the idea. Mother is . . . well, she's what one might call *spiritual.*"

I understand this to be a euphemism for gaga, just like my mother and father say that Grandpa Ed is *afflicted.* Though Mr. Bernard doesn't appear to be concerned about the matter. However if any animal sacrifices will be taking place this certainly looks like the spot. I can't help but wonder if his mother practices witchcraft. She sounds as if she has a New England accent, like those people who say *pahk the cahr*, and as I understand it, that's the birthplace of American witchcraft.

"Mostly Mother just sneaks back here to puff on her Gauloises. She quit smoking a long time ago, but the stress of Father's illness gets to her sometimes."

A few feet away is an as yet uncultivated six-by-six patch of lawn sur-rounded by short wooden stakes that are loosely connected by a weathered length of butcher string. Maybe it's the outline for the goat pen.

"This will have to be turned in the spring," Mr. Bernard explains. "I'm installing a blue garden. I took inspiration from Edith Wharton's French Riviera garden."

Edith Wharton must be one of the neighbors. But a blue garden? I won-der if we're going to apply blue spray paint or add blueberry Jell-O to the soil, like kids at school use it to dye their hair.

Mr. Bernard points to the future home of each plant and optimistically performs a practice roll call. "Anchusa, delphinium, lobelia, bachelor's but-ton, blue browallia." Then he glances up at the sun, which is dipping behind the so-called orchard and casting long shadows across the yard, and he sud-denly seems to realize that it's growing late.

"The implements are stored in there." He points to a dark green shed in the corner of the yard, somewhat camouflaged by overgrown shrubbery. "Can you operate an electric hedge trimmer, Hallie?"

"Sure. I can work anything—power mower, weed whacker, leaf blower, you name it. My dad says I'm mechanically inclined. Sometimes I even fix my brother's car. Last summer I pumped gas at the Sunoco. I can even shoot an air rifle."

"Hallie Oakley," Mr. Bernard replies mysteriously. He looks delighted that I've brought these additional skills to light. "So that must mean you can drive."

"Yeah, I've got a license."

We stroll through the darkening twilight air, around the side of the house, and out to the driveway, where Mr. Bernard politely waits while I mount my bike.

"I'm saving to buy a car," I explain. There doesn't seem to be any point in leading him to believe that I own a car.

"Mobility is a noble cause for which to till the soil."

"I just hope I can do the job okay," I say. "I mean, I've never been a full-time groundskeeper before."

"And that's exactly why you're perfectly suited for it. We need one of Plato's philosopher kings, or a queen, such as the case may be—someone who brings outside beliefs and experiences to the fields in order to effectively rule with a green thumb."

Plato's philosopher kings? Sure, whatever he says. Because for twelve bucks an hour he's the boss and he can call me a yard person or a philosopher queen or anything else he wants. In fact, I'll wear a name tag. Now that I think of it, Mr. Bernard and Ms. Olivia could both be communing with fairies. I've read that dementia runs in families just like alcoholism. He offers a leisurely wave good-bye as if I'm a ship pulling up anchor. The gravel crunches under my tires, and as I pedal past the mailbox at the end of the driveway I notice the name RUSH underneath STOCKTON. Maybe it's a government-subsidized halfway house. Who cares, as long as their checks are good. Though I suppose I'll find out soon enough. In the meantime, I'm starving, and decide to raid the church pantry.

9

The Inside Dope

★

As I'm making a left onto Vine Street I hear a car honking from behind, the horn just barely audible over "We Are the Champions" blasting from the radio. Jane screeches to a halt alongside of me and sprays the roadside ditch with a wave of gravel.

"There you are!" says Jane. She turns down the radio. "Come help us deliver donuts. We had to sell them to raise money for the homecoming dance."

Sure enough, there are at least thirty boxes of donuts crammed into the back.

"Okay, okay. But only if you've got something for me to eat."

Gwen leans her head over to the driver's-side window. "Plenty, if you like donuts."

Jane helps me attach my bike to the roof rack while Gwen throws my bag into the back. Jane and Gwen couldn't look more different. Jane has a short athletic frame and a shaggy chestnut-colored ponytail, and is a full-fledged sleeps-with-a-mitt-under-her-mattress jock. In fact, because Jane constantly needs to be around bats, balls, and sweatbands she works at the sporting goods store for only four dollars an hour when she could make almost twice as much baby-sitting.

Gwen, on the other hand, is tall with violet eyes and a mane of honey-blond hair that falls perfectly around her heart-shaped face and dances on the tops of her shoulders. Meantime, I mostly keep my kinky apricot-colored curls in two braids so as not to frighten people or attract the attention of nesting animals in the colder months.

Gwen and Jane like to insist that I am imagining the ill effects of being sixteen, and so they clip articles for me about how teenage girls with poor body self-image and low self-esteem are twice as likely to develop eating disorders or commit suicide. Does my habit of a half dozen chocolate donuts a day qualify as an eating disorder? And if I eventually choke on one of them will people say it was suicide, or worse, donutcide?

Jane spins the wheel and sings along to Alanis Morissette's *Jagged Little Pill* album while Gwen examines her perfectly sculpted eyebrows using the passenger's-side mirror. It's my job to sit in back and prevent the donut towers from toppling over and also to employ my knowledge of Euclidian geometry and the surrounding environs to determine the best route. On the delivery sheet Gwen has scrawled the mysterious acronym V^2 instead of a street address.

"What's V-squared?" I yell above the music.

"Video Village," she replies. "My mom sold those on her lunch hour."

Gwen will marry a rich man or have a trust fund, or both. So her leniency with the alphabet and numbers won't be a problem. I, on the other hand, am heading to Las Vegas the minute I can afford a car.

The geographer in me dictates that we should first complete our deliveries near Main Street and then work our way out toward the surrounding neighborhoods. At one end of town is a block of municipal buildings. At the other is the high school, Grange Hall, YMCA, and the public library. In the middle section is the movie theater, grocery store, and white stuccoed funeral parlor. The funeral parlor makes me think of Craig. What if I die without ever kissing him again? I eat another chocolate donut. It's just what the magazine articles warn against—substituting complex carbohydrates for love.

"So what do you know about Craig Larkin and Brandt's sister, Sheryl Shaeffer?" I direct this question to Gwen, since she runs the electronic dating bulletin board that tracks couples.

"Splitsville. Sheryl found some college guy whose daddy is a big-deal real estate tycoon," Gwen reports authoritatively. "You know—yellow sports car, winter ski cabin, beach condo in Florida. She must have inherited her mother's expensive tastes," Gwen adds sarcastically. Sheryl's mother is always stylishly dressed in tight-fitting designer suits with short skirts, her nails all lacquered up, and lots of jewelry stapled to her, as if a safe filled with gold bullion split open on her head. Actually, Sheryl and her mom look more like sisters than mother and daughter.

After Gwen returns from making the drop at Video Village, she tosses Jane the money to put into a manila envelope with a thin red string attached to the flap.

"I love your shorthand," I say, once again scrutinizing the delivery sheet. "What do three plus signs mean?"

"They're crosses, stupid. Our Lady of Perpetual Agony." That's Gwen's code name for her church, which is really Our Lady of Perpetual Sanctity.

I instruct Jane to turn left off the main drag. She blasts Madonna's version of "American Pie," spins the wheel with one hand, hides a cigarette below the dashboard with the other, and sings, *"I was a lonely teenage broncin' buck with a pink carnation and a pickup truck. . . ."*

We pull up to the ornate Catholic church that has some housing for nuns in the back, a small primary school attached to the side, and annoying electronic bells that can play all twelve verses of any hymn.

"Do you think . . . that they, you know, Craig and Sheryl, were having sex?" I ask.

"Are you kidding me?" Jane shouts above the radio.

"Of *course* they were having sex," Gwen states authoritatively. "Sheryl flunked seventh grade, so she's, like, almost nineteen. That's why she dumped him. Sheryl's *over* high school guys."

While Gwen walks the donuts to the rectory, Jane and I work on our nun jokes. Only we pretend it's the nuns sitting around in their habits, throwing back a few whiskeys and cracking wise about their students.

"What's green-and-blue plaid and spins around in circles?" asks Jane.

"What, Sister Mary Jane?" I play along.

"A third grader with her homework caught in the wheel of the bus."

Gwen returns minus the donuts and we're off to the outlying neighborhoods.

"Turn right into Mush Acres," I announce. It's what we called Marsh Acres, the most run-down section of town.

"Do you want us to find out if Craig still likes you?" offers Jane.

"Oh please, how could a guy like Craig actually have a crush on me?" I know this is like raising a pink flag to the Oprah-fiers, but sometimes a girl needs a push.

They both make the appropriate sighs and then Gwen goes first. "Of *course* he could still like you. If you hadn't been so idiotic about who was supposed to call who after you made out at that party, then you'd be wearing his football jersey today." Craig and I had briefly exchanged saliva over the summer while Sheryl was off having her dimples bronzed. He was an incredible kisser—just the exact right amount of spit, tongue pressure, and groping. Only we never kissed or even spoke again after that night.

Jane goes next. "Guys don't make out with you where other people can see if they don't want it on the public record. And excuse me, but I'm sure that Craig *did* call your house. You just never get any phone messages with all those kids answering the phone and chanting 'The Alphabet Song' to whoever's on the line."

Jane has a valid point. Communication *is* challenging, with the twins constantly using the cordless phone to play "near" and "far" along with *Sesame Street*'s Grover.

"I'll ask Megan to ask her boyfriend Mike whose older brother Brian is best friend's with Craig's cousin Todd to find out if he likes you," says Gwen.

There you had it. Four Degrees of Gwen.

"Okay, but don't make any calls on my behalf. I mean, ask if you think of it. It's no big deal. Don't go out of your way, like don't go home and phone him *just* to ask."

Studying the list, I say, "The last stop is way out on Ransom Road."

"That's a guy my dad works with," says Gwen. "He can bring them to the office on Friday, when he gets back from his business trip."

I fail to mention that by then the donuts might be, well, they might be better employed as paperweights. But I don't feel like going all the way out there either. Ransom Road is in the boondocks, where all the farm kids live. Though with the current rate of suburban sprawl a lot of wheat farmers are selling out to developers. Sprouting up in place of amber waves of grain are outlet centers and warehouselike bulk supermarkets.

"You know, Hallie," Jane tells me solemnly, "you'd better get a body double if you're going to keep ditching school, because that creepy Attendance Nazi, Mr. Collier, was staking out your desk during first period this morning."

"Thanks," I say. "What a selfless act of devotion on his part. I can feel the love."

Gwen invites me back to her house for a makeover, where she has her own bathroom equipped with klieg lights, foundation for a nation, and rotating magnification mirrors. "If you'd just blow-dry your hair, apply mascara, and use sunscreen so your nose isn't always clown-red, you wouldn't need to spend so much time wondering if guys like you. They'd be *chasing* you."

"Yeah, Gwen, guys will be *chasing me* with Band-Aids, a silver cross, and a handful of garlic is more like it."

"Oh, Hallie," Gwen says, as if it isn't her fault that I'm destined to be a permanent "before" photograph in her hall of beauty.

"You probably *should* stay at Gwen's," advises Jane, though not for cosmetic reasons. "If Collier was stalking you in homeroom, then that means he went to your house today."

The girls offer to drop me at home, but it's Monday night and I have a steady engagement that requires my presence. At least it does if I ever want to be able to afford a car in order to get to Vegas and start my new life.

Only it isn't until the station wagon is out of sight that I realize Jane has accidentally given me *her* World Cup duffel bag in place of my own. Shit. I hope she doesn't have a take-home test or something else she needs in there. Then I realize *I'm* the one in trouble, since that's where I thought I'd put my betting money. However, I relax upon locating my stake in the small pouch attached to the seat of my bike and quickly head around the corner to the church.

Deal Me In

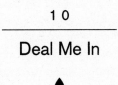

When I reach the back entrance of the solemn granite-faced house of worship, the sun has already set behind the bell tower and though the vestibule light is not switched on there are four cars in the parking lot and the door is unlocked. Inside, deep voices rise from the basement stairwell and I cling to the splintery railing while carefully making my way down the rickety wooden steps.

The basement is dimly illuminated by three bare urine-colored bulbs. Bluish cigarette smoke clogs the air and the scent of freshly opened salt-and-vinegar potato chips competes with the powerful aroma of bayberry coming from an open box of candles that sits on a broken pew next to a dust-coated Christmas manger. In the center of the noxious haze four middle-aged guys huddle around two card tables pushed together while the bulkiest and the only African American, Officer Rich, acts as banker and issues red, white, and blue plastic poker chips in exchange for cash. He's still in his uniform except for the dark brown tie and stiff cap, which hang off the chair behind him.

"Oh great," sneers Herb Rowland, the local pharmacist, seeing me standing at the bottom of the staircase. "It's ladies' night."

"Just think of it as more money for you to win, Herb," Officer Rich suggests. The fact that he's wearing a badge adds a natural diplomacy to his words. "So what are you in for, Hallie? A Jackson Five?"

But I don't have my usual five twenty-dollar bills tonight. "Just a sawbuck." I toss the crumpled ten from my oil strike onto the table and take the empty chair next to Pastor Costello and directly across from Al Santora, a technician at the municipal water-treatment plant. Pastor Costello says hello and Al grunts, anxious to deal the first hand.

"Spend all your money on boxing lessons?" asks Herb, obviously alluding to my shredded elbows and scabbed hands.

"I'd hate to see how the other guy looks," says Officer Rich.

"You won't," I remark dryly. "He's dead."

We play poker for a little over three hours, with a short break for some sandwiches that Father Costello picked up at the deli. The food is usually compliments of God.

Herb wins the first few rounds, which makes him cocky, so he overbets and has to go back to the bank. Al catches a bunch of hands near the end, but they're chump change. Officer Rich folds often and folds early. He has an extremely overbearing wife. But he plays well and manages to win a couple of big rounds. Pastor Costello wins and then loses and then wins and then loses and mumbles, "The Lord giveth, the Lord taketh away." I'd wager that if you calculated his overall balance sheet from playing cards, it'd come to exactly nil. He's proof that life is a zero-sum game.

If it doesn't cost much to stay in, then I don't fold up, or else the guys will think every time I do stick it's because I've got the cards. Sometimes you have to bluff just to get caught bluffing. However, I manage to take three healthy pots, and that puts me slightly ahead.

Finally, it's the last deal of the night. I hold a dead man's hand of two pair—aces and eights. Pastor Costello drops a one-eyed jack in front of me, which he'd called as wild, so now I have a neat boat. I clean up a tidy profit of seventy dollars. Only it's mostly from Al, and so I won't be able to collect until he gets paid in three weeks, on the first of the month.

It was almost two years ago that I'd happened across this discreet low-stakes poker game, which follows the Monday night Grounds Committee meeting. Actually, it *is* the Monday night Grounds Committee meeting. The way the guys figure it is that they all meet on church *grounds*. Also, Grounds Committee is a carefully chosen moniker that brings to mind pruning and snowplowing and therefore doesn't attract the womenfolk.

Most people would probably wonder how a teenage girl managed to get herself invited to a weekly poker game with three beer-swilling locals and a man of the cloth. And the truth is that I wasn't exactly invited. When I don't feel like heading home for dinner I stop by the church to raid the apple juice,

ice cream, and graham crackers, all kept in good supply for the Sunday school. And sometimes, if there's been a meeting of the Ladies' Craft Group, or better yet, a board meeting, I can scrounge up cinnamon swirl coffee cake and even a leftover turkey sandwich. This is all thanks to the fact that the basement window is never locked. Actually, the metal frame is so caked with rust that it won't even close all the way, a little ecclesiastical inside information to which Marty Benson, the town drunk, is also privy.

Anyway, one night I pried open the window, and when this huge cloud of smoke hit me in the face I swear I thought the whole church was going up in flames. Pastor Costello quickly appeared at the back door, probably assuming I was seeking spiritual solace, rather than some old-fashioned appetite appeasement. And after explaining that I was just sniffing around for a crust of bread he quickly trundled me downstairs and offered me access to the seven-card-stud buffet. In fact, I was hustled inside so fast that it seemed he was worried someone might be following me.

Initially the guys denied my request to join in for a few hands. But then I whipped out a hundred bucks and asked if they knew high-low seven-card stud. That definitely swung the mood in my favor. And when I mentioned how it was funny that I'd never heard any of their wives talking about the game, I was immediately offered not only a seat at the table but a stack of poker chips and my own bowl of pretzels.

"I should report you to the cops," Al says with mock disgust when the game is finally over.

"The police are already here," Herb chimes in from across the table. He nods in the direction of mild-mannered Officer Rich.

"Good point," says Al, gathering up the grease-stained red diamond-backed playing cards.

"You're not even old enough to drive," he taunts me.

"Am so! I turned sixteen last Monday, and now that my losing streak is over I'll soon have enough for a used car."

"Remind me again, Rich," Al says dryly. "Why do we let her play in our *guys only* poker game?"

Officer Rich rises and straps on the clunky black belt that suspends his holster and parking ticket book, the latter looking more used than the former.

"You *know* why. Because she knows too much."

Even though the game is over, Al shuffles the cards out of habit before replacing them in the worn cardboard box. He casts an accusatory glance in the general direction of Herb. "That's your fault," he says.

"Goddammit—sorry, Father—*nothing* is going on with Jemma!" Herb declares defensively. "She works for me, and so I just offer her a ride home once in a while . . . when the weather is bad."

"Oh yeah, Herb," I reply and laugh right in his face. "And the entrance to Harriman woods is on the way to *both* your homes."

"I wish you *would* get a car," says Herb irritably. "That stupid bicycle of yours goes too many places."

"Well, it's not as if *you're* out keeping the streets safe for virginity," I retort.

"Jesus Christ—sorry, Father—why doesn't everyone mind their own beeswax," Al says, mostly to me, apparently back on Herb's side. He's aggravated that he has to write an IOU. An IOU to a teenager. To a girl.

"Maybe you should withdraw the money you owe me from your secret Saving-For-A-Boat account down at the bank," I say. "The one that your wife doesn't know about."

"And how the hell did you hear about *that?*" Al stands up and glares at me, not so good-naturedly. "You think you're so smart, don't you, Hallie Palmer?"

"Smart enough not to take a hit playing blackjack when I have seventeen and the dealer is showing a six."

"All right, all right," interjects Pastor Costello. "I think that's enough revelry for one evening, gentlemen." He glances over at me. "And lady."

"Some lady," Herb says and hastily pulls on his windbreaker. "Lady Macbeth is more like it."

"That would be Lady Luck to you," I crack wise.

"Christ—sorry, Father—she probably plays cards every night and shoots craps during the day," says Al. "If I played all the time, I'd be that good, too."

"Yeah, Hallie Capone. You still riding out to the Indian casino?" Herb asks me.

"Nah," I say. "The Feds cracked down on being underage over the summer and I got the boot. They've got my kisser on file at both doors."

"I always said you'd be famous," Al states sarcastically. "Before you go to jail, just make sure to tell us what your favorite kind of cake is so we can bake a file into it. And I'll lay ten-to-one odds it's not *angel* food cake."

"Funny as a leper in a wind tunnel, Al," I say.

"It takes a child to raze a village," Herb comments wryly.

Choosing to ignore him, I say, "You'd be surprised at who goes to the casino. A few times I saw Brandt and Sheryl Shaeffer's mother there in the middle of the day. Once when they were taking my mug shot up in the crypt I had a chance to watch her play blackjack. And let me tell you, she's no casual cardplayer. She bet big and knew not to split an ace-eight combination."

"I'm glad she's good with numbers," says Al. "She's my stockbroker."

"I hope she makes more money for you than you make playing poker," chimes in Herb.

Officer Rich is just about to take off when he turns to me and the good humor of the evening promptly vanishes from his pillowy face. "Uh, Hallie, I'm getting complaints from the school and it's only the second week of September. Did you forget your homeroom number or else relocate to Randolph County without telling them?"

"I'm sixteen now and you can't make me go to school anymore." This is delivered in my best *schools are for fools* tone of voice.

Officer Rich studies me with a mixture of exasperation and resignation, as a man might watch his house sink into the ocean during a tropical storm. Then he turns to Pastor Costello as if to say, *See what* you *can do, because* I *don't get paid enough.*

Pastor Costello raises Officer Rich one glance with his *Jesus, this is a job for Job* look but apparently feels beholden by his occupation to take a stab at it. He leans over and places his arm on the back of my wobbly wooden folding chair and says, "Hallie, why don't I treat you to some cheese and crackers in my study?"

Cheez Whiz on Ritz crackers is Father Costello's on-tap solution to every dilemma, from what size font to use on the weekly church bulletin to a complete loss of faith in God.

"No thanks, Padre," I say. "Save it for the folks who want to be saved." I leap up and dart past Officer Rich, take the stairs two at a time, and make my escape into the crisp fall air.

Herb yells something after me, only I can't tell if it's Hallie or Hellion. Hellion is his nickname for me when we're playing poker. Of course, he never uses it in front of outsiders. In public the guys have to treat me like a regular kid. And I have to be polite and call them Mr. So-and-So instead of Herb and Al. Though we always call Pastor Costello "Pastor Costello." Except for Pastor

Costello's mother, who calls him Arthur. Only she puts the emphasis on the "thur." Ar-*thur*. And it sounds really silly.

I hop on my bike and take the dirt path through the fields toward my house. The night air is rich with the aroma of pine and lingering hydrangea, and underneath my tires fallen leaves and branches crackle and crunch. A dog barks in the distance. Another answers back, as if they're having a conversation. Then a puddle sprays muddy water all the way up to my eyeballs. Gross. One thing is for sure, when I have a car there will be no more pedaling, no more woodland shortcuts with sharp tree branches swiping me in the face, and no more muddy tracks up my ass when it rains, making me look like a frigging inside-out skunk.

The House of Grimm is dark aside from a porch light. Below the picture window there's a rustle in the bushes. Brandt is probably stalking me. When he wants something, like to go to some horrible science fair with me, he keeps popping up every few hours hoping I'll be won over by his persistence. Brandt is a big believer in the Stockholm Syndrome, that given a long enough period of time a captor and his prisoner will eventually fall in love.

But from out of the bushes darts a neighborhood cat. I lean my bike against the cold chunky bark of the oak tree, stand on the seat, and easily hoist myself up to the first branch and then climb up to a higher branch, which is adjacent to the lowest part of our white aluminum-sided house. From there it's a cinch to climb across the eaves and up to the second story. I try jostling open the bathroom window, but it's locked. Shit. I have to shinny up and over the roof and rap on Eric's window with my knuckles.

After a few minutes Eric nudges open the window. He's annoyed, but he pushes it up the rest of the way and moves his desk aside just enough so I can drop into the room and then pull Jane's duffel bag in behind me. "I'm telling Mom and Dad," he threatens.

"And I'm telling them that last year when you said you lost your school ID and had to pay ten dollars for a new one it was because you accidentally dropped Wite-Out on the old one and changed your birthday to make yourself twenty-one instead of sweet-'n'-shady-seventeen. I'm sure that Dad, as a civil servant for the state of Ohio, would keep his job a long time with his darling oldest boy football star, heir, and namesake in the pokey for underage drinking and using fake ID."

"Fuck you," Eric says and slams the window shut behind me. "Get out!"

He tilts his head to one side and runs his fingers through his brush cut as if he's checking to make sure the lobotomy scar isn't showing again.

"What's going on?" Teddy, our ten-year-old brother, sleepily inquires from his position as a lump of blanket in the top bunk.

"Shut up!" Eric and I whisper in unison. No matter what we're fighting about, we always stick together when it comes to torturing the little kids. Whenever it rains, we tell them that God is crying because of something bad that they did.

"Now he's going to wet the bed," a grumpy Eric complains.

"So what else is new?" As I leave their room I switch off the overhead light.

"Hallie?" Eric calls softly. "Just Call Me Dick came by this evening, and Dad's shooting to kill."

"Just Call Me Dick" is how all the kids refer to Mr. Collier, the persnickety attendance officer who is constantly playing cat and nuisance with me. Whenever a grown-up calls him Richard he obnoxiously squirts out *Just call me Dick* before the person has time to finish pronouncing the *D* at the end of his given name.

"I hope for your sake that you've been busy organizing a Braille book drive for the blind over the past few days."

"As a matter of fact, I was. But thanks for the tip. 'Night."

" 'Night," he says wearily. By the dim glow of the Donald Duck night-light I observe him tentatively poking a finger at the mattress above his to test for any leakage before climbing back into the bottom bunk.

Of course, the real miracle of the day will not be to sneak in without my parents' finding out, but to make it to my room without tripping over a PlaySkool lawn mower. Or get a deadly concussion from an Easy Bake oven and then have my corpse sprayed by sixty-four Crayola crayons while the built-in sharpener lodges itself up my nose.

1 1

Betting Against the House

♦

A note on my pillow says, SEE DAD IMMEDIATELY. Yeah, right. As if I'm going to turn myself in after midnight and get even more murdered.

Instead I lie on my bed like a prisoner counting the cracks in the ceiling of my cell and watch the fan turn slowly around and around. What's wrong with me? Why do I feel like I'm in that *Sesame Street* song? *One of these things is not like the others, one of these things just doesn't belong.* I'm part of this family and yet I don't feel as if I am. I never have. From the moment the school bus pulled up on the first day of kindergarten I've felt that everything is wrong—that there's been a huge mistake. And every year it only gets worse. Whenever I read about adopted children reunited with their birth parents I think that something similar will happen to me; that my real parents will show up and it will turn out that there was a hospital mix-up and I'll be whisked off to my proper life, whatever that may be. Or else I imagine that I'm an alien who has been put in this all-American family pod as some sort of an experiment and at any minute a spaceship is going to land and take me back home to Jupiter or the Planet Claire or wherever I'm from.

Last week there was a quiz in *Cosmopolitan* magazine that supposedly determines if you're suffering from depression. It asked questions such as, Do you worry a lot about money? Do minor irritations overly upset you? Are you easily disappointed by friends and family? Do you take yourself seriously most of the time?

According to the test I'm not depressed. In fact, there isn't too much that worries me, especially now that I've purged school from my life. Sure, I care that I lost the money at the track, but I'll make it back. One day last summer I dropped almost a grand on a pool game. There were also days I'd won over a thousand dollars playing blackjack at the Indian casino. That's how it is with gambling. I just need to regroup and recoup for a month or two. And I need to pay Craig back as soon as possible or else he's going to believe whatever Eric has been telling him about how deranged I am.

However, I *do* conclude from the *Cosmo* quiz that my parents would have to answer yes to every question. They constantly worry about money, get overly upset about minor irritations, and are easily disappointed by family. And not only do I think they're depressed, but quite frankly, they're depressing *me*.

Mom and Dad and Eric think the reason I gamble and won't attend school is that I'm lazy. But I'm not. I just happen to think it's a waste of time to write a paper so some teacher can decide whether or not she likes it. Likewise, it's dumb to get paid five bucks an hour for shoveling snow or putting air in people's tires when I can make an easy hundred knowing that Pastor Costello is bluffing whenever he fingers the silver cross around his neck right before he bets. Gambling is how I paid for my mountain bike and my field hockey stick and a lot of other stuff. And after I buy a car I'm going to start investing some money in the stock market.

Further complicating matters is the fact that my parents think gambling isn't Christian. But then they like to tag almost anything pleasurable as unchristian, for one reason or another. If I were a parent I'd rather know that my daughter was out playing in a friendly poker game than listening to acid rock music alone in her room and painting all her Barbie dolls black. Only they act as if by playing five-card draw in the lunchroom I'm going to wind up pregnant. At least that's what my aunt Alice says, that I'm going to finish high school via correspondence courses from a home for unwed mothers.

And what the hell am I supposed to do in my room for the next four weeks? It drives me crazy to be inside with the kids drawing in crayon all over my shit and singing frigging Barney "I Love You" songs while popping cap guns. You can't walk down the stairs without tripping over a Fisher-Price phone or a plastic potty seat shaped like a damn duck. And if my parents aren't going to help me buy a car, what's the point in staying here at all?

That's when it dawns on me. I can leave. Just walk out the door. Well, I'd never walk out the *door*. I'm more of a window person. Actually, I had run away a couple of times when I was thirteen, only I didn't have any place to go. But now I have a plan.

Wow. I've been a hamster sitting in his metal cage while the gate has been open the entire time. Besides, they'll probably be happy to have the extra room for the new baby and one less mouth to feed. Before I can change my mind I haul my knapsack out of the closet and pack up some clothes. Then I toss in Jane's duffel bag—which turned out to contain an Ace bandage, a padlock, some athletic tape, and a mud-encrusted pair of sweatpants.

As for where to go, gosh, I have tons of choices. There's always Gwen's house. Her parents are really cool about extended sleepovers. In fact, I have a couple friends whose folks wouldn't mind having me live with them fulltime. I'm a good guest, too. I do the dishes and they tell me to stay as long as I want.

The only problem with living at other kids' houses is that eventually their parents want to reform me as well. It starts small, with trying to get me to do homework after dinner and watch the Discovery Channel instead of true-crime shows. And then before I know it they're chasing me with *Where There's a Will There's an "A"* educational videos and Bible verse, just like Aunt Polly laying into poor old Tom Sawyer.

Then there's Jane's mom, who was raised in Georgia and can find a way to work scripture into absolutely *any* conversation, even one about the weather. In the hopes of prodding her into offering one of her delicious root beer floats, you might say, "It sure is hot out, Mrs. Davenport." And she'll reply: "But we know a hotter place, *don't we?*"

However, you always got your ice cream float. Everything has a price, at least that's what Cappy says. Gambling. Even people. Or rather, especially people.

I finish packing quietly so that I don't wake Louise. Though she's used to me climbing in and out of the window at all hours. In many ways I actually envy Louise. She's content to attend school, be a cheerleader, edit the yearbook, and go shopping on weekends. Some evenings she sits at the computer writing instant messages to her boyfriend and giggling, or else they have a fight and then make up.

Of course, I don't want to *be* like that. It's my worst nightmare. And yet, at the same time, I *wish* I could be like that—that it *didn't* seem so alien.

Louise is happy. She even says so herself. She always asks, "Hallie, why can't you just be *normal*? You know, just try it, maybe you'd like it."

Climbing down the oak tree, I don't even have to search for my toeholds, I know them so well. The night sky is cloudless and the moon is silvery blue and almost full, and it's easy to retrace my path to Nuthatch Lane. That summerhouse looked awfully inviting. But maybe they use it at night or have floodlights illuminating the backyard. I couldn't remember seeing a dog. A dog could be a problem.

After ditching my bike in the woods I cautiously thread my way around the apple trees. A few lights are still glowing in the main house, but it doesn't appear as if anyone will be coming outside, unless the old lady suddenly runs out of toad's blood or some other ingredient for one of her magic potions.

It's almost ten o'clock. The door to the little fairy tale gingerbread house opens easily. The floorboards creak so loudly that for a second I worry that they might give way entirely. If ever I get to be friendly with these people and can pull them away from their chaise longues and vampire rituals for a minute, I might introduce them to the concept of dry rot.

There's just enough light inside for me to dig out my retainer and lie down on the couch. I don't dare switch on one of the table lamps. However, the glow from the moon casts long shadows on the walls and windows, and I decide that if a person had a faint heart and an active imagination she could start thinking up some pretty spooky scenarios to accompany the sound of energetic night insects sawing away. And from somewhere off in the distance, beyond the dark-topped trees, I hear the faint sound of a choir singing.

Seeing as it's awfully early for me to be going to sleep, I tell myself a story in order to become drowsy. I enjoy updating fairy tales such as "Snow White and the Seven Dwarfs" or "Rapunzel." For instance, I'll have Snow White become pregnant by one of the dwarfs and then there will be a controversy over whether they should do prenatal testing to see if the baby is also a dwarf. Or I make Rapunzel a prisoner-of-color, with her own cosmetics line that she sells via mail order out of the tower unbeknownst to the witch. And the Prince's father, the King, is in an uproar about the prospect of his son and heir having biracial children with a feminist who runs her own business. As anyone can see, the possibilities are endless. . . .

1 2

An Honest Day's Work

♣

When I raise my eyelids a brilliant sun is smashing through a hexagonal window near the roof and causing me to wonder if I passed out in a tanning bed. It's seven o'clock, give or take ten minutes. I don't wear a watch. It's not that I don't own one. It's just that I always know what time it is, even when I first wake up.

In the corner of the room farthest from the door is a large round table covered by a full-length pink and green paisley silk tablecloth, which makes a perfect hiding place for my knapsack. After straightening the cushions on the couch, I attempt to corral my rebellious hair into a braid. Then I retrieve my bike and take the path through the woods back to the street so as not to cut through the Stocktons' yard and risk being seen.

While I wait to pay for my donuts and chocolate Yoo-Hoo at the 7-Eleven, my eyes automatically seek out *The Daily Racing Form*. Even in my effort to go straight for a couple of weeks, it isn't lost on me that today is a perfect day to hit the track. Only now I'm a day laborer with exactly eleven dollars and fifteen cents left to my name. And if I *did* have any more money I should probably be putting it toward a tin lunch pail and a red plastic thermos rather than temptation. This will teach me not to listen to some old fart down at OTB. I am now experiencing the ripple effect, the trickle down of an ill-thought-out wager, just like all the rest of those losers who have duct tape covering the holes in the soles of their shoes.

My thoughts are interrupted by a violent blast of flowery perfume mingled with industrial-strength black coffee fumes blowing in from the northeast. Standing behind me is Mrs. Shaeffer, Sheryl and Brandt's mother, holding a large steaming Styrofoam cup and a folded *Wall Street Journal* in one hand while applying reddish-brown lipstick to her mouth with the other, using the muffin display case as a mirror.

Instinct tells me to drop the donuts and take off. But then I realize the chances of her running into either of my parents are slim to none and Slim just walked away. Besides, after completing the lip-lacquering she's totally wrapped up in the financial headlines and I don't think she even notices me.

On the way back to the Stocktons' I wonder when I'll receive my first paycheck. Not that it's a matter of survival. Fortunately a homeless person can survive quite easily in a small midwestern town, at least until winter. People always wonder aloud why Marty Benson, the town drunk, doesn't move down to Florida. Why bother? The living is easy right here.

Besides, Marty is an institution. Parents needed to be able to threaten their teenage sons: "You're going to end up just like Marty-the-Town-Drunk if you don't straighten up, mister." And everyone knows what that means—a dilapidated vagrant in a stained suit reeking of cheap whiskey propped up on a park bench during the day and sleeping in the courthouse vestibule or, on cold nights, the church basement.

In fact, if it weren't for Marty-the-Town-Drunk there'd be no one for those individuals just scraping by to look down upon. Or else to hand a crumpled dollar bill in order to relieve their guilt for something they did that nobody knows about. Herb probably slips Marty a crisp new twenty every time he drives Jemma home.

As for food, there are still tomatoes in people's gardens and the church larder. I only resort to eating fruit and baked goods at the Star-Mart when it's absolutely necessary. I mean, it's not as if I stand in the aisle rotating a rump roast under a lamp. But it still means exiting with the merchandise *inside* my body. However, friends' houses are out of bounds now that my folks will be on the lookout for me.

At about a quarter past eight I approach the Stocktons' front door and try to appear as if I haven't spent the night in their backyard. Just as I'm preparing to make my knock, a medium-sized man with dark brown hair and a neatly trimmed mustache pushes open the door using an overstuffed tannish-yellow leather briefcase.

"Good morning. I'm Gilbert Rush. I'm the normal one here." He announces this breathlessly and quickly switches his briefcase to his left hand and then extends his right one in my direction. "They"—he indicates with a nod of his head toward the inside of the house—"don't know what day it is."

I shake his hand. "I'm Hallie Palmer, the new yard person."

He laughs good-naturedly. "Yes, I've heard all about you. Welcome aboard. Bertie says he's positive that you're not an alcoholic but you can't move in the morning without a chocolate Yoo-Hoo."

"I guess it's my coffee."

"It's lovely meeting you. I have to run off to a training seminar. Go right in. Bertie's in the kitchen." Just then the high-pitched shriek of an alarm blasts from deep within the house and we both wince. "Follow the smoke alarm," he adds, athletically taking the porch steps in a single leap.

"Hello," I call out as I enter the front hallway and the screen door wails and then slams shut behind me. Whoa, what a bang. They need a new washer behind that spring.

Mr. Bernard appears from the kitchen wiping his hands on a tea towel, seemingly oblivious to the smoke cloud trailing behind him and the deafening blare that's issuing from the plastic contraption above our heads. He pulls a dining room chair into the hallway and calmly steps up and removes the battery from the smoke alarm and then lets out an exhausted sigh. "Mother set fire to a bagel. A *bagel*. Can you believe it? She insisted on heating it in the oven because she's protesting the fact that our new toaster was made in Nepal by some outfit accused of employing child labor."

Mr. Bernard says this with mock despair, as if the entire household is preoccupied with hatching one big conspiracy to aggravate him and he is the voice of reason crying out in the domestic wilderness. "Mother is *not* oven-approved. She burns everything in the large one and then puts tinfoil in the microwave. She's permitted to operate the toaster, teakettle, and the electric can opener. And that's *it*!"

I just cough and wave at the smog streaming out of the kitchen.

But just as suddenly he drops that act and tells me he's going to sing his version of "There's No Business Like Show Business" and bursts into: "*There's no tuna like dolphin-safe tuna, like no tuna I know. The boats, the nets, the harpoons, the killing. One minute you're swimming in the ocean with your dorsal fin, the next you're being sold by Star-Kist in a tin.*"

"I hear you, Ethel Merman!" Ms. Olivia shouts from the other room. "And it's not funny!"

"Mother?" Mr. Bernard says with exaggerated surprise. "What are *you* still doing here? I thought you were scheduled to donate a kidney at half past eight." He glances down at his watch and then turns back to me. "Last week she forgot to poke holes in a baked potato," he reports in a stage whisper. *"Ka-boom!"*

But just as Mr. Bernard throws his arms up in the air to illustrate his story, someone comes up behind me and covers my eyes with his hands, the way you do to a friend until they guess who it is. The fingers are extremely smooth, and I can tell by the coarse wool around the wrists that the person is wearing a thick sweater. Perhaps their housemate came back for a sweater. "Mr. Rush?" I guess.

"Stop that, Rocky!" says Mr. Bernard and I hear him jump down off the chair.

The hands move away from my face and a loud whooping goes up behind me. Standing on a dining room chair is a full-grown chimpanzee, hooting, grinning, and clapping his hands.

However, Mr. Bernard is not amused. "That's Rocky," he says in a curt tone. "I thought he'd be gone by the time you started work. We're just keeping him here temporarily."

Mr. Bernard proceeds to ignore the chimp and indicates that I should follow him by waving his towel in the direction of the burning bread. Rocky darts off in the direction of the living room.

I'm still rather stunned after coming face-to-face with a chimpanzee. Sure I'd seen them in zoos and on television, but I'd never known anyone to keep one as a pet. Furthermore, I can't help but wonder why Mr. Bernard lets his mother in the kitchen at all if she's off her rocker and dangerous. The old lady could kill herself or leave the gas on. But Mr. Bernard blithely pushes through the haze and doesn't appear at all concerned about the prospect of the whole house going up in flames. Instead he smiles at me, pulls back the curtains and opens a window above the kitchen sink, and removes the dark green apron he'd been wearing. Underneath it Mr. Bernard is nattily dressed in black pants with a faint gray check, a cream-colored corduroy shirt, and a gray suede vest.

"I was hoping to devote the morning to acclimating you, but I must scout out an estate sale. However, I've created a list to get you started." He passes me a piece of letterhead stationery on which there's a neatly hand-printed row of five tasks. "You need not accomplish them in any particular order. Do as much or as little as you like today."

The items seem to be pretty straightforward yard person–type tasks such as mowing the grass and turning the gardens.

"Mother," Mr. Bernard calls into the room where we had all met the day before. "Hallie is about to embark upon her work. She'll tell you if she needs anything."

He turns back to me. "She's giving Father his breakfast." He quickly grabs a tweed sport jacket that's hanging over the back of one of the kitchen chairs. It has gray silk threads running through it that glimmer when they catch the sunlight that's now streaming into the room along with the morning breeze.

I see a flash of color and Ms. Olivia appears from around the corner in a bright red dress and places her hand on my elbow. "Good morning, dear. It's splendid that you've accepted the position." She says this with a warm smile.

"*Quel est le date aujourd'hui, cheri?*" Ms. Olivia asks.

"*Je ne sais pas.* Hallie, do you know the date today?" Mr. Bernard translates.

"Eighter from Decatur," I reply without thinking.

They both look at me as if I've sprung another head.

Whoops. Sometimes I forget I'm not playing poker. "The eighth," I say. "Today is September eighth."

"Yes, of course. Thank you," Mr. Bernard says. Then he turns back to Ms. Olivia. "Did the Judge finish his oatmeal this morning?"

"About half."

"Father suffers from Alzheimer's disease," Mr. Bernard explains as he strides toward the front entrance hall. "Mother, *please* call down to the Senior Center and get me into that Hudson estate sale a day early. You've been friends with the sister since the Flood, and if Ethan Hill gets his hands on those Aubusson Oriental rugs I'll have to bite off his right ear in the manner of Turiddu and Alfio in *Cavalleria Rusticana.*"

"Stop being so melodramatic. It's not enough that I keep all of your accounts on my computer. No, you're always wanting me to procure for you among my widow friends." She raises her arms and her delicate fingers flutter about the sides of her head, but without touching anything.

Mr. Bernard just rolls his eyes and pushes open the swinging door.

But his mother doesn't *really* seem to mind the request. At least not like when my mother becomes exasperated by ungrateful, overdemanding children and threatens that she's on the brink of a nervous breakdown. In fact, Ms. Olivia complains as if it's an inside joke. And I decide that she may not be so senile after all.

"Come and meet the Judge," Ms. Olivia says. "I'll introduce you as the county clerk, because whenever we're in the Florida Room he thinks he's in chambers. Or would you rather be a witness for the prosecution?"

"County clerk is fine," I reply. Just Call Me Dick is always saying that I'm about one day of playing hooky away from reform school, and so I figure the judicial exercise will be good practice for my trial.

Sitting in an armchair with a TV tray in front of him, which also acts as a stand for a small wooden gavel and half-eaten bowl of oatmeal, is the Honorable Judge Stockton. He has high prominent cheekbones, a ruddy complexion, and with that beard, mustache, and froth of white hair, holy shit, is he ever a dead ringer for Colonel Sanders. Ms. Olivia introduces me as the new clerk, and Mr. Stockton briefly looks up from sifting through a file folder on his lap.

"Some days he's more communicative than others," she says cheerily. "It probably sounds silly, but we put on his judge's robe every morning and give him a docket to sort through. The routine seems to make him happy."

Wow, if you didn't know something was wrong, he appears pretty normal sitting there—as if he's just about to smack that gavel into the oatmeal dish and send someone up the river for thirty to life. He really looks like a judge, too. Very distinguished, except for a yellow terry-cloth bib covering the front of his black flowing robe. He looks up at me for a moment, as if trying to situate me in the confused map of his memory.

"Does he understand what he's reading?" I ask in a whisper.

"No, I can't imagine he does. But I believe he comprehends that he used to do this every day and so it's familiar. There's always comfort to be found in the familiar," she says in an upbeat voice.

When Ms. Olivia speaks, she's very animated and gestures with practically her entire body and so appears younger than she is. I mean, I don't know exactly how old she is, probably around sixty. Her movements are swift but graceful, almost birdlike.

Not knowing what else to say, I move toward the door. "I'd better get started."

"Be sure to ask if you need anything. There should be a pair of gardening gloves about your size in a basket in the shed, and there are ear mufflers, or whatever they're called, to be used when you operate that cacophonous mower. And don't worry about the rose garden—I'll tend to it this afternoon."

Yeah, sure, I think. And I'll win the Kentucky Derby and buy a brand-new Mazda with heated seats and a CD player.

What Are the Odds?

♥

First I scope out the garage, but it's overloaded with furniture and rolled-up rugs and more old-fashioned lamps with shiny fringe dripping off the shade bottoms than there's crabgrass growing in the entire backyard. It finally occurs to me that this must be Mr. Bernard's business—he must restore old furniture. Only nothing in there is any good for doing yard work, unless I'm supposed to drag out the hundred-pound crystal chandelier and use it as a manure spreader.

The shed, on the other hand, is neatly organized and has everything necessary for industrial-strength lawn care—rider mower, electric hand-push mower, edging machine, pesticide sprayer, and extra lengths of garden hose. There's a tree trimmer, leaf blower, leaf sweeper, two boxes of lawn and leaf bags, and at least six different styles of rakes.

I decide to start by mowing the entire yard—front, back, and sides—since this gives the best visual effect and hopefully they won't worry that I'm another Lars-the-Alcoholic-Lawn-Mower-Man slacker. After checking to make sure no one is watching, I sneak into the summerhouse and retrieve my Walkman to wear underneath the ear protectors. Then I gas up that big Toro, turn on the tunes, and ride away. The sun shines down bright and clear but without warmth.

Almost four hours elapse before I notice Ms. Olivia waving a bunch of scallions at me from the big bay window in the Florida Room. She motions for me to come inside and points to the green and white stalks with her free hand. I guess she's going to feed me scallions for lunch.

"Bernard left us all sandwiches and fruit salad," she explains once I'm inside. "Or you can make some eggs if you prefer. He must have told you I'm not authorized to prepare food. Not even brownies from a mix. Bertie says that I don't cook, I burn." She laughs about the whole situation, as if it's okay to tell your mother that her cooking stinks, even if it's true. "He's right, of course. When I'm reading or writing, I completely forget about what's baking or boiling over in the kitchen."

At first I wonder if I should take my lunch into the backyard and sit under a tree, since I'm just the hired help. But Ms. Olivia has set the table for two.

"Roasted vegetable, roast beef, or tuna?" She passes me the platter.

I carefully remove a tuna sandwich and she selects a vegetable one. I'd never seen a vegetable sandwich before. I mean, one without anything else on it—no cheese slices or Oscar Mayer bologna.

"I don't consume anything that had parents," Ms. Olivia confides to me as if someone might be listening—like the roast beef, for instance. "I'm a vegetarian."

"Oh, you don't eat meat," I say.

"Bertie claims I'm starting to bend toward the window on sunny afternoons. He says we wouldn't have incisor teeth if we weren't carnivores. But I don't believe in unnecessary killing."

She's not normal by any standards, but she's definitely not hiding her own Easter eggs, either. Besides, they wouldn't allow her to care for another senile person if she were senile, would they?

My tuna sandwich is really good, not canned tuna and blobs of mayo. This tuna is brown, not white, and slightly drier and the chunks are bigger. Though I'm not picky about what I eat. Basically, if it's free, then it's for me.

Ms. Olivia calls into the sunroom, "Rocky, do you want a sandwich?"

The chimp comes darting out from the other room, long gangly arms dangling below his kneecaps, and his velvety brown eyes are bright and expressive, incredibly humanlike. So are his hands. He deftly makes a plate for himself with a sandwich and uses the serving spoon to take a big helping of fruit salad. Then he removes a napkin from one of the drawers in the highboy and easily balances the plate as he exits.

"That's amazing," I say. "I had no idea chimps were so . . . that they could . . ."

"Rocky is very special. He's been trained to work with people who have disabilities, specifically paraplegics who require insulin shots."

"Oh. So he helps the Judge."

"No, no," replies Ms. Olivia, "though he's wonderful with him, and the Judge seems to like him. He worked with my friend Geraldine for years, but she passed away last week and so now he's between engagements."

"Sorry about your friend" is all I can think of to say. Just when it seems as if these people can't possibly say or do anything weirder, they do. But the thing is, they act as if it's all perfectly normal!

After a few moments of silence Ms. Olivia politely inquires, "Do you attend school?"

Oh damn. Here it comes. "Oh yeah," I lie. "I go at night."

"Everyone must bow to his or her circadian rhythms," she states breezily.

I don't know what that means, but it doesn't seem to be a question or criticism and she doesn't pursue the school matter.

My sandwich disappears quickly, though I don't talk with my mouth open or anything table-incorrect like that, and then I say how tasty it was in an effort to encourage her to offer me a second one. Over the years I've discovered that the more you compliment the food, the more people *want* you to eat it. It actually makes them happy. And I'm all in favor of spreading joy in this manner. Also, operating as a professional vagrant is like being a bear— you get into the habit of storing up calories for later on.

"Help yourself to another one, dear. All that work must build your appetite."

I thank her and select a vegetable sandwich. To be honest, I had my eye on the roast beef, but as a general rule I never take the most expensive item on charity's plate. And also, now that my hostess has declared herself against slaughter, my good-guest instincts tell me to eat whatever she's eating. Ms. Olivia seems pleased by my selection.

"How's the work going? I saw you riding around on that gigantic machine and it appeared as if you were singing."

I don't mention the hidden Walkman, because the last thing I want her to think is that I'm goofing around on the job. Old people in particular have this habit of assuming that you can't walk and chew gum at the same time—

like if you're playing a video game you can't simultaneously listen to them and concentrate on the screen.

"Yeah, I like a little music," I say.

"It soothes the soul. The term *music* of course comes from the word *muse*, to inspire. Some people are happy because they sing, and others sing because they're happy. Into which category do you imagine you fall?"

Huh? "It makes the time go by fast. But if you mind getting bugs in your mouth, then you shouldn't sing while on a rider mower."

"Excellent observation." She smiles as if this is not the right answer but is just as good as the right answer.

The phone rings and Ms. Olivia hastily rises, places her napkin on her chair, and darts into the kitchen. It's easy to overhear the conversation, since the door between the two rooms is open. Though what she says doesn't exactly make sense. There's some polite chitchat along the lines of "How are you? Fine, thank you." Then Ms. Olivia instructs the caller to stop by in an hour, and that they're to meet in the living room of the main house and *not in the summerhouse.* Apparently she's going to give the person some sort of medication. My imagination returns to the mysterious Druid Circle in the backyard and then to Mr. Bernard's herb garden, and I wonder if she really does sell magic potions. Or have I just been reading too many of my brother Teddy's Harry Potter books?

But then I recall the small brown box on the table in the summerhouse containing pills in individual plastic packages that resemble the allergy medication my doctor gives out as samples. At least I'd assumed it was allergy medicine. I mean, why else would she keep it in the summerhouse? Though I thought it was odd that the labeling on the foil packets and the stack of brochures next to the box were all in a foreign language. Could the Stocktons be *drug dealers?* Does the chimp act as a runner or a lookout?

Ms. Olivia returns to the table, and I decide it's impossible for her to be a drug dealer. She seems like a sweet old lady, perhaps with some bizarre hobbies, but nonetheless, a law-abiding citizen. Besides, she wouldn't do a transaction with me right in the backyard, would she? I hope she doesn't ask me about the meaning of life or if I believe in God or if perhaps I'm in the market for any crystal meth.

Before she has a chance to say anything else, I jump right in with "I'm afraid we're going to need some oil if I'm going to finish mowing today. I searched around but couldn't find an oil can."

"If it's not in the shed, then I don't know. Bertie was always after Lars to make a list of supplies since we were constantly running out of everything, but he never did, except for Aquavit."

Aquavit must be a type of pesticide. I've never heard of it but don't want to let on.

Ms. Olivia's eyes light up as if she's arrived at a solution to the oil problem. And in fact, she has.

"Why don't you drive into town," she suggests. "And go to the hardware store or the gas station or wherever they traffic in mower grease."

She's obviously getting rid of me so the deal can go down within the hour.

I start to clear the table, but she says, "Let Rocky do that. It's good therapy for him."

The chimp is in *therapy*? I want to ask, but I don't.

"And be sure to drop by Bertie's store. He adores visitors. Plus it makes the shop appear busy, which attracts customers."

"Mr. Bernard has a store?"

"Oh yes, almost ten years now. It's a lovely shop right at the corner of North Abbey and Swan Streets. Bertie has a flair for design and window display, and especially the placement of objects. For three years he called it *Avant et Après*, which I thought was charming, but no one understood that it meant Before and After. So he switched to the more straightforward Stockton Antiques and Collectibles and then last year renamed it the Sweet Buy and Buy. With the IRS being the way it is, it's best to close these types of enterprises down every few years and reopen them under a new name."

So that explains all the stuff piled up in the garage. One mystery solved and a new one begun. While Ms. Olivia is busy searching for her purse, I take our plates into the kitchen, rinse them off, and load them into the dishwasher. I'm not stupid when it comes to free food and a roof over my head. Because if there is something for nothing out there, I feel certain I would have found it by now.

Ms. Olivia returns with two crisp twenty-dollar bills and her car keys. Out of habit I hold the Andrew Jacksons up to the light and check the watermark to make sure they're not forgeries.

"Please fill the tank with unleaded gas, but don't tell Bertie, because I keep nipping the cement pilings underneath the fuel pumps and he doesn't want me to drive anymore. There's absolutely nothing wrong with my eyes or reflexes," she insists. "He claims that I just don't pay attention."

She glances around as if to see whether anyone else is in earshot, then giggles girlishly. "He's right, actually. I'm always thinking of a poem or fretting about how the Judge is getting along while I'm gone."

However, I'm not really worrying about whether she's a capable driver or not, because I'm so stunned that this woman who hardly knows me just handed over her money and car keys to me, the local juvenile delinquent. Though it now appears entirely possible that she's the local *senior* delinquent.

"And would you do me another favor, please, Hallie—pick up some fresh lemons and a box of sugar? Bertie keeps buying me those artificial sweeteners. Oh, and procure a gallon of Yoo-Hoo for yourself, or however they sell it."

I'm of course thrilled to be entrusted with a car. But what if there's a kilo of cocaine in the trunk? Or a stack of Mexicali Gold joints in the glove compartment? I mean, explaining that I'm playing hooky is one thing . . .

Letting It Ride

★

Driving the big cherry red Buick Park Avenue feels as if I'm floating down the middle of the street and then docking at the gas station. No wonder she knocks into the pumps. And there could be no doubt she knocked into the pumps—along with anything else that happened to be in the way. The car has more dents in it than my brother Eric's head after a football game.

After running my errands, I pull up in front of the Sweet Buy and Buy. I'd passed it a thousand times but never considered going inside. Mr. Bernard is setting down the telephone receiver as I enter the shop. The phone is old-fashioned, with a scrunchy spiral cord running between the receiver and the handset. The store itself is like a cramped version of the Stockton house, a more dimly lit version of the summerhouse, and a better-organized version of the garage. Only inside the store there isn't an inch of open space upon which to rest the eyes. Paintings and tapestries cover the walls, charging all the way up to the ceiling, interspersed by row upon row of candlestick holders. And the back wall is covered almost entirely with clocks.

"Hallie, *entrez-vous*. Lovely to have you stop by to check on me. And I see you've arrived first class, in the *QE2*."

"The what?"

He nods toward the plate-glass picture window in the front of the store.

"*Queen Elizabeth the Second*, a luxury cruise ship operated by the Cunard Line. It's what we call Mother's car, since as she ages her houses get progressively smaller while her cars get larger. She insists on having the extra trunk space for her community outreach projects."

"Uh, yeah." I can only imagine that extra trunk space would come in handy for moving large amounts of heroin across state lines. "Well, I had to get some oil for the lawn mower. It was low when I started and I didn't want to wreck the engine."

"Yes, Lars probably drank it as a chaser after the ethanol ran out. Did Mother ask you to fill up her car with gas?"

"Uh, I uh—" I don't want to break my promise to Ms. Olivia, and yet Mr. Bernard is my boss and so I stutter while considering how to reply. But he only chuckles.

"No!" He puts his hand out as if to stop a line drive. "Don't answer that. We mustn't compromise your integrity or your ability to keep household secrets. What would a house be without its secrets?"

This particular house would most likely be empty without its secrets. Because everybody would be in the slammer.

"It's pretty neat to have a chimp." I change the subject.

"Oh, that dipsomaniac primate is the bane of my existence." Mr. Bernard places the back of his hand to his forehead as if the very mention of Rocky gives him a migraine. "If I don't lock the liquor cabinet, he destroys the entire house."

"I thought he was specially trained to work with paraplegics."

"Yes, well, it so happens that his last patient was also an alcoholic and they drank Singapore slings all day long for the past five years. The trainer wants to put him to sleep, but Mother insists she can rehabilitate him. I've brought some of my best pieces down to the shop, out of harm's way." Mr. Bernard points to a row of vases with animal designs on them. "Those are very valuable art deco pieces signed by Charles Catteau."

After looking at the vases, I begin to examine the paintings above them.

"Do you enjoy art?" he asks.

"Yes," I say enthusiastically. "I mean, I don't know anything *about* art. I just enjoy looking at it."

"And what kind of art do you take pleasure from—drawing, paintings, sculpture?" Is he just goofing on me or being serious? I keep feeling as if they may all be treating me as a joke, a neighborhood mutt that knows a few amusing pet tricks to perform for food. Then again, maybe they're *all crazy*. But I like them, even though they may be, umm, criminals. So I think hard about the question and wish I'd paid more attention to the little brass plaques next to the pictures when my seventh-grade class went on that field trip to the Cleveland Museum of Art.

"I like, uh, I like art when I can tell, uh, what it is."

"Exactly!" Mr. Bernard declares, smiling broadly. "I don't even carry modern works in the shop. It's not that my clients don't buy them, it's just that the pieces are so trendy and impossible to price. One bad day for the stock market and the bottom of the modern-art market drops out just like that." He snaps his fingers. "Not to mention that very little of the work itself does anything for me, personally."

Then I realize he's not *laughing* at me but *agreeing* with me!

"Oh, well, I don't know anything about all that. I just like to see a stream or a house or a person and not have to try and figure out what it is. Or I like to see something beautiful. I mean, at the Cleveland Art Museum there was this series of paintings of plain old wooden clothespins. But . . ." I suddenly worry about sounding like a jackass.

"Yes, but what?"

"But I like collages and . . . and dioramas. Sometimes I make collages out of pictures in magazines or bottle caps or household items that have been thrown away or dumped into the recycling bin."

"That's wonderful. Do you know what dioramas were called in Victorian times?"

"No." Actually, I didn't even know they had shoe boxes back then.

"They were called shadow boxes. Come with me." Mr. Bernard cautiously works his way between all the furniture, metal stands overflowing with gold-headed canes, and gnarly wooden walking sticks, and then past an enormous painted Japanese screen. He leads me to the back of the shop just as he'd guided me down the garden path the day before.

From behind a tall oval standing mirror he gently removes a box that appears to be very old. It's constructed of light-colored wood that's been sanded smooth and decorated with real lace and pieces of silk so that it resembles a three-dimensional valentine. Mr. Bernard switches on a nearby lamp and motions for me to look inside. Peering through the small square opening, I gaze upon a wonderful panorama of children enjoying a puppet show in a large living room with a blazing orange fire at their backs. Every last detail has been attended to by its creator—wallpaper, grandfather clock, winding staircase with a big landing, large screen in front of the fireplace, and a wide, squat Christmas tree with tiny candles nestled among its branches. The children are meticulously outfitted right down to their white socks and starched collars. In fact, it seems as if the figures might actually come alive at any moment. Or that maybe when we're not peeking inside they actually *are* alive.

"It's beautiful," I say when I finally look up. "There's even a tiny sewing basket next to the rocking chair, with knitting needles and some yarn sticking out of the top."

"A wood carver in the Cotswold Hills in England made it over a century ago. It's not the kind of antique that people around here collect, but it was so enchanting I couldn't resist."

Suddenly Mr. Bernard's shop starts tolling, chiming, and cuckooing, and I realize that he has a lot more clocks squirreled away in here than I'd originally noticed. It's already three o'clock.

"I'd better be getting back. I'd really like to finish mowing the lawn today."

"Certainly. It was good of you to stop by. Tell Mother I picked up two cloisonné Fu dogs for a song this morning."

"Excuse me?"

"Yes, of course. Over here." He threads his way back to the counter where I'd originally found him.

"Cloisonné is the art of making designs on objects by using thin metal wires, filling in the spaces with porcelain, and then glazing them. The best pieces came out of China before World War Two, and if they're handsomely crafted and in good condition they can be extremely valuable."

Mr. Bernard points to a few pieces inside the glass display counter, then carefully removes the tissue paper from a large cardboard box sitting atop the counter, and out come two statues that resemble Doberman-Rottweiler combos, each one about the size of a newborn baby. "Fu dogs," Mr. Bernard says with a flourish as he crumples the last bit of packing paper into a ball. "Normally I would sell these here in the shop, but I already have a dealer in Toronto who wants to buy them. Oh, and be sure to tell Mother I also acquired a Hepplewhite chair."

"Okay. I'll tell Ms. Olivia you've got Fu dogs and a hefty white chair."

Mr. Bernard chortles and comes from around the back of the counter to show me a dark wooden chair with a finely carved back. "Hepplewhite.

Named after George Hepplewhite. A great deal of intricate design work on the legs and back. See the fleur-de-lis on the top here? It's a stylized three-petaled iris. I've already been offered a hundred dollars over what I paid at the auction. What do you think?" he playfully asks. "Should I sell, or wait and see if a better offer comes along?"

"It's better to have a fast nickel than a slow dime." At least that's what Cappy always tells me when it comes to wasting time and money on long shots.

Mr. Bernard politely nods, as if he's never heard it put exactly like this before, but it's certainly one way of viewing the matter. "And tell her I also bought three Louis Philippe urns. They're French, of course."

"Three French urns, two Fu dogs, and one Hepplewhite chair with a fleur-de-lis. Right?" I say this to the tune of "The Twelve Days of Christmas" and the corners of Mr. Bernard's mouth turn up and his eyes twinkle with delight.

"Exactly. And four Sprint calling cards."

I wave and say good-bye.

"I'll see you back at the Manse," he calls after me.

As I reboard the QE2, I spy Mrs. Muldoon, my parents' next-door neighbor, crossing the street directly in front of me. She almost drops her dry cleaning when she sees me pull away from the curb in that big old Buick. Wow, it's worth getting caught just to see the expression on her face. I know she'll assume that I stole the car, especially since it has a bumper sticker on the back saying: A WOMAN'S PLACE IS IN THE HOUSE—AND THE SENATE. Definitely *not* my father's automobile.

All my parents' friends tend to regard me as a convicted felon because I skip school and gamble and stay out all night. For instance, whenever anything is missing, including their husbands, they imply that *I* might know something about it. But the truth is that I've never stolen *anything*, not even a candy bar. At least, I've never walked out of a store with anything I didn't pay for (it doesn't count if it's inside your stomach). Meanwhile, I know kids who have shoplifted fifty-dollar tropical fish from the pet store and expensive bathing suits from the mall. And what about stockbrokers who lose other people's money? Nobody goes around calling *them* gamblers. No, they're *professionals*, who go to work in silk suits and drive fancy leased cars and sit on the school board and spend afternoons on the golf course. Not only that, they get to *keep* all the commissions, even when they lose money for clients. If that's not a life of crime, then I can't imagine what is.

Contemplating how long it's going to take Mrs. Muldoon to have me apprehended, I drive back to the Stocktons' and return to work. An easterly wind makes the leaves rustle in the trees, and the bird feeders rock gently back and forth as if they're boats in a harbor. While dumping the last of the grass clippings into a big olive-colored Hefty bag, I make a mental note to ask when garbage day is so that I can haul everything out front, which I assume is part of my job. I'm relieved that the Stocktons don't buy those cheap trash bags where sticks poke and scratch your hands and you can't fill them to the top or mash down the contents without your foot blowing through the plastic. I'd also noticed that the Stocktons use two-ply toilet paper, which could mean that they're rich. My friend Gwen is the only other person I know who has two-ply, and her father is the vice president of the Ohio Forge Company.

So what if the Stocktons deal a few drugs on the side in order to keep up a certain lifestyle? At least they were pouring their ill-gotten gains back into the economy. In fact, if the Star-Mart started selling steroids and performance-enhancing Brussels sprouts, they'd be able to pay more in line with the Stockton scale instead of those slave wages.

Best Bet

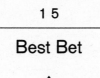

The afternoon slowly curves toward twilight and in the distance the sun begins to sink behind a ragged line of trees dotted with red and brown and gold bouquets of leaves. Once the shed is closed, I head toward the house to replace the washer on the screen door with the new one I picked up at the hardware store while sailing around town in the *QE2*.

Before entering I knock on the door the way neighbors do just to make sure you're not naked. The sound of voices can be heard from the rear of the house, so I remove my muddy high-top sneakers and walk into the living room. Through an archway at the far end of the room I can see Mr. Bernard in the den, leaning over Ms. Olivia, who is sitting in front of a computer and efficiently tapping away at the keyboard.

Mr. Bernard is speaking. "Send him an epistle saying—"

"It's called an E-mail, you Luddite—"

"Saying that I will not accept a farthing less than sixteen hundred non-Confederate dollars and then push the button that beams up the photograph."

"Scans," Ms. Olivia replies as she efficiently plinks away.

"Hello, Hallie," Mr. Bernard calls when he spies me approaching. "That has a nice ring to it, doesn't it?" He cups his hands around his mouth and says, "Hello, Hallie, who enters these hallowed halls." Then he gestures toward Ms. Olivia's workstation. "Do you know how to operate one of these doohickeys?"

"Bertie is under the impression that computer viruses result from not washing your hands after buying a Mandarin palette vase off the eBay Internet auction site," says Ms. Olivia.

"Of course she can use a computer!" Mr. Gil's voice rises from the basement stairwell. He appears from around the corner carrying a stack of newspapers and looking more relaxed than he had that morning. "Hi, Hallie," he says.

"*You*," he says to Mr. Bernard, and points an accusatory piece of kindling in his direction, "are the only person in the United States who cannot operate a computer."

"It's just a fad, like Ashtead Pottery and Kewpie dolls," Mr. Bernard says with a dismissive wave of his hand.

"The computer is the only reason they keep me alive," Ms. Olivia chimes in.

"That's not true, Mother," Mr. Bernard says seriously. "You're the only one who knows how to replace the needle on the record player."

"Bertie, you just *push* the old needle out and *clip* the new one in." She taps one more button on the keyboard. "There," she triumphantly announces. "All finished. Now it's cocktail hour and I'd like an Old-Fashioned, slightly muddled, please."

"Excuse me." I finally manage to get a word in. "But do you have a stepladder? I'm going to put this washer on the screen door." I hold up the small metal ring. "To stop it from slamming."

"There's a stepladder somewhere in Bertie's Museum," Mr. Gil says.

"That's his code name for the garage," Mr. Bernard drolly explains.

"Come on. I'll help you find it." Mr. Gil leads me out to the garage. He runs his fingers across a dusty armoire and then surveys all the furnishings piled up on top of one another. The stacked wooden chairs make it look like a house of cards about to tumble down from the slightest bump. I'd be afraid to use the electric garage door if I were him.

"One of these days when he's at the Armory Antiques Show in Manhattan I'm going to have a gigantic garage sale. Have you ever seen so many gewgaws, lambrequins, and jardinières in one place? It looks as if everything was dropped by a flood."

Just as Mr. Gil finishes speaking, he accidentally knocks an oversize wastebasket with a hunting dog painted on the front of it off the edge of a bureau. A thousand empty wooden spools of every size hurtle through the dank atmosphere, ricocheting off mirrors and china cabinets and raising a roar as if every gun owner in Ohio simultaneously shot off a round.

"Duck and cover!" shouts Mr. Gil. We're both startled by the thunderous noise and have to catch our breath as the last ones eventually settle into dark corners, crevices, and open drawers.

"What are we going to do with the Stocktons, Hallie?" He laughs as he surveys the scene. "Sometimes I wonder if the Judge isn't the only sane person here."

I decide that I like Gil, too. They're all so much more interesting than my parents' friends. I keep feeling as if I'm an extra in one of those Masterpiece Theatre programs.

"I suppose *I'm* senile for staying here," he adds. "It's a Catch-22. Have you read that book?"

"Uh, no." I feel sort of stupid because these people seem to know so much.

"It's a novel by Joseph Heller. The hero is in an impossible situation characterized by absurdity which he calls a Catch-22," he explains. "It's hilarious. You should read it."

I kneel down and start gathering up the escaped wooden spools, though they're everywhere and it's obvious that it'll take all night to round them up.

"Aha," says Mr. Gil. He forces an aluminum stepladder out from behind an old bulky steamer trunk with tarnished bronze fittings and peeling labels with names of exotic-sounding places like Istanbul and Ceylon printed on them.

"Forget about the mess. In the spring all the furniture goes to auction and then I'll make a bonfire out of whatever's left."

It only takes me a few minutes to replace the washer, adjust the spring, and add a little WD-40 so that the door closes less fitfully and doesn't make such a horrific bang.

"Well done," says Mr. Bernard. "Yes, you are indeed good with your hands."

And though I feel pleased to have his approval I modestly say, "It's just a washer. Ten cents at the hardware store."

"But who knew?" he says. "We pay the doctor not for the fifteen-minute consultation but for all those years he spent slaving away in medical school."

Just then Ms. Olivia enters the front hall with Rocky. She takes a key out of her dress pocket and unlocks the liquor cabinet. Rocky excitedly claps his hands and takes two clean glasses from off the top and holds them up to the light as if inspecting for dust particles. Then I see the most amazing sight of my life. The chimp chooses a lime from the fruit bowl and with a vegetable peeler removes the skin in a continuous spiral, taking care that no white fiber adheres to the peel. Once that's finished he sets it aside and from the liquor cabinet takes out bottles labeled gin, cherry brandy, and benedictine.

I whisper to Mr. Bernard, "But I thought he's a, you know . . ." not wanting the chimp to overhear me, since I'm not sure exactly how much he understands.

"Mother found some moderation program on the Internet that she's trying out on him. One cocktail a day and that's it."

Rocky lifts the quart of Gordon's gin at Mr. Bernard and lets out a discontented series of hoots while holding the bottle up to his face as if using a cross to ward off a vampire.

"I'm not going to the liquor store for you, you stupid monkey!" Mr. Bernard says to Rocky.

Rocky curls back his lips if he's going to spit at Mr. Bernard.

"Bertie, he's a *chimpanzee*, not a monkey, and considers the latter designation to be an insult."

"Then let me point out that chimpanzees, along with baboons, are the only primates who regularly kill other mammals, intoxicated or not," says Mr. Bernard.

"You're forgetting about us humans, dear." Ms. Olivia's smile indicates that she's quite pleased with her retort. She turns to me as if Mr. Bernard has ceased to exist. "Rocky always made Singapore slings for himself and Geraldine using sloe gin, and so he prefers it."

The chimp turns back to the bar and carefully combines the gin, cherry brandy, and Benedictine into a cocktail shaker, and then while holding it he jumps up and down for a moment. When that's finished he empties the mix into two crystal cocktail tumblers. Then he deftly opens the ice bucket and actually uses tongs to drop exactly three cubes into each drink, fills the glasses the rest of the way with club soda, and adds the lime peel, half to each. Finally he skewers maraschino cherries on toothpicks, lays them atop the glasses, and with a big smile hands Ms. Olivia her drink.

"Thank you very much, Rocky." They clink glasses and both take a sip.

Rocky looks to Ms. Olivia for a reaction. "Very nice. If Bernard won't buy sloe gin, then perhaps we should try it with ginger ale next time."

"Mother, stop being ridiculous," says Mr. Bernard. "He doesn't understand a word of what you're saying."

But Ms. Olivia ignores her son. "Would you like to stay for dinner, Hallie? We're having—what are we having, Bertie?"

"Ruby-glazed lamb with oven-roasted new potatoes, Mother. And of course for you and what's-his-name I've prepared beans, *haricots verts,* and some other herbivore-friendly fare."

Then he turns to me and announces, "Mother is a *vegetarian,*" in a way that indicates she cannot possibly appreciate good food.

"Leonardo da Vinci said there's no reason for our bodies to act as a tomb for other creatures," says Ms. Olivia defensively.

"Yes, that's probably why Michelangelo outlived him by almost a quarter of a century," says Mr. Bernard, now sounding quite pleased with *his* comeback. "Hallie, you are welcome to stay. We can accommodate a vegan, meat-eater, omnivore, or gourmand. The only menu I'm afraid I can't accomplish on short notice is kosher."

I'm hungry, but I also know that the law is closing in on me and I must prepare. It's doubtful that Joan of Arc was sitting around laughing and eating ruby-glazed lamb when she knew her trial could come up at any moment. "Thanks, but I have to go to the library for an hour before they close."

"Feel free to drop back afterward," Ms. Olivia says. "I give the Judge his dinner at quarter after six, get him settled, and then we dine at around half past seven."

I hesitate. Their suspicions will be aroused if they think I might not have another place to go. On the other hand, it's only a matter of time before the posse arrives and the Stocktons find out I'm between bedrooms anyway. Mrs. Muldoon must have reported her findings to my parents by now. But hunger wins out and so I agree to return.

Then I contemplate my other problem, a shower. I'd purchased some shampoo while doing Ms. Olivia's shopping and planned to bike over to the YMCA after the library, since my friend Donna works at the desk checking IDs and will let me in anytime I want. Only they close up shop at seven.

"I'd hate to eat dinner all grungy," I say, trying to sound casual. "Would you mind if I take a quick shower?"

"Help yourself," says Mr. Bernard. "There's a guest room—"

"Junk room," interjects Mr. Gil.

"Ahem." Mr. Bernard clears his throat for effect. "There's a *guest* room with an en suite bathroom."

"*Oh, Bertie* . . . you have a three-hundred-pound Austrian neoclassical brass-inlaid fall-front secretaire sitting in the tub," Mr. Gil reminds him.

"Storage is such a dilemma. Use Mother's facilities. Just watch out for all the vials and votive candles. She went through an aromatherapy phase last winter."

My project at the library is to verify that the legal age to quit school and work full-time is sixteen and to find out at what age you can divorce your parents, if it's even possible, in the state of Ohio. The librarian helps me find the state legal statutes, and it turns out that child-parent divorce is called becoming an "emancipated minor" and that you have to petition the court in order to get one.

After the copy machine I have exactly thirty cents left to my name. It's a good thing the Stocktons invited me for dinner. Because I've managed to break every rule of gambling, the last being that it's okay to eat your betting money but never bet your eating money. And my current state of famishment makes this lesson all the more memorable.

Leaving the library, I carefully fold the documents for my defense and tuck them into my pocket. But before climbing on my bike, I have another thought and go back inside and locate the librarian who helped me with the law books.

"Excuse me, but have you ever heard of a book called *Catch-22*?"

"Of course. It's in fiction under *H*, for Heller. Joseph Heller."As I get on my bike, it starts to drizzle. Great, my first dinner with actual upholstery on the dining room chairs and I'm going to have a wet mud stripe up my ass.

Where the Action Is

♦

When I return to the Stocktons', Mr. Bernard and Mr. Gil are having drinks in the warmly lit living room while violin music soars in the background.

I'd not really taken a good look around this room during the daytime. It's long and wide and has a high ceiling with intricate molding along the top. In the middle of the wall opposite the entranceway is a cavernous fireplace surrounded by thick dark green marble, and standing on the floor in front is a brass screen with a complicated swirly design on a mesh background.

Above that, resting on top of the mantel, are about a dozen three-inch-high figurines of Asian people that appear to be carved out of ivory. They were probably the Smurfs of the eighteenth century. And hanging on the wall above their heads is a painting of a country church. It's one of those pictures where small brush strokes of pastel colors make everything look fuzzy when you get close up. In fact, there are acres of pictures on the walls, mounted in chunky gold or shiny dark wooden frames. Most are oil paintings, but there's a set of six watercolors featuring those cherubs you see on Valentine's Day cards and also on the covers of books about angels. The paintings must be worth a lot of money. I wonder if the Stocktons worry about getting robbed, especially since I haven't seen a burglar alarm, and they don't bother to lock the doors during the day. Then I contemplate whether the artwork is "hot." Is it possible that the Stocktons are art thieves as well as drug dealers?

It's hard to imagine a burglar robbing *my* house, so tastefully decorated in Early Rec Room. All he'd find is a bunch of action figures, some board games, and a Nintendo. In fact, the TV is so old and banged up that he'd probably leave it behind.

Everything at the Stocktons', on the other hand, looks old but expensive—the maroon-and-chestnut-colored rug with its fancy floral patterns in blue, yellow, red, and beige whirling around as if someone tossed a gigantic bouquet down from the ceiling fan, and all the chairs and end tables and especially the luxurious down-filled couch and matching love seat with the dark wooden feet that resemble animal hooves. It's the kind of furniture you'd expect to be covered in thick plastic so as not to be ruined by people sitting on it and spilling their drinks.

Quite frankly, I'm terrified to touch almost everything, especially the little footstools with their delicately embroidered cushions. But *they* don't seem to care. Nope, they walk right across that fancy rug in the same shoes they wore outside in the rain. Mr. Gil plunks his feet right up on the glass coffee table. With his loafers on! And the living room isn't dotted with circular red coasters the way mine is, as if the house has a case of measles.

Mr. Gil must do some type of corporate training, because he's in the middle of a funny story about a big-shot executive whose colleagues are supposed to carry him over a mud pit but he's so fat that they accidentally drop him in. And when they finally hoist the boss out, his pants have slipped down enough to reveal a woman's name (not his wife's) tattooed on his rear end. It's hilarious the way Mr. Gil recounts the event and describes the sucking sound from pulling the guy out of the pit while his pants and shoes stick in the mud.

Mr. Bernard catches me studying a framed needlepoint sampler on the coffee table. The picture is of a brightly-plumed bird against a background of sky and mountains, and underneath is stitched: *Horas non numero nisi serenas.*

"Mother designed that," Mr. Bernard explains. "When father became ill she took up needlepoint for a time and decided that we needed a Stockton family crest and motto. That's Latin for 'I count only the happy hours.' Apparently she saw it on a sundial while traveling in Italy, somewhere outside of Venice." He pauses to glance at the needlework and then continues, "Palmer sounds like an aristocratic English name. Does your family have a crest or motto?"

I've never seen any crest lying around the house, aside from the toothpaste. "If we have a family motto, I guess it would be *Does the salad come with the meal?*"

Mr. Bernard and Mr. Gil both chuckle at this, and once again I'm not sure if they're laughing with me or at me.

"Don't worry, Hallie," says Mr. Gil. "Bertie's real crest is the letter *S* with two vertical lines running through it."

"What's another name for box?" Ms. Olivia's voice comes from her den in the alcove off the back of the living room.

"What?" Gil calls from the living room.

"What is a synonym for *pussy?*"

"Oh dear," Mr. Bernard says.

My cheeks turn warm with embarrassment, but he only bursts out laughing along with Mr. Gil and almost drops his glass in his lap before setting it down on the end table for safekeeping. "Mother!" he calls into the den. "Hallie's here. *Puh*-leeze!"

"Wonderful. I'm sure she'll know a word. Ask her."

Mr. Bernard pulls himself together and with an air of mock sincerity states, "Hallie, Mother scribes pornography for *Milky Way* magazine . . ."

But Mr. Gil is still laughing too hard for Mr. Bernard to continue.

"Will you hush already," Mr. Bernard scolds Mr. Gil.

Mr. Bernard clears his throat and begins again. "Hallie, Mother is a poet and has had much of her work published in literary journals. Only the compensation isn't very good and she requires the validation of earning an income. Thus for many years she's written *erotic narratives.*"

"Well?" Ms. Olivia impatiently calls out from the den. "It's for a new piece I've titled 'Thong of Myself.' "

"How about *snatch?*" Mr. Gil shouts back.

"I already used that," Ms. Olivia states matter-of-factly.

"And Mother is wondering if you have an idea for a synonym for the female reproductive organ," Mr. Bernard continues. "Only a little less clinical. More risqué, if you will."

"How about *beaver?*" I yell in the direction of the den.

We hear a "hmph" and the sound of more clicking on the keyboard, as if she's trying it out. "No good."

"Or *love muscle*," I add.

"Wonderful!" Ms. Olivia calls back. "I've never used that before. You see, gentlemen, we need a young person around to keep us up to date."

"You're a woman of many talents," Mr. Bernard says to me. "We'll have to show you some of Mother's work." He picks up his drink. "I mean her poetry . . . of course."

"Of course," I reply.

After dinner I help clear the dishes and clean up. Mr. Bernard doesn't try to stop me, but he doesn't turn the job entirely over to me either. He stands in front of the sink rinsing and loading the dishwasher and lets me bus everything from the table and pile the dirty linen napkins in the laundry room.

Ms. Olivia and Mr. Gil sit at the dining room table sipping cappuccinos and animatedly discussing a play that Mr. Gil is directing at the Community Center. It's called *The Glass Menagerie* and it sounds like it's rated X. There's a part for "a gentleman's call girl," and so I imagine that's why he wants Ms. Olivia's expert opinion.

Once everything is straightened up I thank the Stocktons and Mr. Gil, cheerfully say good night, exit through the front door, and ride my bike down the driveway as if I'm heading for home. After about fifteen minutes, I cut back through the woods behind their house and lean my bike against the side of the summerhouse.

However, it's obvious that someone has been inside. Most noticeable is that the box with the drugs and the stack of pamphlets is gone. And there's an afghan sitting on one of the chairs that I didn't remember seeing the night before. Although there's so much stuff jammed into the small room that I could have missed it. I retrieve the flashlight I'd stowed in the drawer of the table and then settle into one of the couches and begin to read *Catch-22*. It opens during a war with a guy named Yossarian who is a patient in the hospital. He no longer feels like writing to his family and friends and so he tells them he's going on a dangerous mission and he'll write when he gets back. Then he gets bored and inks out all the adjectives in the letters written by the enlisted men. And even though there's a war going on it seems as if it's going to be a funny book.

Only my reading is soon interrupted by what is most likely my own war—the crunch of gravel in the driveway followed by the slam of a car door. I quickly switch off my flashlight and take up a battle position behind the couch so that I'm hidden and yet can still peek out the window and observe the back of the Stockton house.

After a few minutes a girl about my age or perhaps a little older appears and tentatively makes her way to the back door. She's quickly ushered inside as if her arrival is expected. Hmmm. I'd have to say that eleven o'clock at night is a bit late to be selling magazine subscriptions. I'll bet she's there to score some hashish.

At least I can rest easy knowing that whoever she is, she isn't looking for me, for a change. Besides, after working in the yard all day I'd rather have a plateful of Mr. Bernard's lamb and a good night's sleep than a line of cocaine. As I understand it, drugs aren't very filling.

Doubling Down

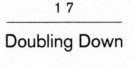

Since my funds are down to a handful of loose change, there doesn't seem to be much point in riding over to the convenience store the following morning. A dollar is pretty much the opening bid at any 7-Eleven. Unless I want to buy a gumball from the machine. Besides, I'm pretty sure the Stocktons won't mind if I bum a Yoo-Hoo and maybe a piece of fruit for breakfast. I mean, they bought the Yoo-Hoo for me. And after the Lars experience they'll probably be relieved I'm not whittling away at a stalk of celery from my wake-up Bloody Mary.

I navigate my bike through the path in the woods and backtrack to the driveway so it appears as if I'm just rolling up from home. However, from the end of the street I can see a squad car, my parents' station wagon, and another car that doesn't belong to the Stocktons, Mr. Gil, or my folks.

Well, hail, hail, the gang's all here. Ambushed. I ride back through the woods and collect the papers I'd copied from the library and then go back around to the driveway. The first dead leaves of autumn scrape along the blacktop and catch in my spokes.

There's a big powwow occurring on the front porch—Mom, Dad, Officer Rich, and Just Call Me Dick appear to be facing off against Mr. Bernard and Mr. Gil. Lots of gesturing is happening on the part of Dad. The fact that the Stocktons haven't invited them in for coffee is a good sign. And so far it's safe to assume that Ms. Olivia hasn't asked anyone to supply a synonym for their genitals.

The hive stops buzzing as my bike pulls to a stop in the driveway and everyone turns to stare. In the direct sunlight Just Call Me Dick appears excessively crustaceanlike, as if he's an advance man for an invasion of fiddler crabs. The sun is directly behind me, and so they all simultaneously shade their puckered eyes with their hands as if I'm an eclipse. In a burst of maternal joy, Mom runs over and hugs me and says how relieved she is that I'm all right and why did I run away and perhaps they were too harsh about the car.

Returning her hug, I try to think of a nice way of saying that I really do love them and appreciate all they've done for me, only it no longer holds any interest for me to be around them on a day-to-day basis. We never agree on anything. And so our relationship has been reduced to one round of fighting after the next. Plus those little annoyances like placing me under house arrest.

After the long-lost mother-daughter *National Enquirer*–style reunion, I confidently saunter up to the front porch with my handful of documents like Nancy Drew preparing to solve the mystery once and for all. Only I don't have a light blue convertible or a drop-dead handsome boyfriend to look on in an admiring fashion. Just an anxious mother wondering if I've eaten anything over the past two days.

Dad appears incredibly angry, as if he's about to say something disagreeable. But when he glances over and notices the tears running down Mom's face, he stops himself. Instead he just stands there glaring at me, feet firmly planted, hands on hips, looking every bit the ex-linebacker daring me to make a try for the end zone.

Mr. Gil and Mr. Bernard study me as if they're not sure if they've hired a convict, and maybe Lars the Lush isn't looking so bad after all. At least he wasn't a minor. Though Mr. Bernard appears vaguely amused by all the drama.

"Okay," I say. "Before you guys read me my Miranda Rights, do you mind if I get something to drink?"

"I'll get it," Mr. Bernard offers.

I take this as a good sign, Mr. Bernard demonstrating that we're in cahoots enough to both know what "it" is.

"How dare you frighten your poor mother, especially in her condition?" Dad can no longer help himself and starts laying into me. "What if Mrs. Muldoon hadn't seen you yesterday? We had the police out looking everywhere for you. We called all the hospitals and checked the Cleveland bus station and—"

"Excuse me, but why don't we all go over and meet in my office at the school?" Just Call Me Dick suggests in his varmintlike way, beady eyes glinting with dark deeds. He's clutching a file so thick that it must include my kindergarten immunization records. "I really must insist we bring in the district psychologist at this juncture. Obviously there are some issues concerning the home environment."

Wrong thing to say, Mr. Collier. This will really piss off Dad. My father faces off with the Attendance Nazi mano-a-mano, or rather bureaucrat-a-bureaucrat. Dad's counted beans for the State of Ohio for twenty years. There's no piece of red tape he hasn't wrapped around someone's neck. Dad takes the two steps across the porch in one and places his arm around Mom. Now that an outsider is threatening the family pod, they're back on the same team.

"Excuse me, Richar—"

"Just call me Dick," Just Call Me Dick interjects. He rubs his hands together like an insect scrapes its feelers against each other.

"Of course. With all due respect, Dick, we have raised seven perfectly well-adjusted children in a Christian home—"

Mr. Bernard arrives with my Yoo-Hoo, and that stops Dad midsentence.

"Listen, I'm going to save you guys a lot of time and trouble," I announce. Of course, this is entirely the wrong thing to say to career paper shufflers, since that's what makes up their workday in the first place, wasting time.

No matter. After taking a big swig of chocolate drink I dig the photocopies out of my pocket. "Number one, I don't have to go to school anymore, Collier, and you know it." I say "Collier" the way they do on police shows—last name only and pronounced with disdain. "Sixteen is the legal age to drop out. It says so right here." I punch the papers with my index finger for emphasis.

"Of course you *can* leave school, Hallie," Just Call Me Dick admits in that smarmy voice he puts on whenever parents are around. "But you're too smart to make such a poor choice," J.C.M.D. continues. "You can't go on to college without a high school diploma."

"Who said anything about going to college?" I quickly retort. "I've got a job."

Mr. Bernard and Mr. Gil observe the exchange as if they're watching a tennis match, heads bobbing back and forth between Just Call Me Dick and me.

"Mr. Stockton, I must advise you that you can't employ a student full-time," J.C.M.D. arrogantly states, as if he's threatening Mr. Bernard with detention.

It's do-or-die time. There's no photocopy that can get me out of this one if Mr. Bernard caves in to the scholar majority.

Mr. Gil puts on his best deferential corporate seminar voice and pleasantly addresses Officer Rich: "Excuse me, Mr. Collier, but I believe we're within our legal rights to employ Hallie if she's *not* in school."

Meantime I remove the next crumpled photocopy from my pocket. "You only have to be sixteen to work full-time." I pass around exhibit *B*.

"I'm afraid she's right," Officer Rich concedes, apparently with mixed emotions. I have a feeling he secretly gets a kick out of me fucking with the grown-ups. As if his job is so boring—cats up trees and housewives locking keys in cars—that I'm his current big entertainment, the ESPN Game of the Week. It's not like we get any homicides, serial killers, or crimes of passion around here, *especially* crimes of passion.

Everybody on the opposing team begins harrumphing and scraping the toes of their shoes into the concrete like agitated horses before a storm. All except my mother, that is, who gives my father the *do something* look. But my father only gives her the *what am I supposed to do?* look in return.

For a moment I feel terrible, torturing my mother like this. She's an awfully nice person. On the other hand, the Palmer household isn't into any of the latest educational theories—for instance, that different children learn differently.

"I don't mind about the school, Hallie." My mother bursts into tears again the way overtaxed pregnant women are supposed to do. "Just come *home.* You can go to a private school. Or attend night classes at the community college to prepare for the high school equivalency exam. We'll hire a tutor."

That's one thing you can say about mothers when it comes to their offspring—while other people are trying to untangle the legal system, they're busy working out practical solutions. And yet how do I explain why I can't live with my parents anymore when I don't completely understand it myself?

So here goes the big one. I offer up the last piece of paper and hope for a better reception than Moses received. "Listen, it says in the state legal statutes that I can apply to become an emanated minor and—"

"*Emancipated,*" Mr. Bernard and Officer Rich chime in simultaneously.

"Anyway, that's what I'm going to do. I'm working here during the day if you need me, I'm going to the track on the weekends, and I'll come home for dinner once in a while if you want."

As I casually fold up the final paper, everyone looks to the gentle-mannered Officer Rich for guidance now that the entire calamity appears to hinge on a legal issue. And I realize that I'd better move things along. Because whether they accept it or they don't, it's not as if it's going to help my case to stand around and give them time to consider other options, like kidnapping. "Well, I've got weeding to do." I finish the last gulp of Yoo-Hoo and hand the empty back to Mr. Bernard. "Would you mind tossing this for me, please?"

He takes it and appears well satisfied, as if he's just witnessed a good per-formance on *Law & Order.* Only now comes the real test. I turn and walk down the front steps. If they're going to try and stop me, then this is it. But they don't. And I don't look back, either. Finally, it appears as if there won't be any more "How I Spent My Summer Vacation" essays penned by Hallie Palmer.

At around noon I get the scallion wave from Ms. Olivia, and it's a wel-come occurrence, because I'm awfully hungry after no breakfast, the surprise front-porch trial, and then unearthing six bags of dead plants with root sys-tems like chain letters. As I enter the house, Ms. Olivia delightedly claps her hands and begins a recitation: "*Hail to thee, blithe spirit! Bird thou never wert, That from heaven or near it—*"

I don't know what it means, but it's definitely not the Patrick Henry High School song. I assume it's some kind of a victory acknowledgment, and so I wash my hands at the kitchen sink while she finishes trilling the last lines.

"*Pourest thy full heart / In profuse strains of unpremeditated art.*"

"Excuse me?" I finally ask when I'm pretty sure she's finished.

" 'To a Skylark,' " says Ms. Olivia. "Percy Bysshe Shelley. I can't tell you how good it is to have a battle raging once again. The only triumph of good over evil around here during the past few months involved trouncing the phone com-pany for overbilling. And even that wasn't tremendously gratifying—just a credit for twenty-six dollars accompanied by a computer-generated form letter."

There's a delicious-looking quiche with a thick light brown crust on the table, and Ms. Olivia catches me hungrily eyeing it.

"Isn't Bertie wonderful? It's like having Meals on Wheels, but with goat cheese, sun-dried tomatoes, and Portobello mushrooms. Sit down and help yourself. The spoils go to the victor."

Ms. Olivia reclaims her spot at the table from the day before.

"I fudged a couple of answers," I admit. "I'm afraid it's only round one."

"Without a doubt. Being a free spirit is never easy. You must constantly battle convention—the gatekeepers, the cage cleaners, the small-minded apparatchiks, the empty suits!"

"You mean, you think it's okay that I don't want to get an education?"

"Don't be ridiculous. Of course you wish to pursue an education. Education gives one dignity. You're familiar with Rosa Parks, are you not?"

"Sure, she wouldn't move to the back of the bus." Everybody knows *that*, whether they went to school or not.

"What is important to remember is that Rosa Parks took it upon *herself* to get an education and this served to give her dignity. When the bus driver threatened to arrest Ms. Parks, she replied, You *may* do that. She did not say, You *can* do that, or You gotta do what you gotta do. Do you see the difference?"

Sort of. But then why did Ms. Olivia take my side instead of the school's? Fortunately I could see she was prepared to answer the question that I could not.

"You just don't want to be brainwashed in their educational institution. And I don't blame you one bit."

"So how do I get an education if I don't go to school?"

"Hallie, learning is everywhere, knowledge is ubiquitous. In fact, the very idea that they can force you into a room and try to befoul your mind with meaningless catalogues of names and dates is preposterous. That's not even thinking—" She suddenly stops. "Isn't that why you won't attend?"

"Yeah, I suppose." I don't want to disappoint her, especially since she seems so thrilled to be providing sanctuary to a radical. And second, I don't feel like telling *anyone* the real reason I can no longer go to school.

Once again, Ms. Olivia doesn't press for details. She offers me another piece of quiche, which I gladly accept.

"Do you know any painters?" she asks.

"You mean who paint pictures?"

"No, houses. Everything needs painting—the inside, the outside, the shutters and trim, the summerhouse."

"The shed," I add.

"And especially the porte cochere and the garage," she says.

I'd noticed the garage is flaking like Herb's scalp. It's a good thing the bushes aren't navy blue like his sport jacket.

"Yeah, me. I paint."

"Excellent! We're in desperate need of a face-lift around here, and though Gil's been threatening to tackle it for over a year now, I don't see how he can possibly find time with Bertie marching him off to rummage sales every weekend."

If nothing else, it sounded as if it would be good for my résumé. After "yard person" I could list "paint engineer." And if the Stocktons continue to promote me at this rate, then I might reach "gutter management specialist" by Halloween.

Pay Dirt

At the close of the workday, when I stop up at the house to say good-bye, Mr. Bernard and Mr. Gil have just arrived home and are laughing about some fur stoles that Mr. Bernard purchased at a garage sale in order to resell down at the store.

"If it isn't Prince Hal!" Mr. Bernard says.

"I thought the British princes were William and Harry."

"It's from Shakespeare's *Henry V,*" Mr. Bernard says.

"Never mind him," says Mr. Gil. "He criticizes Olivia, but in reality he's exactly like her—thriving on a good helping of social unrest with lots of foot stamping, sabotage, and threats of self-immolation."

Meantime, from out of a shopping bag Mr. Bernard removes a black velvet hat with a starburst of rhinestones across the front and places it atop my reddish-blond mop. "Oh, Hallie, it's you!" The hat has a round brim that is at least a foot wide and resembles the top half of a flying saucer.

"Wait," says Mr. Gil. He adjusts the front so that it covers my forehead and I can just barely peer out from underneath the expansive brim. Then he tosses a long billowy black feather boa around my neck. But looking in the mirror, I can only laugh at these movie star accessories combined with my T-shirt, jeans, and high-top sneakers.

"Holly Golightly," says Mr. Bernard. "We just need the sunglasses."

"Definitely," Mr. Gil adds.

"Who's Holly Golightly?" I ask.

"Audrey Hepburn, of course," answers Gil. "Uh-oh," he says to Mr. Bernard. "I smell a movie night."

"Most definitely. Saturday night—*Breakfast at Tiffany's*," states Mr. Bernard.

"Are you free Saturday evening?" Mr. Gil inquires.

"It's not as if they're expecting me at vespers," I say.

"Brilliant! We'll have Cornish hen and I'll make a tangerine upside-down cake for dessert. And this way Mother will stop threatening to go to Havana for the weekend if she knows you're coming. She's taken a shine to you."

"Yes," adds Mr. Gil. "You'd better watch out, Hallie, or she'll have you in Appalachia registering people to vote by Columbus Day."

Mr. Bernard removes a neat stack of twenties from the pocket of his sport jacket and hands me the money. From the height of the pile I can tell that it's $240. I suppose a person should know she's spent too much time at the racetrack and the gaming tables when she's able to identify a stack of cash in any denomination solely by its height.

"What's this for?" I ask. No one gets paid after only two days.

"We'll compensate you every Friday. However, this is a bridge until then."

I guess it doesn't take a genius to figure out I'm on the lam. And probably broke, too.

"Okay, but this is too much. You only owe me a hundred eighty-two."

"Yes, well, Mother told me you changed the oil on all the cars. And refueling the tank on the *QE2* is considered overtime."

"I *heard* that," Ms. Olivia's voice chimes in from the den.

"Go back to smuggling penicillin and schoolbooks into Cuba," Mr. Bernard shouts back.

From the way the downstairs is laid out, with the rooms leading off and making a square around the central hallway, it's pretty easy to hear what's being said anywhere on the first floor. There aren't any doors dividing the rooms aside from the swinging one leading to the kitchen, but that's open most of the time, unless Ms. Olivia has set fire to something.

"Want to stay for dinner?" offers Mr. Gil.

"Uh, no thanks. It's probably best if I go underground tonight. We haven't seen the last of the dogcatchers."

"Be sure to let us know if there's anything we can do to help," Mr. Bernard says.

"Actually, if you don't mind if I take a shower . . ."

"Certainly. Help yourself to shampoo, and there's a hair dryer . . . whatever you need. And feel free to use the laundry," adds Mr. Gil.

I turn to go upstairs to the bathroom.

"Uh, Hallie," Mr. Bernard says. "The superintendent of schools called here today. And then phoned me at the shop. By not agreeing to handcuff you and deliver you to his office by eight o'clock sharp tomorrow morning, I think we're now regarded as the enemy. Or the Principal Revolutionary Party, if you prefer Mother's lingo."

"Listen, I'm really sorry about all this. I didn't mean for you to get involved. If you don't think it's a good idea to have me work here, I'd under—"

"Oh, don't fret about it. Mother hasn't had a satisfying altercation with the authorities since the Judge became ill and had to take early retirement and they refused to cover home health care. I haven't seen her this exhilarated in years. She's back on the barricades. In case you haven't noticed, Mother's a bohemian. Though a rather militant one. Now, go make your toilette."

Following a hot shower, I ride my bike over to the pizza parlor. Hopefully Craig is there and I can pay him back the sixty dollars I still owe him and also return Jane's dirty old gym clothes. It feels good to once again have some presidents in my pocket and actually have a choice as to what I'd like to eat. If I start painting the house on Saturday I'll have a car by Thanksgiving and be celebrating Christmas in Las Vegas.

The minute Jane sees me entering she races across the room and tackles me like a long-lost wealthy relative. She must really be missing those sweatpants.

"Hallie, I've been looking everywhere for you! Where the *hell* have you been?"

"Uh, Jane, I didn't realize we were dating."

But Jane doesn't smile. "Hallie, this is serious! Where's the *money*?" She says "money" as if I'm supposed to understand, as if we hijacked a Brinks truck together and both know about the Secret Hiding Place.

"*What* money?" I am so sick of money. In one way or another everything that's wrong with my life right now has to do with money.

"The *money* from the donuts! Almost three hundred dollars! We swapped duffel bags the day we delivered the donuts—the US World Cup bags I bought for us in New York!" Jane is bopping up and down on her toes as if she's preparing to hit a volleyball serve.

"Jane, will you calm down? In that bag was an Ace bandage, a roll of tape, and some grunged-out sweats. The *money* was in a big manila envelope. Up *front*."

Tears begin to crowd the corners of Jane's eyes. "Oh, Hallie, you were my last hope. What am I going to do? The money is due on *Monday*."

"Did you ask Gwen?" But that was a stupid question. Of course she'd asked Gwen. "Did you search the station wagon?"

"We looked *everywhere*. I thought for sure that it was in my duffel bag."

"Well, I don't know. Maybe I missed it." I remove Jane's crumpled bag from my backpack. No money.

Jane eventually calms down. After all, three hundred bucks isn't the end of the world. Though I know she's saving to attend an expensive sports camp in North Carolina next summer. But her parents both have good jobs. I offer $160 from the money Mr. Bernard just paid me, but she declines, saying that her dad already offered a loan.

Jane and Gwen and the rest of my friends have staked out our regular corner booth, though unfortunately there's no sign of Craig.

"Hallie, where have you *been*?" asks Gwen through freshly applied pink lip gloss. "Eric told me you ran away and your mom is acting totally mysterious whenever I call."

It transpires that a flurry of excitement has surrounded my absence. Gwen enthusiastically recounts how on Tuesday morning everyone in the eleventh grade was grilled by all kinds of grown-ups—teachers, social workers, PTA members—to see if they knew my whereabouts and if anybody thought I was suicidal or had a drug problem. Apparently it was all very thrilling and disruptive, because if you could claim to have spoken with me in the past few weeks you could skip class and tell your story to a counselor. Some top administrator in a suit even arrived and had a janitor cut the padlock off both my hall and gym lockers. I wonder if I can sue them for breaking and entering. Probably not, since it's school property. Oh well, my gym locker needed cleaning out anyway.

Todd Murphy says that someone's mother reported seeing me enter an OTB with a weapon and another kid's neighbor insisted I'd been kidnapped by the Mafia for gambling debts. My life should only be so exciting. I don't bother to tell everyone that I've been busy weeding half-dead flower beds. Because *whatever* they come up with is going to be a lot more interesting than the truth.

Eventually I take the sixty dollars that I owe Craig and hand it to Gwen, since her locker is across from his. "Please give this to Craig and say that I'm sorry."

"All right. But why don't I tell him that you'll be at my Halloween party and then if he still likes you . . . ," says Gwen. "You are coming, aren't you?"

"Of course," I reply.

"Be careful," Jane warns jokingly. "Last year Gwen fixed a cousin up with her biology student teacher and now they're getting married."

Seth Gilmore, who's also a junior and works one period in the principal's office, comes over with a calzone and joins our expanding group. He heard that the principals in all the surrounding districts are worried that if our school doesn't get me back then soon other kids will start taking off, sort of like copycat crimes.

They all want to know if I'm coming back to school. And the truth is, I have no idea what I'm doing right now other than weed whacking and painting the house. I'd always just assumed that after graduation I'd become a professional gambler.

"You're so brave," says Tara, the fullback on the soccer team, with true admiration in her voice. "I wish I had the guts to cut school and just go AWOL. But my parents would kill me."

"It's not really like that, Tara. It's hard to explain."

After dinner I ride my bike to the bookstore, since the library is already closed. I look up this Truman Capote guy and find that he's got a book out called *Breakfast at Tiffany's*. It must be based on the movie.

In the reference section I look up *Bohemia*. It was located in Eastern Europe, but now it's gone. Poor Ms. Olivia. Her whole country was *abolished* in 1948. She must be a refugee. No wonder she's against all forms of government and oppression.

That night I lie on the couch in the summerhouse and read more *Catch-22* by flashlight. Chief White Halfoat just overturned a jeep because even though somebody kept telling him to switch on the headlights, he wouldn't listen.

Outside the clouds travel dark and fast across the moon and it's sprinkling just enough to drown out the usual spooky sounds that come from the fifty or so chipmunks that have built condominiums in the walls.

After reading a few more pages of Joseph Heller, I hear music. At first I think it's the rain hitting the windows, tapping out a melody, like sometimes I

swear I hear songs in the beat of the rain the way you imagine you see cartoon characters in cloud formations. But after a minute I'm positive that the
music is actually playing right inside the summerhouse, and not just inside
my head. Flashing my light around the room, I eventually spy two small
speakers nestled in the far corners of a shelf. They're next to a row of white
porcelain urns with colorful designs of people doing some pretty interesting
things to one another.

I'm no electrician, but I surmise that the Stocktons have a stereo system
with an extension out here that can be operated from within the house. Only
last night when I heard the music, it was coming from an open window of the
main house and not through these speakers.

My radar tells me that I've been busted, only this time not by Officer
Rich or my parents. I switch off the flashlight, lay the book on the coffee
table, and peer over the back of the couch, toward the house. No one is visible
in the windows, but the porch light flicks on and off. Or maybe I'm imagining things. Perhaps I do need to cut down on the Yoo-Hoo. Pointing my
flashlight toward the house, I flick it on and then off again. The porch light
answers back. Which one of them could it be?

I hope they can't get in trouble for harboring a fugitive. I snuggle up under the afghan and the music softly drifts through the room. It's not quite
classical, but more akin to those shows where people holler a lot and then get
bad coughs and die in the end. *Nessun dorma! Nessun dorma! Tu pure, o
Principessa, Nella tua fredda stanza, Guardi le stelle Che tremano, d'amore e di
speranza. . . .*

This whole deal is getting to be more and more like *Alice in Wonderland.*
Curiouser and curiouser. But I'm tired and the song is soothing and so I drift
off to sleep.

1 9

Fast Company

Upon entering the main house the following morning, I find Ms. Olivia and Mr. Bernard are in the middle of a major league quarrel. Only this time they don't seem to be joking around.

"Mother, I won't hear of it!" Mr. Bernard nods toward me as I enter the kitchen, but he doesn't stop arguing, the way my parents always do when one of us kids shows up. "You don't know anything about this *person.*"

"His *name* is Ottavio." Ms. Olivia then turns to me. "Don't you think that's a lovely name, Hallie? He's the eighth child, and in Italian families they sometimes name the eighth child Ottavio, for eight."

"Then I guess I should be named Secondo, since I'm number two out of seven. Actually, make that eight in another few months." I remove a chocolate Yoo-Hoo from the fridge, shake it, and pop off the top. But Mr. Bernard has stopped beating his eggs and is giving me a sideways stare while Ms. Olivia is looking at me as if I'm speaking in tongues. Total silence.

Where the hell did that come from? I wonder. First the joke and then the family update. I was cracking. The first rule of being an outlaw is to never volunteer information. It could end up as ammunition in the hands of the opposition. The old *anything you say can and will be used against you.*

But maybe it's okay. After all, Mr. Bernard said he's on my side. And they're probably risking prison for aiding and abetting a juvenile delinquent by purchasing the very Yoo-Hoos that are keeping me alive.

"Secondo," Mr. Bernard repeats. "That's funny. But of course, it's true—

it's what they often call the second son. Primo for the firstborn, and then Secondo."

Only now I don't really know what to say, so I just raise my Yoo-Hoo in toast fashion and then take a big swallow. However, they quickly recover from my interruption and get back to the business, or rather the altercation, at hand.

"Now, Hallie, if you don't mind, would you *please* tell Mother that these *bounders* one encounters on the Internet are not who they seem. This Ottavio *person* is most likely a swarthy four-hundred-pound transsexual who spray-paints neon Elvis daguerreotypes on a black velvet background."

"Don't be *ridiculous*, Bernard. I made his acquaintance in a Bernini chat room. We happen to share an enthusiasm for Italian baroque sculpture. And we've spoken on the phone. In fact, Ottavio E-mailed me a photograph of himself in front of the Tomb of Pope Urban VIII in St. Peter's." She says this last part with dreamy detachment.

"That's *exactly* what I mean, Mother. It could be a picture of *anyone*. He, she, it, could have cut the photo out of a magazine!"

"Bertie, why don't you just say it? Stop couching the issue in terms of computer security. Just admit that you don't want me to have anything to do with other men while your father is still living and breathing."

"Mother, of course I want you to have *friends*. . . ."

"Yes, but you don't want me to take a lover. And I respect that, Bernard. All I'm asking is that we discuss the *actual issue*."

Mr. Bernard haughtily hands the tray he's just prepared to Ms. Olivia and begins furiously scrubbing a frying pan. "Please, just go and free Father—I mean *feed* Father. I don't wish to consider this matter any further right now!"

I'm hoping that they do decide to talk about it later, because I'm feeling uncomfortable, as if I'm eavesdropping. Transsexuals and popes and lovers. Wow. And it's only half past eight in the morning.

However Ms. Olivia isn't ready to be dismissed. "I love your father very much, Bernard, and I always will, but the man I married has been gone for six years now. I wish you would consider that the heart is not an hourglass filled with only so many grains of sand. And therefore one love does not exclude another."

She purposefully turns and stalks out of the room. Only she forgets the tray and so she has to march back in, retrieve it, and purposefully stalk out all over again. As Ms. Olivia disappears under the archway, Mr. Bernard lifts his head up from scrubbing and says, "Honestly, Hallie, she's going to drive me crazy . . . if it's not already too late." Then, as if he's talking to himself, he continues, "Chat rooms . . . she can chat all she wants right here. It makes no sense whatsoever."

He removes a plate from the oven on which there are two homemade Egg McMuffin–style sandwiches and shoves it firmly into my hand. "Can you believe this? My sixty-two-year-old mother is caught up in some Internet romance with a Neapolitan bricklayer-slash-songwriter and is arranging a weekend tryst in Havana! Of all places! She and the roué are going to wind up in some communist prison and we'll all be sleeping on cots at Guantánamo Bay while mixed up in some type of horrendous international incident."

"So what are you going to do?"

"Do! What's there to do? She does whatever the heck she likes. Always has. Fortunately for us and the rest of the world, she customarily uses her talents for worthy causes."

I don't feel it's my place to say anything. Mr. Bernard puts the pans in the drying rack, checks to make sure the stove is turned off, and then hangs the towel that he's been using over the faucet.

"And heaven forbid Mother ever couches something in a euphemism such as she would *enjoy some companionship*." He exhales dramatically. "No, she has to announce that she's *taking a lover*! And of course Mother can't just have a date, it has to be a *grande passion*, and with a *boulevardier*. Whenever I had boyfriend problems, it was always an *affair de coeur*."

Did he just say what I think he said? Maybe he meant *when he had problems as a boyfriend*. No, of course not. Who did I think Gil was, anyway? Okay, they're a couple. So what?

"I . . . I've never met anyone like your mother," I finally manage to say.

"Neither have I," he answers with exasperation.

"But . . . but I like her. She's nice. And, uh, very unusual. I mean, interesting."

"Her heart is in the right place . . . most of the time. And the worst thing about this Ottavio *person* business is that she's right in theory. Anyway, let's forget about all that nonsense for now. Paint, paint . . ." He fishes through all his different pockets. "Mother said you're up for some painting." He passes me his credit card. "I'll phone the hardware store and tell them it's okay for you to use this. Purchase whatever we need—drop cloths, rollers, brushes. Ivory matte on the inside, eggshell gloss on the outside. And bring Mother some paint chips and wallpaper samples for her den in the most outrageous colors and patterns you can find. Perhaps that will keep her occupied for a few days. And do me a favor and stop at the drugstore." He hands me a neatly printed list containing toothpaste, shampoo, aspirin, and some medication for the Judge.

I wolf down the last bite of egg sandwich and wipe my hand on my jeans before pocketing the list. One thing is for sure, there's never a dull moment in this house. I mean, the big excitement when we visit my grandma is to hear about who in her bridge group is having a hip replacement operation and which of her kids never visits.

The hardware store trip actually turns out to be a revelation. Usually I go in there to buy something inexpensive, like a patch for my bike tire. And then I always have to wait until Mr. Burke finishes with all the grown-ups, even if they come in after me. But today, because I have a credit card and am picking out hundreds of dollars' worth of paint, Mr. Burke is incredibly nice and makes other customers wait while he locates a trim brush out of the stock-room. I never realized how differently a person could be treated just for having a piece of plastic.

Cool Hand Hallie

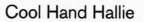

As always, Herb and Al and Officer Rich spend the first few minutes complaining about their wives and the high cost of sneakers and college tuition. Fortunately Father Costello doesn't bring any of his counseling and sermon stuff to the card table.

"So what's the score with the school?" I eventually ask Officer Rich.

"You're here. They're there," he says without looking up from his cards.

It's obvious he's got a crappy hand. He only looks at a good hand for a few seconds. But a nasty one, he keeps staring at the cards, like if he gazes at them long enough they'll transmogrify into a royal flush.

"So?" I ask.

"So you're winning, as usual," Officer Rich replies and throws away an eight of clubs, which is the exact card I know Herb was hoping to be dealt.

"For now," he adds mysteriously.

"What do you mean *for now*?"

"The emancipated minor thing was real cute, but you'd better have a pretty good reason to petition the court."

"Yeah, I knew I was on slightly weak ground there. So why didn't they come and drag me away?"

"Because they figure you'll just jump out the window again. They say you have a problem with windows."

"When the Good Lord closes a door, he usually opens a window somewhere else," Father Costello absentmindedly says as he fingers the silver cross around his neck.

We all give him a funny glance, because normally he doesn't chime in with any religiosity. He catches our looks. "It's not scripture. It's what the Mother Superior said to Maria in *The Sound of Music*. My mother and I watched it on television last night."

We all look relieved. I'm thinking what a fun life Ar-*thur* must have. It's no wonder he never misses a poker game. In fact, I'd bet my winnings that he makes up some lame excuse to his mo-*ther*, like he's running a Bible study group on Monday nights.

"It's your bet, Padre," Herb reminds Father Costello.

Father Costello bets five dollars, positively adventuresome for him. Officer Rich sighs and folds his hand and then turns back to me. "Hallie, do you mind me asking, just as a friend, why you don't want go to school? I mean, Jesus Christ—sorry, Father—did somebody there sexually abuse you?"

I consider spilling the beans but subsequently decide he'll never understand. "No. It's nothing like that. You don't need to dust the girls' locker room for fingerprints."

"They bandied about a trip to reform school today," he says. "All the windows *there* have bars on them."

"My mother will never go for it." I don't look up.

"No wonder you're such a good poker player. That's exactly what happened. She wouldn't even let us *threaten* you with reform school, even as a bluff. She really loves you, by the way. All joking aside, this thing is ripping her heart out."

"I hardly ever saw her when I was at home. I mean, not that I wanted to. We don't have a lot in common, so she can't really *miss* me."

"Well, we could just fill a snuffbox with what you know about raising kids," says Officer Rich.

"Amen," calls out Herb.

"I told them I'd visit," I say. "I mean, hell—whoops, sorry, Father—some kids leave for boarding school when they're twelve."

"Hallie, your parents feel guilty that you're so unhappy," says Al. "Can't you *see* that?"

"I'm *not* unhappy. I wish everyone would stop having my thoughts and feelings for me. They don't have to live my life." It's my deal, and so I riffle the cards. I'm a practiced shuffler and can even triple-cut the deck in the palm of one hand. "So give me the inside scoop," I say. "What's their next move?"

"If you're so smart that you don't have to go to school, then figure it out for yourself," says Officer Rich.

"Yeah, don't tell little Miss Hellfire," says Herb. "She's still young enough to know everything."

I start dealing. Al looks pleased with his ace of hearts.

"They mentioned the car again," Officer Rich says.

"Bribery!"

"Will you do a deal?" Officer Rich casually asks.

"School for car?" I ask but don't wait for a response. "Not anymore. That was last week's pot."

"Between you and me, Hallie . . . ," Officer Rich says slowly, "I just don't want you to freeze to death in the woods. Call me an old softie, but where in the name of God—sorry, Father—are you sleeping? I could lose my job for this, but if you really won't go home," he pauses as if he's seriously weighing up the risk of unemployment, "you can sleep down at the station. There's heat and vending machines."

"That's okay. I've got a place. At least until the snow flies." But it was a big deal for Officer Rich to make the offer, and I appreciate it. He really could get into trouble. I catch his eye so he knows it. "But thanks."

"Sure, no problem." He says this gruffly and looks away, like all big guys have to do so people won't assume they're turning into women.

"Ohio law enforcement couldn't hold John Dillinger," says Herb, "so I don't know how you think they can hold Hellraiser Palmer."

We all ignore Herb, which is easy to do. And now it's Al's deal.

"I thought for sure they'd assume I was staying at the Stocktons'," I say.

"Of course we did," says Officer Rich. "That's the first place we checked. But they swear you ride up at quarter past eight every morning, eat lunch, and then take off at around six. They said you had dinner there one night: ruby-glazed lamb with roasted red potatoes and cherry cheesecake for dessert. It sounded real good."

"It was," I say. Mr. Bernard chose a French Huguenot theme and almost everything, including the bean salad, candles, tablecloth, and linen napkins, were red. But I don't bother telling the poker club this colorful detail.

"I have a pretty good idea of when people are lying," says Officer Rich, "and I don't think that Bernard Stockton was trying to pull one over on me. He's a little eccentric, I'll grant you that, but he's got integrity, just like his old man."

"So the Cosgrove County Inquisition is under way," I sneer. "What else did he say?"

"That you're definitely not an alcoholic. Mr. Stockton made it quite clear that they've had experience with an intoxicated gardener and so they know all the signs. And by the way, how in the heck did you ever hook up with that family?"

"I'll never forget the day *that* wedding was announced," recalls Al. "I was just a little boy, but my mother and her sister, my aunt May, they both needed smelling salts."

Herb takes up the town history from there. "The Judge was a lawyer back then, a prominent young man from a local blue blood family, and he went to Paris on a Farmers' Union case—onions, I think. Anyway, that's where he met the redoubtable Olivia Newton."

"She's French?" I ask. "I thought she was from Bohemia, somewhere near Yugoslavia."

Al and Officer Rich both laugh.

"Yugoslavia?" says Herb sarcastically. "Try Yugocrazia!"

Pastor Costello looks at me quizzically. "Olivia is originally from Cambridge, Massachusetts," he says. "She was studying in Paris."

"Studying, huh?" Herb scowls at his hand. "The way I heard it, she chased some artist guy from Boston to Paris, he promptly disappeared the day after she arrived, and the Judge rescued her from humiliation."

"My mother insisted the marriage to Stockton would never last," says Al.

"It's probably a good thing that the Judge developed Alzheimer's before discovering that his only son and heir is gay," comments Herb.

Pastor Costello peers at Herb in a strange way after that remark, as if he's hoping that someone else will say something so he doesn't feel morally obligated to do so.

"Hey, Herb, just play cards, okay?" Officer Rich admonishes him. Pastor Costello appears slightly relieved.

Herb rises to his own defense. "Oh, hell—excuse me, Father—I don't mean that it's a good thing the old man lost his marbles. Please. And I don't necessarily mean there's anything wrong with, you know . . ."

"Let's just forget it," says Officer Rich.

But Herb isn't finished. "I just meant that I don't know how well the Judge would have handled that information."

Al deals Herb a three of clubs that I know he doesn't want. Pastor Costello looks mournfully at the card and it's obvious that it blew his hopes for a basement straight.

"Okay," Officer Rich says, gathering up the cards. "Deuces wild, last hand."

"No way," says Herb. "I need a chance to win back some of the dough I lost."

"So play better next time and you won't lose so much," retorts Al. "Or bet less."

"It's her!" says Herb. "I know you memorize all the cards played, Hallie, but I've been watching you and there's something else. I just can't figure out what it is."

"Hey, Herb!" says Officer Rich. "Watch what you're saying there. . . ."

"Thank you, Constable," I reply.

"Hallie is just very blessed when it comes to playing cards," says Pastor Costello.

"Thank you, Father," I say appreciatively.

What I don't bother to tell these guys is that I don't play cards so much as I play *them*. Christ, they should look in a mirror sometime. When Herb is bluffing, he drums the fingers of his left hand on the table. If Father Costello needs a card, he moves his lips in prayer and then either thanks God when he gets it or grimaces if he doesn't. When Al has a good hand, he speeds everyone along and tosses his money into the pot real fast, so it practically rolls off the other end of the table. But when he's bluffing, he moves real slow and pauses to fire up a cigarette. I eventually fold. The chances of getting the spade I need to fill out my flush aren't so hot, and I'm ahead for the night. Herb wins the last hand and he's pleased about that and the game breaks up.

"You know," Al says to me, "when my kids told me what was going on with you, I felt bad and I was going to offer you some money if I saw you here tonight."

"Yeah, and . . . ," I respond.

"And now I'm not. You must've taken seventy-five bucks off me."

Herb and Al depart. I know it's a setup, but I don't care. Pastor Costello and Officer Rich are pretty cool.

"Listen, kiddo," Officer Rich begins, "even though this Collier guy can't nail you on legal grounds, he's not going to give up so easily. And I truly wish it was because he's so desperately concerned about your education and well-being. But I'm afraid he views this situation as some sort of a contest between you and him. He doesn't want to lose and he doesn't want to be made to look like a fool. Do you get my drift? The assistant principal is retiring in June, and Collier has his eye on that plum position."

Officer Rich is leaving, and I know that I'd better exit with him or Friar Tuck is going to angle for one of his pew-side chats. Surely my mother's been in touch. However, I figure he can get my parents off my back some if I let him ply his trade. Officer Rich says good night and then looks at me and lets out a gruff chuckle.

"And just what's so funny, Smokey the Bear?" I ask.

"Collier calls you the Artful Dodger." He pauses. "At least that's what he calls you when he's not in a bad mood."

Pastor Costello steers me back to the card table with the gentle *we care* ministerial hold on my elbow. "Hallie, I'm concerned about you. You don't have to bear this burden alone. Now, please tell me if someone has hurt you or is causing you pain in any way—physically, emotionally . . ."

"No, Father. Absolutely not."

He appears as if he'd like to believe me and yet can't quite bring himself to do so. "Would you rather speak with a woman about this?"

"No, Father. I'm not being sexually abused and I'm not pregnant."

He appears rather relieved that I don't start sobbing about missed periods. "Then will you please confide in me why you won't go to school and why you've moved out of your family home if I promise that it won't leave these church walls? I've known you since you were a baby, Hallie. You were christened at this altar. I've always realized that you were a different sort of girl—you're very astute and independent and you do things in your own way."

All this concern is suddenly making me want to cry. I think ministers are like TV interviewers in that they don't feel as if they're doing their job or will get that wink from the Big Guy unless a lot of people are reduced to weeping and thrashing about.

"Hallie," he continues, "your mother says you're upset about the new baby. Should we temporarily place you with another church family while you get some counseling?"

Ugh. Family and counseling are two words I've heard just about enough of.

"Father, if they're happy to have another baby, then that's just fine with me. I stand only to gain another potential bone marrow donor. I just can't live with them anymore, okay?"

I feel a burning sensation on my neck and face as tears spring to the bottom of my eyes. Shit. "Pom-poms and football games and the ten o'clock news," I stammer between sniffles.

Father Costello looks perplexed, as if he's trying to download this eclectic list into his secret Christian clergy decoder ring and come up with a prayer and a self-help group to fix everything.

"Thanks, Father, but there's nothing you can do. I have to figure it out for myself." I blow my nose on the inside of my sweatshirt and rise to leave.

He walks me to the door. "Is there anything you need? Do you have a warm place to stay?"

I don't say that the summerhouse is not going to be so warm in another week or so, since the air goes right through all that glass. "Yes, I'm fine."

"All right, then. I'll pray for you."

"Thank you," I answer sincerely. Although I don't really buy that old-man-in-the-sky God stuff, I find the trees and the flowers are all pretty cool and so a few prayers launched into the universe under my social security number can't exactly hurt anything.

While mounting my bike I notice Father Costello standing in the doorway, a dark shadow outlined by a pale yellow glow. "Hallie . . . if you don't mind my asking . . . ," he says haltingly, "how did you know when I didn't get that other king? There weren't any kings showing . . . and you didn't have any."

"Now, if I told you *that* I *would* have to come here asking for handouts instead of winning your money fair and square."

"I just thought I'd inquire, that's all. . . ." He brightens up and then tosses off that old chestnut, "The Lord works in mysterious ways."

"Let's hope so," I say before rocketing off into the night.

Gods and Odds

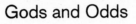

Working as a full-time yard person is not for slouches. Shoulder and back muscles that might eventually qualify me for a women's wrestling team are beginning to fill out my shirts. And by the end of each day I'm physically exhausted. It'll be a relief when all the gardens are pulled up.

Late Saturday afternoon I finish pruning and go inside to take a shower. Downstairs at the dining room table the Judge is about to have his dinner, looking very much the retired Civil War general in starched gray pajamas with navy blue trim. Once inside Ms. Olivia's bathroom I have to move aside this special metal chair with a white plastic seat that they use to sit the Judge under the shower. There are also grab bars along the walls so he doesn't slip and fall.

Even though Mr. Bernard cooks the Judge's meals and helps him up to bed, Ms. Olivia almost always feeds him and sits with him until he falls asleep. She told me he'd been ill for six years. Wow. That means she's fed him 1,095 meals a year, a total of 6,570 to date. I picture my mom always perched next to a high chair and spooning gruel down the throat of the latest addition—but at least she knows they'll outgrow it.

I wonder if Ms. Olivia ever gets depressed by the whole situation. If she does, it's impossible to tell from her behavior. Ms. Olivia is wonderful with the Judge and always speaks to him as if he's a competent adult. When I used to visit my father's aunt Clara in the retirement home, I noticed that some of the nurses addressed the old people as if they were preschoolers. But Aunt Clara died of heart failure last summer and so now I don't know anyone in a nursing home. Though I think about death a lot—that I don't know if I'm going to die when I'm sixteen or when I'm ninety-six. And if I did know, would I be doing anything differently?

At that moment I hear the front door open, followed by Mr. Bernard's cheerful proclamation that he's arrived home. When I greet him at the bottom of the stairs he hands me an envelope containing three hundred dollars, all in twenties. He must assume that I don't have a bank account since I'm living a drifterlike existence.

"If it's easier to write a check, it's no problem. I have an account at the bank."

Mr. Gil nudges the door open with some overstuffed grocery bags just as I say this.

"Bertie, a check?" he chimes in. "*Never.* The IRS is under the impression that he runs a small hobby shop down on Swan Street. Through some astounding feat of bookkeeping legerdemain he's managed to show a loss for the past ten years. Going by his tax returns we're eligible for food stamps and two bricks of Welfare Cheese. Ever wonder why the name of the store changes every few years?"

But Mr. Bernard just chuckles. "Always remember that cash is king in a depression. And I don't see anyone complaining about my monetary contribution to this household—what with Mother sending all her earnings for the upkeep of retired racing greyhounds down in Sarasota. I've a hunch those pampered canines are taking luxury cruises to Caracas and learning the cha-cha."

They *must* be laundering money, I think. First drug dealing, then fencing stolen art, and now tax evasion! How can such nice people be such hardened criminals? And who ever said that crime doesn't pay?

Mr. Gil waves a blue-and-yellow Blockbuster plastic bag like a flag on the Fourth of July. "Movie night! Can you believe our movies were *still* there at five o'clock?" Then he does a few dance steps back and forth and chants, "One-two, cha-cha-cha. Three, four, cha-cha-cha."

"Our choices are *always* there," Mr. Bernard says to me. "When it comes to film appreciation, we're slightly ahead of the town."

"Or behind," says Mr. Gil. "Depending on how you choose to look at it."

Mr. Gil is in a good mood. He takes my hands and starts showing me the cha-cha. "One-two, cha-cha-cha." Only I'm not much of a dancer.

"Hallie, I'm running late," Mr. Bernard interrupts, "and I need you to help in the kitchen, if you don't mind." This is more of an order than a request.

"But it's just that . . . I, uh, I don't know *how* to cook anything."

"Well, come along, then," he continues in a Scottish brogue. "*Give me a girl at an impressionable age, and she is mine for life.* At least according to Miss Jean Brodie."

Miss Jean Brodie must have been his home ec teacher or else the author of a popular cookbook. I follow Mr. Bernard into the kitchen and stand there like a scarecrow while he preheats the oven and fills pots with water.

"We're making Rock Cornish game hen with Israeli couscous, hearts of palm salad, and artichokes stuffed with zucchini, bread crumbs, and Parmesan. Mother, of course, won't consume ornithologia, so I always prepare a vegetable, starch, and salad that can serve as her meal. And I make some extra for the rum bum."

"I like Rocky. Sometimes he gathers the plants after I dig them up and bags them for me. Though I think he eats a couple."

Mr. Bernard rolls his eyes whenever anyone mentions the *R* word. He pulls a carton of cream out of a grocery bag and places it in the refrigerator. "Oh, and I bought some vanilla Yoo-Hoo on the assumption that it's like wine, and that if strawberry goes with meat then perhaps it's culinarily correct that vanilla accompany fish and fowl." Mr. Bernard always pronounces culinary to sound as if it begins with a *q* rather than *cull*, like most people.

Unpacking the bags of groceries on the countertop, I don't recognize half of the ingredients. It seems impossible that we're actually going to make dinner out of all these piles of green stuff, onions, cloves of garlic, tins of anchovy paste, croutons, and cans of beef stock.

"Now take a cup of flour from the canister on the counter and combine it with some rosemary—first chop it into one-inch sprigs."

Rosemary, rosemary, what the hell is rosemary? I know as much about cooking as a lemur at the Columbus Zoo. I pick up a plastic bag with green stalks in it.

"Those are chives." Mr. Bernard hands me another bag that is apparently rosemary. "Then add a pinch of ground pepper and drag the hens through it."

Mr. Bernard appears to thrive on the entire cooking process. He becomes quite animated and hums and sings and dashes around whisking this and tasting that.

"You see, Hallie, cooking is another art form. You combine different elements in an effort to coax your vision into a reality—just as a painting has light, shape, color, and texture, yet at the same time it's also purely the expression of the artist."

After about an hour of dicing and stirring and broiling and basting, we actually have this incredible-looking meal. Though I have no idea how it will taste.

When we finish laying the table in the dining room with what would in my home be considered the "good" dishes and flatware, Mr. Bernard lights some tall ivory candles in silver candlestick holders and switches the radio station from jazz to classical.

"Call Mother to the table, please," says Mr. Bernard. "Hopefully she's not on some sort of fast to protest genetically altered crops. That's her latest."

Ms. Olivia enters the dining room and peers skeptically at the beautifully garnished dinner that is carefully arranged on shiny black china plates with gold rims. "I know exactly what my son is up to. He told you cooking is a form of art, right—light, shape, and color and all that philosophical flapdoodle? Well, it's malarkey. Cooking is a job that you should get paid to do. And just because we're paying you to mow the lawn doesn't mean you have to play kitchen copilot for the Julia Child of Cosgrove County."

"Mother, please!"

"Well, I don't want Hallie to think that chopping celery is part of her job," Ms. Olivia replies and takes her seat at the table. "Not all women are domestically inclined."

Mr. Gil enters the room and takes a seat at the head of the table. "Please say grace, Bertie," he says. "We don't want Hallie to think we're heathens."

I quickly fold my hands and bow my head.

"Yes, of course." Mr. Bernard briefly steeples his hands and quickly clears his throat. "Grace Kelly." Then he passes me the platter with the Cornish hens.

"Did I have a vision of Madeleine on the sun porch last night, or was it just my imagination?" asks Mr. Gil.

I perk up my ears. Madeleine must be the resident ghost. The fact that I'm completely lost doesn't go unnoticed by Mr. Bernard. "Hallie, you know those shell-shaped cakes you arranged on the dessert platter?"

"Yeah."

"Well, they're said to be named for their inventor, Madeleine Paulmier, a nineteenth-century pastry cook in France. Supposedly it was on a visit to his mother that the famous French author Marcel Proust was served the scalloped *petite madeleine*."

Mr. Gil turns to me. "So the story goes that the taste of the *petite madeleine* brought back a flood of memories to Proust, and he went home and wrote his masterpiece, *Remembrance of Things Past*."

"Perhaps you'll write a novel someday, Hallie," Ms. Olivia says enthusiastically, as if this is a perfectly reasonable aspiration for someone who has just dropped out of high school and now mows lawns for a living. "Although Bertie tells me you enjoy creating collages."

"I made a few for school projects and that sort of thing."

"Then I'd love for you to fashion a large collage on the garage door," says Ms. Olivia. "In the spring there's a garden tour that comes down our street, and I want to make a statement next year. Preferably a political one—perhaps a representation of all the spirits of female Chinese babies using plastic dolls, victims of infanticide, or of women bleeding to death as a result of female circumcision."

"Arghh," goes Mr. Gil.

"Ugh," says Mr. Bernard and drops his fork so that it makes a clattering sound on his plate.

Ms. Olivia dismisses them with a wave of her hand. "Pay no attention to those two. If it were up to them, the great Mexican fresco painter Diego Rivera would have had to earn his living sculpting Zapata miniatures out of driftwood and hocking them to tourists." She turns her attention back to me. "As the *artiste*, you must of course select a subject that speaks to *you* personally. It's not supposed to be about me."

"And when is it not about you, Mother?" Mr. Bernard says dryly.

"People who cook with glass mixing bowls shouldn't throw beaters," Ms. Olivia shoots back. "*Si jeunesse savait, si vieillesse pouvait.*"

"If youth but knew, if old age could," Mr. Gil translates.

When he's certain that Ms. Olivia's finished, Mr. Bernard pronounces, "I think a collage is a grand idea. Use anything you want from the garage."

"Use *everything* in the garage," Mr. Gil chimes in. "I'm begging you."

"A garage collage," I say.

"More like a garbage collage," says Mr. Gil.

"Okay," I agree. "If you're sure you don't mind."

"Not at all," says Mr. Bernard. "We haven't had a decent crowd of photographers out front since Mother scribed an editorial protesting prayer in the public school system."

"But it succeeded, didn't it?" Ms. Olivia states proudly. "Besides, I could have taken it much further. You know, the Pledge of Allegiance shouldn't even be allowed in public schools. It clearly states *one nation under God*. If they want to change the law, then that's fine, let them go ahead and try, but in the meantime it clearly calls for separation of church and state."

"If you consider the school board suing us for seditious libel after you handed out those flyers a success, and your having to set up a legal defense fund, then I'd say that it worked very well indeed," says Mr. Bernard.

"What I of course meant was that the resulting fracas forced the state legislature to become involved and start a debate over the issue. And a debate in the public forum is the seed of revolution. That's how the city of Boston started the Revolutionary War."

As if Ms. Olivia isn't even at the table, Mr. Bernard turns to me and says, "Once a guest at a White House reception told Calvin Coolidge, 'I'm from Boston,' and the president replied, 'You'll never get over it.' Well, it's the same way around here."

I'm grateful that I at least know who Coolidge is and that this time I can follow the conversation. I bought a pocket dictionary the other day just to look up the words they use—like *ludicrous*. Mr. Bernard constantly tells Ms. Olivia not to be ludicrous. Also, he said that the hearts of palm salad was *salubrious*. And that the way I edged the front walkway was *splendiferous*.

"Hallie," Ms. Olivia turns to me, "I have nothing against praying privately, but do you think it's fair to have organized Christian monotheistic worship in a public institution where children are Muslim, Buddhist, Skeptic, and Zoroastrian?"

"That's just the point, Mother, there aren't any Muslims or Buddhists or Zoroastrians in Cosgrove County."

Honestly, I need a translator. There are two words in the *question* that I've never heard of before: mono-whatever and Skeptic. Forget about Zoroastrian. Do I ask, agree, or dodge the whole thing altogether?

Mr. Bernard seems to sense my discomfort and kindly gives me an out. "Mother, I don't think it's necessary for Hallie to posit her political platform."

I gather up my courage and ask, "What's mono-whatever and Skeptic?"

"Monotheism is the belief in one God to which the majority of this country—Catholics, Protestants, Jews, and so forth—adheres. Polytheism is the belief in many gods," Mr. Bernard explains. "You'll find it in modern-day India and ancient Greece—you know, Zeus and Eros and all those characters."

"India is an excellent example," Ms. Olivia enthuses. "Agni is the fire god, Vayu the wind god, and Indra is the god of storms."

"And Skeptic?" I remind them.

"Bertie!" Ms. Olivia says.

"What?" Mr. Bernard asks.

"You're a Skeptic," she says.

"Yes, I suppose so. It means that you've not yet reached any firm conclusions about the existence of God, heaven and hell, and so forth."

"Bertie's a fallen Unitarian," says Ms. Olivia.

"There's an oxymoron if I've ever heard one," Mr. Gil chimes in.

They all laugh and so I fake a smile to look as if I, too, get the joke. But I figure I'd better look up the word *oxymoron*, even though it sounds like a new acne medication.

"What's the difference between being a Skeptic and being a Unitarian?" I ask.

"Very simple," Mr. Bernard states. "I mind my own business and that way I don't get arrested." He shoots an accusatory glance at Ms. Olivia. "Mother, your taking on the Boy Scouts is the last straw. Really, they tie knots and cook over campfires and help old ladies to cross the street."

"They shouldn't be requiring boys to pledge themselves to God as part of the inclusion process. And I disagree with the requirements for earning the religion badge. I've told you before, most wars have been fought in the name of God. More people have been slaughtered in the name of God or Allah or Yahweh than anything else."

"Here we go . . . ," says Mr. Bernard.

"If they're going to pray in the schools, then they should offer all different kinds so that no one is left out," I say. "Like we sing Christmas *and* Hanukkah songs."

"Sensible girl." Ms. Olivia smiles at me.

Mr. Gil interrupts. "It's time for some *Breakfast at Tiffany's* and Givenchy.

Let's save the Boy Scout jamboree debate, nuclear nonproliferation, and global warming for a breakfast summit, if that's agreeable to all the delegates."

Ms. Olivia leans across the table toward me and speaks softly, as if she doesn't want Mr. Bernard and Mr. Gil to hear her, but of course she really does. "You see, Hallie, what Gil and Bertie don't understand is that it's our differences that bring us together, and in the end, it's our shared convictions that tear us apart."

After the movie ends and Holly Golightly and her handsome new boyfriend return to the alley and find Cat, I decide that this Audrey Hepburn has some nice clothes for a person who makes only fifty bucks every few days for going to the powder room.

"Why does the older woman give Holly's boyfriend clothes and money?" I ask. "Is he working on a writing project for her?"

"He's a male escort," says Mr. Gil.

"A walker," adds Mr. Bernard.

"He's being kept by her," further explains Mr. Gil.

I must still look confused.

"She pays his bills," says Mr. Bernard.

"Oh." I think about that for a second and wonder how he found such a job. It's doubtful there was a sign at the Star-Mart for *that*. "I like that song she sang on the fire escape."

"It just goes to show you what idiots directors are," Mr. Bernard says knowingly. "They were going to cut 'Moon River' from the film."

When it's time to say good night we act out the charade that I'm going to climb on my bike and ride somewhere other than the backyard. Because we all realize that if they don't acknowledge my living here then they're not really lying to the authorities.

"Get home safely," Mr. Bernard says with a twinkle in his eye.

Since the following day is a Sunday, I'd been considering taking some time off and heading out to the track. After all, it's the last racing day of the season.

"Uh, did you want me to start painting tomorrow?"

"You may have the weekends off. Or if you want to earn extra funds, then you can work," he says. "It's completely up to you."

"Okay, I'll see what I feel like in the morning. If it's nice weather, I might take off and go for a bike ride."

Back in the summerhouse the trees sift the moonlight so that nightfall covers the walls like an intricate tapestry. Drifting off to sleep, I hear the song I liked from the movie playing over the speakers: *We're after the same rainbow's end, waitin' 'round the bend, my Huckleberry friend, Moon River and me.*

I know what a drifter is, but what's a Huckleberry friend . . . I wonder? Walkers and Zoroastrians and a feisty old lady who sells drugs out of her summerhouse. Wow. There are so many different occupations. Who knew?

Leaving It to Chance

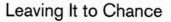

The temptation to begin my garage collage is too great, and so I skip the final day at the racetrack even though it's the Thurber Stakes. While sanding the peeling paint off the old wooden doors, I contemplate what type of a statement to make. Unfortunately an enlarged photo of Just Call Me Dick with bars painted over his face to make it appear as if he's trying to escape from prison is out of the question. I'm in enough trouble. About hitting a streak of bad luck Cappy always says: "Know when to cash in your chips."

It's a big space to fill. I've never seen a real-life collage the size of a garage door. Though I'd seen murals on the sides of buildings and on water towers. If only I had a thousand marbles or seashells or even pennies. Not that I had to cover every last inch of it. Less is more, as my mother likes to say. Though obviously this maxim doesn't apply to having children.

Mr. Bernard comes out to get the newspaper and invites me in for breakfast. Rocky is in his usual spot sitting next to the Judge and playing that hand game that little kids often enjoy, where you keep lifting your hand off the bottom and putting it on top of the other person's. Only today Rocky is actually dressed in a suit and tie. He looks just like a small human except for the extended tan snout and big ears.

In the dining room I eat some of Mr. Bernard's French toast, which is very thick and tasty. He makes it from special bread called challah. "Um, why is Rocky all dressed up?" I ask.

"He's a practicing Catholic," says Mr. Gil seriously but unable to keep the corners of his mouth from turning up.

"Rocky took Geraldine to church every Sunday for years," explains Ms. Olivia. "He has a lot of friends at Our Lady."

"Friends," scoffs Mr. Bernard. "If one of the deacons hadn't vouched for Rocky after Geraldine died, the humane society would have put him to sleep on the spot. He went on a bender the likes of—"

"Now, Bernard," Ms. Olivia interrupts him.

"Well, let's just say the only thing missing was Giuseppe Verdi's drinking song from *La Traviata*," Mr. Bernard says with a *you know what I mean* roll of his eyes.

"Rocky wasn't born knowing how to mix a cocktail, though I admit he's quite a gifted bartender," says Ms. Olivia. "Someone *taught* him those behaviors."

"I hope they keep him away from the communion wine," says Mr. Gil and releases a suppressed giggle.

"I hope they don't suddenly start believing in evolution, realize that they're descended from his ancestors, and excommunicate him," says Ms. Olivia, joining in the spirit of fun. "I've always found there to be an uncanny resemblance between Rocky and Monsignor O'Flaherty, especially around the jaw."

The church bells begin to chime "Stand Up, Stand Up for Jesus," indicating that Mass begins in fifteen minutes, and sure enough, Rocky passes through the dining room in his gray slacks, navy blue jacket, and red tie, looking absolutely presidential, but for the fact that he isn't wearing shoes, and heads out the front door.

I return to the garage door, and after about two hours of scraping and brooding Mr. Gil and Mr. Bernard exit the house carrying a jumble of newspapers covered with red Magic Marker *X*s and thick neon yellow highlighter circles and a pile of haphazardly folded road maps. At first I worry that they're off to hunt for a new house. But I can't imagine Mr. Bernard giving up his herb garden or Ms. Olivia her Druid Circle. And besides, we'd just planted fifty tulip bulbs on Wednesday.

"Oh my, look here, if it isn't Hallie Longstocking!" Mr. Bernard says as he passes my ladder. I assume this is a reference to Pippi Longstocking because my hair is tied up in two braids to keep it from collecting paint crud. He and Mr. Gil open the car doors.

"Now wish us luck," says Mr. Bernard.

"Where are you going?" I ask.

"Picking," Mr. Gil answers.

"Please." Mr. Bernard scoffs at him. "We're scouting for undiscovered and underappreciated treasures."

"More like *underpriced* treasures," Mr. Gil corrects him.

Mr. Bernard amiably disregards this comment. "And we must hurry if we are to arrive before the vultures."

"Yard sales," Mr. Gil informs me. He comes over as if to inspect my work and whispers, "Use everything you can from the garage and throw the rest away. I'll pay you a bonus to dispose of it *all.*"

"Come along, Tonto," Mr. Bernard says impatiently. "I have a presentiment that somewhere out there in this great land of ours an old dowager who accidentally drove her car through the back of the garage is being forced into a twilight home by her mendacious offspring and her Regency mantel clock with the satinwood balloon case, sunburst inlay, and pineapple finial is slightly dusty but priced to sell. And I intend to be the best offer."

Before Mr. Bernard backs his silver Alfa Romeo roadster out of the driveway, he pulls right up next to my ladder and rolls down the window. The car is incredibly cool and he says I can drive it anytime I want. But I'm afraid to. Mr. Bernard claims it's a "vintage automobile," though Mr. Gil says it's more like "previously owned."

"Be sure and join Mother for lunch. I've made some absolutely brilliant stuffed peppers and a lentil soup. And if you can talk Mother out of rendezvousing with the Italian gigolo in Cuba this weekend, there's an end-of-the-month bonus in it for you." He turns the radio up full blast and I can hear some opera singer blowing out a lung. Then they speed out of the driveway at about forty miles an hour, a cloud of gravel dust like a desert sandstorm rising behind the wheels.

He can't seriously expect me to change Ms. Olivia's mind or travel plans, *can he?* And I don't know—if she wants to go off and meet a boyfriend somewhere I guess that's her business, isn't it? I can't exactly blame Ms. Olivia for wanting a friend her own age.

Inside the house I find her serenely filing the Judge's nails and trimming his cuticles while harp music plays softly in the background. It's rather sweet to watch the two of them together. The Judge sits there like a complacent three-year-old and lets her fuss over him. Yet it's also sad. This man must have gone to school forever to become a lawyer and a judge, and then he made so many important decisions and now he doesn't remember any of it, or even know what's for breakfast, or worse, who's feeding him breakfast. Ms. Olivia speaks to him as if they're going to enjoy a special day together and he needs to look his best. Once I watched her comb the Judge's hair and then hold up the hand mirror for him to check the results. And I felt sure that she was hoping against hope for a response, some small sign of acknowledgment. But the Judge only stared vaguely past the glass to the television set, even though it was turned off.

Ms. Olivia eventually senses my presence. Without glancing up, she begins talking to me, her nimble fingers still gently doing their work while the sunlight that manages to sneak through the blinds paints distorted cracks across their bodies like rivers on a map. As if she's reading my mind, she says, "It's not as bad as it seems, dear. I have my memories to comfort me. That's the part you can't see. And sometimes the most essential things, the ones that make all the difference, are the ones we can never see."

She looks up at me before moving on to the next finger. "Have you ever read *Peter Pan*?"

"Yeah." I nod my head affirmatively because I know the story, though on second thought I've probably only seen the movie.

"The man who so famously created the boy who wouldn't grow up was a well-known Scottish dramatist back at the turn of the last century. He once wrote that God gave us memory so we might have roses in December. A lovely thought, isn't it?"

Ms. Olivia carefully completes her manicuring and returns the Judge's hand to his lap and smiles warmly up at him. "Now do make me a cup of Darjeeling tea, please—it's in the blue-and-gray tin with the picture of Mount Everest on the front."

I have the table laid by the time Ms. Olivia enters the dining room and takes the chair across from me at the lace-covered mahogany table. She carefully administers a heaping spoonful of sugar to her aromatic tea. There's a large oval-shaped walnut table in the kitchen, but Mr. Bernard has it completely covered with his Cuisinart attachments, an industrial-size blender, shiny aluminum mixing bowls, a knife sharpener, espresso maker, old copies of *Bon Appetit* magazine, about ten cookbooks, and lots of loose recipes clipped from newspapers. It's more of a storage area than a place for casual dining.

"Surely Bernard suggested you persuade me into calling off my Havana excursion," she states rather than asks. But before I can determine how to play this one without betraying either side, Ms. Olivia announces that she isn't traveling to Cuba after all.

"I'm meeting Ottavio in Orlando at the end of October and we're going to motor down to Vero Beach. If the trip goes well, I may invite him to visit after the holidays."

"Oh well, uh, then why . . ."

"It gives Bertie an opportunity to vent. It's difficult for him to let his father go. That's the problem with being an only child—once you let go of your parents you're suddenly alone in the world. I'll always have Bernard, God willing, but he won't always have me." She gently rotates her spoon in her teacup and sighs. "At the time I thought I was being socially conscious—zero population growth and all that. Though in retrospect perhaps it was selfish of me not to have more children."

However, Ms. Olivia looks up and brightens, as if she's decided not to worry about all of that anymore. "So, do you have a boyfriend or girlfriend?" she inquires.

I almost choke on a chunk of pepper. A girlfriend! "No!" I cough up a hunk of green and put my hand up to my mouth in case it decides to take flight.

Uh-oh, I don't want her to think that I think it would be wrong to have a girlfriend, seeing as her son obviously has a boyfriend.

"I have friends who are girls. And then there's this guy Craig Larkin who I made out with at a party over the summer."

Did I just tell a sixty-something-year-old lady that I "made out" with a guy? My parents don't even know that I've ever held hands with a boy.

"Then why aren't you entertaining his offer of romance? You must have experiences if you're going to be a great artist." Her voice soars on the word *experiences*.

"There was this thing with some money I owed him. I mean, I paid it back. Maybe once things settle down with school. I wouldn't want to get him into trouble."

"But it's a braver thing to love knowing that disaster may strike at any time, to love what death can take away at any moment." Her eyes sparkle briefly while conjuring up the possibility of a doomed romance. "Seeing as you brought up your state of affairs, I think you should be aware that what's-his-name, that quisling-education-bureaucrat Mr. Presumed Ignorant, paid a call on me yesterday in order to enlist my services in this conspiracy to repatriate you to their youth indoctrination compound."

I take it that she means Just Call Me Dick and the school.

Ms. Olivia thrusts her right hand upward as if to trap a fly ball in a catcher's mitt. "Not that I have anything against schools, mind you. In general, that is. Nonetheless, I felt compelled to remind him that children are human beings protected under the constitution, and not government chattel, and that it's obvious that you do not want to participate in his Marionette Dance."

"Marionette Dance?" Homecoming is over and the prom isn't until spring.

"Expectations, my dear. They don't want a freethinking person in their establishment. No, absolutely not. They want blocks of soft, malleable clay that they can carve and shape into their own images. People have a child and then set about tugging the strings to make that child dance to their own tune—become what *they've* envisioned a child of theirs should be. I said to him, 'Mr. Collier, with all due respect, one of your trained seals has risen up from the man-made pool and spat in the eye of the zookeeper.' "

"Do you think I should go back there?" I honestly believe that if Ms. Olivia told me to return to school then I would. Because although I won't admit it, this situation has gotten *way* out of hand and I have no idea what my next move should be. I never dreamed it would get this crazy, with half the town involved. The owner of the local Chevy dealership wrote an editorial in the newspaper about *me*, saying that if we let social problems get out of control now it's just going to cost the American taxpayer more money to deal with them later. Surely he was using me as an example of a *social problem* as opposed to that of an American taxpayer.

Ms. Olivia is the first person to articulate anything close to expressing how I really feel. Suddenly I experience this surge of relief, because if she doesn't think I'm crazy then maybe I'm *not*. Sort of like the bombardier in *Catch-22*. But then a lot of people in this town, including her own son, seem to think that Ms. Olivia is crazy. And I occasionally wonder the same thing. I mean—poetry and pornography and Druid Circles and aromatherapy. And if she *is* crazy, then it doesn't help that she thinks I'm *not* crazy. In fact, it probably makes things worse. If a crazy person thinks I'm not crazy, then for sure I most likely *am* crazy. It's all so confusing.

"Do I think you should go back?" Ms. Olivia repeats my words. "Oh, Hallie, it doesn't matter what *I* think. You must follow the beat of your own heart."

Wouldn't you know it—the *one time* I decide to take advice from a grown-up, the well all of a sudden dries up. And instead I get some funky answer right out of *The Wizard of Oz*. The Flying Monkeys are probably waiting for me inside the summerhouse along with a message in the sky written in black smoke saying "Surrender Hallie!"

"And now what about that garage door?" Ms. Olivia inquires with gusto, as if tourists are going to be lined up around the block to see this so-called collage and we'll be able to charge admission. "Have you settled upon a motif yet? Every great work of art must have a theme—you know, destruction, despair, reckless abundance."

"Actually, I was just about to ride over to the library to search for some ideas."

"There's an entire wall of art books in the den. Why don't you glance through those for inspiration when you have a moment?"

That's another thing I enjoy about the Stocktons and Mr. Gil. They treat a sixteen-year-old as if she has meetings to attend and a busy schedule and always add "when you get a chance" or "if it's convenient," even though I'm an employee and only a teenager. Even when assigning my yard duties Mr. Bernard will often ask me to do such and such when I can "see my way clear."

Upon finishing my lunch I say that I'd better get back to stripping the garage door.

"Ottavio wrote me the loveliest poem. Would you like to hear it?"

"Sure," I say. But I decide that if it's pornographic I'm going to be awfully embarrassed, like when my art teacher put up the Titian slides and the entire drawing and painting class snickered. Ms. Olivia removes a folded-up paper from her dress pocket and carefully smooths it out. It's a computer printout, so I assume he sent it to her via E-mail. "He wrote it in Italian and so I've tried my best to translate."

Rose Moon

The moon has lost its luster and the stars have dimmed their lights
Because my lover and I cannot share the Salerno night sky.
Absence is the breeze that fans the flame of burning passion

Or else snuffs the embers out.
That's how it must be for my lover and me.
And though you remain in my soul after we say good-bye,
When it's time to part, oh how my heart does sigh.

"He wrote that for you?" I ask when she finishes.

"Yes. I'm not so sure about the rhyme scheme or the meter, but it's the thought that counts." Ms. Olivia looks like a schoolgirl who's just stolen her first kiss. I guess this love thing can afflict people of all ages.

"Cool. I can't imagine someone writing a poem for me."

"Don't be *ridiculous*, Hallie. You'll be the object of many a heart's desire. Especially with your capabilities in math and operating power tools and lawn mowers. And *you'll* write love letters, too," she adds.

Somehow I doubt that. I can barely put the bibliographies and footnotes together for a simple book report.

On the way back outside I poke around the garage. Perhaps I could do something with all those wooden spools. Wouldn't Mr. Gil be relieved? Though I think he'd truly be ecstatic if I could find a way to incorporate that dining room set with the twelve chairs so that he could park his nice white Land Rover in the garage instead of under the cherry tree.

Down and Dirty

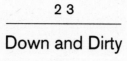

While scraping the garage door all sorts of thoughts run through my head about Ms. Olivia and love and poetry and the realization that I won't be six-teen forever. Eventually I'm going to grow up and have experiences, and I start to consider what kind of experiences I'd like to have.

It's in this state of artistic dreaminess that Officer Rich finds me when he pulls into the circular driveway. At first I think Mr. Bernard and Mr. Gil are returning from their travels early, but I immediately recognize the old blue Ford pickup. He must be off duty. I wonder if it's something to do with Mon-day's poker game.

Officer Rich studies me chiseling away and then scrutinizes the rest of the house and grounds in that coplike way, as if counterfeit presses are hid-den in the bushes.

I put down my scraper and sit on the top rung of the ladder. "Resting, roosting, or just nesting?"

He has to look up to see me. "I think you and I had better have a little talk down at the station." Urgency underscores his woolly voice.

"What's wrong with right here?" I ask.

"What's wrong with down at the station?" he counters and glances around to see if anyone is in earshot.

"You don't have a warrant for my arrest. And besides, only Ms. Olivia and the Judge are here, and they're inside."

"All right. But come sit in the cab of the truck. I'm not yelling up a ladder."

The front seat houses mostly paperwork and stained coffee cups. The only ornamentation aside from his PBA stickers and a twisted wire hanger for opening car door locks is a sun-faded plastic St. Christopher statue stuck onto the dashboard.

"Did you stop in at Jerry Exner's store on Saturday morning?"

I have to think for a second, because the name Exner doesn't even ring a bell without *cheap* and *old* preceding it. "Oh, you mean Cheap Old Mr. Exner, at the sporting goods store. No, I didn't."

But Officer Rich only scowls at the steering wheel. "Well, *cheap old* Mr. Exner is also the treasurer for the annual charity golf tournament and raffle to raise money to help build a new hospital at the edge of town. And it so happens that on Saturday morning Mrs. Shaeffer, the chairwoman of the event, dropped nineteen hundred dollars off with Mr. Exner, so he could deposit the money at the bank on Monday morning. Only the money was stolen."

"So, what's that got to do with me?"

"Hallie, you were the only one in the store between the money being dropped off and disappearing."

"Says who?" I ask.

"Says Mrs. Shaeffer. She saw you go into the store."

I become indignant. "She should get glasses because . . ." But I hesitate, because I suddenly remember that I did stop by the store on Saturday morning. "Well, I did ride my bike over there and look in the window to see if Jane was working. But she wasn't and so I left without going inside."

"That's not what Mrs. Shaeffer said."

"Even if I did go in, which I *didn't*, that doesn't prove anything." But Officer Rich just turns down his mouth as if he's already decided to doubt anything I might have to say. And of course it just makes matters worse that the whole town, including Mr. Exner, Mrs. Shaeffer, and even Officer Rich, know that I'm a homeless gambler and therefore assume I am in desperate need of currency. Or else that as a result of being associated with gambling I must automatically be in possession of a criminal underbelly.

"Officer Rich," I say and give him my best *I am not bluffing* stare, "I did *not* steal any money. Jesus, I stopped to see if Jane found this envelope of donut money . . ." But this only makes it sound even more like I need money, that I went in, saw the cash, and couldn't believe my luck.

"Hallie, I just came from your folks' house." He gazes out the front windshield rather than at me. "They said the amount they recently declined to front you for a car was two thousand dollars."

This is unbelievable. My life will *not* stop going downhill. It's as if a spell has been cast on me. At every turn the problem has to do with money, and somehow my name is attached to it.

"Officer Rich, I *swear* to you that I didn't take that money. Besides, if I had two thousand bucks you can bet I wouldn't be sitting here right now." I deny the crime using several different phrasings. "I can't believe I'm being accused in the first place. There's no videotape. There aren't any fingerprints. And it's not like Cheap Old Mr. Exner even has an alarm system. *Anyone* could have walked in there during the night or after the store closed and stolen that money."

But Officer Rich claims that the locks weren't jimmied and there are no signs of an intruder. And nothing else is missing.

Well it doesn't take long for me to develop a theory. Whoever took the money must have a key, unless Mr. Exner just misplaced the dough, which isn't entirely out of the question since he must be pushing seventy, or pulling eighty is probably more like it. However, I happen to know there's another person with a key. And that person is my best friend Jane. That's because Mr. Exner is too cheap to keep his store closed on Sunday when all the business guys head out to the golf course. Only he's a Fundamentalist, which means he can't work on Sunday morning, and so he has Jane operate the store from seven until noon. But would Jane *steal* money? Could she be that desperate to pay back the donut money she lost? Oh shit.

When Officer Rich sees the look of consternation on my face as I put all this together, he probably thinks it just confirms that I did indeed swipe the dough. I vaguely hear him say stuff like "No hard evidence . . . The proprietor has agreed not to press charges . . . Simply return the funds."

Then I realize that the worst thing about all this, aside from the possibility that one of my best friends is a criminal, is that Officer Rich, who has stood up for me until now, believes I'm guilty!

I rack my brain to think of another scenario that could explain the missing money. Because even if I can prove that I didn't do it, then they're going to get to Jane pretty soon. Maybe Cheap Old Mr. Exner is trying to frame her and keep the money himself? Since the new outlet center went up, his store doesn't do much business. Or *did* he just misplace it?

"And what if I didn't take the money?" I ask.

"Then I'd of course be interested in hearing your theory on where it went," Officer Rich replies. "You'd need some sort of evidence to corroborate your story. And it's pretty serious to accuse someone of a crime that they didn't commit." He stares down at his coffee-colored arms and sighs as if he knows a thing or two about assumptions made based upon a person's looks.

"Yeah, no shit," I concur.

I can tell that Officer Rich is disappointed I won't just confess and return the money. And I can't help but wonder if my parents also believe I carried out the dirty deed and presume that I have once and for all turned to a life of crime.

"All right," Officer Rich eventually says when I don't respond to his plea bargain. "I was hoping we could just settle this quietly, between the two of us. Why don't you take a day to think about it, Hallie? Because believe me, you don't want this to go any further than it already has. And I'm serious about that."

I turn away from him and stare out the side window.

"And I don't think you'd better come to the poker game," he says. The final insult.

Officer Rich departs, and of course I can no longer concentrate on the garage. My first instinct is to ride to my parents' house and proclaim my innocence. However, on the heels of Officer Rich's visit a cameo appearance at this moment may very well be counterproductive.

Instead I hop on my bike and ride to Jane's house. I can tell by the tense and phony friendliness that her mother is wary of my arrival, as if I'm a bad influence. God only knows what stories she's heard by now.

After Jane learns what's happened, she swears up and down that she didn't take the charity funds. "Besides, I had a cold the past few days and didn't even go to the store."

"It's not that I really thought you *stole it*," I say apologetically. "But with the donut money . . ."

The donut money! She waves an empty manila envelope in my face. Sure enough, it's the dreaded donut envelope. As it turns out, Jane's mother accidentally took the money to work in a pile of folders that were in the front seat. Mystery solved. And I'm incredibly relieved that Jane's been cleared, because that points to Cheap Old Mr. Exner himself and I care a lot less about him.

However, it's obvious that Jane isn't as convinced that *I'm* in the clear. "You know, Hallie," she says, "I'd understand if you needed the money . . . if you just borrowed it and you plan on paying it back as soon . . ."

Oh damn. Not her, too. "Jane, I swear to you that I didn't steal any money."

"I just meant that it doesn't look very good . . . to other people, you know?"

Yeah, I know exactly. She thinks that I did it.

When I return to the Stocktons' I'm not at all in a cheerful mood and in no way prepared for what greets me. Mr. Bernard and Mr. Gil and Ms. Olivia are gathered in the living room having a discussion, and they all stop talking and stare up at me the minute I walk in, as if I'm breaking and entering. Talk about the pot calling the kettle black! Maybe they consider larceny to be tackier than dealing drugs or selling forged art or laundering money or whatever it is that they do.

"Uh, sorry," I say. "The door was open . . ."

"No, of course, come in," says Mr. Gil.

"It's only fair to tell you that Officer Rich phoned," says Mr. Bernard.

Gee, I never would have guessed. I don't even bother to enter the living room, because I figure I'll be leaving momentarily anyway.

"Listen," I say, still standing in the front hall, "I didn't do it. But I totally understand if you want me to quit."

"See, I told you," says Ms. Olivia and taps Mr. Bernard on the knee with her fingers.

"What do you mean you *told me*," Mr. Bernard snaps back. "I never said she took the money. I merely answered the phone, then related the officer's remarks to you."

"Of course we don't want you to resign," says Mr. Gil. "In fact, come and sit down."

"You don't?" I plop down on the couch, exhausted and defeated from all this craziness.

"No, no," agrees Mr. Bernard. "I told Officer Rich that with my business I leave hundreds of dollars lying around here all the time and that since you joined us nothing has ever gone missing and we trust you implicitly."

It's a fact that Mr. Bernard leaves money scattered all over the place. And it's true that I've never touched it and never would, though I rather doubt he would notice if I did. Just last week I handed him four fifty-dollar bills that I found sticking out from under a vase on the piano and he didn't even remember leaving them there.

"And tell her what you told him about the salary," prompts Ms. Olivia.

"Oh yes," says Mr. Bernard, "I explained how you've been laboring so intently for twelve dollars an hour in an effort to save for an automobile that I thought it highly doubtful you would be inclined to embezzle."

I'm grateful that the Stocktons have rallied around me, even if it's only an honor-among-thieves type of camaraderie. But I can't help sensing that the tide of public opinion has turned against me for good and even the people on my side must be having their doubts. When I stopped at the convenience store on the way home Hal the counter guy watched my every move, as if I was about to stuff a box of Twinkies under my sweatshirt. It's obvious that I have to determine what happened to that damn money, and not just prove that I didn't take it, but find out who did.

The Best Game in Town

★

The beginning of October brings many new experiences and surprises into my life. For instance, the discovery that small-town suspicion can wash a person away like a sand dollar in a tidal wave. The bell no longer tolls for me. Not the doorbell and not the phone. However, the fall does deliver an extraordinary amount of leaves that need to be raked, blown, and bagged.

The most exciting occurrence is full-time access to the *QE2*. At breakfast Mr. Bernard announces that Ms. Olivia is no longer approved to drive. Though he insists that she's perfectly *capable* of driving if only she'd pay attention "in lieu of composing heroic couplets in her head."

"Don't be ridiculous," she says. "There's nothing wrong with my driving."

"Mother, you hit a *deer* yesterday."

"Oh, Bernard. It was *ceramic*."

"That's exactly my *point!*"

Frankly, I don't understand how he knows whether she's composing poetry or pornography behind the wheel, but I have to agree with him that Ms. Olivia tends to be what my mother would call a daydreamer. Sometimes she's so lost in thought that it appears as if she might actually vanish into the air like a sigh.

It's a lovely fall morning at the start of Columbus Day weekend and we drive to Pymatuning State Park in Ashtabula County near the Pennsylvania border to watch the leaves change and try to spot a bald eagle. Ms. Olivia doesn't believe that bald eagles should be taken off the endangered-species list and that industrial lobbyists are fudging the increase in their numbers and therefore insists upon seeing one for herself.

A visiting nurse comes to stay with the Judge and so we're all able to leave the house for the entire day and experience autumn face-to-face. At least this is what Mr. Bernard claims is our mission; that we're setting out upon a journey of self-improvement and self-renewal through the appreciation of nature and all the earthly delights that we normally cavort right past in our frantic daily lives.

Only I wonder if this outing is in part to lift my spirits about the missing money, as Officer Rich has been phoning with pacemaker regularity to remind me that the longer I wait to confess, the worse the consequences will be. The past week I'd been moping around the kitchen and studying architectural drawings of the golf shop procured from town hall. I was testing a theory that someone could have tunneled in from the bookshop next door, or else lowered himself in through the skylight. Such exercises, combined with being the town pariah and family outcast, overwhelm all of my private moments with dread.

To whatever end Mr. Bernard is working to take my mind off this predicament, he also manages to map out a route that takes us past a large number of flea markets and tag sales. At each stop he organizes us like a military platoon commissioned to hunt for objects such as paperweights with silhouettes inside the domes, Bakelite jewelry, old jelly glasses, and lunch boxes from the 1970s. At least those are what he deems to be my areas of expertise. Mr. Gil is instructed to search for fountain pens, turn-of-the-century optical toys, clockwork cars, and something called Liberty pewter.

Meanwhile Ms. Olivia floats around and browses through old books. Mr. Bernard attempts to have her look for soup tureens and sauceboats, but she's continuously sidetracked by stacks of old *Life* magazines and hand-inked poetry chapbooks to the point where I have to hunt her down when it's time to leave. By the time we've scoured and plundered four garage sales, two flea markets, and one musty antique store and have our dusty treasures packed into the trunk, Mr. Bernard is in high spirits.

"Okay, Hoke, make a hard left at the purple wisteria and then a beeline toward the heliotrope." Mr. Bernard is always calling me names from movies such as *Driving Miss Daisy*. It amuses me, because after all his carping about Ms. Olivia being chauffeured around town from "protest to prison" he doesn't seem to mind being driven around himself.

Mr. Bernard's idea of a picnic is definitely not the annual exercise in soft-ball playing and charbroiling hamburgers that my dad's office sponsors at the town park every August. He brings tins of caviar and serves it in a raised silver dish that comes with its own delicate shovel. After warming toast triangles over a can of Sterno, he applies a thin layer of tiny black marbles and then sprinkles it with chopped egg and onion. Following that we have marinated artichokes, oysters on the half shell with lemon juice, fresh ground pepper, and cocktail sauce, and smoked turkey sandwiches on French bread with a thick crust.

From crystal champagne glasses we sip mimosas or delicious sparkling lemonade that Ms. Olivia mail-orders from some village in France. And for dessert there are strawberries and star fruit dipped in rich dark chocolate that Mr. Bernard and I had stayed up late the night before to make.

"Hallie, while you're up please liberate my sunglasses from the glove compartment," Ms. Olivia politely asks.

Ms. Olivia never asks anyone to *get* or *fetch* an item. She says *free*, *emancipate*, or *unfetter*. I had to look up the last one when I first heard it. And it's a good thing I did, because I almost plucked all the feathers off her hat in addition to removing it from the top shelf of her closet.

During lunch Mr. Gil plays Chopin études on his boom box. "Prelude in E-flat Minor" is his favorite. Ms. Olivia reads a few poems; something dreamy by William Wordsworth and an Edmund Spenser sonnet about death and decay and love and virtue. Ms. Olivia knows lots of poems about these subjects and many take place upon a strand. I kept thinking *a strand of what* until Mr. Gil informed me that it's a beach.

Ms. Olivia recites "Noon Walk on the Asylum Lawn" by Anne Sexton. It's very short and sounds almost like a church prayer. After this she has me read a poem by Sylvia Plath about a lioness followed by a child's cry and then suicide, or what Mr. Gil deems as a real *womb-jerker*. I can't help but wonder if my mother will eventually have a nervous breakdown from constantly giving birth and thawing chickens and eventually just toss off a sonnet or two before shoving her head into the Diaper Genie.

During the car ride home Mr. Bernard trills along to *La Bohème* and he has this hilarious falsetto voice that he uses for the girl who dies at the end. Then Ms. Olivia recalls the time Mr. Bernard was a toddler and they traveled by steamer to Ethiopia to protest corporate America's distribution of infant formula. As with most of the stories she recounts about her life and times as a young firebrand of a mother, she concludes by saying, "You certainly had an exciting childhood, Bernard."

It's at this point that we pass a sign for a triple yard sale—three neighbors pooling their castoffs—and Mr. Bernard excitedly yells, "Ready about, turn to starboard." And off we go.

Now, normally if someone had suggested a picnic and leaf drive with two guys in their thirties and an old lady I would have developed acute appendicitis real fast. But the Stocktons and Mr. Gil have a talent for making an ordinary afternoon into a once-a-year day, a unique experience that could never be replicated, but would provide pleasant memories for many months, like scoring a soccer goal from midfield.

Later that evening I'm in the living room giving Mr. Bernard his poker lesson when Mr. Gil asks me to help him decide whether he should exercise the stock options he's been issued at work.

"I don't even know what a stock option is," I tell him.

"It's just a matter of doing some math, which you happen to be very proficient at," he explains. "And then deciding whether the company is going to do better or worse than it is right now."

After reading the explanatory documents from his company, we look up the stock in the newspaper and also the fifty-two-week high and I try to determine the probability of the stock doing what the analyst in Mr. Gil's finance department thinks it should do, based on the current earnings and future projections. It's amazing how similar the stock market is to playing cards; so much of it depends on odds. And that's when it finally hits me—how to find the missing golf money. All this time I've been thinking in terms of *MacGyver* reruns—cat burglars climbing along the walls using shot put gloves as suction cups and a fishing rod to lift the cash from behind the counter so as not to leave a trail. When the solution is really just a math problem.

Sweetening the Pot

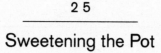

The minute the library opens the following morning I locate every book that they have on the stock market, spread out the *Wall Street Journal,* and spend more than half the day poring over the jumble of numbers and definitions.

When I arrive at the Stocktons' at four in the afternoon to use their shower, Mr. Bernard asks me if I'm going to help him prepare dinner. After a month of slaving away as Mr. Bernard's cooking assistant, I no longer pose a health risk in the kitchen. At least not of the magnitude that Ms. Olivia does. The worst thing that's happened so far was putting the *turkey en croûte à la Oranges Orientales* in the oven and turning on the light instead of the heat. But Mr. Bernard whipped up an appetizer of celery root pancakes and then served the turkey about half past ten. He insisted that it was more European to dine late anyway.

However, in spite of a sometimes painfully slow learning curve and a few minor setbacks, I am learning to cook. It's doubtful I'll ever have Mr. Bernard's passion for food preparation. Then again, I won't have to subsist entirely on Yoo-Hoo shakes and peanut butter sandwiches, either. Or else cook for my family in an Easy-Bake oven.

When we prepare dinner Mr. Bernard always puts on background music, Yo-Yo Ma playing Bach on his cello, Andrés Segovia's Spanish guitar, or if he can't get the stereo to work right, which is often, the jazz radio station. Above the music he offers a steady flow of comments about the state of American produce and the progress of the meal. Mr. Bernard delights in knowing all sorts of unusual details about different foods. He discusses dinner the same way he piques the curiosity of his customers down at the store with engaging anecdotes about the history of any object in which they express an interest. When Mr. Bernard embarks on a story, I've noticed that people gather to him like iron filings around a magnetic pole.

"Chickpeas have of course killed people," he vigorously declares while I'm slowly stirring a pot of tomato lentil soup that smells delicious even though it's the color and consistency of what you'd expect to see splattered around a crime scene. Between making sure the hemoglobin soup doesn't permanently clot and burn, I stand next to him at the counter and mash cloves of garlic for the hummus. I've learned that if one is craving a supremely entertaining story from Mr. Bernard's repertoire, it pays to reward him with plenty of disbelief. And there is never a time I don't want him to tell a story, since once he gets started the time flies by, no matter what we're doing: planting bulbs, polishing brass, or just cleaning the icky old oven. He makes everything fun. And no matter how far-fetched Mr. Bernard's stories sound, they are almost always true, or at least they've been officially documented as hearsay. Like the fact that Oscar Wilde's final words were "Either this wallpaper goes or I do."

"You mean that people were shot with chickpeas out of a gun and died!" I say.

"Chickpeas shot out of a gun! Heavens to Betsy, no."

He turns and drops one of the raspberries he's washing into my mouth. To be honest, Mr. Bernard and I eat more food in the kitchen than we do at the table. And it's not like at my house, where you have to sneak food from the kitchen. He's constantly taking out forks and spoons and saying try this and test that and do you think this needs more anchovy paste? As if I would know.

By now I am desperate to discover how you can kill someone with a chickpea. It might be one of those life skills that could come in handy later on, like knowing how to remove chewing gum with lighter fluid. "So how do chickpeas kill people?"

"The Latin word *cicer*, or chickpea, found its way into Old French as *chiche*," Mr. Bernard announces as if he is making a proclamation, which in a way he is. "But speakers of Middle English adopted this name for the legume and tacked onto it a redundant *pease*, which is the same as pea—leave it to the English to complicate the language. Anyway, it wasn't long before the resulting compound transformed into the now familiar chickpea."

"But I don't see how anyone died by adding *pea* onto the end of chick." He purposely leaves out the good parts to see if I'm paying attention.

"Ah yes. In the Sicilian uprising against French rule in 1282, Sicilian rebels had orders to kill every French person on sight. But they were faced with the problem of determining who was or was *not* French. So they commanded every stranger they met to say *cecceri,* the Italian dialect expression for *chickpeas.* Strangers who failed to pronounce it correctly were killed." And with that Mr. Bernard switches on the Cuisinart with a flourish, as if to theatrically punctuate the end of his story. Mr. Gil often refers to Mr. Bernard as "Our Lady of the Cuisinart."

"How do you know all this stuff?" I shout above the whirring avocado paste in progress.

"Much of it I learned from Mother. She home-schooled me for a year while protesting the local district for not wanting to integrate. First she transferred me to the all-black school the next town over, but the children's parents were told that I was an informant from the FBI and so no one would speak to me. Then Father put his foot down and said he wouldn't tolerate his son being used as a political platform."

"Is it legal to keep a kid home from school like that?"

"I thought you were the expert on the truancy laws in the state of Ohio," Mr. Bernard replies humorously. "Actually, believe it or not, Mother is a certified educator, though she's only worked a few years as a substitute teacher, and that was just to antagonize Grandfather Stockton, who believed that married women should remain in the home. She initially earned her teaching certificate to be able to join the Peace Corps, which she did. Mother worked in Burkina Faso in Western Africa to form farming cooperatives as a way of breaking the grip of the warlords."

"She's a certified teacher!" I exclaim in disbelief. I mean, I just can't imagine it.

"I appreciate your shock. The *certifiable* part is of course entirely believable," he says with a twinkle in his eye. "It's the teaching part that throws people."

Mr. Bernard demonstrates how to chop peaches for his "famous" raspberry-peach cobbler, just so. Too thick and you can't cut them properly with a fork; likewise, too thin and the crust flops.

"Peach is from the Old French *peche,* which is ultimately from the Latin for peach tree, *persica,*" he says. "That's because it is a widely held belief that the peach has its origins in Persia, now Iran." Then he asks, "So what's happening with school?"

He catches me completely off guard and I accidentally allow the paring knife to fling a peach pit onto the floor, and it skids into the bottom rungs of the metal refrigerator grille. Up until tonight no one in the house has mentioned my ditching school. I'd assumed they'd all accepted it. In fact, I thought they rather prided themselves on being open-minded and tolerant about truancy.

"Uh, what do you mean, school?"

"I'm not referring to those public school mandarins in their brick and mortar pagodas. I'm talking about an education for *yourself*—knowledge for the sake of knowledge. You're too intelligent to allow your mind to languish."

"But I learn stuff here. Every day. And Mr. Gil gives me all those books to read—*Catcher in the Rye* and *Vanity Fair* and Dickinson's stories about other runaway kids."

"It's Dickens. Charles Dickens. Emily Dickinson is a poet who Mother frequently quotes."

"So you want me to go back *there?*" I can't believe what I'm hearing. "Besides, everyone thinks I'm a criminal now. I don't even have any friends left."

"No, of course that's not what I meant. It's just that I've been thinking . . ."

Tears well in the corners of my eyes. I was having such a good time gardening and painting and learning to cook and being around the Stocktons and Mr. Gil. And I *was* getting some education—okay, so maybe it wasn't exactly what they taught at Patrick Henry High School.

"You need an English and a social studies credit to get a high school diploma, right?" he asks.

"I suppose so, if they bend the rules a bit. Why?"

"Well, what if Mother were to apply for permission to tutor you here at the house and then you would sit for their exams at the end of the school year?"

"They'll never go for it," I say. "The last thing they want is for me to graduate."

"Ah, for someone who is a skillful poker player you disappoint me."

"Huh?"

"What's the first rule you explained when showing me how to play five-card-draw poker?"

"Never throw away a king? Don't bend the cards?" But I'm no longer in the mood for games. "I don't remember."

"Play the *person*, not the cards," Mr. Bernard reminds me.

"Play Mr. Collier, you mean?" I try to consider it in terms of a card game. Just Call Me Dick looks bad because I'm not in school. But if there were a way for me to graduate the school wouldn't have to record a dropout. In fact, if I were on the books as being home-schooled they could probably even still collect their precious dollars in state funds.

But would the school allow it? I know my parents would be nothing less than thrilled, even though they've written me off for good now that they think I've gone to the dark side by stealing from local charities.

Wow. Eric and I would graduate on the same day. Too bad his first name starts with an *E*. I'd give anything to graduate before him. And then it strikes me that Mr. Bernard appears extremely confident about this "new" scheme, as if he's already put a lot of thought into it. And perhaps a few phone calls as well. I give him a horse trader's glance and see a smile of satisfaction on his face as he deftly kneads the dough that will become the cobbler crust.

I want to be mad. But I can't. After two months of mowing and turning flower beds and scraping paint, I've realized that although this manual labor routine may be good for the body, and possibly even nourishing to the spirit, it would not be so good to have to do it for the next forty years in order to earn a living. Not that I don't have complete confidence in my gambling abilities, but all those dilapidated horse players down at OTB must have at one time felt they possessed the Magic Touch. And so it might not be a bad idea to be qualified for a desk job in case I ever have to ride out another losing streak. However, I rather question Ms. Olivia's ability to teach anything that is a part of the public school curriculum.

"You've already worked this whole thing out, haven't you? You've talked to the school and my parents and even signed up Ms. Olivia?"

"I hope you're not cross. Normally I don't believe in meddling in people's lives."

"I'm not mad. But can I at least think about it?"

"Certainly. The school has even offered to pay Mother a small stipend for tutoring."

"No kidding?"

"Yes, they're required to, actually. And they have to list you as being out on some kind of psychiatric disorder. If you're only disordered, and not a dropout, then the school district is responsible for supplying a tutor."

"Mr. Collier will *never* go for Ms. Olivia. I wish they would just fire him," I say.

"There you go again. That's the second rule of gambling you taught me: When you find yourself wishing or praying for a certain permutation to occur, it usually means you're in trouble."

"But I *am* in trouble." You know your life is bad when you get thrown out of your weekly poker game and even your pastor is looking down at his shoes when you pass each other on the street.

"Forget about Mr. Collier being dismissed. He's protected under the Americans with No Abilities Act. And it just so happens that Mr. Collier is thrilled at the prospect of marking you present and accounted for by way of home schooling and will be delighted to have this entire mess off his aluminum desk."

"What type of psychiatric disorder do I need to have?"

"It doesn't matter. You could be agoraphobic—afraid to leave the house. Or pogonophobic, possessing an abnormal fear of worms."

"But I leave the house every day. And I work outside. I work *with* worms."

"Good point. Just say you saw God in the shed or that the lawn mower is telling you to bake poppy seed muffins in order to prepare for the end of the world."

"Oh, I *like* that last one."

"Yes, it has a nice Rod Serling feel to it."

"And what happens if I don't do it and they call in the police?" I ask.

"Two words: Oliver Twist."

I take it that he means reform school or the workhouse. "Well, when you put it that way . . . okay."

Table Stakes

♦

By the time Mr. Bernard and I finish preparing dinner, word has somehow traveled through the house that a plot is being hatched. As we all gather at the dinner table, Ms. Olivia immediately throws in her two cents.

"I was dead set against it," she firmly states. "I just want that to be perfectly clear. I'd rather have been on Nixon's cabinet back in the seventies than participate in engineering someone else's destiny."

"So you don't want to do it, then?" I ask her.

"Oh, I think it's a wonderful solution, if it's what you're after. I just object to Bertie running around pushing buttons behind the scenes here like Big Brother. Though he probably envisions himself more as Audrey Hepburn playing a nun or an angel. No matter, if you don't want a high school diploma, then you shouldn't get one."

But the more Ms. Olivia rails against it, the more I decide that I really do want a high school diploma. And as much as I hate to admit it, with this missing-money accusation hanging over my head, it's actually a relief to have some grown-ups taking charge of my situation. Because whenever I allow my attention to turn inward for even a second the world suddenly flip-flops and the Stocktons seem only a dream, everything else seems real, and the tears will not stay back. Especially when I try to sleep at night. Sleep has become the enemy. But here, sitting with them around this table, I'm secure against the outside world.

"I'd like to give it a try, if that's okay with you," I say.

Mr. Bernard smiles down at his perfectly browned Tuscan pork chops.

Without even glancing at her son, Ms. Olivia admonishes him. "Don't look smug, Bertie. It's unbecoming. And besides, if it's meant to be then it's meant to be, and there's nothing you could have done to stop or start the process."

However, it's obvious that Mr. Bernard doesn't buy this fatalistic approach. "Yes, of course you're right, Mother. *Que sera, sera.* Why don't you two do lessons in the afternoon while Father is resting? It will be just like the Roosevelt children's tutorial schedule—lots of exposure to the natural world in the morning and then inside to feed the mind. And on weekends you can perform your trust-busting, battle police corruption, and go on safari."

"Hallie and I won't be going big-game hunting anytime soon," harrumphs Ms. Olivia.

"Mother, you're aware that you have to meet with her teachers and get the curriculum. So please *try* to be normal."

"I hardly think I need someone to tell *me* what makes for a suitable English and history plan of study for a young lady."

"Oh dear, I was afraid of this. Mother, the objective is for Hallie to pass *their* tests at the end of the year. You must teach her what's going to be on the final examinations," states Mr. Bernard.

Ms. Olivia runs a butter knife across her roll and serenely declares, "Tests are ridiculous. They have nothing to do with learning."

But Mr. Bernard apparently decides he's made enough progress for one day. He turns to Mr. Gil. "Tell us how the play is coming along."

"The gentleman caller is a mailman named Josh, and though his résumé says he's thirty-five I think he's more like fifty-three. He's going to need *lots* of makeup."

"It's a small role," says Mr. Bernard.

"Yes, but extremely important. In fact, I could use some help if you feel like looking at the set one evening this week."

"Of course, I was planning on it. I'll bring some period pieces from the shop, and I'm sure there's something in the garage—" But a look of dread crosses Mr. Bernard's face the second he utters the *g* word.

"I don't believe we're that desperate yet," Mr. Gil rescues him. "And Mom, perhaps you can rehearse lines. Amanda needs to sound more like Joanne Woodward and less like Woody Woodpecker."

It's the first time I've ever heard Mr. Gil refer to Ms. Olivia as *Mom*, which is kind of weird. Although if they were married she *would* be his mother-in-law. And Ms. Olivia doesn't seem to mind, or even notice, for that matter. But then, a lot of odd things happen around the Stocktons, like the constant stream of pill poppers showing up at the back door during the night. And last Saturday Mr. Bernard woke Mr. Gil and me up at two o'clock in the morning to go and "borrow" a stargazer lily bulb from Mrs. Graham's garden since she wouldn't sell him any or trade for one of his rare Casablanca lilies.

"Hallie, perhaps you can bring that toolbox and paintbrush of yours and tart up the scenery?" suggests Mr. Gil.

I'm flattered that he invites me to help with the play. Though I can't decide whether he really needs my assistance or just doesn't want me to feel left out. "Sure. But I've never worked on anything like that before."

"Don't worry, you'll be in good hands with Joey, the set designer. He's the best chicken coop builder this side of the Mississippi. And we're in desperate circumstances for warm bodies who know what a lug wrench is."

It's nice the way they all help one another. The household swirls and tilts around the Judge as if he's a dead leaf in the middle of a whirlpool. Ms. Olivia does the computer correspondence for Mr. Bernard's business and pays all the bills. Mr. Gil assists with caring for the Judge on weekends if Ms. Olivia gets the urge to protest inhumane animal slaughter or acid rain while Mr. Bernard is off giving someone an estimate on their antiques. Mr. Bernard cooks for everyone. And I'm the yard person and chef's helper, which suits me just fine.

"Speaking of projects, how is the collage coming along?" Mr. Gil inquires. "I saw an outline of what looks like some stick figures on the garage door and a lot of sawed-up spools. What's the theme? Eating disorders?"

"Anorexia!" Ms. Olivia cries out enthusiastically. "How engaging— women's self-image destroyed by the media. That's magnificent!"

"Actually, it's not about eating disorders. It's a surprise."

"How about we guess and you only tell us if we're right?" Mr. Gil suggests.

"Adam and Eve get chased out of the garden?" Ms. Olivia asks.

"A tribute to Modigliani?" Mr. Bernard asks.

"Who?"

"An Italian painter and sculptor. He specialized in thin, elongated figures," Mr. Bernard explains.

"He crafted *Walking Man*," adds Ms. Olivia. "Don't worry, we'll do an art history section in our tutorial."

Mr. Bernard shakes his head as if it's just dawned on him that the home schooling idea might not proceed exactly as he had envisioned it.

"Is it a ballet?" asks Mr. Gil. "*Giselle* or *Don Quixote*?"

"Nope."

"Stop annoying the *artiste*," says Ms. Olivia. "How would you like it if I stood over you in the kitchen and peppered you with questions the entire time you were cooking?"

"Don't be ridiculous, Mother, by the time you finally found the kitchen, dinner would already be finished."

"*Gil?*" Ms. Olivia turns to him for an ally.

"You're a poet, Olivia," Mr. Gil replies diplomatically. "A devoted sonneteer cannot be bothered with such mundane tasks."

"Indeed," adds Mr. Bernard. "Mother is single-handedly trying to put *whorl, frond,* and *limn*—the three favorite words of the nature poets—back into popular usage."

After dinner, when they're upstairs checking on the Judge and bringing him a dish of ice cream, I'll go and look up the word *mundane*. And also the ones Ms. Olivia is supposedly attempting to reissue, if I can spell them.

"Speaking of your writing, Livvy, why don't you share with us something that you're working on?" Mr. Gil suggests. Though I wonder if he means poetry or pornography. And I can't decide which I'd rather hear, either. Sometimes I see people kiss and feel a pang in my chest and wish that I could get up the courage to call Craig.

"All right. But it's still in the embryonic stage," Ms. Olivia replies. She takes a sip of tea and then recites from memory:

> How would I know thee
> in a rail station dense with
> bustling crowd?
> Wouldst thou don a red boutonniere,
> a silken ascot plumed
> or a boldly checked bow tie?
> How would I know thee
> in a foreign land
> under cover of the night?

Wouldst thou imitate the mockingbird,
whisper my name in an exotic tongue
or limn the sky with flares?

I'm surprised when Mr. Bernard quickly retorts:

Thou will know me right away, dear one
By the devotion of my son
Who will be standing right in front of me
And pointing a loaded gun.

Gil and I both burst into laughter.

"Very funny," Ms. Olivia says sarcastically. But I can tell by the way she's suppressing an encroaching smile that Ms. Olivia secretly appreciates his clever response. "At least *I* don't go dashing around the house shouting 'WWMD,'" she retorts.

Mr. Gil lurches forward with laughter so that his nose almost lands in the leftover pool of gravy in the center of his plate.

But Mr. Bernard looks serious and says, "That's enough, thank you, Mother."

Meantime I have no idea what's going on, as usual. "WWMD?" I ask. "What's a WWMD?"

"Nothing!" Mr. Bernard says hastily, and I see that his cheeks are starting to resemble a raspberry patch.

Only by now Mr. Gil is thumping the tabletop because he's laughing so hard. "Oh my, Livvy, I'd forgotten about that. The day the fruitcakes exploded just as all the guests were ringing the front doorbell!" Mr. Gil has to catch his breath before continuing. "And Bertie standing in the hallway yelling, '*What would Martha do?*'"

On the Make

♣

It's Halloween, and so after I finish working in the yard Mr. Bernard invites me to stay for dinner and help pass out his homemade toffee to all the trick-or-treaters. However, I politely decline since I'm off to Gwen's party. Gwen was at least honest enough to tell me that her parents thought I should be un-invited, due to the missing money. But Gwen believes that I didn't take it. Or at least she says she believes me, even if she doesn't call to go out anymore. And she insists I'll look even guiltier if I skip the party.

Meantime Mr. Bernard becomes excited about the prospect of a costume party and asks if I want to go through Mr. Gil's theatrical wardrobe rack. It's not *that* kind of a party, I explain, just a bunch of teenagers hanging out and listening to music.

Gwen lives outside of town on what local Realtors refer to as a "farmette." Even though they don't have more than two acres of land, they're zoned to keep farm animals. Gwen has a horse named Mayday and her little brother has a Shetland pony named Peanuts. Mayday is a tall, beautiful, and high-spirited horse of Spanish lineage and Gwen lets me ride him. Peanuts, on the other hand, looks incredibly cute with her chocolate-brown eyes and velvety tan coat with white socks, but she's a mean cuss, always trying to bite and kick everybody. Most people think ponies are adorable and that big horses are scary, but anyone who knows anything about horses will tell you it's usually just the opposite.

There's a big barn with a hayloft and an attached indoor riding ring, and that's where the party is held. Gwen's parents are that rare breed who actually want to be around teenagers. So unlike most of our parties, we can't get drunk and smoke pot and then pair off and make out for the entire night. No siree. Mr. Thompson is right there with the grill sizzling, his tall white chef's hat cocked to the side, turning out hot dogs and cheeseburgers while Gwen's mom oversees the make-your-own-sundae bar on top of some haystacks and her little brother runs to and fro in his cowboy outfit. As if that's not super-vision enough, Mr. Thompson invites his sister and her husband over and they string a net between the wooden posts and organize games like volley-ball and badminton and, later on, capture the flag. And whenever a kid walks past with a couple of hot dogs the husband shouts, "Squeeze your buns tight!" and then chuckles like crazy.

Of course, we all make fun of the arrangements because we're between fifteen and eighteen and it's like a party for five-year-olds. I mean, last time they put a bull's-eye on Mayday's side and made us play pin-the-tail-on-the-horsey. But the funny thing is, once we start playing games and doing the hokey pokey it turns out to be tons of fun. No one wants to admit it, but the parties where you just sit around and talk about school and drink beer get really boring after about an hour, and if you don't have anyone to suck face with you just end up watching MTV and gnawing on pizza crusts and pret-zels all night long.

By the time I arrive, about forty kids are eating and bouncing around the barn and Mayday is dressed up like a bullfighter with a red cape, black boots, and an eye mask. He's wandering around the barn mingling and mooching handouts. Peanuts is dressed like a clown, but fortunately she's locked in her stall.

A record player blasts limbo music while Mrs. Thompson and her sister-in-law have corralled about twenty kids into doing backbends and slither-ing under a bamboo pole they're holding. After each successful passage the crowd whoops with delight. After a fall they laugh uproariously and make catcalls. No, the Thompsons were never going to get irate calls from parents asking, "What goes on in that barn of yours? Is there no adult supervision?"

Normally I'd be on the receiving end of a nice friendly welcome from Mr. and Mrs. Thompson. They greet all their teenage guests individually, the way salespeople make eye contact when a customer enters a shop, partly as a courtesy and partly to signal that they're watching every move you make. However, this evening I receive only the forced smiles, furrowed brows, and hasty hellos that mean: You're a bad influence, and one bad banana can ruin the bunch.

I immediately locate Gwen and a few other friends.

"Is it true that you took the golf money to pay gambling debts?" Mary-Ella immediately chimes in. "And that—"

"A loan shark is threatening to break your knees?" Seth finishes for her.

As I explain my total lack of involvement with the theft I feel as if they really want to believe me, but that at the end of the day they probably don't. It's hard not to turn around and leave and forget about the party altogether. I should have taken Mr. Bernard's advice and worn a costume—for instance, a sheet over my entire body.

However, they eventually drift to other subjects, and if they believe I'm guilty they don't appear to hold it against me. Or else they decide Mr. Exner is so stingy that being robbed serves him right.

Real relief arrives in the form of Jane. She takes me aside and says, "Hallie, I'm sorry that I initially thought you stole the money. I've since realized that if you had taken it then you never would have come over to my house that day thinking that *I* took it. You were trying to protect me—you didn't want to rat me out or else let me get caught."

"Thanks. That makes two people who know I didn't steal it—you and me—and how many who think I did take it? What's the population of the United States these days, around two hundred and eighty million?" And though I say this sarcastically, it's a good feeling to have Jane certain of my innocence. Because the Stocktons would have to be categorized as hopeful, almost sure, but not proof positive. How could they be?

"Then it must have been Cheap Old Exner," declares Jane. "He's always rounding down my time sheet so that he doesn't have to pay me for the half hours. And he rips people off in all sorts of little ways—selling factory outlet stuff, you know, slightly irregular sneakers and socks, at full price."

"He repackaged the golf balls I found and sold them as new!"

Gwen and a group of friends begin to migrate in our direction.

"The only way to fix this is to find out for sure who did steal the money," Jane says quickly.

"No shit, Sherlock," I reply. "Will you help me?"

"Of course."

"Keep an eye on Cheap Old Exner, look around the stockroom, ask him what he thinks happened to the money, and see if he acts at all nervous."

"You got it." Jane gives me a quick hug as the rest of the crew arrives, biting into burgers hot off the grill.

For a while we all stand around the jumping hurdles eating and talking. Sheryl Shaeffer wouldn't dream of coming to a kiddie carnival like this, especially with her new Big Time college boyfriend, though I spot another member of her family whom I try my hardest to ignore. To no avail. Brandt eventually slinks over and there's something weirder-looking than usual about him, but I can't quite put my finger on it. Oh, he's wearing those stupid Mr. Spock ears. If nothing else, they at least make him look a little older.

"Can I make you a sundae, Hallie?" he earnestly inquires in that trombone voice.

With the way I've been getting the cold shoulder around town, I don't have the heart to give it to Brandt. Fortunately Jane doesn't have the same problem. And also she is holding the piñata bat. "Mr. Spock," she says, "the whole point of a make-your-own-sundae bar is to do exactly that."

He looks fearfully at Jane and then turns back to me. "Hallie, I just wanted you to know that I'm sorry about what my mother said, and that I know you didn't do it."

"Thanks," I say politely and look past him to where the limbo is morphing into a conga line with Mayday prancing in the lead.

But Brandt doesn't appear satisfied and nervously glances up as if a vulture is circling overhead and casting dark shadows on the earth. Then he stares directly into my eyes. "No. What I mean is . . . that I *know* you didn't do it, and if you want to call me . . ."

This time I solidly meet his gaze. "Okay. I understand."

Jane taps her bat on the ground as if she's warming up to whack him over the head, and he scurries away at warp speed. "First it's a sundae, and next thing you know he's doing the Vulcan Meld on you," she says after he's gone.

"Look at the bright side. I've just increased the number of people who don't think I stole the money by fifty percent."

I don't see Craig anywhere, but then those football guys usually arrive in a pack around eleven o'clock, as if it's not cool to show up before then. However, when he does turn up it's with Julietta Tarnasas on his passing arm. Gwen comes flying over to give me the scoop. It seems the new object of Craig's affection is a *freshman*, of all things. An exotic and stunning exchange student from Buenos Aires, certain to be discovered by a modeling agency within the next week or two. So much for Gwen's matchmaking skills.

"When did *this* happen?" I ask.

"Last weekend," says Jane.

"We were afraid to tell you," says Gwen. "She got drunk at a church re-treat and *threw* herself at him. My mom says that Argentineans are very social people."

"It'll never last," adds Jane. "After they hooked up, he probably felt bad because she doesn't know that many kids and her host family is this boring Methodist couple in their sixties."

"Oh right, so he's just doing a good deed, a form of community service," I say.

"If you like him then *why* didn't you go to his football game when he in-vited you?" Gwen demands, as if it's all *my* fault.

"Because he didn't *ask* me to his game!" I shout over the Hawaiian drum-beat. "His exact words were 'maybe,' 'perhaps' he'd 'hopefully,' 'possibly' see me there."

Gwen does her combination sigh, shrug, eye roll that means *how dumb can you be?* "That's how a guy asks you out, Hallie. What were you waiting for, a subpoena?"

I look to Jane for help, but she nods in agreement. "It's like a dog scratch-ing at the back door," says Jane. "It's their way of telling you they want to go out."

"My older brother is dating a girl because she looks good with his car," comments Gwen, as if this explains everything.

Across the room Craig and Miss Argentina share a banana split, feeding each other off the same spoon and giggling. Gross. And of course he looks as if he just jogged off the cover of *Sports Illustrated*, with the kind of per-fect muscles and ruddy tan that only guys who never think about building muscles and getting tan seem to possess. He glances up and catches me look-ing directly at him. I wave and mouth "Hi." He nods and turns back to Evita. A chilly reception, and that isn't even taking the ice cream into account. I assume that Craig has been informed of the latest addition to my criminal record. And he certainly has no reason to believe otherwise. "So now what?" I ask.

Gwen eyes the crowd like a hungry Komodo dragon. "See Seth over there?"

Seth Gilmore is playing volleyball with some of the swim team and other guys who don't play contact sports.

"Yeah, what about him?"

"Make out with him," Gwen instructs me.

"No way!"

"Well then get him up to the hayloft long enough so that I can spread a rumor that you're making out with him so that Craig will hear about it."

Again I look to Jane to rescue me and again she does just the opposite. "My father says that at his company they prefer to hire people who currently have jobs. It's the same for dating. You look more appealing when you're on someone else's payroll as opposed to being unemployed."

"What makes you think that Seth will make out with me?" Actually, he isn't all that bad. Seth has straight brown hair and hazel eyes, and though he had bad acne freshman year it's all cleared up now. Besides, I haven't kissed a guy since the summer. And I don't want to get completely out of practice.

"Seth will swap spit with anyone," Gwen assures me.

"Thanks a *lot*," I say.

"No, I just mean he went out with Paula since, like, eighth grade, and they broke up last month and so now he's on a rampage. Trust me," says Gwen.

"Trust her," agrees Jane. "Though there's always your boyfriend from the starship *Enterprise*." Jane nods in the direction of the makeshift volleyball court where Brandt happens to be serving. One of his triangular rubber ears drops off into the dirt just as I look over. Brandt would of course interpret this as a sign that we're destined to be together. I take it as just the opposite.

And that's how I end up making out with Seth Gilmore in the Thompsons' hayloft while "The Hokey Pokey" blares down below and pigeons scratch around above and I spend the next day picking little pieces of yellow straw out of my hair and fingernails.

The following morning Ms. Olivia looks up from her tea and asks if I've spent the night in a Monet painting. Then she inquires if I'm ready to begin our tutoring session. I say sure, even though it's Sunday and I thought we'd have the day off. Ms. Olivia keeps to a rather odd schedule, and she certainly doesn't abide by the notion of working Monday through Friday and then having weekends free. Sometimes she gives me Wednesday or Thursday as a vacation day and then decides to teach me about Herodotus at noon on a Saturday. She says that the body feels the pull of the moon, like the ocean has tides, and therefore certain subjects are best absorbed in the evening while others are best mastered during a storm. Likewise, she claims that the American Revolution is best studied on a farm or in a public park so that you can experience the trees and the sky and the grass and everything that the colonists were fighting for.

Also, Ms. Olivia doesn't believe in alarm clocks. She claims that they leave the people who depend upon them in a constant state of nervousness.

I for one couldn't agree more.

Under the Gun

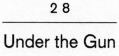

By the time I finally move into the main house it's the first week in November and the summerhouse is turning chilly, with morning frost flowers etched onto the windowpanes. Even the space heater I'd located in the shed can't prevent my breath from rolling out like gray mist across the green woolen blanket while I wait for sleep to come. As I patch together the pieces of the golf money scandal and finalize my plan to resolve it, most nights sleep doesn't arrive for a very long while.

Nor am I the only one feeling the onset of winter. Alvin and his merry band of chipmunks have gone so far as to borrow one of my socks for added insulation in the rafters, where they've set up light housekeeping. However, they're in the habit of dropping a few nuts on my head in return, and so I guess it can be considered a fair exchange. I take it as a good sign that my roommates are willing to have open trade relations.

After I'd finished painting the upstairs bedrooms, moldings, and radiator covers, Mr. Bernard, Mr. Gil, and Ms. Olivia set to work converting Mr. Bernard's junk room into a bedroom. Granted, a bedroom with a lot of junk in it. The makeover was supposed to be a secret. But first of all, nobody in that house is very good at keeping secrets. And second, it was hard not to hear Mr. Bernard in there cursing while he was trying to assemble the antique four-poster canopied twin-sized bed and then arguing with Ms. Olivia about the color scheme. (She wanted carnation pink, while he insisted upon deep jade.

She won.) But I don't want to spoil the surprise, and so when they lead me upstairs, open the door, and shout "Tada," I do my best to look astonished.

Next to the bed is a round wooden nightstand with scalloped edges, a little drawer near the top, and a utility shelf at the bottom. On the table sits a dainty lamp with a white porcelain base covered by a pale green silk shade trimmed with red velvet brocade. Opposite the bed stands an elegant rosewood bureau with an oval mirror in a gilt-edged frame hanging above it. On the wall perpendicular to the bed and opposite the door are some matted and framed samplers of embroidered flowers I'd seen down at Mr. Bernard's shop.

"So, Nell, will you finally come in from the wild?" Mr. Bernard asks after I finish absorbing the transformation. Mr. Bernard often addresses me as Nell because he claims that Jodie Foster and I are the only two girls in America who have perfect teeth despite having lived in the wilderness.

"And look," exclaims Ms. Olivia, "there's a drainpipe located directly outside your window so you can come and go at any time without using the front door."

I glance at the escape hatch with approval but also wonder how she knows about the erratic comings and goings at my previous dwelling.

"This is wonderful. You're very generous." I don't really know what else to say. It is truly an odd moment when you officially move in with a bunch of eccentric older people who you met through an advertisement at the Star-Mart.

"Now it's just like a kibbutz!" Ms. Olivia says delightedly. "I always wanted to live in a commune, but the Judge would never allow it. He said it was bad enough having to share a bathroom with just *one* other person."

I notice that someone, probably Mr. Gil, has placed a worn copy of *The Adventures of Huckleberry Finn* on the nightstand. I walk over to the bed and examine the beautiful soft white coverlet with tiny pink roses stitched into it that match the canopy.

"Wow, this is gorgeous. It must have cost a lot of money. Please let me help pay for it."

"Don't be ridiculous," snaps Mr. Bernard. "Mother has fantasized about decorating a girl's room for over three decades. In one month you've removed all the pressure on Gil and me to have grandchildren. We should be paying *you*."

Mr. Bernard catches me eyeing a huge marble statue of an angel that has been pushed into a corner behind the door.

"I haven't found a place for that yet," explains Mr. Bernard.

"We thought we'd just try to hide it back there for the time being," says Mr. Gil. "Maybe you can hang some dirty clothes on it or make it into a Rococo belt rack."

I nod in agreement. Obviously it's a challenge to camouflage a two-hundred-pound, six-foot-high marble statue.

I walk over to the window, part the lace curtains, and peer down at the driveway where the silver birch trees, now spindly and naked, cast thin shadows. They'll be pretty again once the snow comes. For a moment I feel slightly guilty. Not for accepting the Stocktons' hospitality so much as for betraying my *own* mother and father. Forsaking them because they couldn't provide individual rooms for their children and one-on-one parenting. But deep down I also know that the real reason I left isn't that simple. And now that they believe I'm a criminal-at-large they probably wouldn't let me come home again anyway.

My resolutions are suddenly interrupted by a tan and white squad car pulling into the driveway and then the familiar heft of a resolute-looking Officer Rich hoisting himself out of the vehicle by using the top of the door-frame for ballast.

"Uh-oh," I say. For some reason I suddenly doubt I'm going to get a chance to sleep in my new room, because there's already a narrow cot with a lumpy mattress waiting for me somewhere else.

The crunch of wheels on gravel brings Ms. Olivia to my side.

"Who is it?" inquires Mr. Bernard.

"The gendarme," replies Ms. Olivia in a voice I think is more eager than apprehensive.

"I'm pretty sure that this time he's going to take me," I worry aloud.

Mr. Gil and Mr. Bernard arrive at the windowsill in time to have a look for themselves. Officer Rich ambles up the driveway, pausing every few feet to take a breath and glance toward the front door, as if considering a hundred things he'd rather be doing.

"Whatever happens, don't go quietly," Ms. Olivia firmly instructs me. "In fact, run out barefoot and shackle yourself to the front porch right this minute." Her voice trills as her fingers dance up to her pearl necklace and begin twisting the knot on the end of it. "I'll call the newspapers and the local TV. Better yet, try to persuade the constabulary to handcuff you to the porch themselves." She prances over to the doorway.

"Mother!" Mr. Bernard practically shouts. "Just hold it right there. This isn't a game. It's someone's *life.*"

"That's *exactly* what you don't understand," Ms. Olivia replies. "It's never about one single action, it's the larger picture, the broader implications."

Then she turns the beam of her enthusiasm back to me. "Now, after you've secured yourself to the rail the reporters will arrive and you must inform them that you're initiating a hunger strike."

"Yes, tell them you're only fortifying yourself with chocolate Yoo-Hoo until a settlement is reached," Mr. Gil adds nonchalantly. He's acting as if the police pulling up in the driveway is a daily occurrence around here and nothing to get alarmed about.

The doorbell chimes. From the window I can see Officer Rich shifting his weight from one foot to the other and scratching his head. He certainly doesn't appear to be relishing the task ahead.

"Now, Gil, if you and Mother will only stop this foolishness we can create a plan . . . ," begins Mr. Bernard.

Only Ms. Olivia has already darted off, most likely to alert the media.

"What do I *do?*" I ask the two of them.

"Stay right here and let me handle this," Mr. Bernard says authoritatively.

But I'm worried about Ms. Olivia and the fact that I'm supposed to be wrapping myself in garden hose and somehow attaching myself to the front stoop. Because suddenly I don't want to go to prison, especially for something that I didn't do. I look over to Mr. Gil, as if he's the tiebreaker.

"Don't ask me, kiddo. Take your pick—the barricades and the evening news or Bernard Stockton, professional mediator and hostage negotiator. He cuts a mean deal on an antique armoire."

The bell rings again. Oh damn. I don't know.

"I'm going to answer the door. You stay here!" Mr. Bernard says to me. To Mr. Gil he says, "You go spy on Mother and report back to me all of her movements."

Mr. Bernard straightens his posture, adjusts his shirt collar, and exits my new bedroom. Mr. Gil follows him. I quietly trail after them but stop at the top of the stairs so I can eavesdrop while my fate is being bartered away.

It's impossible to hear every word, but Mr. Bernard sounds polite and helpful, just like he does with his customers, and Officer Rich sounds apologetic, just like he does when he wins at cards. It's possible to make out the words "so sorry" and "it's not up to me" and then "warrant for arrest." *Warrant for arrest.* Holy shit. I race back to my room and open the closet door to see if there's space for me in there. No dice. It's packed with rolled-up rugs, an antique wire birdcage, and about twenty old-fashioned wall barometers.

I hear the gravel crunch again and wonder if Officer Rich might be leaving. Out of the window I can see the Channel 7 news van pulling into the circular driveway. So much for sliding down the drainpipe. My stomach is in knots and my legs are turning to soup. I wasn't made for the renegade life like Ms. Olivia. Playing blackjack at the hundred-dollar table never made me this nervous. I'm positively frantic. I dash back to the top of the stairs.

"Mother!" I hear Mr. Bernard call.

Mr. Gil trots up the stairs and practically trips over me, since I'm now crouched on the landing, chewing the cuticles off my fingers.

"I was just coming to get you," he says calmly. "It's not you. They're arresting Livvy."

"Ms. Olivia!" I stand up. "What for?" I ask. I'm dumbstruck.

"The usual, Olivia Disobedience. Interfering with police procedure. She has a habit of going into town on Saturday afternoons and putting quarters in all the parking meters that are about to expire. Then she leaves a mimeographed note on the windshield explaining what she did and saying that before that driver leaves he or she should check the other meters and deposit a quarter in someone else's if it's about to run out. She calls it her traffic collective. Anyway, the town is losing money in ticket revenues. She's been doing it for years and they've been threatening to arrest her almost as long. But you know Olivia."

I was certainly beginning to.

"C'mon." Mr. Gil leads the way down the steps. "But brace yourself. Olivia is like a tea bag—she's very strong when placed in hot water."

Out front there's a tremendous commotion under way. Ms. Olivia is insisting that Officer Rich drag her away in handcuffs and with his gumball lit and siren blaring.

Mr. Bernard is courteously but firmly explaining that Ms. Olivia can't go to the courthouse because she must tend to her ailing husband.

Ms. Olivia demands to be taken into custody, claiming that as an American citizen she's entitled to be arrested and read her rights and have due process.

The crew from the news van is capturing the action on camera while a TV reporter approaches the porch carrying a big black microphone. A female journalist from the *Cosgrove County Register* arrives on the scene with a tape recorder slung over her shoulder and a notepad in hand. The front yard begins to resemble a presidential press conference.

The TV reporter holds out the microphone and shouts questions. "Wasn't Olivia Stockton the lead activist for separation of church and school?" And "Mr. Stockton, are both of your parents currently suffering from mental illness?"

Ms. Olivia automatically moves toward the microphone like a smart bomb approaching its objective. Mr. Bernard agilely pulls her back.

The reporter aggressively continues. "Are you aware that your mother is known as the Cosgrove Car Angel?"

"Yes, of course." Mr. Bernard raises his hands to silence them.

Then the guy holding the klieg light for the cameraman suddenly swings around and fixes his gaze on me with more than a passing glance. "Who are you? His kid? The granddaughter?" While pointing a finger at me he hollers to the cameraman, "Hey, get a shot of the kid."

"I'm just the yard person!" I say and shield my eyes from the blinding light that is now shifting in my direction.

Meantime, Officer Rich appears to be refusing to arrest Ms. Olivia. And he seems alarmed by the sudden media frenzy, anxious to make it disappear at any cost. Ms. Olivia, on the other hand, is visibly energized by all the commotion. No stranger to the power of the press, she takes the newspaper reporter aside and gives her an earful.

Mr. Bernard eventually ends the circus by waving his hands and shouting at everyone. "Okay, you've got your footage. This is private property and everyone must disassemble immediately."

Then he turns to Mr. Gil. "Take Mother inside, please."

But Ms. Olivia is enthusiastically conversing with the female reporter, and so he takes them *both* by the arm and steers them toward Mr. Gil and the front hall. "My alleged mother can finish making her proclamations over a cup of tea at the dining room table."

To me he says, "Hallie, please go retrieve the checkbook out of Mother's secretary and bring it to me. I'm going down to the precinct with Officer Williamson in order to straighten out this *misunderstanding*."

To himself he mumbles, *"Après Mom, le déluge."*

When the TV crew realizes that they're not going to witness a white-haired old woman being forcibly dragged off to a squad car in handcuffs, they pack up their equipment.

Mr. Bernard walks over to the cruiser accompanied by an obviously relieved Officer Rich. Meantime, Mr. Gil graciously escorts Ms. Olivia and the reporter into the dining room. Only instead of discussing her near-arrest, I hear Ms. Olivia congratulating the young woman on her choice of career and for having the courage to speak out on behalf of the oppressed at the hands of a greedy municipality.

I don't like the look of the woman and wish that she would leave. But then I realize it's impossible to dislike her because I've never met her and don't know a thing about her. Perhaps it's just the idea of Ms. Olivia having another student that I resent. I vow to try harder in my studies. I don't want her to find a more willing pupil.

Next I hand Mr. Bernard his checkbook through the window of the police car and am pleased to find that he's sitting in the front seat, and not behind the Plexiglas partition and the wire cage. No, they're chatting amiably and Mr. Bernard is shaking his head in disbelief and Officer Rich is nodding as if he understands. Like we *all* have a nutty relative and what *can* you do?

"Don't worry," Mr. Bernard reassures me. "I'll get it knocked down to a fine."

But I feel better knowing that due to his father having worked in the courts, the family must still have connections and maybe the fix is in. I mean, I know Ms. Olivia was hoping to go to prison and all, and that I should probably respect her wishes, because essentially I'm in the same boat. Only she wants to go where everyone doesn't want her to go, while I *don't* want to go where everyone wants me to go.

"I think you'll have to agree with me that she costs us more in fines and bail than she saves anyone in parking tickets." Mr. Bernard opens the checkbook to glance at how much money is in the account.

I assume he's talking to Officer Rich because of the way he says "we," but when he looks up from the leather folder he's staring right at *me*. I'm the other person in "us," and I nod my head in agreement to both his proposition and to us being *us*.

"Hi, Hallie," Officer Rich says to me as he turns the key in the ignition and starts his engine. But he says it with a dismissiveness that makes me feel like an outsider. I suppose he can see my relief that he isn't there on my account.

"Hey," I say.

"I'll be in touch." He starts pulling away.

And I know that he will be, too. Officer Rich has made it quite clear that I don't have much time left to either produce the money or come up with a good explanation for where it went. Or else . . .

Now that I think I've figured out who did it, all that's left is to prove it. The only problem is that I need to be eighteen in order to execute my plan. There's always Eric. Though he would probably squeal to Mom and Dad and they'd call Officer Rich. Craig is eighteen. Only I'm probably still on his shit list for borrowing the money for the racetrack, even if I did pay it back eventually. But it's worth a try.

In or Out?

★

Saturday night Mr. Gil invites me to watch *Gigi* with Mr. Bernard, Ms. Olivia, and the Judge. The Judge has been weary lately, and so Mr. Gil and Mr. Bernard set up the VCR in their bedroom and bring up some chairs from the living room. I politely decline, because it's time to finally get to the end of the missing money trail.

After dinner I drive over to Craig's house. I don't know what made me think he'd be home on a Saturday night. He must get invited to tons of parties just like my brother Eric and sister Louise. I can tell his mother is reluctant to help me locate her son. Obviously she's heard about my colorful résumé. But she gives me the name, address, and phone number of where he is, which I find totally fascinating. My mother would need a computer and a full-time assistant to keep track of where all her children are. But I suppose if you only have one kid then surveillance is much easier.

I drive to Scott Kirkland's house. He's in my brother's class and also on the football team, so I know him well enough to knock on the door. It's cold outside and he invites me in. Craig is there watching one of the Scream movies along with a bunch of guys and Scott's older sister, Trish, who is visiting from college and has one of her high school girlfriends over. Either they're too involved in the movie to say much or they've heard that I'm the town exile. I suppose I should just be flattered that the women don't grab for their purses and hide their jewelry.

I ask Craig if I can talk to him privately, and so we go to the kitchen together and he offers me a beer. Scott is the youngest of four, and so his parents treat everyone like grown-ups. And both his parents smoke, so you can smoke and drink and watch adult movies and they don't run around banging on locked doors, turning on lights, and carding everyone.

Craig looks more perplexed than pleased to see me, and so I wonder what he's heard. The stories about me being abducted by aliens were fun in the beginning, but I'm getting tired of people treating me like some sort of freak in addition to a hardened criminal. I can't decide which is worse. I mean, you always hear about people writing to prisoners and wanting to marry them, and in movies the bad characters are often sexy. But who wants to date a freak?

"So what's going on?" asks Craig.

"Depends on what you've heard," I say. "There's an ugly rumor going around that I cadged some cash from the sporting goods store."

"I heard that," he says. Then he raises his right hand and ticks off with the forefinger on his left while presenting the rest of the list. "I heard you were involved with the Mafia. I heard that you dropped out of school to become a jockey at the racetrack." He eyes me skeptically. "Though you appear tall for that." He pauses, and I think he's finished.

"That's all?" I ask sarcastically.

"Actually, no. I heard that your parents threw you out of the house because they found pot in your room."

"You have to wonder how I find the time to fit it all in," I say. "Especially with my glamorous full-time job as a housepainter."

It isn't the welcome wagon I'd hoped for, but Craig is my best shot at a partner in reversing crime.

"I sort of need to ask you a favor."

"Okay, but why me? Why not Eric or your boyfriend Seth?"

"What's *that* supposed to mean?"

"It was pretty obvious you two were an item at Gwen's party."

I'm surprised he even noticed me, he was so busy spoon-feeding What's-Her-Name, but I figure that mentioning this is not going to score any points.

"Yeah, well, Seth is over," I say. "And I need your help, because you're eighteen. You are eighteen, aren't you?"

He nods affirmatively but hesitantly, like an impatient loan shark being forced to wait through another tale of woe.

"This is going to sound really weird," I say. "And I'll understand if you don't want to do it."

"It's nothing illegal, is it? Because, you know, I'm sending out college applications and my parents—"

"No, no. Just the opposite actually." I remove eight hundred dollars from my coat pocket and Craig puts his hand out as if to stop me from going any further or else he'll be forced to call the police.

"Just hang on a second. If this is the money you stole—"

"No," I practically shout. "I mean, that's what I have to ask you—I *didn't* steal the money. I need you to help me prove that I didn't . . ." My voice breaks and I'm practically in tears. Craig still looks skeptical. After composing myself, I explain what I think happened to the money and that what I need now is for him to open up a stock-trading account.

He appears to believe my explanation, although I can tell he thinks the whole scheme sounds pretty far-fetched. "All right," he agrees.

Craig offers to give me a ride home, and so now I wish that I hadn't brought the Buick. I consider lying and saying okay and then doubling back later to pick up the car.

"So, uh, how come, you know, where's what's-her-name, Julia?"

"Julietta," he corrects me. "She's a good friend."

Good friend. The two most misunderstood words in the language of love. But I'm not about to ask.

"That's nice, just like you and Sheryl," I say. "So anyway, I'd better get going. I borrowed a car." He probably assumes that *borrowed* is a euphemism for *carjacked.*

"Are you sure you don't want to watch the rest of the movie?" he asks.

"Uh, no thanks. Actually we're watching something back at the Stocktons'."

"Oh, you guys probably have one of the Chucky movies. We tried to rent those, but they were all out."

"Probably. It's impossible to get a good horror film on a Saturday night."

Craig walks me to the front door.

"You've got the money?" I ask.

He dutifully reaches his hand around and pats his back pocket.

"Okay, well then, uh, thanks," I say.

"No problem," he replies.

I look up at him, way up, since he's so tall. He reaches out his hand, and I shake it. But it feels as if we're sealing a business deal. I highly doubt that this is what Ms. Olivia was talking about when she said that I'd have lovers and experiences and write poetry. I suddenly want to say something to express the way I really feel, not just some platitude or jokelike sarcastic remark.

"You know, I can really use a friend right now," I finally say. "Will you be my friend?" No sooner is this gem out of my mouth than I decide it probably won't become a tag line in any romantic comedies.

"Of course," says Craig. And fortunately he doesn't say, "I'll love you like a sister." Because that isn't what I have in mind.

When I arrive back at the Stocktons', Mr. Gil and Mr. Bernard shout for me to come upstairs and watch their favorite number with Maurice Chevalier and Hermione Gingold singing "I Remember It Well." The Stocktons look like the three bears. It's actually quite funny. The Judge, Ms. Olivia, and Mr. Bernard are all squeezed together in the big sleigh bed with Rocky sound asleep at the bottom, and Mr. Gil is right next to them in a chair with his feet up on the bed across Mr. Bernard's shins. And except for the Judge, who's just smiling vaguely in the middle, they're all three happily singing right along with the television: *We met at nine. We met at eight. I was on time. No, you were late. Ah yes! I remember it well.*

But all I can really think about is how this stock scheme better work, and work fast, since I doubt any musicals are shown in reform school.

3 0

House of Cards

♠

On Sunday morning Mr. Bernard rushes around the house frantically searching for his bank card and car keys in preparation to storm the rest of the weekend garage sales, while Mr. Gil and I sit at the dining room table and finish eating our Eggs Bernard on toast. I'd agreed to go over to the Community Theater with Mr. Gil and paint the sets while he organizes the box office.

"Hallie, your mother phoned last night," Mr. Bernard calls out from the front hall. This is followed by a series of crashes—the familiar sound of everything tumbling from the flimsy overloaded shelf above the coats and onto his head. A silk scarf sails through the entranceway to the dining room like a magic carpet and settles on the rug.

"Oh horrors!" he yells out in dismay. "My cloisonné for a map of Cleveland Heights."

"It's in the glove compartment," Mr. Gil calls out. "And just leave everything in the foyer. I have to reorganize that closet anyway."

"Hallie, please do ring *Mamacita* back. She's been calling with telemarketer reliability," Mr. Bernard continues. "I can no longer bear to hear the sorrow in that woman's voice."

Three days ago I'd written my mother a letter explaining that I didn't steal the money, and that I knew who did, but it was going to take me a little while to prove it. Because if I'm murdered between now and then I'd rather not go to my grave with her believing I'm guilty. I don't care so much about the rest of the town. As a postscript, I'd reminded her of the time she'd accused Eric and me of drinking the brandy and it turned out that Aunt Vi had used it to bake fruitcakes.

Mr. Bernard appears wearing his normal weekend outfit of chinos, light blue cotton button-down collar shirt, and tweed blazer, only dangling from his ears are an enormous pair of orange and red rhinestone earrings shaped like ripe peaches. They're the size of silver dollars and heavy enough to weigh his earlobes down so that the fruit is practically bouncing up and down on his shoulders.

Mr. Gil chokes on his coffee, and I find Mr. Bernard's clownish appearance so unexpectedly hilarious that I allow myself to slide off the chair and onto the floor, since it's easier to laugh this hard lying down, especially after having eaten three eggs.

"What's wrong?" Mr. Bernard inquires with a perfectly straight face. He uses his hands to still both earrings and then lightly touches the top of his head with his fingertips. "Is my coiffure out of place?"

Mr. Bernard *loves* to do this—surprise us by suddenly modeling some bizarre item he's purchased at a garage sale and pretending that nothing is amiss. And no matter how many times he does it, it never fails to crack us up.

Just then Ms. Olivia enters through the swinging door from the kitchen carrying a teapot. However, she pretends to take no notice of me, still on the floor howling with laughter, nor of Mr. Gil blotting up the coffee running out of his nose and the tan spots he's sprayed across the white linen tablecloth. After casually glancing at the main attraction, she remarks in a perfectly modulated voice, "Darling, I've told you a million times that orange is not your color. You're a winter. Try ice blue, dove gray, and ivory—whatever Grace Kelly and Helen Hayes looked good in. *Those* are the proper hues for you."

This only causes Mr. Gil and me to laugh even harder.

"Really, no one else in this house has the slightest sense of style." Mr. Bernard says this with mock disdain and continues to ignore the earrings, though he purposely moves around and tilts his head in order to achieve maximum jiggle from the ornaments. "Now, Hallie, why don't you invite your mother here for a luncheon on Sunday?"

"*Here?*" I rise back up to a sitting position.

"Yes, of course *here*. Tonight we'll prepare a lovely quiche Lorraine with Gruyère cheese and pommes soufflés. And for background music I'll have Berthe Sylva singing 'Les Roses Blanches.' "

It's not that I don't want to see my mother so much as I'd rather wait until the money situation is cleared up. I'm also still fearful that they're trying to declare me mentally incompetent in order to pack me off to a psychiatric hospital. That's what Ms. Olivia said European monarchs oftentimes did to get rid of their wives when they wanted to remarry.

I glance around the room for a way out of this proposed luncheon. But Mr. Gil has finally stopped laughing and nods in my direction, as if it's a good idea. Ms. Olivia doesn't say anything. But of course it's her credo not to become involved in other people's business.

"Okay," I acquiesce. "Quiche Lorraine it is."

"Tallyho, then, off I go!" Mr. Bernard grandly scoops up his haphazardly folded pile of newspapers with the sale notices circled in bright red ink and sweeps out of the room.

"Darling," Ms. Olivia calls after him. "You may want to drop your baubles, bangles, and beads back in your jewelry box before you leave." She serenely takes a sip of her tea.

Mr. Bernard darts back into the dining room and stands in front of the mirror. "*Oh my Lord and Taylor,* I almost forgot."

"In the meantime, you've certainly given new meaning to the line 'He glittered when he walked,' " Ms. Olivia says. She turns to me and says, "That's from the poem 'Richard Cory' by Edward Arlington Robinson. He dropped out of Harvard."

I'd noticed that Ms. Olivia is in the habit of pointing out to me Ivy League dropouts who became successful, like F. Scott Fitzgerald and Bill Gates. I guess she thinks it will help my self-esteem.

"Who dropped out of Harvard?" I ask. "Richard Cory or Edward Arlington Robinson?"

"Robinson," she says. "Cory committed suicide," she adds matter-of-factly.

Mr. Bernard tugs the big peaches from his lobes and plops them down on the table in front of Mr. Gil. "It's like the old stripper said: *You either have it or you've had it,*" he says and exits once again.

"You're looking a bit fatigued," Ms. Olivia says to me and then places her dainty hand up to my forehead. It's funny how she can be a revolutionary one minute and then slip into some typical grandma behavior the next, such as examining me for a fever.

"I feel okay," I reply. "Maybe I'm getting a cold."

"I suppose," she says. "You're not used to sleeping indoors. It's probably been a shock to your system. Have Gil examine your teeth."

"What?"

"Gil can tell everything about one's health by scrutinizing the teeth. He grew up on the most famous horse-breeding farm in Northern Kentucky. Isn't that right, Gil?"

Mr. Gil nods his head in agreement.

"Gil is to tooth prognostication what Nostradamus is to historical prophecy," continues Ms. Olivia.

Mr. Gil wipes his mouth with his napkin and then walks over to where I'm sitting. "Open wide," he says and tilts the chandelier in the direction of my head.

He moves my chin around in a circle, furrows his brow, squints, then stares in my mouth and says, "Hmmm, mmm, hmm," as if he's choosing between two competing laundry detergents. "You've contracted an upper respiratory infection," he finally announces. "And you have a slight iron deficiency. Drink lots of juice and pick up some One-A-Day vitamins for women at the drugstore."

"General Cuspid is never wrong about these things," Ms. Olivia states sincerely.

"You can tell a lot from the mouth," Mr. Gil says as he returns to his chair. "It's the nourishment center for a person's health and well-being."

But I'm not convinced that this isn't some sort of a parlor trick. They probably pull this old chestnut on every yard person. No wonder Lars started to drink.

"What else can you tell about me from my teeth?" I skeptically ask. "Do they say if I'm going to get married and have kids?"

Mr. Gil laughs. "Sorry, Hallie, but it's not like palmistry or looking into a crystal ball. I can't foretell the future, only examine the past. For instance, I can see that you had scarlet fever as a child and that you're allergic to penicillin."

My mouth almost drops onto my plate, exposing *all* my teeth. "C'mon," I insist. "Cut it out. You can't tell that stuff from my teeth. You must have seen my medical records."

"Certainly I can tell. There's some graying from the penicillin, and I can glean from the condition of your gums that you had scarlet fever. Otherwise you're the picture of good health. And you had braces for about two years.

That's the other thing, you can often determine a person's socioeconomic background from the amount of dental work they've had."

"And of course he can tell your age," Ms. Olivia adds. "That's why I make it a point never to smile around Gil."

"You have lovely teeth, Livvy," Mr. Gil replies.

"Thank you for the compliment," says Ms. Olivia.

"They look exactly like your real ones did."

"Thank you again."

Well, I'll be damned. Just when I thought Mr. Bernard and Ms. Olivia were the entire show around here, it turns out that Mr. Gil is a toothsayer.

Long Shot

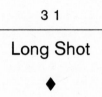

This Saturday night Craig *is* expecting me. When I arrive at the house his mother and father are pleasant and so I can tell that he must have laid some groundwork by making a few positive remarks on my behalf. For instance, that I'm not really a convicted felon.

After the first half an hour I think we're all going to spend the evening double-dating—me, Craig, his mom and dad. They even ask if we want to join them to see a movie over at the multiplex in Timpany.

Thank God Craig says no. I've never been out with a guy *and* his parents. Actually, I've never been on a real date. All I ever manage to do is hook up with guys at parties and then the following week at school I avoid them or they avoid me. Usually both.

After Craig's parents depart for the movie he takes me up to his room and removes an envelope from underneath his big double bed. Craig's room is huge. It has a skylight and its own adjoining bathroom. He has his own TV, VCR, computer, and telephone. It's like an apartment. I mean, if you had food delivered you could live in here for months and never need to go out.

Craig has done everything just as I'd asked. He's opened up the trading account and told the broker to invest in stocks with major growth potential, like the ones that discover new drugs and make people into millionaires.

"Did you get the canceled check back?" I ask. "You didn't pay with the cash, right?"

"No, Hallie. I did everything just as we agreed. In fact, I had to open up my own checking account at the bank to do it. I told my parents I was writing a lot of checks for college applications so it'd be easier, which is true."

Craig proudly shows me his new checkbook with his name, Craig T. Larkin, printed across the top in bold letters. "Look, I ordered the blue checks with the sailboats. I thought they were really cool when I first saw them at the bank, but now I think they may be sort of stupid." He looks back up at me as if I'm the final word when it comes to check decoration.

I take a good look at them. "I think they're terrific. Why would you want checks that look like everyone else's?"

"Yeah, you're right," he agrees.

And it's funny, but there's a lilt to his voice as if we're on some type of adventure together. Once again I survey all the only-child perks in his room, the stereo and hundreds of CDs, a room that if my brother Eric were to awaken in all by himself, without Teddy peeing in the bunk bed above him, he'd think he'd died and gone to heaven.

Craig turns on his state-of-the-art computer and we look up the stocks the broker has chosen and read on-line reports that explain what the companies do, how much money they expect to make, and who their major competition is. Most haven't been in business long enough to have a one-year performance record. Then Craig pulls up some Web sites to show me the colleges he's looking at.

"Don't you ever miss your parents?" Craig asks.

"Sure, I mean . . ." But then I have to think what I mean. *Do* I miss my parents? "Yes and no, I guess. By the time I left they were on my case, like, *all* the time."

"Sometimes I think that when my parents die I won't have anyone else," he says. "No brothers or sisters or nieces or nephews."

"You'll have your own family by then. And you have a million cousins. I can't believe your mother has five sisters."

"She loves her family. They all baby-sit for one another and talk on the phone practically every day."

"Ask her how she felt back when they were all sharing a bathroom."

Craig switches off the computer and we watch TV for a while. There doesn't seem to be any easy way of transitioning from friend to girlfriend. Gwen is probably right. I blew it when I had the chance. And I'm not about to ask about Miss Argentina again. Though I haven't seen any pictures of her around. And she's the kind of girl that if you were dating her you'd want everyone to see an eight-by-ten glossy on your dresser so that they'd know about it.

When Craig's parents eventually return from the movie, Mrs. Larkin makes us all some of those Pillsbury turnovers that you heat up in the oven and frost from a plastic pouch. Then they proceed to give a rundown on the film and who they ran across in the lobby after the show.

"Craig tells me the two of you are working on a project involving the stock market." Mr. Larkin catches me by surprise. But I guess Craig would need a way to explain receiving statements from a brokerage firm. After all, it doesn't appear as if there is much about Craig's life that goes unmonitored.

"Uh, yeah," I lie. "It's the latest trend, you know, to try and teach teenagers stuff they can actually use in the real world."

"Well, I think it's a capital idea for young people to learn how to invest. My parents gave Mary and me some Procter & Gamble stock when we got married, and by gosh if it didn't pay for this entire house. Isn't that right, Mary?"

"It certainly did, Dan." Mrs. Larkin circles the table and refills our glasses with iced tea. "I have an idea—how about we all play some cards? Hallie, do you know any card games?"

"Sure," I say. "Blind openers, Texas hold 'em, Canadian stud, low-hand stud, table stakes, freeze-out, deuces wild, dealer's choice, jackpots—"

However, Craig interrupts with a massive throat clearing and so I don't even have a chance to get started on types of gin rummy. "Actually, Hallie and I have to finish up the project."

But we don't really have anything more to do, and so I assume that Craig wants to go back upstairs and make out. Only instead he leads me to the parlor off the living room. However, before opening the French doors he hesitates. "Promise you won't tell anyone about this."

"Of course." This is said with a minor note of disgust in my voice, since in my former business people who don't keep confidences don't keep breathing. They die of lead poisoning. The kind you get from bullets.

Craig swings open the doors and before me is something you just don't see in Cosgrove County. Large moon-shaped globes suspended from the ceiling and pole lamps in corners that cast a rosy glow on fifty or sixty plants. But they aren't houseplants. They're Disney trees and bushes—topiaries of all different shapes and sizes, the taller ones in black pots on the floor and the smaller ones in square ceramic dishes resting on sculpted white plaster columns of varying heights. One corner of the room is covered in cacti, some topped with bright orange flowers like clown noses. And along the far wall is a giant terrarium illuminated with a fluorescent blue light that makes the rocks and plants in it appear to be lavender-colored.

"Wow." It's the only thing I can think of to say.

A relieved smile appears on his face.

"How come you don't, I mean . . . I don't even think my brother Eric knows that you—"

"Uh, Hallie, it's not really considered cool for quarterbacks to be into horticulture . . ."

"But this isn't . . . I mean this is . . ." But I don't know what I mean.

Craig takes me on a tour of his enchanted forest. He explains the different types of soil that he uses and shows me all the varieties of topiaries and cacti that he's "hybridizing." His husky baritone voice lifts with excitement as he demonstrates how to prune a Japanese dwarf tree in the "clasped-to-rock style."

Along the far wall is a large window hung with a wooden blind that allows long silvery-white slants of moonlight to stretch across the floorboards. The bright gro-lights overhead cast grayish-pink shadows while a humidifier softly hums in the corner and makes it all feel very romantic. I think that perhaps Craig will kiss me, especially when he places his hand on mine to show me how to plant a tufa rock with flowering quince and moss. But instead we move on to the proper care of the night-blooming cereus and the correct method of watering a bonsai tree. Not only does Craig not kiss me, but he doesn't even attempt to put his arm around me, not even after he closes the blinds so that I can get a good look at the terrarium.

Eventually we walk to the front door and the entire family stands in the vestibule waving good night and telling me to drive safely and to watch out for deer. It feels more like a scene out of the three-hour driver-safety course I had to take to get my license than the passionate parting I'd been daydreaming of all week.

Full Table

My mother is scheduled to arrive at noon on Sunday. At a quarter to twelve Mr. Bernard is enthusiastically demonstrating the proper way to place a slice of quiche on a plate and then garnish it with purple kale and sprinkle rosemary on top. "A successful presentation includes serving the courses at the right temperature with the right beverage and in keeping with the theme."

"What do you mean *the theme*—like runaway adolescents?"

"No, silly. The continuity, the total ambience—*par exemple,* at Christmastime you have a decorated tree and certain traditional dishes, drinks, and songs. Today we're going *française,* à la *Gigi*—a *petit déjeuner* of beet vichyssoise and niçoise salad with quiche Lorraine and *croustade aux pommes avec crème glacée* for dessert. And of course you'll offer your mother a glass of Beaujolais."

"But she's going to throw a foal in the spring."

"*Pardonez-moi?*"

"She's pregnant."

"Ah oui, *enceinte,* but of course. Offer her sparkling or spring water with a slice of lemon or a wedge of fresh lime. Then we'll sing 'La Marseillaise' for the baby's listening pleasure. It's beneficial for unborn children to hear music.

"*Marchons, marchons,*" he sings, while making the whipped cream for dessert.

Mr. Bernard has tactfully offered to leave Mom and me on our own for lunch, but we all end up dining together, which I think is rather how he planned it in the first place, since he had plates for all of us stacked in the kitchen and ready to go. The guys appear keen to demonstrate that I'm not residing with weirdos. Mr. Bernard and Mr. Gil may be different, but they're not stupid. They know what people like Herb and Al say about them. Thus Mr. Bernard has emptied the downstairs of funny hats, suggestive paintings, and the nude statue in the guest bathroom has mysteriously been replaced with a clipper ship in a glass bottle.

When my mother arrives they don't model earrings, do the can-can, or perform movie scenes. Even Ms. Olivia is in on it. She doesn't start railing about her latest cause, which happens to be the unfair government representation and land appropriation of the Chiapas villagers in Southern Mexico. I'd spent the morning helping her write a petition to be passed out at her church so the members can collect signatures at their respective workplaces. Ms. Olivia is chairperson of the Chiapas Right to Fight committee. Actually, she's the only person on the committee. Apparently the church has eighty-seven members but over a hundred committees.

Before lunch we show my mom around the downstairs of the house and give her a tour of the backyard. It's obvious that she finds Mr. Bernard to be charming. But then most women do. In fact, the older and more affluent ladies in town often stop by his shop just to gossip or complain about their kids and marriages. Not surprisingly, he usually manages to sell them something before they leave.

True to form, Mr. Bernard politely holds the doors for my mother and gracefully motions for her to precede him as we enter each room. Once we're all seated in the Florida Room, Mr. Bernard offers everyone a "preprandial drink." He graciously rises whenever my mother stands and also when she returns from the powder room.

It's doubtful that my mom really had to use the bathroom, since she always goes before she leaves the house in order to avoid public rest rooms. She probably wanted to do some investigating on her own and to see if the Stockton household met her standards for cleanliness. And maybe go through the medicine cabinet. I wouldn't put it past her.

Ms. Olivia has trimmed the Judge's hair and beard so that he appears shipshape even though his recent behavior has been erratic. Up until a few weeks ago he was content to sit quietly when left alone for an hour or so, but now he keeps rising from his chair and walking from room to room and opening drawers, as if he's searching for something. He's also taken to crashing through the house in the middle of the night. The doctor says the Judge may have experienced a mild stroke. He's scheduled to make a house call on Monday to review the Judge's medications.

However, this afternoon the Judge sits calmly in his armchair with the sun's rays sifting through the blinds to form bars of light across his chest and face. He vacantly stares at Court TV, though Ms. Olivia has muted the sound. I catch my mother furtively glancing over at the Judge whenever she goes to sip her tea.

Ms. Olivia of course notices my mom attempting to evaluate the Judge. "It wasn't so bad up until this past fall, since he still delighted in his surroundings," she explains cordially. "He enjoyed watching the birds, strolling outside, and sitting and watching the fountain in the mall. The worst part is he no longer smiles, much as I try to engage him."

"I'm sure the doctor will adjust his medication, Mother," Mr. Bernard says with encouragement.

"I believe he's fading, dear," Ms. Olivia says and looks over at the Judge. "And maybe it's just as well. This is a life sentence that he shouldn't have to endure. He was a dignified man, your father."

"*Is* a dignified man, Mother," Mr. Bernard quickly corrects her.

But Ms. Olivia just sadly turns her head back to us.

From my mom's point of view I expect it's a good thing that we have the Judge here. He lends an air of credibility to the entire household, even though he's out of it. And Ms. Olivia earns plenty of points, too. I'm always amazed at how easily grown-up women can converse with each other, even if they've never met before. It seems as if Ms. Olivia and my mom might chat until the six o'clock news comes on. They talk of children, husbands, how much the town has grown, and the proposed Grocery Depot that everyone has been fighting over and editorializing about the past few months. In fact, I start to worry that they're getting a bit too chummy—that they may start to conspire against me. Could that be my mother's hidden motive in coming over—to turn the Stocktons against me so I *have* to go home?

However, I'm reassured by the knowledge that my mother has *no* idea what she's up against. I attempt to view Ms. Olivia through my mother's eyes, that is, if you don't know about the Druid Circle, pornography, Mexican Revolutionaries, Italian lover, and the like. Aside from all that, she seems fairly credible as a representative of what my father calls a Responsible Adult in Charge. And the fact that she's at least twenty years older than my mother probably helps, too. This way it doesn't appear as if I bolted my house for the home of a competitor. It's more like I moved in with an eccentric grandma.

Had the lunch ended there things probably would have been fine. But when Rocky arrived home from church in his three-piece suit, mixed himself a Singapore Sling, and then actually served the luncheon, I think she would have felt as if she were being a good Christian by having us all committed.

33

Stacked Deck

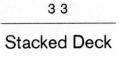

Immediately following lunch Mr. Gil and the Stocktons discreetly disappear, making the appropriate noises about errands to run and accounts to balance, and they leave Mom and me to the fresh apple dessert.

"I haven't had real whipped cream since I was a girl," she says appreciatively. "My grandmother used to make it. She also made a delicious bread pudding. I wish I had her recipes."

"It's not very sweet," I say.

"No, but it has a lovely fresh taste. This is how we served it during the seventies when sugar became so outrageously expensive."

"I prefer Cool Whip," I say softly so that Mr. Bernard can't overhear me in case he's spying from the foyer. Because these walls don't have ears, they have stethoscopes.

"I see you still enjoy chocolate Yoo-Hoo," Mom says diplomatically.

"Yeah. I haven't changed or anything like that."

"I'm just pleased that you're back in school." But then she apparently remembers that I'm not exactly *in* school. "I mean, of course, that you'll graduate."

"I don't gamble much anymore." I think this will please her. Besides, if anyone in my family is going to win the Breeders' Cup it's Mom, not me.

"Oh, really? Why is that?"

I'm reluctant to bother her with the details of being thrown out of the Indian casino, barred from the church poker game, and the fact that with the track closed for the season I'm pretty much out of options. So instead I just say, "I'm busy painting the interior and we're building a small greenhouse out in the backyard. And I'm doing a three-dimensional mural on the garage door."

"I noticed that. Very interesting. It reminds me of the flexible wooden figures that art students use as models when they're learning to draw the human figure."

"It's not done yet. I'd like to finish before it snows, because there's this silicon spray down at the hardware store that can be used to protect wood from the weather."

"I'm pleased you're doing something with art. I've always said that you have a natural ability. I took some drawing classes as electives at Cleveland State and I think you're probably more accomplished now than I was in college."

"Oh, I didn't know that."

"It was just a hobby. And your father will certainly be pleased that you're no longer gambling. He heard a rumor at a Kiwanis meeting that you won eighty dollars from Father Costello. I told him I was sure that it was just a joke and that the pastor would never play cards, at least not for money."

"He's not a very good poker player. I could teach him a few things."

"Oh dear," she says, her worst fear confirmed. "I'd rather you didn't."

"It's funny, because no one believes it, but the only reason I gambled was to make money. It isn't that I enjoyed it so much as, you know, that I was just good at it. It's not as if I'm addicted to it the way some people are."

"You used to win more money from the baby-sitter playing Rummy Five Hundred than we paid her for watching you and your brother. It was embarrassing to have to warn her not to gamble with an eight-year-old."

"She used to bite her nails when she was one card away from getting gin. And she held on to aces, even when it was obvious there was no chance of getting another one."

"Speaking of money," says my mother in a failed attempt at nonchalance, "you mentioned that you found out who took the charity funds . . ."

"Um, yeah. But I can't say anything until it's all been resolved."

"And you feel sure that you didn't do it? Because it's probably not too late to . . ."

"Mom, I don't *feel sure* . . . I *know* that I didn't do it."

"Then I believe you. I must say that you've never really lied to me about anything. Well, except about playing hooky, of course. You weren't hard to *handle* so much as hard to *find*."

Apparently this is supposed to be a compliment. "Thanks," I say.

My mother proceeds to catch me up on the progress of my brothers and sisters. But it's not long before her agenda surfaces once again.

"So then, now that all this nonsense is almost over with, when do you think you'll be coming home?"

Just when I think that the reunion is going really well I realize that the entire afternoon has been a scam. "Mom . . . I'm not coming home."

"Now, Hallie, I've spoken with the school psychiatrist and they can prescribe Ritalin to help you concentrate."

"I can't believe this!" I raise my voice. "You want to drug me so I can sit at a desk all day?"

Now I'm irate. I push my chair back from the table, stand up, and almost hurl the china dish full of whipped cream against the wall. But it's not my home and so I don't.

My mother is angry, too. She purses her lips and rises from the table. "You know, you can't just *live* here, Hallie . . ." She lowers her voice. "I'm sure they're very nice people and all that, but . . ."

"But *what*?"

"Well, you know, people talk . . ."

"Yes, Mom, and what are people *saying*? That you're a bad mother, that you can't control your children. Is *that* what you're worried people are saying? That your daughter is a dropout, a vagrant, a runaway, a *thief*?"

"Hallie, you *can't* stay here!"

"Oh, so you came to take me home, is that it? To *your* home."

"There are things you don't understand, Hallie," she hisses back, as if she doesn't want to be overheard by our hosts.

But I don't bother to lower my voice. "Things like what? That Mr. Bernard and Mr. Gil are *gay*? That they enjoy art and music and theater and watching old movies instead of frigging football games? That they eat hors d'oeuvres and drink Merlot instead of sloppy joes and Juicy Juice? Well, then maybe I'm gay, too!"

"Oh, *Hallie!*" My mother's hands fly up to her face as if she's just witnessed a car wreck, and then she glares at me as if the home for unwed mothers or the women's prison farm would be a *relief* compared to this.

"You'd better go," I say.

"I didn't mean there was anything immoral about them—it's just not the kind of place for a young woman to be staying, that's all. You've been raised in a *Christian* home, Hallie—"

"Is that what this is about? Religion? Are you afraid I'll become a Unitarian?"

My mother keeps putting her index finger to her lips in an effort to signal that I should lower my voice, but this only makes me want to yell even louder. "Hallie, they're different from *us*," she says forcibly. "Surely you under—"

"No, *you're* different from *us*," I shout back.

Silently and hastily I escort her to the door, still seething. How did this go downhill so fast? Only ten minutes ago we were talking about the upcoming baby and Eric's football playoffs and Louise's latest boyfriend.

Mr. Bernard appears in the front hall before my mother has even started her car. "I guess we won't be shopping for mother/daughter jumpers today. What a shame."

"You heard?"

"Enough to get the general idea."

"I'm sorry." I'm truly embarrassed by my mother's remarks. However my anger disintegrates as soon as I see her car turn out of the driveway. Only now I feel as if I'm about to start sobbing. "I think I'll go for a walk."

"Why do you want to go for a constitutional?" Mr. Bernard asks. "It's a cold and damp November day out there. It might creep into your soul. Take the *QE2* if you need to set out to sea for a while."

Mr. Gil arrives in the front hall and also appears concerned. "We're just about to watch a movie," he announces.

Mr. Bernard joins in, "Yes, why don't you watch the movie with us?"

"What are you going to watch?" I ask. Because I'm not sure that I'm in the mood for Rosalind Russell as the overbearing Mama Rose in *Gypsy*.

"What movie were we going to watch?" Mr. Bernard asks Mr. Gil. It doesn't take a particularly high IQ score to figure out that this spur-of-the-moment entertainment is being introduced on my behalf.

"*Harold and Maude*, of course," Mr. Gil replies as if he's been planning this all weekend.

"*Harold and Maude?*" I say. "What's that about?"

"It's hard to explain. But . . ." Mr. Bernard lowers his voice and says conspiratorially, "There's always been a rumor that Maude was based on Mother. The writer met her at the Village Vanguard down on Bleecker Street in Manhattan during her hippie salad days in the sixties."

"Are you kidding me?" I can't tell if Mr. Bernard is just trying to liven things up in order to get me interested in the film, like when he's selling his antiques and says he's quite certain that such and such a Sheffield plate was once owned by Jackie Kennedy and used in the White House.

"I'll locate the videotape and see if Mother Jones can steal a few minutes away from coordinating her Chiapas firebrands," says Mr. Gil, as if it's a done deal. "Why don't you make tin roof sundaes?"

But just then Ms. Olivia wanders through the front hall as she goes to prepare the Judge's medication and pauses next to our huddle. "Have I interrupted a Freemasons meeting?" she inquires. Then she shields her eyes with the back of her hand and says, "Don't let me see the secret handshake. Knowledge is responsibility."

With Ms. Olivia getting in on the act, I *know* it's a conspiracy to cheer me up.

"We're going to watch *Harold and Maude.* Why don't you and Father join us in the living room?" Mr. Bernard inquires enthusiastically.

But she politely shakes her head no. "I'm on a deadline for *Milky Way* magazine. I'm taking a story I wrote a long time ago and updating it—you know, removing items like Grape Nehi, Etruscan vases, parlor games, and rumble seats. Otherwise, it's remarkable how little has changed. Though of course nowadays everyone has to jump up and fetch condoms. Making prophylactics sexy—that's the trick to writing erotic literature today."

"Mother," Mr. Bernard exclaims, pretending to be shocked. "Amorous tales on a *Sunday.*"

"Bertie, how many times have I told you to read the Bible? If you would, you'd find that the Old Testament is positively teeming with sex."

Ms. Olivia says all this as she carefully counts out the Judge's pills onto the heavy oak dining room table. "Sarah giving a concubine to Abraham or Rachel giving a concubine to Jacob. Then there's Absalom, up there on the rooftop having sexual relations with not one but *ten* of his father's concubines, Lot committing incest with two of his daughters and still walking away from Sodom and Gomorrah unscathed. And when it comes to first-rate erotic verse, you have to search far and wide to beat the Song of Solomon."

"I always thought there must be a reason that the acronym for Song of

Solomon is SOS." Mr. Bernard says this and then heads toward the kitchen. "Would you care for an ice cream parfait, Mother?"

"Not one of those dreadful white-on-white-on-white monstrosities you make. They're much too sweet."

"But I love the way they *look*—tone on tone on tone in scalloped glass with a long silver spoon."

"Just give me two dishes of vanilla, please, and I'll have it with Father. And put cherries on top."

While they're busy bickering, I'm wondering how soon I can start reading the Bible, like maybe right after the movie. Ms. Olivia keeps a copy filed under "fiction" in her library, between the Bhagavad Gita and the poems of Elizabeth Bishop. I'd attended religion classes every Wednesday afternoon all through elementary school, and now I finally understand why we were only allowed to read the Children's Bible.

"Hallie, please retrieve the parfait glasses from the top shelf of the china cabinet," Mr. Bernard instructs me from the kitchen. "And attempt to locate the long spoons in the silver drawer."

"Let that be a lesson to you, Miss Hallie," Ms. Olivia continues.

"Huh?"

"People are too quick to condemn things of which they have no knowledge."

"Oh, now I'm to be made an example of," Mr. Bernard says jokingly, his head inside the freezer.

To me she says, "Hallie, pornography has been on the forefront of every major revolution. Just look at photography and the Internet."

"Yes," says Mr. Bernard. "I'm certain that erotic narratives have saved countless lives." Mr. Bernard smiles sweetly at his mother and hands her two dishes of vanilla ice cream with chocolate sauce and a cherry on top.

"I didn't ask for chocolate syrup," Ms. Olivia objects, though she doesn't look at all unhappy about the added touch.

"I know. I did it out of love," he says and gently shoos her into the hallway.

"Hallie," Mr. Bernard says to me conspiratorially as we assemble the sundaes, "you and I both have mother problems."

"I think mine is worse," I say. "My mom is trying to control my life. Yours at least allows you to do whatever you want."

"I suppose. It's like what Lyndon B. Johnson said about J. Edgar Hoover when he ran the FBI—I'd rather have him inside the tent peeing out rather than outside the tent peeing in."

"Then mine's more like *Fiddler on the Roof*," I say, referring to the musical we'd all gone to see at the revival house in Cleveland the weekend before.

"How's that?" Mr. Bernard asks with great curiosity. "Is your mother keeping a kosher kitchen these days? Are you living here to escape an arranged marriage with the butcher?"

"No. Remember that part where they say 'God bless the Tsar but keep him far away from us'? Well, that's pretty much how I feel about my mother right now."

"Yes, of course," Mr. Bernard says with apparent delight as he scoops the ice cream. "We must remember to tell Gil. And of course those tsars got their just desserts."

At least Mr. Bernard and his mother have figured out how to compromise. In fact, they actually *like* living together. Sometimes they pretend not to, but anyone can tell that they really enjoy each other's company. My mother, on the other hand, is the most stubborn woman in the entire world. Even when I was little, there was just no chance of getting my own way with her. Strong-willed and stubborn, stubborn, stubborn. That's what she is and always will be.

Then again, I'd heard the same thing said about myself.

3 4

Risky Business

★

Even after the movie I can't sleep. Visions of Mom loom large and a feeling of disconnectedness overcomes me like a fever. My mind reels back to when I was a little girl and I try to pinpoint where it all went wrong. I suppose it started with the fights about dresses, which I refused to wear after age six. And then it was about skipping Sunday school. Following that were endless arguments about making my bed and not wanting to take those stupid ballet lessons. Then it was everything. She said black and I said white. She said to go left and I went right. Eventually I couldn't tell the difference between what I was doing to make myself happy and what I was doing just to annoy her.

The only argument Louise and Mom ever have is about baby-sitting. Louise hates baby-sitting Francie and the twins, even if Mom pays her. And Eric hasn't fought with Mom *or* Dad since he was in middle school. Though once Eric came home drunk and Dad made him get up at six o'clock the next morning and work *all* day—mowing the lawn, cleaning the garage, washing the cars. He looked as if he was going to die.

My thoughts are interrupted by the phone ringing. Someone in the living room picks it up and the sound of a short muffled conversation drifts up the stairwell.

Eventually I turn on my light and pick up boring old *Jude the Obscure*, which Ms. Olivia is making me read for school. If this doesn't put me to sleep, then nothing short of a lethal injection will. Only I can't concentrate on the words long enough for them to work their anesthetizing magic. I pick up *The Adventures of Huckleberry Finn* and reread my favorite line, "Then Miss Watson took me in the closet and prayed, but nothing come of it." I put this book down as well. I'm restless, like in the old days, and need to be outside. Over my T-shirt I pull on paint overalls and tiptoe down the stairs. Then out the front door in order to go and work on my garage mural. It's better to view it at night anyway, without the sun causing a glare.

The air is frosty but refreshing and I take a deep breath. There's a faint hint of smoke, only it's not the kind you get from a chimney or a campfire. Before turning on the garage light I see the dark outline of a figure standing in the garden, right in the middle of the Druid Circle, just like a statue. In fact, I'd think it *is* a statue if I didn't know that there isn't one in that spot. But perhaps Mr. Bernard recently brought some plaster of paris figures home from an estate sale and ran out of room in the garage. This is *entirely* possible.

The moon is low and casts an otherworldly glow across the yard and the gardens look like patches of worn gray corduroy. And it's a good thing I don't believe in ghosts, because the statue slowly moves its right arm and takes a drag off a cigarette, the orange tip pulsing in the darkness like a firefly. Aha! So this is when Ms. Olivia smokes.

I contemplate joining her, not for a smoke, but just for company. However I don't want to frighten her. She appears lost in thought, with her back to the house and eyes searching the black branches of the trees and beyond.

The rasp of gravel churning under hesitant tires draws my attention and I quickly move to the side of the garage. Perhaps it's just a car turning around in the driveway. Or maybe Ms. Olivia is meeting someone. I hide behind the bushes as headlights illuminate the driveway but are switched off as soon as they cast a reflection in the front windows.

A petite woman slowly climbs from the car, gently closes the door, and is met by Ms. Olivia. Together they walk toward the summerhouse. There's no way I can observe what's happening from my current post, blocked by the garage, and so I decide to go back inside the house and peek out the kitchen window that overlooks the yard.

As I enter the front door I can hear noises coming from the kitchen. Perhaps Mr. Bernard is doing more of his middle-of-the-night therapeutic baking. In this house a person can easily wake up to three key lime pies, pear strudel, and a batch of macadamia nut cookies.

Pushing on the swinging door to the kitchen, I see the pantry door is ajar and the interior light is on. I expect to find Mr. Bernard searching for flour, but instead I start to scream. A man in a ghostlike nightdress with blood dripping from his hands and face turns toward me and with his right hand raises what appears to be an ax.

"Mr. Bernard!" I yell and slam the pantry door shut. I run toward the stairs in order to awaken someone or call the police or find an exorcist or I'm not sure what. Because if I didn't believe in ghosts fifteen minutes ago, I sure as heck do now!

Just as I turn to dash toward the hallway, Mr. Bernard and Mr. Gil come flying into the kitchen. Mr. Bernard is in his boxer shorts, and Mr. Gil is also in his underwear with a maroon robe attached to one arm that's flying behind him like Superman's cape.

A second later Ms. Olivia darts around the corner, pulling Jemma the twenty-something clerk from Herb's drugstore along behind her like an animal trapped in a snare, eyes wide and cheeks as red as taillights. Even in my panic I manage to note that Jemma is the only person who actually appears more fearful than I, which is quite a feat, under the circumstances. Mr. Bernard and Ms. Olivia both utter "pie filling" simultaneously and reopen the pantry door.

Inside the small room the Judge is tranquilly eating strawberry pie filling out of a Mason jar, using a large black-handled bread knife as a spoon, blissfully unaware of all the commotion. His white beard and nightshirt are splattered with red goo and fleshy chunks of berry. He looks like Father Time caught in the crossfire.

Rocky now bounds in from where he sleeps on the couch in the sunroom, wearing his green flannel nightshirt with King Kong on the front, and a terrified Jemma lets out a shriek.

"Nothing to worry about," Mr. Bernard says, though he sounds as if he's actually becoming *more* agitated upon learning that a bloodthirsty, ax-wielding maniac is *not* on the loose. That's when I notice Jemma clutching the small plastic pack containing the pill as if it's her last dollar bill.

"Oh my God," I say without thinking, "are you a drug addict?" I know Jemma, because she normally checks me out at the drugstore while Herb runs the pharmacy and does back office work. However, my insane remark only terrorizes her further, and she drops the pill on the floor and appears ready to flee.

"I'm sorry," says Jemma and doesn't close her mouth even after the "y" has been out for almost a full five seconds.

"No one here is a drug addict," Ms. Olivia says sharply and stiffens with dignity. She wraps her arm around the alarmed and now falsely accused Jemma. "I'm so sorry, dear," she says comfortingly. To me she says, "Hallie, why don't you fetch some washcloths from the bathroom to help clean up the Judge?" She points to the sunroom. "And Rocky, back to bed!"

Meantime Mr. Gil reaches down and retrieves Jemma's pill and hands it back to her, while Mr. Bernard gently leads his bewildered father over to the sink. Mr. Bernard is *awfully* quiet. He surely realizes that each one of these incidents, and there have been more and more lately, mean that the Judge is another day closer to being put in a home.

Ms. Olivia shuttles Jemma into the living room while Mr. Gil and Mr. Bernard get the Judge sorted out and I prepare to clean up the pantry.

"I'm—I'm sorry," I say. "I just thought . . ."

"Don't worry about it," says Mr. Gil. "I'm sorry the Judge gave you a fright."

"I'm going to allow Mother to explain this one if you don't mind." Mr. Bernard rinses his father's hands and wrists under the kitchen sink the way one washes finger paint off a kindergartner. "I'm just too exhausted."

A few moments after I crawl back into bed, Ms. Olivia taps lightly on my bedroom door. "Hallie, are you still awake?" she whispers and opens the door slightly.

"Unfortunately," I say and pull the covers up over my head as she enters. There could be no doubt left in anyone's mind that my life had all the makings of a country-and-western song.

Ms. Olivia sits on the edge of my bed the way my mother used to in order to read Louise and me a story when we were little.

"Oh dear," begins Ms. Olivia. "I apologize for giving you the wrong impression."

Everyone has apologized to everyone else by this point, and I'm still not sure what we're all sorry about.

"I saw the box in the summerhouse and someone go to the door one night, and I just assumed you were a . . . ," I start. But now I can't manage to get out the words *drug dealer*.

"Hallie, do you know what a morning-after pill is?"

"A birth control pill?"

"Not exactly. It prevents implantation of a fertilized ovum and is therefore effective as a contraceptive *after* sexual intercourse. You do know what a contraceptive is?"

"Sure," I say. Though coming from a family of seven kids, soon to be eight, I can certainly appreciate why she might ask the question. "But can't you buy that kind of stuff at the drugstore?" At least that's where my brother Eric gets his condoms.

"It's all very political," Ms. Olivia says, as if the entire system exasperates her. "The pills are legal, but there's pressure not to sell them. And so they can be difficult to obtain in a timely manner, if you know what I mean, especially for a young woman."

"So you sell them," I surmise.

"No, no. That would be illegal, since I'm not a pharmacist. I give them away. Just think of it like sex—it's perfectly legal to give it away, one just can't sell it."

Did she just say what I think she said? It's not as if I have anything against contraceptives, or even prostitution, for that matter. But why did it all have to be so complicated and tied up in legal mumbo jumbo? Ms. Olivia rises and smoothes my bedcovers and kisses me good night.

Of course, I think, *Ms. Olivia doesn't deal drugs, she only gives them away.* Now why hadn't I figured that out? What next? Perhaps they'll all be sitting around the table in the morning speaking Hindustani and explaining that it's perfectly fine to *give away* an antinuclear defense system, just so long as you don't *sell one.*

Well, once again I'd forgotten a page out of the Gambler's Bible and lived to regret it: Believe nothing of what you hear and only a quarter of what you see. And when you *assume* you make an *ass* out of *u* and *me.*

Life's a Trade-Off

♠

Ms. Olivia may be the Robin Hood of birth control, but she's also the only teacher I've ever had who makes learning fun. Lessons with her are like sailing along the cloudy coastline of a dream. Ms. Olivia can even make science interesting. "Did you learn about Carl Sagan in school?" she asks me.

"Sure—*billions* and *billions*, the astronomy guy."

"Well, he was a marijuana *fiend* and did much of his best work under the influence. Now don't get me wrong, I'm not suggesting you get yourself an absinthe habit in order to paint like Toulouse-Lautrec or Van Gogh. However, it's my view that young people are quite capable of absorbing this sort of information and coming to their own conclusions about substance abuse. In fact, Van Gogh is probably a better example of why *not* to do drugs than all the celebrity public service announcements combined."

"Did it affect his work?"

"No one really knows for sure if there would have been one star more or less in *Starry Night*. However, he became depressive and killed himself at thirty-six. A terrible shame."

Even though I now know Ms. Olivia isn't dealing drugs, I still can't tell if she's for or against them. What I really want to ask is if she's done any of the drugs she just mentioned and if they'd made her more creative. Only I'm afraid it would come out wrong, like I was just being nosy. And I suppose I would be.

"Was Maude really modeled after you? She *seems* a lot like you. I just wondered . . ."

"Well, I hardly think so." Ms. Olivia begins closing and stacking the books we've been using. "I only met the writer on a few occasions in New York City. Besides, Maude was a Holocaust survivor, whereas I am merely a Watergate casualty."

"But you *remind* me of Maude. Or Maude reminds me of you."

"Thank you. I'll take that as a compliment. But there are plenty of Maudes out there, Hallie." Ms. Olivia pauses a moment. "Just maybe not right here in Cosgrove County."

"Ms. Olivia . . . I—I've decided . . . that I want to become a bohemian."

Ms. Olivia laughs airily. She's not *exactly* laughing at me, because she's too kind for that. But sort of.

Her light voice tinkles like glass chimes. "Oh, Hallie, one doesn't *decide* to become a bohemian. It's not like joining the Rotary club or signing up for a political party."

"Oh." I imagine I look disappointed, because Ms. Olivia places her hand on top of mine as if to reassure me that the door isn't completely closed to me. Then she laughs once more. Ms. Olivia has an enchanting musical laugh, one that would make the bells in heaven sound like a tugboat's horn.

"Hallie dear, you *are* a bohemian."

"I am?" For some reason I'd assumed that you had to be at least twenty-one.

"Of course. A bohemian is simply someone who disregards convention."

"Is Mr. Bernard a bohemian?"

"That's a difficult one." She furrows her brow slightly and brushes a wisp of yellowy-white hair behind her ear. "Most children rebel against their parents, so the best bohemians usually come from straitlaced Protestant stock. However, if your parents are already bohemians, then I suppose you must rebel by joining the Young Republicans or the Moral Majority."

"Sort of like a Catch-22?" I ask.

"Exactly right," Ms. Olivia replies, obviously pleased that I've been following her logic. "It's been difficult for Bertie. I'm sure I don't have to tell you that not many people would choose to live an alternative lifestyle in Cosgrove."

"Do you mean that for Mr. Bernard to be different he has to try and fit in?"

"Whereas you and I have to work hard to make sure that we *don't* fall into lockstep with conformity," she says. "It's one thing to feel that people are small-minded, but it's quite another to know that their eyes are boring holes into the back of your tweed sport jacket when you're standing in line at the bank."

"Was the Judge a bohemian?" I ask. However, it's difficult to imagine a Cosgrove County judge as a bohemian. It would be like discovering that the tub-shaped Officer Rich is a nudist. Or that my mother works nights as a lap dancer.

A shadow briefly crosses Ms. Olivia's face and I'm sorry I brought up the subject of the Judge, especially since he's been getting on so poorly lately. Yet I can't envision Ms. Olivia allowing him to be put into a nursing home. She'll handcuff herself to his wrist and they'll have to drag her along, too. And we'll all be on the news again.

"Oh, I wish you could have known the Judge when he was in his prime." Her face brightens as she reminisces. "He was a truly remarkable man. I prefer to think of the Judge as more of . . . an armchair revolutionary. Some children are raised to lead a particular type of existence, and it's really impossible to alter that course . . . for instance kings and queens, and oftentimes the sons of presidents and senators. Businessmen who own companies look forward to their sons succeeding them, and ministers, doctors, and military men often expect their offspring to follow in their vocational footsteps. And that's what was expected of the Judge."

"My dad doesn't want any of us to do his job. He hates it."

"Parents who aren't satisfied with their jobs or education can become even *more* hopeful and determined that their children will fulfill all of the dreams they couldn't."

"He's convinced my brother Eric is going to be a nuclear physicist just because he won the contest for best science project back in the ninth grade."

"That's rather how it was for the Judge. Only multiply those expectations by a hundred. Abelard Kendall Stockton the *Third*, a.k.a. the Judge, was raised right here in Cosgrove County. His great-grandfather was mayor and then started a law firm and the sons were expected to carry on the political and legal tradition."

"*Oh!* Kendall Airport!"

"One and the same."

Ms. Olivia goes to the bookcase and brings back a photo of the Judge as a young man in a letter sweater holding a pigskin and standing between two serious-looking older men in dark suits who also resemble Colonel Sanders.

"Didn't he *want* to become a lawyer?"

"Yes, he very much enjoyed the law. But there's something slightly stifling about being put in Kenyon College training pants and a Yale Law School sweatshirt when you're eighteen months old, and going with Daddy to the office and being shown where your desk will eventually be. Though I must admit that the Judge, before he was a judge that is, took some civil rights cases that did not make anyone in the firm especially happy."

"Do you think he would have been a bohemian if the family hadn't had so many plans for him?"

"Let's just say he always followed his heart and mind when making an opinion, and that he appreciated other open-minded individuals."

"So he was sort of a closet bohemian?"

She gaily tosses her head back and chuckles. "That's a good way of wording it. Or as Tennessee Williams once said, 'Bohemia has no banner. It survives by discretion.' You see, we need people like the Judge who can work from the inside. He was instrumental in ensuring that the students in this area had an open forum during the Vietnam War, even though he didn't necessarily agree with what they had to say, especially coming from a long line of distinguished veterans."

She glances at me, with my shoulders hunched over the table, digesting all this and intently making notations. "He would have enjoyed you, Hallie."

"I wish my parents would enjoy me," I say sadly.

"Mr. Emerson said that it's better to be a thorn in the side of your friend than his echo. And that can be true for parents, too, don't you think?"

I nod yes, though I'm not so certain whether I agree or not. Mostly because I hardly have any friends these days.

"And Hallie, we mustn't forget that not everyone is designed to run the gauntlet. The poet John Milton said that those who only stand and wait also serve."

Though from the way she says this I can't tell if she means I'm designed to run the gauntlet or to stand and serve. Being a lawn person seems to fall firmly in the latter category, unless you include the tractor pull at the state fair, which might marginally qualify as an agricultural gauntlet.

We then turn to English literature. I'd just finished *Henry VIII*, though Ms. Olivia says it's doubtful that Shakespeare actually wrote that one, or at least all of it. She reads a speech from the play that she claims is written in the style of John Fletcher, another English dramatist, and one who was known to collaborate, and then proceeds to read a similar bit from Fletcher's *The Faithful Shepherdess*.

However Ms. Olivia says not to mention this fact on my exams because public schools don't go in for speculation and gray areas, such as Thomas Jefferson fathering children with his slaves. And quite frankly, I don't really give a damn who wrote *Henry VIII*. I just enjoy all the gory death scenes.

"Why don't they want to teach the truth?" I ask.

"Truth and beauty don't necessarily go hand in hand. For instance, Shakespeare's loveliest sonnet, 'Shall I Compare Thee to a Summer's Day?,' was probably written to a man."

Ms. Olivia goes to the bookcase and removes a slim volume titled *A Treasury of the World's Best-Loved Poems* and reads the sonnet aloud and then points out the parts that historians believe were later transposed to disguise this fact.

"But why was it changed?" I ask.

"Because in this supposedly *free* country we've elected senators who believe that same-sex desire is on a par with alcoholism and kleptomania."

"I thought it was illegal to alter someone else's writing." Maybe Eric using Wite-Out on his school ID and me forging attendance notes wasn't so terrible after all.

"Or else they practice censorship by omission. For instance, they don't teach you that Percy Bysshe Shelley, who wrote this lovely poem 'Ode to the West Wind,' was an outspoken radical who championed free speech and vociferously attacked the death penalty, as well as Great Britain's subjugation of Ireland, and even Christianity."

However, Mr. Bernard is now in hearing range and he diplomatically chants, "Mother, teach to the test, please!" And I decide it's probably a good thing he wasn't around when Ms. Olivia was explaining how the ancient Greeks exercised naked.

3 6

Front Runner

♦

True to her word, the final week in November Ms. Olivia prepares to meet Ottavio Vespignani in Florida. The days leading up to her departure are the first time I wished that I *wasn't* overhearing the squabbling between her and Mr. Bernard. Because this week I get the feeling that they're serious.

On this particular morning the war is being waged in the sunroom while I make chocolate and butterscotch chip pancakes in the kitchen.

"I should have named you Hector," Ms. Olivia barks at her son. "Because that's all you've been doing to me the past three days."

"Mother, how can you possibly abandon us like this?" Mr. Bernard soberly retorts.

"Call the Children's Welfare Society immediately," she scoffs. "Explain that I'm deserting my thirty-five-year-old son, his husband, and my own husband who hasn't recognized me in more than three years, to go on a five-day vacation."

"This is not a joke, Mother—you running off with some . . . some Lothario. And leaving us to cope with everything."

"Bertie, Nurse Radcliffe is coming and your father will be in far better hands than he is with me. After all, she's a professionally trained care provider."

"But *Mother*, what will the neighbors say?"

"Oh, be serious! Since when have *you* ever cared what the neighbors think?"

Mr. Bernard trots out twenty more excuses why his mother shouldn't go on vacation, from the somewhat reasonable (how will he get his E-mail? answer: Mr. Gil or me) to the totally ridiculous (what will happen to the leftover Halloween candy?). But he can't sway her, or even lay a guilt trip on her, for that matter. In fact, Ms. Olivia appears perfectly at ease with her plans. After lunch she ushers me into her room to show me the two nightgowns she's purchased for the trip. One is a flowing floor-length silk negligee with a scoop neck, the color of cotton candy, and the other is a gold, tan, black, and cream leopard print.

"Wow!" I envision my mother in her sensible plaid flannel pajamas with a generous helping of Francie's yogurt smeared across the front of them.

"Whoever said love is blind was either extremely out of shape, incredibly hopeful, or a bit of both," Ms. Olivia remarks as she carefully wraps the dainty garments back up in their white and maroon polka-dotted tissue paper.

Even though the satiny leopard print with the spaghetti straps might be considered daring for a woman in her sixties, I imagine that Ms. Olivia can easily pull it off since she has a trim figure and moves so gracefully. Every delicate step and every turn of her head is worthy of attention, like that of a ballet dancer. And since her beau—that's what she prefers to call him—is foreign, I picture him having an appreciation of the exotic.

"Now, Hallie darling, please don't misunderstand me—those football jerseys, cotton Jockey underwear, and high-top sneakers you have a predilection for are perfectly fine—I don't believe women need to go around in lipstick and pearls all the time. And certainly if there's a fire you'll be the first one out, or if the Cleveland Browns suddenly need a quarterback you'll be prepared to hit the field running. But when you take a lover you must really treat yourself to a few nice peignoirs and undergarments. A boudoir ensemble that says 'come hither' as opposed to 'fourth down.' "

"I hate dresses and nightgowns. I can't take two steps without tripping."

"It's just something to keep in mind for later on. They were only able to convict Joan of Arc for wearing men's clothing, which was illegal for a woman back in the fifteenth century."

"They burned her at the stake for wearing men's clothes?"

"They were after her for other minor irritations—starting wars, crowning kings, and hearing voices saying the wrong side was going to prevail and the like. But I tend to think that if the Maid of Orléans had in her possession just one frock or a nice peasant skirt, she would have had a much better chance of getting off with just a warning."

I hear Mr. Bernard's agitated voice echoing in the stairwell. "At least leave me a phone number so that when they find your pocketbook floating in the Gulf of Mexico I can give the information to the police."

"He's coming around," Ms. Olivia whispers to me. *"N'entrez vous pas!"* Ms. Olivia calls out toward the closed door. *"J'ai en déshabillé."*

"Don't tell me things like that!" His voice fades down the hallway. "I don't even want to *know* about it."

I sit in the small chair with the heart-shaped back in front of Ms. Olivia's vanity table and watch as she finishes packing. She removes the red satin case from the pillow on her bed and places it in her carry-on bag and then zips up her luggage. "Well, that should do it."

Up until the very last minute Mr. Bernard is dashing around banging doors and cupboards and emitting the sighs of one who is overworked and exasperated in order to appear as if he has no time in his busy schedule to accompany us to the airport.

It isn't until Mr. Gil and I put on our coats and load the car that he performs a mock capitulation and says that he *supposes* the garage sales can wait. Then he begins clucking like a mother hen: "Tickets? Sunscreen? Tylenol? Passport? Rain bonnet?"

"Rain bonnet?" Ms. Olivia and Mr. Gil say in unison.

"Of course. A woman of a certain age should always carry a rain bonnet and have a twenty-dollar bill pinned to the inside of her sweater in case she has an altercation with her escort and needs to hail a taxi."

"It's Florida," Ms. Olivia reminds him. "It's sunny, I don't need a passport, and I have traveler's checks in my purse."

"And what if you're at sea and The Individual kidnaps you and sells you into white slavery in South America?"

All week Mr. Bernard has been referring to Ottavio as "The Individual" or "The Swarthy Individual." However, Ms. Olivia only chastises him for the latter depiction since she doesn't mind defamation of character for personal habits or backward beliefs, but she vehemently disagrees with stereotyping along the lines of race, religion, or gender.

After we arrive and gather to say good-bye at the departure gate, Ms. Olivia turns and addresses us wistfully: "I love you all very much and I know you think that I'm deranged and irresponsible. But you're all young. The bluebells and the hollyhocks, the dogwood trees and the iris spears all bloomed this year, but not for me. For me it's been winter for the past six years." And with that she waves a book of D. H. Lawrence poetry at us, gracefully turns, and disappears down the jetway.

On the escalator Mr. Bernard actually sheds a tear and doesn't bother to wipe it away. Mr. Gil places his hand on Mr. Bernard's shoulder.

"I just wish she wasn't so *blithe* about leaving," Mr. Bernard says sadly.

At least I now know that blithe means "carefree." And Ms. Olivia wasn't so excited about her vacation that she'd forgotten about our tutorials. While she's away I'm supposed to read *The Cherry Orchard* and a thirty-page chapter in *The American Pageant* about the Spanish-American War. Then I have to E-mail her my questions and observations and she's going to find a cyber-café in Florida where she can retrieve them, make comments, and suggest an essay topic. The Age of Technology definitely has its drawbacks.

"Your mother has a point, Bertie," Mr. Gil eventually says. "We don't live this thing day to day the way she does. Olivia is sixty-two," he pauses, "by her own count," he adds doubtfully, "but she looks fifty-five and has the energy of a forty-year-old."

"That's because she doesn't eat her own cooking and she possesses the common sense of a teenager."

"Hey!" I say. "I'm a teenager and I have common sense."

Mr. Bernard looks over and smiles at me. "*Excusez-moi*, I meant the common sense of a ten-year-old. *Your* ear is so close to the ground that it probably has ticks in it."

"Thank you," I say.

Mr. Bernard mumbles something about "growing old disgracefully."

"Yes, but what would we do without Olivia?" says Mr. Gil.

"The more appropriate question is what do we do *with* her," replies Mr. Bernard.

We walk the rest of the way through the airport and out to the parking lot in stony silence, concentrating on stepping over pools of salty slush and avoiding small but murderous patches of ice. Mr. Bernard and Mr. Gil clamber into the backseat of the *QE2*.

"I just pray that he's not a psychopath," Mr. Bernard finally says, exhaling loudly. "We should have made her leave behind that photo of him that she has in her computer in case we need to file it with Interpol."

"I don't think Ottavio is a psychopath." Not only have I seen his picture and read some of his letters, but I've even talked to him on the phone for a few minutes. He sounds normal enough to me, aside from the broken English and heavy Italian accent.

Mr. Gil states in what I assume is intended to be a reassuring voice, "I'm sure he's quite affable, and a real gentleman."

"That's what I'm afraid of," Mr. Bernard forlornly admits, then suddenly perks up. "To the Garden of Eatin'! We will drown our collective sorrow in blueberry blintzes with sour cream and Barry Manilow ballads from the wall-mounted jukebox. It's the only suitable course of action to take at a time such as this."

We pig out on blueberry blintzes and then go back to the house. Almost as soon as we walk in the door the phone rings. Mr. Bernard frets that Ms. Olivia's plane has gone down but then is elated by the possibility that she's changed her mind about the trip.

But it turns out to be Craig. "Your plan is working." His voice is eager with excitement. "I just received another statement. All three stocks have gone down in value, and one sunk by almost half. Now what?"

"Time for phase two," I say softly. "After school tomorrow, go to the brokerage firm and say you want to cash out your account." I look around to make sure that Mr. Bernard isn't within earshot. "Then ask for a check to be mailed to you for however much is left."

"What if they ask why I'm closing the account after such a short time?"

"It's your money, you can do whatever you want with it."

"You mean it's *your* money," says Craig. "Are you sure you can afford to lose it? Don't you want to wait and see if the stocks come back?"

"I can't imagine they will, at least not in our lifetimes."

"Do you want to go out on Friday night?"

Do I want to? Oh, I want to a lot, but I hesitate. "I promised Mr. Gil I'd help paint one of the backdrops for his play. What about Saturday?"

"Basketball," says Craig.

Just then Mr. Bernard enters the kitchen.

"I'll call you tomorrow," I say and hang up the phone.

Mr. Bernard wears a funny expression, as if he's got some big secret on me.

"What?" I say defensively.

"Lots of mysterious phone calls lately," he says. And then he starts teasing me by singing a song from *Gigi* using a fake French accent: *Zhank heaven, for little girls! Zhey grow up in ze most delightful way. Those little eyes so helpless and appealing, one day will flash and send you crashin' through the ceilin'.*

Pretending to ignore him, I walk out of the room, but my face feels hot all of a sudden, so I glance in the mirror only to discover that I look as if I've just blown twenty bucks at the rouge counter in Nordstrom's.

Playing Close to the Vest

♣

It's been almost a month since Ms. Olivia returned from her vacation with eyes sparkling like blue cake-icing and a mysterious extra tote bag. However, because of Bernard's feelings about Ottavio the subject of the trip is never mentioned.

On the Sunday morning before Christmas, which falls on Tuesday, we all lounge around the living room in our pajamas. Normally Mr. Bernard and Mr. Gil would have bounded out of the house by 7:30 A.M. on a holiday weekend, but there won't be any more garage sales until January. Instead they just lie around exchanging sections of the Sunday *Cleveland Plain Dealer* while I plow through *Anna Karenina*, since Ms. Olivia hasn't seen fit to declare a Christmas break from our tutorials.

When Mr. Bernard hears her delicate step on the stairs, he looks up from the magazine section as if he's been waiting for her. "Did Dad eat anything?"

"Not a bite."

She detours toward us, still carrying the silver tray that holds a glass of orange juice, a plate of scrambled eggs, and toast, all untouched.

"He took a few sips of water, but I think that's only because his mouth was dry."

"Do you think he's in any pain?" Mr. Gil looks up from the sports section. "Should we call the doctor?"

"No, no. We've hit bad patches like this before. But we must accept the fact that he's declining faster than the doctor predicted."

Ms. Olivia sighs and appears tearful, but then moves her fluttery hand up to her mouth, takes a deep breath, and composes herself. "I think it's partially because he no longer comprehends what food is . . . why one needs to eat."

Mr. Bernard sets down his newspaper and clears his throat as if he's about to say something but doesn't. Instead he just stretches out on the floor and stares up at the ceiling as if he's always envisioned himself as being marked for tragedy and the moment is finally upon us. Ms. Olivia shifts her concern from the Judge to her son. "Bertie, I want you to get out and do something this afternoon. You sat around here all day yesterday, and it's making me feel as if we're holding a death vigil. Go to the art gallery."

"The gallery is closed. It's Sunday, Mother. If you'd been brought up in a proper churchgoing family, you'd know that."

Ignoring him, Ms. Olivia rests the silver tray on top of the banister. "Then go look at the store windows or else see a film."

Mr. Bernard places his hands behind his head and addresses the ceiling. "I shop for a living, Mother. I own a shop. And I'm certainly not about to patronize one of these holiday blockbusters where a hundred million dollars is spent on explosives detonated to a backdrop of movie stars making cops and robbers quips."

Just then Rocky comes down the stairs and appears worried at the sight of Mr. Bernard sprawled on the floor. He scampers over and checks his wrist for a pulse and puts his ear to Mr. Bernard's chest.

"Get out of here, you drunken gorilla," snaps Mr. Bernard and pushes Rocky away. The chimp whimpers and retreats to where Ms. Olivia is standing and hides his face behind her skirt.

"That wasn't necessary, Bernard!" she says in a terse voice that I've never heard before. "I will not tolerate unkindness, especially to animals. Now, I'm telling you once and for all, I want you *out* of here today. And that goes for you as well." She lifts the tray slightly and aims it at Mr. Gil. "And you, too." She points her silver tray in my direction as if it's a cattle prod.

Mr. Bernard abruptly sits up, scrutinizes his mother, and then narrows his eyes. "Are you sure you don't have some euthanasia scheme up the sleeve of your flowered housedress?"

"Don't be ridiculous!" replies Ms. Olivia. "However, I'd better see a car pulling out of the driveway in exactly one hour! I'm not kidding," she says and stalks out of the room.

"Mother, I'll have you locked up if you're planning a murder! I swear to God I won't cover for you. It's not like slipping quarters in expired parking meters. You'll do hard time!"

"Bertie, you're being paranoid," Mr. Gil states calmly. "She's not going to knock him off. She loves your father."

"I *know* she does. That's what I'm afraid of . . . she doesn't want him to suffer."

"You've been in his room today. Does he appear to be in pain?"

"No."

"And she certainly isn't trying to organize an elopement with Ottavio."

"My nemesis. The swarthy soldier of fortune waiting in the wings of the stage drama that has become my life."

"Good heavens. You really are losing it. Livvy's right. Let's go somewhere. I'm getting dust mites in my Docksiders from sitting around here. What do you think, Hallie?"

I'm actually thinking how yesterday Ms. Olivia confided in me that she and Ottavio did indeed meet on the Internet, but it wasn't about art; it was about her looking for a new courier for the morning-after pills. Ottavio was more than glad to oblige. He started sending them by mail. And then after they met in Florida Ms. Olivia arrived back with a fresh supply in her extra tote bag. Only I had a feeling he'd become much more than a courier and a poet to her.

"Hallie, what do you think we should do?" Mr. Gil asks again.

I don't know what to suggest, because I haven't a clue as to what gay guys in their thirties do for recreation. They both enjoy the ballet and garden shows and Mr. Gil likes baseball, but I don't exactly have any ideas for a cold December afternoon two days before Christmas.

"Want to go look at the decorations in the mall?" I ask.

"Too crowded," says Mr. Gil.

"Too much materialism," laments Mr. Bernard.

Then I do get an idea. Bernard is always telling me that I should learn how to apply makeup and discover my feminine wiles. So I offer to get a makeover from one of those painted ladies down at the cosmetics store.

"You're pretty the way you are," Mr. Bernard tells me. "Don't get involved with those Lancôme Jezebels. You'll only end up overplucking your eyebrows and developing an eating disorder."

Boy, Mr. Bernard is really in the dumps if he's rejecting the quest for greater cosmetology. He loves to bring home magazine photos of hairstyles for Ms. Olivia and me to try.

"Does anyone like to ice-skate?" I ask halfheartedly.

Ms. Olivia reenters the room carrying a cup of tea that smells of freshly sliced lemons. "That's a wonderful idea. Then come home and have chili and a hot toddy."

"I don't feel like skating," Mr. Bernard announces like a sulky teenager.

"How about the Rock and Roll Hall of Fame?" Mr. Gil suggests. "We haven't been there in a while. I'll give Hallie a guided tour of the Rolling Stones display."

"After he *ruined* the Louvre?" Mr. Bernard raises his voice, as if he's suddenly awoken from a nap.

"Mick Jagger trashed the Louvre?" I ask.

"No, the architect I. M. Pei. I refuse to look at tinted glass pyramids while in an unmedicated state."

"We could watch *My Fair Lady* again and look for more clues that Professor Higgins and Colonel Pickering were more than *roommates*," I say. That was one of Mr. Bernard's favorites. He insisted there was a lot more to the song "A Hymn to Him" than the average viewer realized.

"*As if* we need more proof. They can't show *her* boudoir enough, but never *theirs*."

"Then what do *you* want to do?" asks Mr. Gil. "Because Livvy is right. We need to get out for a while."

"If only Judy Garland were here," Mr. Bernard replies forlornly. "We could all go into the summerhouse and dress up and put on a show." Mr. Gil ignores his reference to *Girl Crazy*, which Mr. Bernard had made us all watch on video the day before. Mr. Bernard loves Judy Garland and claims he holds a master's degree in "Judyism," only he warns me not to use her as a role model because she didn't live a healthy lifestyle, and also, she let people take advantage of her.

"I know!" Mr. Gil exclaims. "Let's play Jew-Christian. We haven't done that at all this year."

Ms. Olivia arrives back at the bottom of the stairs carrying a stack of fresh linens. "Oh, that inane game! You don't even know the difference between the two."

"Of course I do," says Mr. Bernard indignantly. "When the Messiah comes the Jews will say, 'It's lovely to see you,' while the Christians will say, 'It's so nice to see you *again*.' "

"Very well, then," says Ms. Olivia. "Anything to get you all outdoors."

"It's too homogeneous around here," Mr. Bernard complains. "Plastic Santas and those awful strings of white lights that are supposed to resemble icicles. We'd have to drive to the Cleveland suburbs."

"Splendid!" says Ms. Olivia. "I'll pay for the gas. Now go and play your game in Shaker Heights."

"Excuse me," I finally manage to interrupt the organizers. "But what the heck is Jew-Christian?"

"You drive past a home and from the holiday decorations you see who can be the first to determine whether it's a Jewish or Christian home." Mr. Gil explains this as if it's the national pastime after the Super Bowl is over.

I'm just glad to be doing something that Mr. Bernard is enthusiastic about. When he's depressed it drains all the fun out of the day. And I've never driven the Buick to Cleveland before.

"Mother, I have a wonderful idea. Why don't you join us? I'll call Nurse Ratched to come over."

"Thank you, dear, but I don't need anyone *spying* on me. And it's Nurse *Radcliffe*, Bertie, and you know it. Stop that name nonsense this instant or you're going to accidentally say it wrong in front of her," Ms. Olivia chides him. "Remember what happened with Esther Anne Dingman? She was one of your best customers, only you called her Esther Anne Dingbat around the house so often that you eventually said it right to her face."

"Well, she didn't have good taste—always buying that dreadful Depression glass." He makes the face he reserves for when the liver pâté for the beef Wellington has spoiled. "Nurse *Radcliffe* can sit with Father and we'll all go for a drive in the countryside and chop down a tree."

"If you want I can stay here," I offer.

"That's very considerate of you, Hallie, but the best thing you can do is get some fresh air." She eyes my open copy of Tolstoy's novel. "I'm sure you've had enough Russian tragedy for one afternoon." Ms. Olivia turns and starts back up the stairs.

"You see, Mother, even Hallie's anxious about leaving you on your own here and she's never even *seen Arsenic and Old Lace*," Mr. Bernard calls after her.

"Shush now, all of you," she says. "I'll see you after dinner. And not a moment before."

After Ms. Olivia disappears, Mr. Gil says, "She can be a trial."

"More like a jury," Mr. Bernard answers. But he rises and folds up the scattered newspapers, and I assume we're off to Cleveland in search of the holiday spirit.

Losing Streak

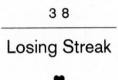

The day before Christmas the Judge is diagnosed with pneumonia. He won't eat or even take a sip of juice when Ms. Olivia puts the straw right up to his chapped lips. Eventually she has to dribble a teaspoon of water into his mouth every half hour or so. But I don't see him swallow. The water is only absorbed by his parched tongue. When the doctor arrives, Ms. Olivia and Mr. Bernard discuss inserting a feeding tube in hushed tones outside the Judge's bedroom door.

Ms. Olivia blames herself for his illness and keeps insisting that the house is too drafty, that cold air is leaking in from all sides and we need new insulation. By now she has caulked the bottom of every doorjamb with a towel or bath mat, and then she has me go around and tape plastic over all the windows.

This is all despite the doctor explaining to her that the Judge's sudden and rapid decline isn't anybody's fault. Sick people just contract pneumonia when their bodies can no longer fight everyday germs and the lungs can no longer filter air, he says. And even though the doctor hooks up an oxygen tank for the Judge and gives him shots filled with large doses of antibiotics, I understand that recovery isn't in the cards. At this stage of the game it's about comfort, not convalescence. I'm standing in the kitchen when the doctor murmurs to Mr. Bernard, "Pneumonia is a friend to the very old and to those who are suffering."

Everyone quietly pads around, not at all filled with the Christmas spirit, but trying to fake it for the benefit of everyone else. Mr. Bernard distracts himself by whipping up a batch of highly decorated yet androgynous "gingerbread persons" for the Unitarians who regularly stop by to visit.

After lunch Mr. Gil arrives home with a lovely and delicious-smelling Douglas fir tree so fresh that it still has lots of sticky pinecones hidden within its branches. He attempts to rally us into tree-trimming mode by building a roaring fire in the living room and then playing Angela Lansbury singing "We Need a Little Christmas" on the stereo. By working together, Mr. Gil and I somehow manage to unearth the boxes containing all the decorations from out of the bowels of the garage. Everything is gorgeous—antique handblown colored glass ornaments housing miniature Christmas scenes, individually wrapped in yellowed tissue paper and then packed in their own cardboard boxes. There are strings of lights where each bulb is surrounded by a hand-stitched red poinsettia and three dark green leaves. At the bottom is a porcelain angel in an ivory-colored moiré gown trimmed with gold lace.

Ms. Olivia and Mr. Bernard remain upstairs with the Judge while Mr. Gil and I set the tree in its stand. After we've watered it and strung the lights Mr. Bernard comes down, hangs one ornament, and then dejectedly goes back upstairs. Even Mr. Gil loses interest and excuses himself to go buy more starter blocks for the fireplace.

I end up hanging most of the decorations by myself. It's the first time I've ever single-handedly trimmed a tree. At my house the installation of the Christmas tree is more like a seven-car pileup—kids accidentally smashing ornaments while crunching on all the candy canes that were supposed to be for the tree. Then there is the baby choking on tinsel and Dad stabbing himself while crafting makeshift ornament hooks out of paper clips.

Though I must admit, it could be fun. Mom makes colored popcorn that we're supposed to string on red thread and hang on the tree, only we end up eating most of it or using it for ammunition in a war. I now realize how an only child must feel. Sure, you get to do everything all by yourself, but somehow it isn't quite the same.

Eventually the tree looks festive enough, though it's still a far cry from the one in Mr. Bernard's shop window. After dinner we pull chairs around the Douglas fir and sip eggnog. Everyone appears slightly less pale in the soft pink glow cast by the tree lights.

When Mr. Bernard is angry or upset he tends to prepare incredibly complicated desserts. The more layers of puff pastry, chocolate sauce made from scratch, and flambéing, the better. He's currently working his way through a Neapolitan cookbook, and so he goes out to the kitchen and comes back with slices of freshly made zuccotto on Christmas plates. It's an Italian dessert that's similar to a chilled pound cake, but with lots of nuts and basted with brandy. Mr. Bernard and Ms. Olivia take just one bite before abandoning their plates on the coffee table. Then Ms. Olivia heads back upstairs.

After clearing up, we all gather in the Judge's bedroom and take turns reading from A Christmas Carol. Every year as far back as Mr. Bernard can remember the Judge read the Dickens story aloud on Christmas Eve. As a boy Mr. Bernard took the part of Tiny Tim and Ms. Olivia would play Mrs. Cratchit and also the Ghost of Christmas Past.

Outside the window dazzling fairy tale snowflakes fall gently to the ground like white ashes, while the Judge sleeps through most of the half-hearted performance. And when he's not dozing he only peers up at us sleepily. Mr. Bernard is becoming more stressed out by the minute. He wants to do something. Mr. Gil says that Mr. Bernard has what is known in business as an "activist" personality—in other words, he's not happy unless something is happening. But there isn't anything to be done.

Ms. Olivia has spent the better part of the past few days sitting next to the Judge's bedside and stroking his forehead and gently running her fingers through his thick white hair. His features appear faded, as if his entire being is slowly vanishing before our eyes. Rocky usually sits on the bed and holds one of the Judge's hands between both of his, as if mourning the fact that they can no longer play their favorite game of placing hand over hand.

"Do you think he knows you're here?" I ask, trying not to sound impolite.

"He may not know it's me, but he's aware that someone is here with him." Ms. Olivia is looking drained, too. Her normally cheerful voice crinkles like wax paper.

"Oh. I'm sure he knows it's you and not some nurse in a hospital," I try to reassure her.

She places her finely boned hands around one of his. Just beneath the surface of his practically transparent skin are purplish veins knotted like earthworms.

I hope that if I ever go senile someone will be kind enough to care for me, rather than leave me arguing with an imaginary friend on a park bench. How do you arrange such things, I wonder. Obviously it pays to be nice to people since you don't know how, when, or where the chips are going to fall. Would my mother and father take me in if I were sick, or even dying? I feel sure they would. In fact, my mother would probably give me one of her kidneys if I needed it. Maybe it's time to grow up and take the long view on the family situation. Though it would be a lot easier if they'd quit telling me what to do all of the time. Eric tried to negotiate a truce so I could visit them on Christmas. But my parents said yes only if I promised to spend the night, a major deal breaker.

With a little luck I won't get terminally ill until my mid- to late twenties—giving me at least a few more years to iron things out.

Covering All Bets

★

On Christmas morning the Judge is drifting in and out of consciousness. A few presents have appeared under the tree. Mr. Bernard is in the kitchen making meringue cookies and Mr. Gil is chopping wood in the backyard with Rocky, who is getting some exercise by climbing the trees.

After a late lunch we sit around the living room listening to Mr. Bernard's favorite recording of the *Messiah*, by the Christ Church Cathedral Choir, and I enjoy a slice from one of his freshly baked pecan pies.

For Christmas I give Mr. Bernard a large metal organizer grid that attaches to the wall in the kitchen. It has adjustable plastic hooks for hanging all the pots, pans, ladles, and colanders.

Mr. Bernard appears to truly admire my gift and declares, "It's wonderful! I'll install it immediately."

"Sure you will," Mr. Gil says sarcastically. "Hallie, I give you permission to put it up tonight. Bertie organizes the kitchen about as often as Livvy remembers to take care of her rose garden. Whatever did we do without this during last summer's gelled food phase when stainless-steel molds took over the entire first floor?" he says to me.

"It was an unseasonably hot summer," Mr. Bernard defends himself.

"Gelled food?" I ask. "Like Jell-O?" I can't imagine Mr. Bernard allowing the use of Jell-O in his sophisticated menus.

"Gelatin, when used properly, is the basis for many epicurean delights.

Past generations that were culinarily in the know feasted upon tomato aspic. And what about that vegetable terrine, Gil? You enjoyed that."

"What about the smoked fish consommé and the shrimp jelly and the yogurt-cucumber gelatin and the jellied mango fruit soup?" Mr. Gil says and grimaces at the recollection.

"You should be grateful I didn't prepare a repast of gellied eels. Back in the twenties they were considered a Sunday-morning treat for London's East End working class. I think this coming year Hallie and I will cook only for ourselves," harrumphs Mr. Bernard, "while you and *Maman* feast on Swanson Hungry Man frozen dinners with tinfoil tops and little squares of peach cobbler held together by molecules of nuclear waste. Or perhaps Mother can whip you up one of her special vegetarian *E. coli* cassoulets."

I can't help but giggle. I love it when Ms. Olivia and Mr. Gil torture Mr. Bernard about his cooking and he finally retaliates by threatening to send them to the Wendy's drive-thru for a Frosty with a taco salad for their Sunday dinner. He loves to tell me that Ms. Olivia never uses four-letter words—specifically cook, wash, iron, and dust.

Mr. Bernard presents me with the Victorian Christmas shadow box that I'd admired in his store way back in the fall, the first week I worked for the Stocktons. He's wrapped it beautifully in black tissue paper and a wide silver lamé ribbon. I'm flabbergasted.

"This is worth a lot of money!" I exclaim. "You could sell it."

"No, no. I want you to have it. We antique dealers are a funny lot. When it comes to a special piece we're like dachshund breeders—the most important thing is that it goes to a good home where it will be cared for and appreciated."

"Speaking of dog breeders," Ms. Olivia interjects, "did you read about the three puppy farms that the police disbanded outside of Dayton? Squalor, neglect, and inbreeding. It's all so terrible. I don't understand why more people don't adopt from animal shelters. There are so many unwanted pets."

"They want purebreds, brand names," explains Mr. Gil.

"Well, if it's good enough to take potluck when you have a child, I can't see why we need genetically engineered pets."

It was the first I'd heard Ms. Olivia rail about any of her causes since the Judge had taken ill, and frankly I was more than a little relieved to hear the start of one of what Mr. Bernard referred to as her "fireside harangues." I've heard stories about people who've been married a long time, where one gets sick and dies and then the other person croaks right afterward.

"I think we should organize a boycott of the pet stores that patronize these horrible places," Ms. Olivia states.

"A capital idea, Mother," Mr. Bernard says diplomatically. "But let's rather just try and make it through to Groundhog's Day without having you placed in a maximum-security rest home."

"Sometimes I don't know why you bother living in a democracy when you never want to participate in it," says Ms. Olivia.

"I'm registered to vote, and I think the public library is a wonderful institution," says Mr. Bernard.

"Bertie would much prefer a monarchy," says Mr. Gil. "More commemorative tea towels and spoons and hot plates to sell to tourists down at the shop. All with a royal seal on them."

"How would you like that, Hallie?" Ms. Olivia asks. "A monarchy?"

"I don't think so," I reply. "There's a saying in poker, you know, that you shouldn't put your trust in kings and queens because three of a kind will take them all."

They all think this is amusing, though I don't quite understand why. Obviously they've never dropped a whole pile of money to some jerk's three deuces against their pair of cowboys in a poker game, or else they wouldn't be laughing so hard.

And although Mr. Bernard jokes that he's renewed Ms. Olivia's membership in the Revolution of the Month Club, she doesn't give or receive any holiday presents. At first I assume it's because she's been preoccupied with the Judge's condition. Only it turns out that she *never* gives Christmas presents. Ms. Olivia believes that gift giving is preposterous and that people should exchange tokens of their affection when they feel moved to do so and not because of some holiday on the Gregorian calendar. Also, she insists that Christmas is discriminatory to minorities.

Mr. Bernard informs me that back when Ms. Olivia was in her prime, she actually managed to get a referendum placed before the county in order to declare public institutions "Yule-Free Zones."

"It'd be a better idea to install Yule-Free Zones in the stores," offers Mr. Gil. "Pity the poor Jew or Hindu who is trying to buy a tube of toothpaste on December 24 and having to wait in line behind fifty Christians with all of their double-sided Scotch tape, honey-glazed hams, and mistletoe."

Mr. Gil presents Mr. Bernard with a singing bird clock. It's in the shape of a cuckoo clock, except instead of a bird popping out every hour you're treated to a nine-second live recording of one of twelve North American bird songs. Fortunately a built-in light sensor hushes the tweeters when the room goes dark.

Mr. Bernard adores the clock and claims that it will make a wonderful conversation piece for the front of his store—right up there with the pair of antique Van Erp lamps that Mr. Gil had jerry-rigged with clappers. "Perhaps my next window display will be Chia pets grown in porcelain marriage pieces from the Ming dynasty." He looks up at Ms. Olivia in what I think is a rather hopeful way in order to gauge her reaction to this silly suggestion.

She laughs. This appears to satisfy Mr. Bernard, and he finally smiles and takes a bite of his pie. Then he says, "Hallie, go and get Rocky." I'm surprised, because the two of them have been steering clear of each other the past few days.

I find Rocky sitting in the chair at the Judge's bedside. When Ms. Olivia needs to get up he usually takes her place and mimics her exact movements, putting his hand to the Judge's cheek and then gently stroking his head. We come downstairs and Mr. Bernard hands Rocky a box. He sniffs it before ripping open the top and pulling out a bottle of Hiram Walker sloe gin. Rocky immediately recognizes the label and begins to hoot with excitement. He runs over to Mr. Bernard and embraces him with those long furry arms. Mr. Bernard hugs him back and says with ceremonious gravity, "I wish to formally apologize for the remark I passed the other day. You're a good chimp, and I'm only sad that Charles Darwin wasn't able to enjoy the fruit of his labors by watching you mix a Harvey Wallbanger."

4 0

Lucky Stars

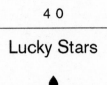

It's five o'clock when we finish talking and opening presents. Just as Mr. Gil is about to venture out and retrieve more firewood I hear the faint strains of "God Rest Ye, Merry Gentlemen" approaching the front porch. Pushing back the thick brocaded curtains reveals a group of carolers bundled up in colorful hats and scarves and carrying old-fashioned oil lamps.

"Let nothing you dismay, born is Christ our savior upon this Christmas Day."

Ms. Olivia practically leaps from her chair to swing open the front door and welcome the impromptu performance. I've noticed that even though she claims to be against Christmas in principle, Ms. Olivia appreciates all the trappings—candles in the window, the lighted tree, watching a performance of *The Nutcracker* on public television.

Aside from ruddy cheeks and fresh snow caked on the bottom of their pants, the carolers appear warm and cheerful. It's a clear evening, and though an early-morning snow blankets the neighborhood, it isn't too cold outside and a glorious winter sunset is painted across the sky.

"Dad used to love to go caroling," Mr. Bernard says wistfully to no one in particular. "He used to pull me along in that old-fashioned wooden sleigh, singing *dashing through the snow, in a one-horse open sleigh, laughing all the way, to Grandma's house we'll go.* I believe he rather fancied himself a Clydesdale horse."

"I saw the sleigh in the garage," I say. "With the bright gold stars painted on the sides."

"That was my own added touch," says Mr. Bernard. "I think by then Father was getting the idea that I wouldn't be applying to law school."

Ms. Olivia turns and gazes toward the staircase as the first verse of "O, Come All Ye Faithful" rises from the front walk.

"I can't stand this anymore," says Ms. Olivia. "This is *not* the way your father would wish to die."

"What *are* you talking about, Mother? He certainly wouldn't want to die in the hospital. There's nothing they can do for him there that we can't do here at home."

"I don't mean that. We're going caroling," says Ms. Olivia, her airy voice rising with excitement. "Bernard, get his coat and find a warm blanket. Gil, fetch a couple of flashlights. Hallie, take the sleigh out of the garage."

At first Mr. Gil and Mr. Bernard and I just stand around like lawn ornaments and stare at one another. But then Mr. Bernard opens the closet door and Mr. Gil goes toward the cellar and so I throw on my coat and head for the garage. Outside the last pale colors of the day are crushed on the horizon. Dark will come quickly, as it always does in wintertime.

Soon Mr. Bernard is gently arranging his father's frail body in the old wooden sleigh and Ms. Olivia carefully tucks a blanket around the Judge. Mr. Gil has dug up some old lanterns that he hangs on the back of the curved wooden handles.

Then we put the rope around Mr. Bernard as if he's a team of oxen and he pulls the sleigh in the direction of the carolers. As we move down the driveway a string of rusty bells attached to a cracked leather bandeau ring out as they bounce against the tops of the runners. The sleigh glides easily across the snow-covered lawns, as if the Judge weighs hardly an ounce. In fact, the Judge doesn't weigh much more than a hundred and twenty pounds now, and I'd rubbed some cross-country ski wax onto the bottom of the runners.

By the time we reach the next house the dull cast to the Judge's eyes seems to have been replaced by a faint glimmer of recognition and a smile, as if the shock of the cold air has momentarily sparked his system back to life. He gazes up at the snow-crusted pine trees and then at the moon rising and the frosty stars beginning to wink overhead. Ms. Olivia trots a few paces ahead, humming "Angels We Have Heard on High" along with the carolers.

We only follow the merry band to the end of the street. They turn left down Sandpiper Lane and we swing around and head for home. By the time we carefully put the Judge back into bed, he falls into a peaceful slumber.

Everyone is exhilarated from the outing and it feels as if the spirit of Christmas has finally come to 48 Nuthatch Lane.

4 1

The Final Round

♦

The Judge fades away an hour past dawn on the morning of December 26. The funeral is scheduled for Friday, in two days' time. The forty-eight hours leading up to it are a blur of preparations, phone calls, running errands, and making lists. There's a tremendous sense of relief in no longer waiting around. We're like a battalion of soldiers that has finally received orders and, though not cheered by the cause, are thankful to be mobilized.

Ms. Olivia unplugs her computer from the second phone jack and sets up an auxiliary telephone which she uses to deliver the sad but inevitable news to friends and relatives, organize the newspaper obituary, and arrange the order of the service with her minister. I notice she's making a lot more trips to the backyard, and I can smell the leathery richness of her French cigarettes when she comes back inside.

Mr. Gil mans the constant stream of deliveries to the front door—flowers, food, fruit baskets. And he answers a continuously ringing main phone line—condolence calls, people needing the details of the funeral, and out-of-towners wanting directions.

Meanwhile I shuttle back and forth to town, picking up whatever items appear on the lists that the three of them keep feeding me. Mr. Bernard plans to have family members and select funeralgoers back to the house, and so there's a great quantity of provisions needed. Having completed one list, I am immediately de-bagged and sent back out with the next one. I must admit, I feel like a grown-up standing in line at the delicatessen asking for fresh pork tenderloin and three pounds of Norwegian smoked salmon. "Anything else for you today, ma'am?" the counterman asks, as if I'm thirty-two years old.

When I return from a mission to the Party Place in order to load up on paper cocktail napkins and to the hardware store for Sterno cans to put underneath the chafing dishes, Mr. Bernard is waving a hanger holding one of his father's blue serge suits at Ms. Olivia.

"So what if it's too big," Mr. Bernard is saying. "No one will notice the length of the sleeves when he's lying down."

"Why waste a good suit that we can otherwise donate to the Helping Hands so that some young man can use it for a job interview or wear it to his arraignment?" Ms. Olivia argues. "It's going to be a closed casket anyway."

"If it's all the same to you, Mother, I'd rather have an open casket."

"I'm sorry, dear, but it's already been settled," Ms. Olivia says firmly.

"Well, I'll just call the funeral director and change it and run the suit over," says Mr. Bernard.

They're arguing in the dining room, but I don't want them to think I'm eavesdropping and so I enter the kitchen and allow the clatter of the Sterno cans hitting the sink basin to announce my arrival. It's the only available space left.

"Oh, Hallie's back," Mr. Bernard says. "She can run his clothes over to the funeral parlor right now.

"Hallie . . . ," Mr. Bernard calls into the kitchen.

I enter the dining room, still wearing my winter coat and carrying a fistful of dry cleaning.

Mr. Bernard turns to me. "Hallie, would you mind taking Dad's suit, a clean shirt, and his good patent leather shoes over to the funeral parlor? Let me just dash upstairs and find his favorite cuff links—the ones shaped like gavels."

"Bernard, I'd really rather leave things as they are." Ms. Olivia frowns and glances down, clasping and unclasping hands as fragile as moth wings.

"Mother, I don't understand what difference it makes. I would like to see my father one last time if it's all the same to you. And to see him as I remember him."

I gently remove the suit from Mr. Bernard's hand, since he's only using it to gesticulate and emphasize the points of his argument. Besides, if he wins I'll be the one to take it to the funeral home. If Ms. Olivia wins, I'll take it back upstairs with all the dry cleaning.

Ms. Olivia fingers the tattered address book she's been using all afternoon to make phone calls and then puts it back down on the sideboard and sighs. "Bertie . . . ," she begins tentatively, "your father is gone."

"I *know* that, Mother. I'm not entertaining the idea that he's going to leap out of the casket and dance a jig. I just want a proper funeral, that's all."

"Bertie dear, I mean he's gone. The casket will be empty."

"What do you mean he's *gone*?" Mr. Bernard asks, stunned. He places both hands on the dining room table for support and leans forward.

"*Gone* where?"

"I donated him to the University of Ohio for Alzheimer's research."

"But the hearse—"

"The hearse took him to the university."

"Jesus Christ, Mother! How could you do this without telling me?!" He yells at her like I've never seen before, all the distress of the last few days finally coming out in a torrent of rage. Even his forehead is clenched.

But Ms. Olivia remains perfectly calm. "I didn't want to upset you."

"Upset me?" he shouts.

"Yes," Ms. Olivia says. "Upset you. And I'm sorry, Bertie, but there's nothing to be done about it now. You must think of your father as a flower that propagates by dying." She glances up at the black mahogany grandfather clock. "He arrived at the university late this morning. His brain is already in a jar of formaldehyde with a masking tape label on the top."

"Mother, don't make jokes. This isn't funny. I can't believe you did this! Get him *back*!"

"Bernard, darling, your father didn't know he was going to get Alzheimer's disease, so this wasn't something we discussed. But you must believe me when I say that I based my decision on what I know he would have wanted."

Mr. Bernard collapses into the nearest dining room chairs as if his legs have suddenly given way.

"Do you remember that time when you were a boy and your father ran in front of a streetcar and saved the life of that little girl?" Ms. Olivia continues. "And a photographer happened to be nearby and his picture was on the front page of the newspaper the next day?"

"Of course. The title was THE VERDICT IS IN: JUDGE IS LOCAL HERO."

"Your father didn't know that little girl from Eve, Bernard. He didn't know her parents or anything about her. And he never saw her again after that day. The family wasn't even from Ohio. Are you going to tell me he risked his life to have his picture in the newspaper?"

"Certainly not. But that's different." He appears to regain his composure slightly. "I—I only wish that you had discussed this with me."

"I'm sorry. I was wrong not to do so. But you know as well as I do that by donating his brain to medicine your father will be helping others. And someday it could be one of us who has Alzheimer's disease, perhaps you or Gil or Hallie, or even Hallie's children."

"Or you," Mr. Bernard adds philosophically.

"Perhaps me, too," she says brightly. "Only I'm afraid that I'm a little old to benefit from the current round of medical advances. In fact, why don't you donate my brain to the university as well? That way your father and I will be together."

"Ohhhh, Mother," Mr. Bernard exhales for a long moment, "I highly doubt the government is going to permit anyone to go poking around inside that mind of yours once you've finally finished with it. Were it to fall into the wrong hands it would most certainly constitute a threat to our national security."

The Fix Is In

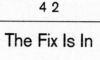

The morning of the memorial service dawns blustery and gray. An ice pick of a wind is screaming off Lake Erie and a storm is forecast for the afternoon. It's slow going to the funeral parlor, and Mr. Gil says he regrets not bothering to put chains on the tires.

Inside the funeral parlor it's humid and there is an aroma of 409 cleansing spray combined with my grandmother's Chantilly perfume. As we walk into the room reserved for the Judge I have a sneezing fit. There aren't any other names spelled out in removable white plastic letters on the black felt board other than Stockton, and so I assume that Christmas is a slow time for death, unlike the Fourth of July, when lots of people drown or blow themselves up with fireworks.

Mr. Bernard ushers me into the small private grieving alcove where there's a cubbyhole for personal belongings and strategically placed tissue boxes. He whispers that he's not convinced the casket is empty and wants me to go up and peek inside.

"Why me?" I whisper back.

"Because *you're* the reformed con artist," he says. "You can appear nonchalant while casing a coffin."

"I never did anything *illegal*," I argue. "I was just underage, that's all."

"Okay, I take it back. You're the one who's skilled at sneaking into betting parlors, pool halls, poker games, casinos, and other places where you're not supposed to be. You're the one who can pick the window lock when I forget my keys. You're the one who knows how to get free long distance on any pay phone."

He says all this in a complimentary manner; therefore, I feel more inclined to help him.

"All you need to do is lift the casket lid slightly and see if you can identify an arm or an ear or something. I'll distract Mother so that she doesn't see you."

"Okay, but I want a raise."

"Deal."

"And an electric hedge trimmer."

"*And* an electric hedge trimmer."

I put out my hand and Mr. Bernard shakes it. Then I head toward the front of the room and Mr. Bernard walks quickly to the rear, where Ms. Olivia is greeting the attendees as they slowly file in through the vestibule.

Sidling up to the casket I consider how to negotiate the huge memorial wreath with the big molded-plastic spray- painted gold scales of justice wired to the top of it. It's pretty tacky. In fact, it looks like the logo for the Libra astrological sign that they use on the horoscope vending machine at the 7-Eleven. I doubt that Mr. Bernard has seen it. If he had, it would have been discreetly relocated behind the pulpit.

Apparently the Judge's sister, Nora, converted to Catholicism upon marrying and had nine children and so a lot of relatives have sent Mass cards. One in particular has a foot-high cardboard cutout of a bare-chested Jesus affixed to the cover, and I wonder if inside there are different outfits for him, like you get with paper dolls.

On closer inspection, the wreath appears heavy enough to hold its own and not slide off the casket, and so I face out toward the gathering mourners, slide my right hand behind my back, and attempt to raise the wooden lid with my fingers. But it's much too heavy to move with one hand, and so I check to make sure that no one is staring directly at me. Mr. Bernard has captured Ms. Olivia's attention, and he's waving his left hand behind his back like a coach signaling me to steal second base. I turn so that I'm facing the casket and use both hands to raise the top an inch.

But it's dark in there and so far I can't see anything. I lift the heavy lid another few inches. Damn, I wish I had a penlight. Suddenly the wreath slides off the back of the casket. It hits a low-slung silver candelabrum and then tumbles to the ground with a loud crash. The domino effect goes to work, and as the candelabrum strikes the floor it slides into the base of the aluminum Mass card stand and knocks that over with another round of heavy-duty clattering which echoes like buckshot fire throughout the chapel. Mass cards fly across the casket like a flock of seagulls coming in for a landing. Shit! I drop the lid and it slams shut with a voluble *thwack.*

I feel the eyes of every person in the room on my back. The minister is already running toward me from where he was organizing his papers behind the podium. I start making sobbing and wailing noises in an effort to appear distraught. It's the only dodge that comes to mind on such short notice. Flinging my entire upper body across the top of the casket, I stretch my arms above my head like an Olympic diver. The sound of people gasping resonates throughout the room.

Azure-haired old ladies arrive at my side from every corner, embroidered hankies flying behind them like flags. They all try to console me at once. When eventually I rise, a woman with white hair towering on her head like a wedding cake shoves a bottle of smelling salts in my face. Other lavender-scented dowagers dig tissues out of their sleeves and sweater pockets, and our expanding huddle of suffering starts to resemble a giant wad of toilet paper. Meanwhile, the men busy themselves gathering up the wreath and collecting all the scattered Mass cards. It looks as if I just finished playing a game of fifty-two pickup beneath the casket.

A rotund middle-aged woman I've never seen before hugs me so close that her pocketbook feels like an overinflated football being jammed into my rib cage. In a thundering whisper that arises from somewhere in her vast bosom, she announces: "There, there now, it's going to be all right. Come have a sip of seltzer and a breath of fresh air." Over her bulky shoulder pad I spot Rocky sitting in the front row all dressed up in his suit with his hands covering his face like the see-no-evil monkey.

During the car ride home, Mr. Bernard endeavors to be serious and suitably mournful, but he keeps bursting into laughter and then apologizing.

"I'm sorry. It keeps reminding me of the funeral for Chuckles the Clown on *The Mary Tyler Moore Show.* You know, after the minister explains how poor departed Chuckles was trampled to death by a rogue elephant while dressed as Peter Peanut."

Meanwhile every two or three minutes Mr. Gil also erupts with loud snorts of laughter but immediately pretends he's coughing and eventually clears his throat and politely says, "Excuse me."

But that only gets Mr. Bernard guffawing again. They both sound as if they're choking on extra-hot chili dogs.

"I know. It's terrible," Mr. Bernard finally admits. "I don't have any idea what the minister said. I ran to the men's room, but Uncle Oscar was in there doing something with his colostomy bag, so I dashed out the front door. Every time I attempted to stand in the back of the room, I just burst out laughing again."

"Well, we couldn't wait any longer. I just said that you'd taken ill from the stress of it all," says Ms. Olivia. She seems neither angry nor amused by the entire incident.

"I'm sorry, Mother. Really, I am."

"I can't believe you put Hallie up to that," Ms. Olivia scolds him as I glide the Buick into our block. "What's wrong with you?"

"I just wanted to be sure," Mr. Bernard replies.

"The Second Stockton Theory," Mr. Gil says and then cracks up again.

"And when have I ever lied to you?" Ms. Olivia asks.

"That's it exactly. You never have, and I *still* can't believe the things you do."

Then Mr. Bernard and Mr. Gil burst into gales of laughter, and I'm not far behind.

Blackjack!

The day after the funeral Mr. Bernard sends me off to the Star-Mart for cardboard boxes so that he can pack up his father's law encyclopedias and donate them to the Judge's alma mater. When I arrive back at the house the front door is wide open and the downstairs is ablaze with lights. Officer Rich's blue pickup truck is parked in the driveway.

I assume the worst—that Ms. Olivia has collapsed from grief—and rush toward the house in silent panic. But Ms. Olivia is standing inside the vestibule and assures me that everything is all right. In fact, she says that everything is more than all right, that Christmas has come a bit late this year. And it's then that I notice Craig's black Audi parked on the other side of the circular driveway. What is *he* doing here?

The first truly explanatory words come from Officer Rich, who is waiting to greet me in the living room. "I'm so sorry, Hallie," he says. But not in the way that you would say, "I'm so sorry to hear that you're going to prison for good."

Craig appears from the dining room and out of nowhere gives me this big hug, though I can't get the full benefit because with all the commotion I still haven't taken off my coat. However, it feels good all the same. And I can see that this public display of affection does not go unnoticed by Ms. Olivia. Thank goodness Mr. Bernard is banging around in the kitchen, or else he'd probably be pulling faces over Craig's shoulder.

"Sit down, everyone. I'll make us all some tea," Ms. Olivia announces.

"Now, Hallie, I've already heard how you tracked down the thief who stole the golf money, but I'd like Officer Rich, Craig, and you to explain it again. I'm still not positive I entirely grasp the entire escapade. And get Bertie. I want Bertie to hear every word."

Once we've all gathered in the living room and Ms. Olivia has made tea and Mr. Bernard has brought out a plate of petit fours, Officer Rich unravels the mystery step by step, just like they do on television.

"Well," Officer Rich begins, but then takes out a handkerchief and mops his moist brow, apparently a little uncomfortable with so many eyes intently staring at his flushed face and bulky self. "For background you need to know that Lorraine Shaeffer is the Chairwoman of the Golf Tournament Committee—Hallie goes to school with her kids, Sheryl and Brandt." He nods in my direction. "At least she used to." Officer Rich takes a sip from the teacup Ms. Olivia has passed him, but he's a large man and looks silly drinking out of a dinky china teacup. Apparently sensing this, he quickly sets it down on the coffee table.

"So Lorraine dropped the money at Mr. Exner's store, since he's the treasurer, and watched him put it underneath the counter," Officer Rich continues. "Then she asked to see some ladies' golf gloves that she knew were kept in the back area and simply took the money and put it right back into her purse. She also knew that Jane Davenport would be working at the store that afternoon and thus would probably be blamed, unless Mr. Exner assumed that he'd mislaid the money and decided to replace it himself to avoid the embarrassment of having to admit his own carelessness."

Craig is bouncing up and down on the ottoman and leaning forward as if he's about to jump in at any moment but restrains himself.

"Anyway, she bought a pair of gloves, said good-bye, and went to her car. Only as she was pulling out of the parking lot, she saw Hallie turning in on her bicycle and couldn't believe her luck—the town miscreant—sorry, Hallie—had turned up at exactly the right moment."

"But I still don't understand how Hallie connected Mrs. Shaeffer to the money," says Mr. Gil.

"Hallie," Officer Rich says and still looks dubious, no longer about my innocence but by the resolution itself, "I wonder what could have possibly led you to believe that Sheryl and Brandt's mother might be commingling funds at the brokerage firm? Did one of her kids say something to you?"

"Brandt was willing to spill the beans, but I didn't need him to," I say. "I'd seen Mrs. Shaeffer out at the Indian casino a few times. And I saw Brandt at the track once. I just started to wonder if maybe the whole family has a gambling problem."

I catch Mr. Bernard glancing at Mr. Gil as if to say, *Indian casino?*

"But Hallie," says Officer Rich. "What was it about being at the Indian casino that made you suspect her of stealing the money? Lots of people from town go there. It's not illegal."

"For one thing, when we were playing poker Al made that comment about Mrs. Shaeffer being his stockbroker and losing money for him. Then whenever Mrs. Shaeffer ran into me at the casino she left right away, which I thought was kind of strange. It was the middle of the day when most people are working, but hey, it's a free country. So I just assumed it was because I went to school with Sheryl and Brandt and she didn't want *them* to know what she was up to. But there was this time I was watching her play from the Crypt, you know, when they were processing me right before barring me from the casino for good . . ."

Once again Mr. Bernard's expression distracts me. Upon hearing "the Crypt" and "barring me from the casino," his eyebrows shoot up like window shades.

"So I was looking down and I could tell that she was leaking twenties. Because she was hunched over the cards all tense-like and clutching her purse real tight to her lap. You know, with that hollow expression of a loser who's betting money she doesn't have. And so after the golf money went missing it just occurred to me that if she had a gambling problem and needed money badly enough to steal it from the store, then she might be filching it from her customers as well. Only it didn't all come together until I was looking at Mr. Gil's stock options."

Officer Rich finally understands the missing link. "So *that's* what made you ask Craig to go down to Mrs. Shaeffer's brokerage firm—"

"It was Hallie's money," Craig interrupts him, obviously wanting to be sure to give credit where credit is due. "I just did it the way she told me to."

"Right," acknowledges Officer Rich. "Hallie had Craig open a trading account and instructed Mrs. Shaeffer to use her own judgment as to what stocks to purchase. It's called a discretionary account."

"She told me to say that I was interested in high-growth companies," adds Craig, not wanting any of the pieces of the puzzle to be overlooked. "You know, genetic engineering and biotechnology." He looks over at me with pride.

"But here's the clever part," says Officer Rich. "Hallie had Craig write the check to Mrs. Shaeffer personally, knowing full well that she couldn't legally cash the check on behalf of the brokerage house she worked for. So she *should* have asked Craig to rewrite it payable to the firm."

"But she didn't!" says Craig, eager to get to the good part.

"Right," says Officer Rich. "Mrs. Shaeffer deposited the check into her personal account. And then she sent Craig statements indicating that he'd purchased stock in some extremely risky companies that just happened to be trading near their record-high prices."

"The statements were bogus," adds Craig. "Computer generated."

"And when he closed the account Mrs. Shaeffer sent a generic bank money order with the little cash that remained, which a brokerage firm would never do, of course. They have their own official checks and drafts and so forth," explains Officer Rich.

"So the firm investigated her records and found that she'd been losing money for people and trying to cover the losses with funds from other accounts," says Craig.

Mr. Gil and Mr. Bernard just sit there with astonished looks on their faces, as if Officer Rich has suddenly morphed into the sheriff on the television show *Murder, She Wrote*. Meanwhile, Ms. Olivia serenely sips her tea and appears as if she knew it would work out like this all along.

"Calamity Hallie," Mr. Bernard finally says, happily, and gives me a round of applause as if I've just performed in a show.

"But how does the fact that this Shaeffer woman was embezzling prove that she took the golf money as well?" asks Mr. Gil.

"Oh, she confessed to that right after the manager was shown Craig's cashed check and reviewed her accounts," says Officer Rich, though not as cheerful sounding as when first proclaiming her the culprit. "I—I sort of felt sorry for her . . ." But then he apparently recalls that my life hasn't exactly been a *Brady Bunch* rerun the past few months. "My gosh," says Officer Rich. "And to think that I gave you such a hard time about this, Hallie. I feel terrible."

"It's not really your fault," I say. "I mean, if I didn't get into so much trouble and cut school, then you wouldn't have suspected me in the first place."

"Thanks, kiddo, but that's no excuse," replies Officer Rich. "Innocent until proven guilty."

"All's well that ends well," says Ms. Olivia.

"Onward and upward," adds Mr. Gil.

"Exactly right," says Mr. Bernard. "Life is too short to be anything but gay."

Mr. Gil shoots Mr. Bernard a look.

At this point I'm the only one who hasn't thrown in my two cents, though I've donated my eight hundred dollars, which Officer Rich promises I'll get back.

However, it's Officer Rich who has the last words, which for once I don't mind a bit. "Case closed," he says.

And I realize it's the first time in almost a year that I'm not being hunted down for something or other. At least that I know of.

4 4

Deal Me In

★

The week following the funeral we all sit around the house encouraging one another to go out and do something, but no one does. Except for Ms. Olivia. She ventures outdoors to shovel the front walk every morning, and then heads over to her church to sort and price junk for the yearly white elephant sale.

I'm afraid she'll have a heart attack doing all the snow removal, but when I rise early to beat her to the job Mr. Bernard stops me. He explains that Ms. Olivia always recovers from tragedy through manual labor and that we should just let her go at it.

Otherwise, the gloom of the Judge's last weeks begins to fade and life gradually returns to normal. At least by Stockton standards. Mr. Bernard and Mr. Gil are both back at work. I paint trim, run errands, and work on the garage collage in the mornings. Ms. Olivia tutors me during the afternoons and writes pornography or poetry in the evening while Mr. Bernard and I prepare dinner. To provoke Mr. Bernard she threatens to pass a petition to change the name *women* (look what it ends in!) to Estrogen-Americans. But Mr. Bernard doesn't take the bait. He simply suggests that Ms. Olivia and her Unitarian feminist cronies start speaking in *Shebonics* so they'll no longer have to concern themselves with how the rest of the world labels people.

The day before New Year's Eve, Mr. Bernard appears to finally run out of steam in the kitchen and he actually orders a pizza. Even the bread machine has gone cold for the first time in months. The last few days we've been subsisting on "chicken déjà vu," Mr. Bernard's code name for leftovers.

That night I head off to the New Year's Eve party at Jane's house. Mr. Gil and Mr. Bernard are both pleased that I have a function to attend. However, they aren't going anywhere. Mr. Bernard claims that once you're over thirty, New Year's Eve is amateur night. He and Mr. Gil prefer to stay home and have a nice dinner of ragout of veal and watch old Alfred Hitchcock movies.

It's the first time seeing my friends since the criminal charges against me have been dropped. Jane greets me at the front door with a big hug and hangs several black and white leis around my neck. "I heard all about it," she says excitedly. "What an incredible story! Poor Sheryl and Brandt. I invited them to the party weeks ago, but I doubt they'll come now."

Guests pile up behind me, and so we agree to catch up later.

Next I have to pass Jane's parents in the family room in order to reach the basement door. Mrs. Davenport is extra nice, and it's obvious that she's trying to make up for all the thin-lipped smiles and terse telephone greetings from when it appeared as if I was in possession of the golf money. Or worse, that by regularly conferring with Jane I was insinuating that her daughter, the only person other than Mr. Exner to have a key, had something to do with the theft.

"How's school, sweetie?" Mrs. Davenport asks me in her friendliest Southern accent and pats the empty couch pillow next to her ample behind to indicate that I should settle in for a nice long chat.

Standing with my hand on the doorknob to the basement, I start to explain my situation. "I don't exactly go—"

"Oh yes, yes of course." She laughs as if this was a silly thing to ask. "And how's your mom? Jane tells me she's expecting . . . again."

"I haven't really seen much of her lately."

Mrs. Davenport is obviously reminded that I no longer live with my folks and appears flustered as the conversation takes yet another wrong turn. "Well, I'm sure the young people are expecting y'all in the rumpus room." She seems to have changed her mind about the heart-to-heart talk, and so I finally open the door and follow the rising roar from downstairs.

Jane's parents have refinished the basement of their sprawling brick ranch house in a teen-friendly way, with a Ping-Pong table, pool table, foosball game, and even the arcade version of Donkey Kong. There's a downstairs refrigerator stocked with all kinds of soda pop, and they have accounts at the local submarine shop, video store, and the Mr. Cluck Chicken Wing Hut.

Once I said to Jane, "Your parents must know that kids smoke and go to third base down here every weekend." Because there are enough large throw pillows scattered around the floor to sleep about twelve. And the basement windows are always open, even in the middle of winter. Jane explained her parents' philosophy, which is basically that kids are going to get into stuff no matter where they are and so it may as well be in a place with adult supervision nearby so they can be driven to the emergency room if necessary. Her parents have promised never to go downstairs unless there's a three-alarm blaze.

The party is in full swing. Teenagers are dancing and music is playing and the boys are throwing a Nerf basketball around the room and trying to hit the girls in the boobs with it. Jane has hung thick curtains of black and white streamers in all the corners to create private make-out bungalows, and the ceiling is dotted with helium balloons that we're all supposed to pop at midnight. Only a few boys are slowly deflating them and inhaling the helium and then singing "Volare" duets in high squeaky voices. Meanwhile the junior class president, Paul Ryan, has mushed a thick layer of devil's food cake into his braces and is running around grinning at people.

Apparently everyone has heard that I solved the mystery of the missing golf money. Though that's largely my doing. The minute the cloud was lifted I told my parents and then I phoned Gwen, knowing full well that she'd have the news out within an hour. Absolutely everybody wants to talk to me about it, but when I see Craig across the room, I excuse myself and go over to him. We shoot a game of pool and I don't purposely try to lose, but I take some shots that are pretty tough, instead of the easy ones, and because I'm out of practice and miss a couple, Craig manages to win by one ball.

The Stocktons would probably find it all pretty juvenile, but I think it's a good party. Besides, it's not as if I no longer enjoy being with people my own age. I just can't tolerate school, that's all. And now that the money has been recovered and I'm no longer a pariah, people don't pretend that they're about to miss their ride as soon as I walk over.

Jane plays a CD of television show theme songs and offers prizes to the first person who can correctly name each one. Four people play Strip Ping-Pong, except they use the Nerf basketball instead of a regular Ping-Pong ball. One of the competitors, Heather Johnson, is already drunk and has her socks and shoes and sweater off, and it's pretty obvious what the guys are trying to accomplish with that one. Mary-Ella grabs the Polaroid camera off the top of the VCR and snaps a photo of her.

The purpose of the Polaroid camera is to watch for a couple to sneak into the laundry room and then after they've been in there about ten minutes three people work together to document their level of commitment. One person swings open the door, one switches on the light, and a third takes the photo.

Brandt rolls up around ten o'clock looking more than a little stoned, or else like he accidentally inhaled a tube of model-airplane glue. He moves hesitantly down the stairs and across the room, with pupils like eight balls and his wiry frame pressed up against the wall as if he'll topple over without the added support of cement pilings. I wonder if he's mad at me for getting his mom into trouble. A relative had to come all the way from Philadelphia to post bail.

"Hey, Brandt," I say and approach the back wall. "Are you okay?"

He appears surprised not so much by my voice but by the words themselves, as if he's trying to make sense out of the question. "Yeah . . . I'm just going to get something to eat," he finally replies.

"The food is over there." I point to the far wall. "You're going the long way, don't you think?"

"I'm not bisecting any parallelograms tonight, if you know what I mean."

I take that to mean that he is indeed wasted. "I just wanted you to know that I'm sorry about your mom and everything," I say.

"I should be the one apologizing to you," he mumbles.

"*You* didn't do anything."

"I guess it was hard for my mom to get used to living on one income after my dad left." He stares down at the indoor-outdoor carpeting and traces an imaginary pattern with his toe. "Not that it's any excuse."

"Sure, I understand."

Brandt nods without looking up and then continues his tentative skulk along the perimeter of the wall.

After a few games of darts, a feeling of guilt about having fun starts to creep over me with every laugh and joyous shout. It's only been five days since the Judge passed away. And so I mention to Craig that I'm tired and about to head home.

"But Hallie, you *have* to stay until midnight," he pleads. "We're going to have tequila shots and light firecrackers out in the backyard. It's going to be a blast."

It's tempting. Craig looks awfully good in a white turtleneck and navy cable-knit sweater he probably received as Christmas presents from his mom and loose-fitting faded blue jeans; his butterscotch-colored hair has grown out of the brush cut he sported during football season.

"I'm sorry," I say. "But I just don't feel much like a party tonight. Maybe we can see a movie tomorrow."

I head upstairs to Jane's bedroom to dig my winter coat out from under the pile of down parkas and fleece pullovers on her bed.

Craig follows me. "I was really hoping you'd stay until midnight."

"What's the big deal about midnight? New Year's Eve is just a celebration that we're one year closer to our deaths." Gosh, I was starting to sound like Ms. Olivia.

"I'll walk you home." Craig proceeds to excavate his ski jacket from the bottom of the heap. "I just had this idea that I'd be standing next to you at midnight."

Now I comprehend the Cinderella-like significance of the witching hour. I suddenly feel a twinge of regret about ruining the moment by making an early exit. The party is reaching full throttle and the glass doors in the china cabinet rattle as kids dance to Elton John's "Crocodile Rock" in the basement directly below us.

We exit the Davenports' house into the clear, cold winter night. All the rooftops are coated with snow and the sky is crowded with stars. The rich aroma of burning firewood lingers in the air while smoke climbs lazily up from the chimneys and sketches fuzzy gray ribbons onto the black sky. No cars are coming down the street and no one else is out wandering around. By now everyone is where they're supposed to be. The only noises come from other houses, where the booze is flowing and the festivities are well under way.

Our breath makes gauzy clouds in the frozen air and I toy with the idea of saying, "We don't have to wait until midnight." But I can't bring myself to spit out the words. Craig threw his love life on the line back there by asking me to stay at the party, and that's encouraging. So technically the ball *is* in my court. And if I don't say or do something soon, it's not likely I'll ever see him again. I'd noticed that if you don't show guys you like them at the right moment, they have a way of suddenly pretending they never cared about you in the first place. In other words, there's a narrow window within which one needs to respond to an advance from a teenage guy.

As Craig and I stroll side by side down the middle of the street, I reach out my thickly gloved hand and grasp his. Only he's wearing waterproof ski mittens and holding on to one of them feels as if I'm squeezing a bag of marshmallows. It's not a particularly romantic moment.

"Hang on a second." Craig reaches over with his opposite hand, removes the offending mitten, and places his bare hand back into my gloved one. Only it's really cold out, below zero. Even inside the gloves my fingers have started to go numb. I recall reading how people in warmer climates become sexually active at a much earlier age, and it now becomes obvious why this is so.

"Your fingers must be getting cold," I say after a few minutes.

"No, no. I'm fine."

But I look down and his fingers have turned a corpselike yellowish-white. I come up with the idea of putting both of our hands in my coat pocket, and this seems to work well, only walking becomes somewhat awkward. I slip and lose my footing and automatically try to throw my palms out for balance, but I can't get the one that's entangled with Craig's out of my pocket and together we tumble forward into the snow-filled street, hands still intertwined.

We both laugh. Craig leans over and tries to kiss me, but our jackets are bulky and it's difficult to get close enough. It's more like the Pillsbury Doughboy trying to slow-dance with Mrs. Potato Head. Winter clothes are definitely an effective form of birth control.

Finally we both thrust our faces forward like hungry ostriches and Craig manages to put his mouth on mine. His nose is an ice cube against my cheek. His breath has the faint scent of peppermint Life Savers and his lips feel cool and moist. He must have wet them first with his tongue. This is one of the advantages of dating a senior. They know such tricks. The downside is that they also have higher sexpectations.

Before venturing outside I had applied a generous coating of Blistex to my perpetually chapped lips. So I can't imagine that I taste very good. But we somehow manage to hold the kiss for over a minute so that it counts, like a wrestler pinning down his opponent until the referee declares it official.

Eventually the cold creeps in and we unsnarl ourselves and rise from the snow-packed tire tracks. Craig retrieves his mitten, which landed under a nearby parked car when we fell. Then I playfully grab his arm and we run the rest of the way to the Stocktons', through drifts of sequined snow that twinkle in the moonshine as if flecked with tiny clusters of diamonds. It's a relief to have that business of the first kiss out of the way. Now it's legitimate, we're "going out." Gwen can mark it on her electronic love bulletin board with a pink pushpin.

We arrive at the end of the driveway giggling and out of breath. With the back of my hand I surreptitiously wipe away the remaining layer of lip salve, just in case.

Craig kisses me for a long time while we are standing together on the front porch. It's nice, but he's so tall that my neck eventually starts to ache, and I'm relieved when we finally need to break in order to inhale and swallow and cough and wipe our noses.

"I'd invite you in, but Ms. Olivia's husband just died," I say.

"I know." Craig places a sympathetic hand on my shoulder. "My parents went to the funeral. Uh—they said that you were pretty upset."

"I made an absolute fool of myself is what I did. It will be a long time before I attend another funeral, unless it's my own."

Craig looks into my eyes with great sincerity. "My mother said that everyone felt your outpouring of grief was extremely moving, that older people keep their emotions inside too much, and it exemplified how the Judge had touched so many lives."

"Your mother is very kind," I tell him.

"She tends to see the best in people," says Craig.

He removes his hand from my shoulder. The moment of intimacy is over. But I determine that it works in my favor if he believes I'm still in mourning.

"Do you still want to see a movie tomorrow?" he asks.

However, the front door swings open and standing in front of us is Ms. Olivia, dazzling in a red angora sweater and a long black silk skirt that rustles as it settles around her calves. Her blue eyes are highlighted by brush strokes of gold shadow with coppery flecks in it.

Craig and I stand there startled and look at her as if she's the host of the *Wheel of Fortune* and we're waiting for the giant wheel to stop spinning.

Oh God, I think. Did she see us making out? First I'm falling into her husband's casket, and now I'm defiling her front porch not even a week after the funeral.

Chances Are . . .

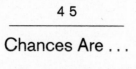

"**I** *thought* that I heard someone out on the porch," Ms. Olivia trills, joyfully clasping her hands together as if she's just captured an elusive butterfly. "I wondered if it was Mrs. Shondra from across the way coming to borrow some ice or vermouth."

Craig extends his hand to Ms. Olivia. Then he realizes that he's still wearing his mitten and glares down as if it's already caused him enough trouble for one night. He towers over Ms. Olivia and has to bend down slightly just to shake her hand. She warmly takes his big paw in both her hands. "Your parents were at the funeral. I believe your father worked with the Judge down at the courthouse."

"Yes, ma'am. I'm sorry to hear that he passed away."

"Thank you, dear. Though I prefer to think of him as recycled. It's less final sounding, wouldn't you say?"

Craig politely nods his head in agreement, even though it's obvious he hasn't made sense out of her remark. He probably thinks it's the grief talking.

"Well, it's much too frigid to be standing outside. Of course, we can't compete with the aroma of wood smoke, moonbeams, starlight, and privacy," she says with a knowing smile, "but there's soft music and mulled cider, peach schnapps, and Bertie's homemade Tokay wine."

We clump into the house and begin the ten-minute ritual of removing all our contraceptive outerwear.

"How delightful to have young people here for New Year's Eve," Ms.

Olivia exclaims. Then she lowers her voice. "Hallie, I'm so pleased you came home early. Bertie is terribly downhearted. He's been lying on the chaise longue listening to the Broadway cast recording of *Les Misérables* all night, and it's driving Gil and me to madness."

In the direction of the living room Ms. Olivia announces with exaggerated volume, "Turn that off this instant and put on some nice party music, Bertie! Hallie has brought her beau along, and I don't want them thinking we're running a mausoleum."

Mr. Gil emerges and shakes hands with Craig. "Thank heavens you've arrived. The Prince of Chintz has been playing 'On My Own' over and over for the last four hours. It's driving me to the Bailey's Irish Cream."

"I *know*," says Ms. Olivia cheerily. "Let's have a dance."

"Yes indeed," agrees Mr. Gil. "What kind of music do *you* like, Craig?"

"Chumbawamba," replies Craig. "Rancid. And Fine Young Cannibals."

Mr. Gil and Ms. Olivia look at each other quizzically.

"Of course," Ms. Olivia replies enthusiastically. "We'll check and see if we have any of that. Bernard is in charge of all the cooking and cleaning." Then she calls into the living room, "Bertie, Hallie has arrived home with her gentleman caller. We're going to have a soiree."

Mr. Bernard suddenly appears in the archway. "A gentleman caller?" he says excitedly as he comes face to chin with Craig and shakes hands. "It's delightful to see you again. Please come in and make yourself at home."

"Bertie, we're going to have a dance," announces Ms. Olivia as she excavates a box of votive candles from the sideboard in the dining room. "Gil, go put on some swing music and get Rocky off the Etch-A-Sketch. Have him help you fetch all those paper lanterns from last year's production of *A Streetcar Named Desire*. They're in the Wellington chest at the top of the stairs. I'll make some snacks."

"Don't go *near* that kitchen, Mother," threatens Mr. Bernard. "I have some prawns in the freezer. It'll just take me a moment to whip up some cocktail sauce."

With that Mr. Bernard charges off like a steam engine preparing to go uphill. Mr. Gil and Ms. Olivia look at each other with obvious enjoyment, then she ushers us into the living room.

I can tell that Mr. Bernard is searching for something in the kitchen, because I hear all the cupboard doors slamming.

"What?" I call out in the direction of the clatter.

"My kingdom for the horseradish." He pokes his head around the corner and looks at me hopefully.

"Refrigerator," I say. "Top shelf in the side door on the far left. Next to the relish."

"*Pickle relish* is one of the French people's favorite American words. Isn't that odd?" remarks Ms. Olivia. "Pickle relish, windowsill, and elbow. They love the sound of those three words."

If Craig thinks I live in an insane asylum, he doesn't let on. Within twenty minutes he's drinking beer from a chilled stoneware tankard and the rest of us are having wine or mulled cider. I help Mr. Bernard serve his homemade porcino mushroom spread, imported water crackers, two kinds of goat cheese, and a large bowl of shrimp cocktail. Mr. Bernard makes the best shrimp cocktail, because he boils the shrimp in Perfect Addition brand fish stock mixed with one cup of white wine instead of just plain old water. He says that shrimp boiled in plain water is for "philistines."

Next Mr. Bernard offers to make us both a plate from the dinner left-overs or else some roast beef sandwiches. I can tell that he's getting back into the swing of things when he starts explaining to Craig that the Earl of Sandwich, the inventor of the sandwich, was inspired by his propensity for gambling. Mr. Bernard claims that the Earl was looking for a way to eat without having to leave the gaming tables.

Meanwhile, along with the decorations, Mr. Gil has found Rocky a top hat and bow tie from his costume rack. Together they string the pastel paper lanterns throughout the room and build a roaring fire. Ms. Olivia has dotted the tables and mantel with twenty or so of her aromatherapy candles. The room, awash in this delirious glow and slowly filling with the scent of jasmine, appears to waver, while in the background Duke Ellington plays "C Jam Blues" and the fire crackles with warmth. Alongside the front windows the tall plush-velvet burgundy drapes are pulled back so that they look like women curtsying to each other before a dance.

"Now push the furniture to the sides and roll back the Savonnerie," Ms. Olivia instructs us. "You know, the pagans observed death with a celebration. I think this is much closer to what the Judge would have wanted than that maudlin service and those old gasbag legal cronies of his."

"I believe the pagans also sacrificed a virgin to the moon gods," retorts

Mr. Bernard. Craig shoots me a quick look to make sure that he's kidding, and I shake my head and roll my eyes to indicate that they always say crazy stuff like this.

"Now, can you two do the Lindy?" Ms. Olivia asks us.

Craig and I look at each other and then back at her and shake our heads to indicate that not only can't we do it but that we don't even know what it is.

"Put on Glenn Miller's 'In the Mood,' " Ms. Olivia says and then she and Mr. Bernard begin to dance together in the center of the room, where the coffee table had been. And oh, can they dance! Mr. Bernard twirls her and dips her and they spin around separately and then together, the shimmer of a dozen candles pinwheeling across their faces. He is surefooted and graceful while Ms. Olivia floats in his arms, light as a silk scarf. The candles flicker in the rectangular mirror above the couch, causing their every movement to dance in shadow against the walls. On the long Spanish baroque library table off to the side sit two lamps with black onyx centers from which chandelier prisms dangle and dance like jeweled icicles.

Halfway through the song Ms. Olivia comes over and takes Craig's hand and shows him the steps while Mr. Bernard instructs me. I notice that he doesn't attempt any of the fancy double spins and dips that he performed with his mother. But it's fun, and I don't step on his toes too much. Then Mr. Gil cuts in and gets me to bring my knees together and quickly swings me between his legs and then back up on my feet again. I have no idea how he made that happen, but Craig thinks it's hilarious. And Rocky jumps up and down on the sofa clapping his hands, occasionally doing a somersault or a handstand.

Mr. Gil, the resident rock and roll fan, manages to sneak in Lynyrd Skynyrd's "Freebird." And after that Mr. Bernard declares us ready for Fred Astaire and plays an old song from the '30s called "Beginner's Luck." *At any gambling casino, from Monte Carlo to Reno, They tell you that a beginner, comes out a winner . . .*

When the song ends it's midnight and the grandfather clock chimes and we all kiss and cheer and clink our glasses. "That was a delightful party," Ms. Olivia says. "But I'm afraid I must take my leave of you."

"How come the redoubtable Ottavio didn't call to wish you a Happy New Year?" Mr. Bernard curiously inquires.

"He's in Sorrento. It was New Year's there six hours ago. We chatted online before dinner while you were preoccupied with *Les Miz.*"

Craig turns to me and quietly asks, "Uh, where did you say you met these people?"

"Through an ad at the Star-Mart."

"Oh, right."

We all take turns kissing Ms. Olivia good night.

"I hope you'll join us for dinner one evening this week," Ms. Olivia says to Craig.

As she waves to us once more from the top of the staircase, Mr. Bernard says, "I pray she's not preparing to do a Barbara Stanwyck in *The Thorn Birds* and go up and off herself while the band plays on."

"Bertie, your mother is *not* suicidal," Mr. Gil replies firmly. "It was *her* idea to have a party."

"You heard what she said—that the pagans love a good jamboree. She just failed to mention that they concluded by sacrificing and vivisecting one another," Mr. Bernard replies skeptically. He turns to Rocky, who is pretending to play chess at the table in the corner, mimicking the way Mr. Bernard and Mr. Gil move the pieces around the board. "Rocky, go up and keep an eye on her." The chimp obediently scoots up the stairs after Ms. Olivia.

"Okay, last dance," announces Mr. Gil.

Since Ms. Olivia has gone upstairs, I wonder if he means that he's going to dance with me. He goes to the stereo and puts on a duet called "Baby, It's Cold Outside." As the syncopated jazz beat drifts through the room he and Mr. Bernard begin to waltz across the hardwood floor together. They are both graceful dancers, and it's exotic to watch these two attractive men hold each other close while swaying to the strains of a saxophone, backlit by the otherworldly glow of a dying fire.

Craig has a look on his face that must resemble Alice's right after she crashed down the rabbit hole. But I take his hand and together we rock back and forth to the music, while every so often Mr. Bernard and Mr. Gil glide elegantly past us. Craig and I don't try anything more daring than the universal high school slow-dance position where you embrace and keep turning a few steps to the right. But I enjoy the feel of his arms around me, and so what if we're not going to win any contests. The sultry music is accompanied by smoky-voiced lyrics: *I really can't stay (baby it's cold outside). I've got to go 'way (baby it's cold outside). The evening has been so very nice . . .*

And I realize that this is the happiest New Year's Eve of my life. It's a night out of time and a time out of place.

Observing the Play

◆

Between painting the bookcases, studying, and working on the collage when it's not snowing out, the final two weeks in January fly by. Mr. Bernard stays late in his shop to do inventory and prepare for a sale, while Mr. Gil frantically makes the schedule and budget for all of his upcoming training programs. The dining room table and chairs are covered in receipts, folders, and big calendar pages that he's brought home from the office.

Most mornings Ms. Olivia busies herself with the poem she's writing in memory of the Judge, and in our afternoon tutorials she's dragged me up through the 1800s in history, art, and English literature. Unfortunately writers back then were paid by the word, which makes for some pretty gluey reading. But as if to compensate for that, wars were breaking out all across Europe and the Americas, so there are plenty of bloody revolutions, traitors, duels, and beheadings to enjoy.

The Judge's absence is still deeply felt, especially since the daily rhythms of life until so recently revolved around him, like planets circling the sun. And yet somehow the household manages to reconfigure itself, and the business of living carries on. After a few weeks the twenty or so pill bottles disappear from the countertop. One evening the TV tray in the Florida Room is returned to the closet. And early one Saturday morning the hospital supply equipment people arrive to collect the bed rails and bathroom shower seat and other items that had become part of the furnishings.

At the beginning of February, *The Glass Menagerie* opens at the Playhouse. The show receives a good review in the local paper, but Mr. Gil doesn't take much pride in it because his largest benefactor, the one whose son stars in the play, is also a golf buddy of the editor. However, the theater is filled every night and this pleases Mr. Gil, since he says that a director's validation must come from his public and not the critics.

After finishing the sets I'm drafted into being the assistant stage manager and assigned my very own walkie-talkie. During intermission it's my job to set the table, switch on the chandelier, put out the flower centerpiece, turn on the streetlamp, and drop down the neon sign for the girlie parlor that's supposedly across the street. Mr. Gil talks Craig into working as an usher, passing out programs beforehand and then selling popcorn and soda between acts.

Following the last performance there's a cast party back at the Stocktons' and all the actors and crew and even the members of the five-piece orchestra get terrifically drunk. Mr. Bernard takes three big antique coffee urns he bought at an ecclesiastical going-out-of-business sale and converts them into fondue pots. We set out big trays of crudités, a fruit basket in a watermelon shell, and bread cubes for the guests to dip into chocolate, cheese, or raspberry sauce.

At around one in the morning Terry, the lighting guy, sits down at the piano and starts playing songs like "Yankee Doodle Dandy" and "Meet Me in St. Louis" and everyone gathers around the old Chickering upright and merrily sings along in liquor-enhanced voices. Eventually a few people begin chanting *"Judy! Judy! Judy!"* And Danielle, who had the part of Laura in the play, goes to the piano and sings "Over the Rainbow." Mr. Gil switches off all the lights except for a halogen reading lamp, which he turns upward, covers with pink cellophane, and converts into a jerry-rigged spotlight.

At the opposite end of the room Rocky and I work as bartenders. Ms. Olivia decided that the best way to keep Rocky from getting into the booze was to put him in charge of it. Nowadays he enjoys mixing cocktails more than drinking them. And the guests are really amazed to watch him work. Granted, they can't order exactly what they'd like, but if they point to a particular bottle Rocky will make them something good.

While I'm serving drinks, Joey, the set designer, comes over and tells me that I should consider becoming a graphic artist. Only I don't know what one does. What I do know is that I especially enjoy it when Craig comes running over as soon as he spots me talking to Joey. *As if* I would be interested in Joey; he's like thirty years old and always trying to get me out to his place to see these deluxe chicken coops that he builds. Furthermore, even though his last name is Chimera he tells everyone to call him Joey Chickens.

Mr. Bernard eventually relieves me at the bar, and this gives Craig and me the opportunity to sneak off to my room to fool around. With the lively music and the laughter rising from downstairs, there's a feeling of romance in the air almost as pungent as the perfume from the six dozen fresh gardenias that Mr. Bernard specially ordered for the party.

At least it's romantic until Craig wants to go all the way and I tell him I'm not ready and he gets all mopey-assed. Oh well. It was a nice evening up until then.

47

Good Fortune

♣

Over breakfast the following morning I casually mention that Joey Chickens said I should become a graphic artist.

"I think that's an interesting suggestion," replies Mr. Gil. "Computers are where all the action is these days." He shoots a glance at Mr. Bernard as he emphasizes the word *computers*.

"What exactly do graphic artists do?" I ask.

"They create visual presentations," explains Mr. Gil. "Everything from detergent boxes and album covers to gravestone markers, coupons, and dog food cans. All companies employ them. And the people who work in the profession can earn darn good money."

"You'd make an excellent graphic designer," says Mr. Bernard. "One needs an eye for object arrangement and a flair for color. Though Gil is right." He glances over at Mr. Gil as if to confirm that it just about kills him to admit it. "Imaging is mostly done electronically now. One would have to attend college to become a graphic designer in this day and age."

So much for on-the-job training.

"Bertie," says Mr. Gil, "I believe you always had to go to college to become a graphic designer. The days of the artisan apprenticeship went out with Johnny Tremain." Then he tells me to call the Cleveland Institute of Art for information. "It's one of the best schools in the country. And practically right here in our own backyard."

"I'm sure they have a Web site," says Ms. Olivia. "Pull it up on the computer."

"Maybe," I reply. I haven't really considered going to college. It'll be a big step just to graduate from high school in the spring and get this mob of people off my back.

That evening we celebrate Ms. Olivia's birthday, which falls on the fifteenth of March. Over dinner she takes pride in pointing out to us that her birth month is the only one that also serves as a verb, as in *to march into battle*, from the Old French *marchier*. And Mr. Bernard is quick to add that in Latin it is the month of Mars, the God of War.

Mr. Gil and Mr. Bernard split the cost of a membership for her in the Hemlock Society as a present. At first I think it's a gardening club, until I see the pamphlet about making an up-to-date will. It turns out that the organization provides all the latest information on death and dying—committing suicide, in particular. Mr. Bernard says it's the first gift membership they ever sold and that an administrator had to create a new form because people generally sign themselves up.

Ms. Olivia explains that normally she doesn't care to receive presents, just like at Christmas. However, she seems thrilled with her death kit.

By now I've finished painting everything inside the house that can possibly be coated with premium interior latex paint, including the basement, kitchen cabinets, bookshelves, baseboard, and radiator covers. So when old man winter finally blinks at the end of the month, it's a relief to spend time outside scraping the shutters and also finishing my garage door mural. And Mr. Bernard announces that it's time to convert the summerhouse into a temporary greenhouse and start the annuals along with some tomato plants, green peppers, squash, and romaine lettuce.

As the days grow longer Ms. Olivia's school sessions also seem to be casting a lengthier shadow. However I don't mind since she keeps the lessons lively. And we're finally reading some fun authors, such as Jane Austen and Katherine Mansfield. Though I'm certain that I've disappointed her with my stabs at poetry.

Ms. Olivia seems to agree that I'm not destined to become a sonneteer, especially after I rhyme "turkey gobbler" with "blackberry cobbler." But she is nonetheless optimistic and insists that everyone has within himself an epic poem, only some people are destined to live theirs as opposed to just write it out on paper. And that this can present an even greater challenge.

Craig often stops by after lacrosse practice and we hang out in the living room and watch a movie or listen to music while playing the board game Clue. Mr. Bernard is fond of coming in and with great acclaim pronouncing: "I know! It's the Duchess of Uranus in the vomitorium." Then he'll raise the back of his hand to his forehead, pretend to concentrate incredibly hard, and announce, "With the macramé plant hanger!"

Sometimes we just laugh. Other times we tell him he got part of it right, that it was the Duchess of Uranus with a wire coat hanger and the murder took place in the sanitarium. And then he'll say, "Curses, foiled again!" just like Daffy Duck.

The hanging-out part of my relationship with Craig is terrific. Especially at the Stocktons', because they all appear to enjoy his company and we feel comfortable eating out of the fridge and lying around the living room floor doing homework. It's when we go up to my room that things become problematical. Craig hasn't let up on wanting to get more serious, and I'm afraid that if I don't relent soon he's going to give me an ultimatum.

One rainy Saturday afternoon Ms. Olivia brings out a set of worn but large and colorful cards she'd acquired in Paris and proceeds to tell our fortunes. Mr. Bernard implies that she once worked as a psychic in a carnival. Ms. Olivia refuses to confirm or deny this rumor, but she is nonetheless convincing. My fortune, at least according to Ms. Olivia, is that I am to be a "keeper of the flame."

But when I ask what flame I am to keep and where and how am I to keep it, Ms. Olivia cannot answer, or if she can, she chooses not to. Instead she speaks of roses. Ms. Olivia says that the Romans were extravagant in their love for roses; rose wreaths were awarded for great military achievements; Nero showered rose petals on his dinner guests, and the poet Horace wrote that too many roses were grown in Rome and not enough corn. But then during the rise of Christianity roses fell out of favor because of their close association with pagan Rome and almost vanished completely. In fact, it was only because a few monks in monasteries kept some, mainly for medicinal purposes, that roses were able to once again flourish throughout Europe after the medieval period.

However I still don't understand what flame keeping has to do with roses, or what *I* have to do with either one. Maybe I'm supposed to tend Ms. Olivia's rose garden after she's gone. Or better yet, Ms. Olivia is probably just using this whole fortune business as a way to sneak in an extra history lesson.

All I know for sure is that it's a lucky thing Ms. Olivia wasn't one of those monastery monks, because under her watch all the roses would have checked out for good.

"But Ms. Olivia," I ask, "how can you believe in fortunes if you're an atheist?"

"They fill a need, just like religion. Besides, people often come unglued if they realize that life is random. And you'll notice that there are far more working astrologers than astronomers in this country."

"You mean you believe in *astrology*?" I ask. Pinning Ms. Olivia down on her beliefs is like trying to catch a fish with your bare hands.

"Of course not. But the unknown is an intimidating destination, and so a reading helps us to focus, like looking at a road map. Fortunes of great wealth and renowned artistic accomplishment don't just occur on their own, you know, out of thin air, as if by magic. You have to work at it. Luck favors the prepared mind. And thus when I tell your fortune it makes you consider what you really want to do with your life as you compare it to my prediction."

To me it sounded more like she was saying that life is a stacked deck and all you can hope to do is play the odds as best you know how.

"Livvy is really an agnostic," Mr. Gil offers by way of further explanation.

"No, I'm not," she retorts. "Agnostics don't know what they believe in."

"Yes, that's never been a problem with Mother," agrees Mr. Bernard. "She'd be classified as more of an *antagonist*, I would imagine."

"I despise spiritual indecision," Ms. Olivia states as she systematically lays down her tarot cards. "Personally, I'd rather someone be a devout numerologist or a serious gymnosophist and thereby at least have the courage of their convictions."

"You can't possibly mean that," Mr. Gil scoffs at her.

"She's a heretic," says Mr. Bernard.

"Of course I'm a heretic! The word *hairesis* in Greek means choice, from the Greek verb *hairein*, to take. A heretic is one who is able to choose."

"Then if you don't believe in Christmas or in heaven or God, do you worship anything?" I ask her.

"The weather."

"The *weather*?" I ask incredulously.

"Certainly. The weather provides us with everything we need to live—food, light, heat, water, even flowers."

"Mother adores nature," Mr. Bernard interjects. And then in his best stage voice he adds, "Despite what it's done to her."

"Bertie thinks the four seasons are salt, pepper, oregano, and saffron," jokes Mr. Gil.

"But what about when we die?" I ask.

"People squander their time concocting postmortem scenarios because they're uncomfortable or unfulfilled in their current lives," says Ms. Olivia. "Forget about the afterlife and make the current one a success and death will take care of itself. Say what you will, but unlike your gods, the weather will never let you down. And though you may not always like what you get, you'll always get something."

Mr. Bernard glances up at the grandfather clock and I can tell he's thinking that it's time to start preparing dinner. "You're going to hell, Mother," he proclaims and then rises from the table.

"Well, Bertie, which do you think came first, Christianity or the elements?"

"God," Mr. Bernard firmly replies.

"Sorry to disappoint, darling, but weather worship predates your Protestant version of heaven and hell. In fact, long before the Christians co-opted December 25 for themselves it was a Roman pagan holiday marking the winter solstice for the sun-worshiping Mithraists. But if it gives you comfort to believe in heaven and hell, then don't let me stop you. At least there will be interesting people in the fiery core with whom I can converse, and we'll have nice books and good light to read them by. Thomas Edison thought God was bunk. So did George Bernard Shaw."

Mr. Bernard interrupts her. ". . . and Clarence Darrow and George Santayana and Bertrand Russell. Yes, Mother, I know your list of skeptic scholars and heathen helpers by heart."

"Then why do you have a Druid Circle in the backyard?" I ask.

"Oh, the pagans had some good ideas, but that's really just to ward off undesirables—lonely men from the seniors center and women wanting me to join their bridge and book clubs. You know, I just take them on a tour of the yard and they immediately think *Waco, Texas,* or *Salem witch trials* and I never hear from them again. It's really quite wonderful. And in my den I have a lovely majolica urn containing the incinerated ashes of my older brother Charles—he died in the Korean War—that serves to scare away most Catholics, except for Rocky."

Oh my God, I'd thought that urn was filled with potpourri!

"You see, I'm the keeper of my brother's flame—his life, his stories. They're all in here." She lifts a delicate hand to her heart.

And the keeper of the remains of his dead body, I want to add. It's then that I wonder if maybe Ms. Olivia is appointing *me* to be the keeper of her flame. Oh shit. What if she *is* getting ready to commit suicide after all, just as Mr. Bernard had said? Only now she has a book explaining exactly how to do it!

An Ace in the Hole

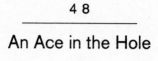

Around the middle of April Craig stops coming by, but I don't mention anything about it to the Stocktons or Mr. Gil. When Mr. Bernard suggests inviting him for dinner, I just say he's too busy with lacrosse and preparing for final exams. So of course Mr. Bernard immediately begins making it his mission in life to find out what happened.

One night at the dinner table he starts in on me with a fresh line of questioning. "Now, aren't you going to invite Craig to the flea market this weekend? It's the first Saturday that the outdoor stalls will be open. And he loves to collect those old postcards . . ."

"Football cards," Mr. Gil corrects him.

"Leave her alone," warns Ms. Olivia. "It's none of your business."

"But I approve of him. He's *good* for her," complains Mr. Bernard, as if I'm not even in the room.

"Good heavens, are you planning an August wedding in the gazebo?" Ms. Olivia replies. "She's only sixteen."

"I just thought he'd look marvelous in the prom pictures. A black Armani tux with a teal cummerbund, matching bow tie, powder blue carnation boutonniere, shiny black wing tips. And perhaps we could have a little punch party here beforehand." But then he turns to his mother. "Since when do we have a gazebo?"

"Craig's eighteen," Ms. Olivia says, again as if I'm not there. "He's probably pressuring her about sex. You know, blue balls, and *needs* and all that testosterone."

I am astounded that Ms. Olivia knows what happened. It's as if she'd overheard our conversation from a week ago. But I know she couldn't have, because we had it outside the boys' locker room at school and no one else was around. It wasn't exactly the ultimatum I'd been anticipating, but Craig more or less said that he has "needs" and he is eventually going to have to fill them "one way or another."

"*Mother,* please." Mr. Bernard quickly glances over at me as if he's going to catch some revelatory expression on my face. Then he goes back to pretending I'm invisible. "Did she tell you that?"

"She doesn't have to tell me. You men can get annoying sometimes. I don't blame Jane Bowles and Susan B. Anthony for seeking the company of women. And I've been meaning to tell you that we need a gazebo. We can't be hosting punch parties and debutante balls without one. Call that carpenter, the one we like so much, and tell him to do a late-eighteenth-century Lake District–style gazebo with plenty of latticework, a trellis roof, and a pergola leading to the garden path."

"One gazebo coming right up," barks Mr. Bernard like a lieutenant receiving orders from his captain. But then he sarcastically continues, "And maybe a merry-go-round for the driveway. And perhaps you'd like me to move the garage several feet to the left."

"Why don't I just blow up the garage?" offers Mr. Gil.

"All I'm asking you to do is make a simple phone call," says Ms. Olivia.

"Oh, all right. I'll try to reach him." Mr. Bernard rises and carries the remains of the rib roast into the kitchen. "Lake District–style gazebo," he mutters on his way toward the kitchen.

Mr. Gil stacks up the dinner plates and follows him.

"Why do I feel as if Bertie wants us to have some sort of a talk?" she inquires.

"I guess he likes Craig."

"Well, the important thing is whether *you* care for Craig. We're not running a matchmaking service here."

"Do you like Craig?" I ask Ms. Olivia.

"He's a sweet boy. And there's something compassionate about him that appeals to me—he'll sit in the yard and talk to a sick tree when he thinks that no one is watching. But he's not trying to sleep with *me*. At least not that I'm aware of."

The idea of Craig making a pass at Ms. Olivia starts me giggling. "I do like him. But you were right—what you said at dinner." I lift the edge of the lace cloth and traverse the beveled edges of the polished wood table with my fingers. It's kind of strange talking about sex with a woman my grandmother's age. "I mean, he . . . he entertains lots of impure thoughts." Shit, now I sound like a total prude. "I mean, I do, too . . . maybe not just to the same extent . . ."

"I'd think it unusual if you weren't entertained by a certain number of impure thoughts," says Ms. Olivia.

"But I . . . I'm just not ready yet."

"Want advice from an old woman?"

"Sure. You know more about men than I ever will."

"In some circles that's not considered an accomplishment," Ms. Olivia says with a sparkle in her eye. She leans toward me as if Mr. Bernard is standing on the other side of the door with a glass pressed to his ear. Which he probably is. "Give him a hand job."

Oh God. If my face is turning the color of Mr. Bernard's beet soup right now, then Ms. Olivia pretends not to notice.

"But he says that guys his age have needs . . ."

"Trust me on this one, Hallie. And not to sound cliché, but if that isn't enough until you *are* ready, then forget about him, because he doesn't care about you. And now I must get to work."

"Are you working on the Judge's poem?"

"No, a letter to the editor. They've dismissed the leader of a local Boy Scout Troop because one of the parents saw him participating in an AIDS fund-raiser and he privately admitted to being gay."

Ms. Olivia disappears through the tall wooden swinging door that leads into the kitchen. She always brews a fresh cup of oolong tea before embarking upon a new writing project.

"I couldn't catch everything you said," I hear Mr. Bernard complaining to her in the kitchen. "Something about a saraband or a Lindy hop. Does he want her to take dancing lessons?"

"Mind your own business," Ms. Olivia replies.

"I'm only trying to help," Mr. Bernard insists.

Mr. Gil reenters the dining room with a cup of coffee for himself and a hot chocolate for me. I can still hear Mr. Bernard grilling Ms. Olivia on the other side of the door. Mr. Gil carefully adds exactly one teaspoonful of sugar to his coffee and then clinks his spoon twice around. "I think it's safe to say that Olivia is making a good recovery now that she's back to writing blistering editorials."

"Will the newspaper print it?"

"Of course. Olivia's editorials are famous, or maybe I should say notorious. They boost circulation by almost fifty percent. Then the paper receives another hundred outraged letters in response to whatever point she's trying to make. Advertisers threaten to pull their accounts. Subscribers threaten to cancel their subscriptions. And so it goes."

"Wow," I say.

"Boyfriend problems . . . ," he states philosophically and sighs as if he's been there and done that. "Are you okay?"

"Pressure. Ms. Olivia said to give him a hand job. What do you think?"

"Good advice—like when slacks are too casual and a dress is too dressy but a skirt is just right."

Mr. Bernard pushes through the kitchen door with his back and enters the room with an ornately engraved antique silver coffeepot he recently bought but can't find a storage place for. "She won't bleed a drop. Your womanly secrets will go with her to the grave."

Mr. Gil and I just look at each other and laugh. I guess that no matter what I decide to do about Craig, one thing is for certain—I sure am living in a good place to get advice about dating men. I don't know why I waited so long to ask.

4 9

The Undealt Card

★

Mr. Gil is as right about Ms. Olivia's editorial as the local weatherman is always wrong about when it's going to rain. The day after her letter about the dismissed scout leader runs in the local newspaper, the phone is jangling away with people saying that she isn't a Christian and that she should mind her own business or else move to California. I'm surprised that Mr. Bernard isn't sympathetic to his mother's current cause, especially since he makes no secret about, well, his own lifestyle.

"Technically, the Boy Scouts are a private club and they can do whatever they please, Mother," he says matter-of-factly.

"I cannot believe what I'm hearing!" Ms. Olivia practically shouts at him. It's the first time I've ever seen Ms. Olivia actually appear to be infuriated, as if she's going to box his ears. "Whose child are you? *You!* You of all people, Bernard."

"I'd rather my life not become part of a cause célèbre, Mother. As soon as that occurs then it's no longer my life. I'm no longer a person. And I don't want the lead in my obituary to read *activist.* I'm an antiques dealer. It's bad enough they're going to find a way to work in the word *flamboyant.*"

"Does this mean you're not attending the meeting tonight?" Ms. Olivia asks with disbelief.

"You're on your own this time. Of course I'll send Gil to post bail if it comes to that." He exits the room in a huff.

"What good is knowledge without the wisdom to use it?" Ms. Olivia calls after him.

Meantime Mr. Gil explains to me that about a third of Ms. Olivia's editorials result in calls for a meeting down at the old Grange Hall, since townspeople become so agitated that they have to vent before a commerce war erupts and all the locals on the political left refuse to patronize businesses whose merchants are on the right. He says it was actually the Judge who started the town meeting tradition to prevent his house from being burned to the ground when Ms. Olivia became overly embroiled in politics.

"Bertie is like Thomas Jefferson," Ms. Olivia says to me, sounding annoyed. "Not only can he simultaneously hold two contradictory ideas in his head but he can also act upon both.

"And what about *you*?" she pointedly says to Mr. Gil.

"Please, Livvy, this is Bernard's hometown. You know that I'm behind you one hundred percent, but this time it's too personal."

"Of course it's personal! It's about the right of every American to have a *personal* life!"

But Mr. Gil doesn't rise to her battle cry.

"The Book of James asks what good is it if a man claims to have faith but has no deeds," she continues. Ms. Olivia could usually rouse Mr. Gil with a smattering of scripture, since it was not lost on her that he was raised a Disciple of Christ, and therefore guilt was always percolating only slightly beneath the surface.

He silently shakes his head as if to simultaneously decline and apologize. Ms. Olivia turns to me. "Well, are *you* coming with me?"

"What should I do?" I ask Ms. Olivia, my teacher who has taught me so much.

"You know that I can't tell you that, Hallie," she says.

I look to Mr. Gil. "Why don't you go and ask Bertie," he suggests. "He adores dispensing advice."

Mr. Bernard is sitting in the sunroom in the exact same spot where the Judge patiently waited out his final years. The television is on, I assume to avoid hearing any further commentary by Ms. Olivia. His chin is cradled in the palm of his hand and he's staring out the window to where the gardens are still dotted with grayish patches of melting snow and a late-winter sun melts into a gauzy white fog bank above the summerhouse.

"Hi," I finally say.

"Hi back," he says as if we're teenagers arriving in the lunchroom at the same time.

"She asked me to go with her."

"So go."

"I don't know."

"I think you do. You're just worried about me. Go with her. Unless you think it will get you into hot water with your folks."

"I don't care what they think."

"Then Godspeed. It's your big break to becoming an official rabble-rouser. I'm sure the evening news won't want to miss a shot of the Artful Dodger protesting next door to her former prison."

"How'd *you* know they called me that?" I ask.

"I had a meeting with your folks and the school administrators at the offices of your parents' lawyer."

Mr. Bernard rises and slowly walks over to the antique secretary where Ms. Olivia used to do paperwork and pay bills while she sat with the Judge. He rolls back the wooden top and slides a manila envelope out from one of the compartments and hands me a sheaf of about twenty papers neatly stapled together. Shuffling through the forms, I see my name typed in several places and also both my parents' full names and Mr. Bernard's name (oh my God, his middle name is Etienne), and there are legal-looking stamps in red ink throughout.

"I don't get it . . ."

"I'm your legal guardian," he says in a serious tone. "I apologize for not telling you earlier."

"Oh." I flip through the papers again but nothing really registers.

"It was the only way to make the whole arrangement work—the tutoring, the job—you know, insurance and liability and all that. The reason I didn't bother mentioning it is that it doesn't grant us permission to order you around."

"Of course not."

"You—you just seemed rather antiauthority at the time. And then, with Dad dying and all that, there just never seemed to be the right moment to bring it up."

"I wouldn't have minded." And this is the truth.

He takes my hand and says wearily, "I know. It's just that I didn't want you to ever feel that you had to stay here if for any reason you no longer desired to."

Staring back at me from the bottom of the last page is my dad's signature scrawled in thick black felt pen. For a moment I can't believe he actually agreed to put in writing that he was giving me up. It's official. I'm a foundling.

Mr. Bernard catches my eye. "It's just a formality. You know, if you need to go to the hospital in the middle of the night we'd have to be able to sign in order for you to receive proper medical treatment."

"Or if I get thrown in jail for disorderly conduct or assembling without a permit."

"Exactly." He cheers up considerably. "Just the pratfalls of daily life. Speaking of which, you'd better go and get your picket signs loaded into the *QE2* or you'll be late for the town hall extravaganza. *Courage, mon brave!*"

I dash back toward the living room to inform Ms. Olivia that I'm coming with her. But Mr. Gil announces that she's already in the car waiting for me.

"I'm honored to be here to see you off on your first protest," he says with mock seriousness. "I'll be sure to set the VCR to record the evening news."

Over at the Grange Hall the decision to dismiss the scoutmaster is upheld despite what I consider to be a brilliant plea from Ms. Olivia. She argues that a verdict based on sexual orientation is the same as firing someone for being handicapped and therefore is unconstitutional and will never hold up in court.

But people stand up one after another and for the most part say this case is different because it involves children and the scouts are not a public institution so they aren't required to follow the same federal laws that govern taxpayer-funded institutions.

When we arrive home Mr. Bernard has made peppermint tea and double fudge brownies for what he dubs a post-protest party. As we enter the living room, still carrying our leftover pamphlets and Ms. Olivia's speech notes, Mr. Gil bangs out "We Shall Overcome" on the piano. Then we all gather around the coffee table while Ms. Olivia and I enthusiastically recount who said what to whom and which factions came out in favor and against.

Mr. Bernard and Mr. Gil caught a snippet of Ms. Olivia's speech on the evening news. Mr. Bernard reports that the cinnamon-colored cardigan sweater set off her eyes nicely. I am so thrilled with Ms. Olivia's performance that I make them play back the video right away. And there I am in the opening shot, standing in front of the Grange Hall wearing a suit of mail on top and bright red tights on the bottom, holding a lance in one hand and in the other a shield with a placard on the front saying: "The First Amendment Is Not a Shield."

The armor was Ms. Olivia's idea. She claims that 90 percent of effective protesting is about marketing the message properly and so she keeps a store of props in the basement for such occasions.

Then the newscaster stops talking and they cut to the final few seconds of Ms. Olivia's speech. Following that the business news comes on and Mr. Gil switches off the television. Mr. Bernard passes the brownies and then sits back down on the couch, looking pleased. "Back when Father was an up-and-coming lawyer Mother used to assist in researching his cases. In fact, she's a charter member of the Institute for First Amendment Studies. Father may have been charismatic and imposing in the courtroom, and he had a brilliant legal mind, but he was a horrendous researcher."

"Yes, but he wrote wonderful opinions that displayed his airtight logic, much better than anything I could have produced," says Ms. Olivia. "I always became too emotionally involved."

Ms. Olivia sips her tea and attempts to recall for Mr. Bernard which of his customers attended, how they voted, and if they said anything worth repeating.

"Did anyone with a Pennsylvania Dutch bedroom set in good condition happen to appear at all pale and sickly?" he asks. "I have a wealthy client over in Youngstown, an oilman, who will pay a nice price for one."

"Oh, will you stop," Mr. Gil scolds Mr. Bernard. "The Judge would be so proud of you both," he says and smiles at Ms. Olivia and then at me.

"Why is everyone so happy?" I finally ask. "The vote was two thirty to forty-eight in favor of dismissing the scoutmaster. We failed—"

"We didn't fail. We just lost round one, that's all, dear," Ms. Olivia tells me. "There'll be appeals and petitions and protests. Don't be so quick to declare the victors and the vanquished."

"But I wanted to *win*," I say despondently. "How can you *live* in a town like this?"

"Yes, Mother," Mr. Bernard chimes in, "how *can* you live in a town like this? Why don't you and Hallie leave this hotbed of social rest and ship off to Berkeley and see how the lettuce pickers are getting on?"

"There's nothing wrong with this town that's not wrong with any other town," Ms. Olivia replies. "A town is made up of people who want the best for their children. And so they have fears. We must demonstrate that they have nothing to be afraid of."

"But everyone knows that you can't catch being gay. It's not like a cold. I mean, if it were, I mean, I would be . . ."

"And you don't think *your* parents are wondering if you're over here reading Gertrude Stein and using power tools?" asks Mr. Bernard.

"You don't really think . . . my parents . . . ," I muse aloud. And then I realize that yes, that's probably *exactly* what they think between my poker playing and the steel-toed hiking boots. And I suddenly start to laugh. "So they think I didn't want to go to school anymore because I'm a *lesbian*," I say incredulously.

"I think it's safe to say that's one theory which has been bandied about," Mr. Bernard says with a grin. "And you've not taken the time to enlighten any of us as to exactly *why* you took leave of public education."

Mr. Bernard occasionally attempts to trick me into telling him why I stopped going to school by asking questions about my teachers and if I missed playing sports and stuff like that. But I've never told him the real reason.

"It's nobody's business but your own," Ms. Olivia states with quiet conviction. "I swear, Bertie, the title of your autobiography will be *Too Nosy to Die*."

This last line makes Mr. Gil practically choke with laughter.

"Besides," Ms. Olivia continues, "I don't see how anyone can expect you to go to that hideous, hard-featured building every day in the first place. You shouldn't attend on aesthetic grounds alone."

"That's preposterous, Mother. Learning can take place in any surroundings, just as you're always insisting that one can worship anywhere."

I love it when Mr. Bernard uses Ms. Olivia's own theories against her. Though she usually finds a way to wriggle out of it.

"Look at the bright side," says Mr. Gil. "If the communists take over they won't have to change a brick."

"I'm being serious," says Ms. Olivia. "They load students into buses and march them through lovely museums to enlighten them about beauty and then dump them back into that steel-and-concrete morgue. Art and life must be experienced as intertwined."

"I'll messenger over a copy of Edith Wharton's decorating book to the superintendent in the morning," Mr. Bernard announces flippantly.

"That's an admirable first step," agrees Ms. Olivia. "Edith understood that life's handmaiden is art. And that the agony and the ecstasy can only exist side by side."

I'm not sure about ecstasy, but I *am* sure that the red tights are starting to itch something awful and that if I don't go upstairs and change in another few minutes I'm going to be in serious agony.

5 0

On the Outside

♠

By the second day of May there's been no sign of morning frost silvering the brown grass for two consecutive weeks and Mr. Bernard declares it officially safe to begin planting the outdoor gardens. We buy flats of flowers from the nursery, carefully bury the roots of the tiny seedlings in the freshly turned earth, and transfer the small but sturdy plants we'd been nurturing in the summerhouse. The porch pots are taken from the sunroom and placed at various points along the meandering garden path.

And by the second week of May, my back is aching, my fingernails are permanently stained brown, and I practically fall into a coma the moment I lay my head down on the pillow at night. There are nightmares about giant pachysandra trying to smother me and bury my worn-out body in the damp soil to be used as fertilizer for their offshoots.

One night I'm so exhausted that I go to my room directly after dinner. I can't even wait for the apple strudel to finish baking in spite of the fact that it smells delicious. Mr. Bernard kindly offers to save me a piece for breakfast.

Propped up between the lamp and clock radio on my night table I find an information package from the Cleveland Institute of Art. A bright purple Post-it marks a summer program where you put together a portfolio that can be used to apply to the regular four-year program. Anyone can sign up. I read about this for a few minutes and then pass out from exhaustion, thereby quickly clearing the way for the sinister pachysandra of my horticultural dreamscapes.

A gentle tapping on my door awakens me. At first I think it's morning or else the pachysandra have taken to clumping around the house in the middle of the night, foraging for boxes of Miracle-Gro.

"Hallie, are you awake?" It's Ms. Olivia.

I open the door wearing the red practice football jersey Craig gave me before his raging hormones totaled us. It has his number, 22, in peeling black iron-on fabric across the front and back. Ms. Olivia is wearing a bright orange tracksuit and carrying a flashlight.

"Hurry up and put some pants on," she urges me. "It's a moonless night, perfect for Conrad."

One thing about Ms. Olivia is that she isn't affected by daylight savings, normal working hours, alarm clocks, or anything else that has to do with time.

"Okay," I agree. "I'll be downstairs in a minute."

The thing I should be most worried about, however, is not that we are going to trudge into the middle of the woods, just the two of us, and read from Joseph Conrad's *Heart of Darkness*, but that I actually knew what Ms. Olivia's cryptic statement meant when she summoned me in the first place.

Together we tramp through the backyard with the beam from the flashlight bouncing along ahead of us like an unsecured moon. I enjoy the great outdoors as much as the next person, but must admit that even I feel spooked reading Conrad in the forest at midnight. Especially the part about coming across a remote outpost with a row of human heads mounted on poles.

And it only makes the reading scarier knowing that on this very same ground, in these very same woods, Indians were once slaughtered by Europeans. Eric had found an actual Indian arrowhead back here when we were in elementary school.

I read aloud the dying words of Kurtz, *The horror! The horror!*

Ms. Olivia stubs out her cigarette and shreds the butt into the grass. Then she explains that *"The horror!"* represents despair over the encounter with human depravity, and that's what the heart of darkness is supposed to mean. And also that powerful people shouldn't go around trying to civilize others. Then she tells me about the author. And when she talks about Joseph Conrad, quite frankly, it's easy to understand how he became preoccupied with despair and depravity. According to Ms. Olivia, his father was a poet and Polish patriot arrested for his politics and sent into exile in northern Russia. And it was there that both Conrad's parents died of tuberculosis. Ms. Olivia especially admires Conrad for refusing an offer of knighthood from the British government.

During the trek back home Ms. Olivia smokes another cigarette. She says that she hopes I'll never start since it's a terrible habit and will probably give her lung cancer. "There's nothing worse than a dead Unitarian," she jokes, "all dressed up with no place to go."

By the time we arrive back at the house it's only one o'clock, but after reading all that macabre Conrad it feels as if it should be much later. Mr. Bernard is sitting downstairs in his bathrobe paging through a coffee-table book about Biedermeier furniture.

"Have Thelma and Louise returned from their adventures? I'm so jealous that you girls never invite me to your Wiccan rituals and coven meetings. Did you have a séance or just talk about boys and do each other's nails?"

"I told you not to wait up," Ms. Olivia dismisses Mr. Bernard's teasing.

"I was listening for the beating of the drums. And also, you had a customer." We all understand this to mean that someone stopped by for one of Ms. Olivia's morning-after pills.

"Good night," says Ms. Olivia as she begins to climb the stairs.

"Oh, Moth-er," Mr. Bernard calls after her with exaggerated sweetness.

"Yes, dear?"

"The pet store next to my shop has a going-out-of-business sale sign in the window."

"Oh, Bertie, I'm just not ready for another dog right now."

"That's not what I meant." Mr. Bernard pauses. "You haven't been down there freeing the birds again, have you?"

"Of course not!" Ms. Olivia replies indignantly. "Don't be ridiculous."

"*Ridiculous?* What about—"

"Those were *toads*, Bernard. Common garden-variety toads, and they never should have been incarcerated in the first place."

"*All right, all right.* I just wanted to make sure."

"And I *bought* the toads before I returned them to the earth."

"Yes, of course. Please accept my apologies."

"I have a receipt for the toads," Ms. Olivia calls out from the top of the stairwell.

After we hear the door to Ms. Olivia's room close, Mr. Bernard asks, "So were you scared?"

"A little bit," I admit.

"Once when I was about ten years old we had a power failure," Mr. Bernard recalls. "Father was out of town and Mother had me make popcorn and then took me down to the basement and lit a few dozen candles and read 'The Murders in the Rue Morgue.' Mutilated corpses, scalped women, an escaped orangutan, the whole kit and caboodle. It made *Psycho* look like a romantic comedy."

Sometimes I can't help but wonder if Ms. Olivia knows more about witchcraft than she lets on. There's a boxful of odd-looking charms and trinkets on her bureau, and a whole shelf of books on mystical writing in her library. She claims it's all research for her poetry.

"Uh, Mr. Bernard . . . ," I whisper.

But he's lost in his book. "Uhmmm."

"Your mother . . . I, uh . . . she's not a witch, is she?" But I don't want this to sound like an insult, because I really do love Ms. Olivia. So I quickly add, "I mean, not that it would matter."

Only Mr. Bernard doesn't even look up from the page. "No, no," he replies offhandedly, as if this is the most natural question in the world and doesn't even require his full attention to properly answer it. "Mother abhors dark clothing. She favors a bold palette—lots of vermilion, marigold, and magenta. Furthermore, I'm quite positive she has no idea as to where I keep the brooms."

Cleaning Up

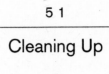

One evening at dinner Ms. Olivia casually announces that the mysterious Ottavio Vespignani will be paying us a visit beginning May 25, in just one week's time. Although she hasn't mentioned him since the Judge died, I know that they send E-mails to each other and occasionally speak on the phone. Ms. Olivia talks on the phone wherever she happens to be and doesn't seem to care if the conversation is overheard.

The only way I can tell that Mr. Bernard is anxious about the visit is by the cooking and housekeeping frenzy that ensues. Using the excuse of "spring cleaning," he hires every possible local service—chimney sweep, window washer, a driveway-sealing company, and eight German-speaking cleaning women who scrub, wax, and shine the place from top to bottom in a single hour. Mr. Bernard dubs them the Luftwaffe and makes us all evacuate the premises while they scour and carpet-bomb. Another van pulls up and two burly men march into the house and take down all the drapes and remove the bedspreads and whisk them off to be sanitized and deodorized.

Ms. Olivia appears unfazed by Mr. Bernard's purification rituals and sloughs off his occasional outbursts about the general squalid state of the household the way a Labrador retriever shakes off its bathwater. Though when he attempts to line all of our drawers with oilcloth she says that angst has finally overcome his innate sense of decor.

Two days before Ottavio's arrival, Mr. Gil and Mr. Bernard sort through all the Judge's clothes and take them to the Salvation Army bin behind the

Star-Mart. Then Mr. Bernard, Mr. Gil, and I sit around the dining room table polishing the silverware while Ms. Olivia alternately works a crossword puzzle and reads to us from Robert Herrick.

> *That age is best which is the first,*
> *When youth and blood are warmer;*
> *But being spent, the worse and worst,*
> *Times still succeed the former.*

"How does a person write a great poem or novel?" I ask.

"Oftentimes they're inspired by earlier works or a heroic figure," explains Ms. Olivia. "Remember the Italian renaissance poet Francesco Petrarca? He inspired Chaucer."

"Like Elton John wrote about Princess Diana?" I ask.

"Quite right," says Mr. Gil.

Of course, the real question on our minds at that moment is not poetry but where Mr. Ottavio Vespignani will sleep. There has been no move by Ms. Olivia to move Rocky off the pullout couch in the Florida Room, and I haven't been asked to donate my bedroom. And even though Mr. Bernard and I scrubbed the summerhouse from the skylight right down to the natural wood flooring, we haven't been asked to prepare a bed out there either.

Anyway, nobody dares to ask Ms. Olivia, though Mr. Bernard has poked around a few times by pretending to mull over the purchase of new linens at one of the white sales at the mall.

"Does Ottavio enjoy seafood, Mother?" Mr. Bernard inquires the morning of the big arrival. "I was thinking of making madrilène with red caviar and Dover sole in a shiitake mushroom sauce."

"I'm sure that will be fine," Ms. Olivia replies. "Ottavio appreciates any and all good cooking."

"Does he have any food allergies?" Mr. Bernard asks.

"Not that I'm aware of," she says.

"I know!" Mr. Bernard appears to have solved the problem. "Crabmeat Monterey! Where can I find Grandma's recipe?"

"I haven't seen that recipe box in a month of Sundays."

"Of course you haven't seen Grandma's recipe box. I hid it because you were always taking out the index cards and scribbling quatrains on the back of her recipes and then misplacing them or using them as bookmarks.

However, the one for Crabmeat Monterey was jotted down on a piece of notebook paper and I thought for sure it was tucked inside one of her old cookbooks. Gelatin, tomato soup, green olives . . . eggs, I can't remember if there were any eggs in it."

"Bernard, it's ridiculous to go to all this trouble."

"Mother, I'm not going to have him think we live like a bunch of hillbillies. I thought I'd reserve tickets for *Swan Lake*. There's a performance at the Cleveland Playhouse on Friday night. And now that Craig has been welcomed back into the fold, perhaps Hallie can invite her beau and the six of us can all go together."

Ms. Olivia's advice has alleviated the sexual Cold War between Craig and me, in that I've promised Craig to deliver her sex cure shortly, as soon as exams are over.

Mr. Bernard looks to me for approval of this ballet trial balloon. "Ever been on a triple date?"

"No. I've never even been to a ballet. I don't think Craig has, either. But sure, we were only going to play miniature golf on Friday."

Fortunately Craig doesn't seem to mind the Stocktons and all of their idiosyncrasies. In fact, he actually enjoys coming here, because they encourage him to practice doctoring the trees and to try different fertilizers of his own concoction. Mr. Bernard even pays him to restore birdhouses. Craig is extremely patient with detail work. Whereas if I can't fix a thing within five minutes I want to smash it with a spade.

"And we'll need new slipcovers in the solarium." Mr. Bernard abandons Crabmeat Monterey for the moment and returns to his catalogue of preparations.

"Oh, it's the *solarium* now, is it?" Mr. Gil says with great exaggeration. "And I imagine it overlooks the *arboretum*," he teases.

Mr. Bernard ignores him and leans over his shopping list for Ottavio's arrival dinner, only by this time he has more items crossed out than left on since he keeps on overhauling the entire menu. He's poking his lip with the back of his pen and muttering, "Lemons, acorn squash, baby onions, pineapples for sorbet . . ."

Ms. Olivia asks if I'm ready to begin our tutoring session. I'd assumed that with Ottavio arriving soon she would have wanted the evening to herself. But she says it's slightly overcast and therefore we should go to the cemetery on the edge of town to study World War I. Ms. Olivia says that you should always discuss war on foreign soil in a cemetery under leaden skies right before sunset so you don't regard human life as expendable.

Before I can answer Ms. Olivia the telephone rings. Mr. Bernard motions to me with his right hand like the Pope waving to his subjects from the balcony, only without looking up since he's still concentrating on his list of ingredients.

"Would you mind answering that, Hallie? It's probably a long-distance salesperson offering to come over here and do our laundry if we'll switch to AT&T." I go to the kitchen, pick up the phone, and find that the person on the other end isn't a telemarketer at all, not by a long shot.

5 2

The Only Game in Town

♣

"Hey, Hellcat?" the voice of my old track pal Cappy croons through the receiver. "What's the skinny? You on the dodge from some Yoo-Hoo bootleggers or the bicycle repo man?" He laughs heartily at his own jokes. "I scrounged this number from your kid brother, what's his name, Freddy? Cost me twenty bucks—I hadda buy him a baseball cap."

"Teddy. Sounds like him. Naw, Cappy, I don't owe nobody any spondulicks."

"Well how come I haven't seen you wagering on the glue pots? What? Didja hit it big on the Preakness?"

"I didn't follow any of the Triple Crown this year. I had stuff to straighten out."

"Listen, kiddo, I got a gig for you. Totally legit. Two words for you, my bookmaking brainchild. *College basketball.*"

"So, what about it?"

"*So,* remember that day you showed me how to enter all the past histories for the ponies and track conditions into the computer and to generate probabilities?"

"Yeah."

"Well, I've been working on that for roundball."

"It's illegal to take bets on basketball in Ohio, you know that," I remind him.

"Who said anything about taking action? You'd just be crunching some numbers, kiddo. C'mon, Hallie. What do ya say? Two grand a week in cash during the season and then we'll do soccer and a little rugby in the summer and winter. Rugby's gettin' real big in the minimum-security slammers—all the rich guys have ESPN nowadays."

Wow, two grand a week! That's over a hundred thousand dollars a year.

"I'll let you know, Cappy. Finals are in a few weeks. I'll call you when they're over."

"Finals? I thought you bagged that school shtick. Lemme know soon. It took me a coupla weeks to track you down. Jumpin' Jehoshaphat, where are you, some sort of mental institute?"

"It's complicated," I say.

As I'm talking to Cappy, Mr. Bernard enters the kitchen as if on a mission from the cooking gods. He climbs up on the stepstool and from the top shelves pulls out a tangle of wire cooling racks, several of which go jangling to the floor.

"Incoming!" he shouts as one of the thin metal racks bounces off my shoulder and a few more clatter into the stainless-steel sink. "*Excusez-moi.*"

He leaps down and spreads the contents of a folder on top of the range, the only available surface space, and after hastily paging through yellowed newspaper clippings and index cards inked in flowery blue script he gleefully shouts, "Here it is!" Mr. Bernard proceeds to remove a square piece of cardboard that's labeled Crabmeat Monterey.

"Uh, I've got to go," I say into the receiver and then disconnect.

"Everything copacetic?" Mr. Bernard asks me.

"Sure," I say, still holding the receiver in my hand. "Why do you ask?"

"Because you look as if you've just heard bad news." Mr. Bernard gathers the cooling racks from off the floor.

"It was just . . . it was just an old friend from . . . from the track."

Mr. Bernard stops what he's doing, stands up, and very seriously says, "Hallie, do you have gambling debts? If you need a loan, it's not a problem."

"No I don't, dammit!" I say angrily.

"Did I say something wrong?" Mr. Bernard appears stunned by my outburst.

"Why does everyone always think the worst of me? I haven't laid any action in months—I mean, not that there's anything wrong with betting. But I haven't so much as played penny-ante Hi-Lo. And I have more than two thousand dollars in the bank . . ."

Mr. Bernard walks over, and I don't know why but I start to cry.

"No one thinks anything bad about you," he says. "It's just the opposite. We care so much. Everybody . . . your parents, Gil, Mother, Craig, me, your teachers at the high school. Even your brothers and sisters. Look how Eric and Louise invited you to the Bulldogs' playoff game in Cincinnati."

At that moment Ms. Olivia waltzes into the kitchen wearing her red pea-coat and carrying the American history review book. However when she catches sight of me wiping my eyes she turns right around and says, "Whoops, I thought the car keys were in here," and quickly exits.

"Mother, wait—" he calls after her. But she's gone.

"It just seems," I tearfully continue to Mr. Bernard, "that whenever I don't show up on time people immediately assume that I'm in reform school or a halfway house. You know, even after I solved the golf money mystery, if something is missing . . ." But I start sobbing and can't finish.

"Oh, dear." Mr. Bernard hands me a tissue and puts his hand on my shoulder. "How can I put this, Hallie . . ."

"Put what? That *is* what you think, isn't it? And Mr. Gil. And Ms. Olivia. That I'm destined to be a vagrant and a criminal!"

"Of course not, don't be ridiculous. Why would Mother spend all that time tutoring you if she thought you were going to end up behind bars?" Mr. Bernard says gently. "Hallie . . . you . . . how shall I say . . . you hold your cards awfully close to the vest. We don't always know what you're feeling or thinking or what it is that you wish to do."

"So you're suggesting that if I said more of the stuff that I'm thinking, people wouldn't always assume I'm going to end up in prison?"

"Try to look at it from my point of view. You receive a phone call and speak in hushed tones so that I don't even realize you're still on the phone. And then right after I arrive in the kitchen you hurriedly tell the caller you have to hang up and look as if you've been caught fixing the World Series."

"But I was just—"

"Wait a second. Now add to that how I've seen you shuffle cards while you're watching television, practically throwing them up over your shoulder and reeling them back in like a scene out of *The Sting*. When you and Gil are playing gin rummy you call the queen of spades 'dirty Dora' and refer to aces as 'oil wells.' And I've seen you tote up a pile of receipts or the columns in my ledgers, add the tax in your head, and then take a ten-percent discount off that before I've had time to enter the first number into a calculator. And your answer is always correct. If the calculator says something different, then it needs a new battery."

After some more snuffling I slump my head down onto the kitchen table. Mr. Bernard puts on the kettle, even though he drinks only brewed coffee. I attempt to suck up a string of snot that's escaping through my nose and then decide to come clean.

"This guy I know from the track is offering me a job for a hundred grand a year as a bookie. I mean, it's not really as a bookie. He's the bookmaker. My job would be more as a systems analyst to the bookie."

"Really?"

"A hundred G's is a lot of scratch," I add.

"It's more *scratch* than Gil and I make combined," says Mr. Bernard.

"I told him I'd think about it. You don't think I should take it, right?"

"I didn't say that."

"No, but I can see it in your face."

"That's not fair. Talking with you is like trying to pull one over on a mind reader." He sits down across from me at the table. "Of course, I'm not going to advise you to become a bookie or a gambler. But I know so little about that life. Maybe it's all very thrilling and glamorous, like in *Guys and Dolls*."

"Glamorous?" I laugh out loud. "A bunch of old guys smoking and crabbing about their wives and trying to catch one another bluffing. Yeah, it's *très* glamorous."

And then it occurs to me: *Why not show Mr. Bernard just how* glamorous *it really is*? I look up at the cuckoo clock on the wall. It's a quarter to eight. "C'mon," I say and push my chair back from the table. "I'll show you."

"What do you mean you'll show me? It's Monday night. Are we going on a junket to Las Vegas?"

"No, to church."

"To church? Is there a high rollers' bingo game in progress?"

"Not bingo. Poker. Now go get a hundred dollars to bet with and meet me in the driveway, or we're going to be late. The guys hate that."

"What *guys*?"

"The *guys* I play poker with." At least I can play again now that I'm no longer banned from the game because of the golf money. "You already know Officer Rich."

"You play *poker* with Officer Rich?" he repeats with alarm.

"And Pastor Costello. And Al Santora and Herb Rowland."

But Mr. Bernard sits back down when he hears the name Herb Rowland.

"Uh, Hallie, it's a nice idea, but Herb Rowland and I don't exactly travel in the same circles," he says hesitantly.

"I don't get you," I say. "You're the one who's always saying that you and Mr. Gil have just as much right to live in this town as anyone else and blah, blah, blah, and people just have to accept that."

"That's correct. But I meant people in general. I never named Herb specifically."

"Listen, Mr. Bernard, he likes to give everybody a lot of shit, but he's okay once you get to know about him."

"I don't think I want to get to know him any more than I did back in high school," says Mr. Bernard. "He was a year ahead of me."

"I didn't say *know him.* I said know *about* him."

"I don't see what the difference is. He's still a closed-minded brute."

"The difference is that, yeah, he can be a pig-headed bully. But his wife makes him sleep on the porch, his daughter was picked up for shoplifting over in Timpany last year, and he's having an affair with Jemma, the cashier who works for him at the drugstore. You know, *Jemma,* the young woman who was here that night to pick up her *medicine.*"

"Really?" Mr. Bernard brightens. "How . . . how do you *know* all this?"

"Same way you get gossip from all your little old ladies down at the shop. With guys you just have to watch more than listen. Now, come *on.* We're going to play a little five-card stud."

Mr. Bernard looks down at his blue-and-white-striped button-down shirt and gray flannel slacks. "All right, but what should I wear?"

I grab the keys off the counter and move toward the archway. "What *are* you talking about? Wear what you have on. We're not playing strip poker. The only thing that matters is putting your money on the table. It's a card game, not a fashion show."

We pass Mr. Gil in the living room. He's sitting in the big armchair next to the fireplace and sorting through a pile of paperwork.

Mr. Bernard clears his throat. "Hallie and I are going to a poker contest."

Mr. Gil glances up as if to make sure the body matches the announcement. Then he matter-of-factly replies, "Yes, of course. It's your poker night. Just remember to remove your reading glasses if you're going to smash beer cans against your forehead."

"Of course," says Mr. Bernard. "We'll be back . . . I don't know." He turns to me. "How long do these matches last?"

"It's a game, not a match or a contest. A couple hours, until Herb wins and wants to quit or until Herb loses and gets cranky and makes everyone else want to quit." If you ever walk in on the middle of a poker game, it's easy to tell who's ahead. The winners lean back and tell funny stories, while the losers shout, "Deal the damn cards already!"

Mr. Bernard shoots me another worried look about the dreaded Herb encounter as we head toward the front hall.

"Oh, Bernard," Mr. Gil calls after us. "Is *that* what you're wearing?" He furrows his brow while giving Mr. Bernard a sartorial once-over.

Mr. Bernard frantically looks down at his slacks and shoes as if he's checking for stains, tears, and iron-on patches. "Yes, why? What's wrong?"

"Nothing," Mr. Gil says and returns to his work.

"C'mon!" I say. "Any faster and we're going to catch up with yesterday."

"What?" Mr. Bernard pleads with Mr. Gil, panic edging his voice. "Should I put on khakis?"

"I was just joking!" says Mr. Gil and laughs.

"But how do I *look*?" Mr. Bernard says.

"You *look* like you're about to meet your *parole officer*," replies Mr. Gil. "Now will you *go* already."

Knights of the Card Table

♥

Outside dusk is falling, gentle and cool. On the way over to the church I can tell that Mr. Bernard is nervous, not just about encountering Herb but also because I only recently taught him the game. Still, the Herb factor is powerful.

"So *that's* why you won't go into the drugstore," I say. "You're afraid of running into Herb. I was wondering what you were doing driving practically to the next town for Band-Aids."

"That's not true. That drugstore was built in the fifties. The ceiling is probably dripping with asbestos. I'm surprised the EPA hasn't closed it down by now."

I begin to feel guilty for torturing Mr. Bernard like this. Thank God I never got bullied in school, at least not by the students. Though I sure knew how it felt to have my parents and teachers all come down on me.

We pull into the driveway of the church. All the guys' cars are there, including Officer Rich's squad car. He must have come directly from the station.

"Okay," I say. "Do you have your strategy down?"

"Yes," he replies. "I'm supposed to concentrate on getting three of a kind. And if I don't make it, then I relinquish. Unless I have a pair of aces, right?"

"Right," I say. "And definitely don't do that thing where you hold your breath while you're being dealt your cards and then sigh or smile depending on what you get. That's a dead giveaway. Do it like the time I watched you buy that jeweled cigarette case at the garage sale, you know, where you appeared totally disinterested even though you knew it was worth a lot more money than they were asking."

"Got it. That's my dealer face."

"And don't raise more than five bucks no matter what you have."

"Right, five dollars is the limit."

"And the word is *fold*, not *relinquish*."

I walk down the stairs ahead of Mr. Bernard.

"Look what the raccoons dragged in," Al says sarcastically.

"Good to see you, Hallie," Pastor Costello says sincerely. "It was a shame about all that missing-money business."

"Well, if it isn't Dirty Hallie," Herb says as he opens a bag of pretzels and proceeds to help himself, his way of welcoming me back into high-stakes society.

"Yeah, thanks, Herbicide," I shoot back. "And I guess you look okay for someone who hasn't slept in his own bed for over a year."

Herb has a face full of chewed pretzels but manages to give me a nasty scowl just the same. He knows that his kids tell stories about him in school. I usually don't lay into Herb for the little stuff, but I figure I'd better get the upper hand right away before introducing Mr. Bernard, whose feet are now coming into view as he slowly descends the narrow stairwell. The dim lighting is made worse by large silver foil-covered pipes suspended from the ceiling that serve to layer the room in a web of confusing shadows. And the fact that Al's already got his Marlboros fired up, sending a steady stream of smoke heavenward, doesn't exactly help to improve visibility.

"I brought a friend along," I announce.

They all look toward the tasseled loafers on the stairs as if we might be getting busted by the Feds, or worse, their wives. The voices of the men fall silent, like birds at sunset.

"Don't let him take all your money," I say.

Officer Rich takes in the scene with a glance, like a lasso. "Ahoy there, Bernard." He stands and shakes hands with Mr. Bernard as if he's welcoming him to a business meeting. It must take a minute for Mr. Bernard's eyes to adjust to the smoke and mottled illumination because he squints and looks around as if he's accidentally stumbled onto a subterranean city.

"Nice to see you, Mr. Stockton," says Pastor Costello. He also rises and offers his hand. For a second I can tell he's concerned that Mr. Bernard may snitch to certain townspeople, specifically the kind of ladies who would frequent Mr. Bernard's shop, about his hosting a game of chance on sacred ground.

"Don't worry," I say, not just for Pastor Costello's sake but also for the benefit of Al and Herb. "He's cool."

"Yes, yes, of course," says Pastor Costello apologetically, as if he's just been caught having impure thoughts. "Have a sandwich. I apologize that we've already taken our repast. However, I believe there's some tuna left."

"Thank you, but we had dinner," says Mr. Bernard as he eyes the crumpled deli wrappers oozing mayonnaise and wilted lettuce. "And please call me Bernard."

Of course, Pastor Costello doesn't say, "Please call me Pastor Costello" to Mr. Bernard, because he just *is* Pastor Costello. "You've been so kind to offer our Hallie food and shelter during these past months."

"Yes, well, it's included in her employment contract," says Mr. Bernard. "But she's a free agent, of course."

"Yes, of course," agrees Pastor Costello.

"This is Bernard Stockton," I say to Al and then to Herb.

Fortunately for Herb, Al is busily shuffling the cards and organizing the poker chips, and so Al just smiles his hello and that gets Herb out of offering a handshake. If Al had stood and extended an arm, then Herb would have been forced to follow.

Officer Rich pulls another brown metal folding chair from the stack against the far wall and sets it up for Mr. Bernard. "I wasn't aware that you were a poker player."

"Actually I just recently learned the game," says Mr. Bernard. He sits down next to Officer Rich. "Hallie taught me over the winter. After she got bored beating us all at gin."

"If you learned from Hallie, then we'd better be careful," says Pastor Costello proudly, as if I'd won awards in the Sunday school for memorizing the most psalms.

"The lessons certainly weren't cheap," he says with a laugh.

This actually makes Al chuckle, and Herb relaxes enough to unfold his crossed arms. "I'll bet," says Al. "But she's right about that. You can't learn real poker with paper money. Playing for matchsticks and pennies is for girls." Then he apparently realizes that he's talking about a girl, and so he corrects himself. "I mean sissies." But then he must realize that Mr. Bernard may construe this as an insult because he's gay and so he starts mopping up after himself once again. "I mean—"

"Just deal the cards," Officer Rich interjects to everyone's great relief.

"Yeah, okay. Five-card stud to begin with, deuces wild." Al passes the deck left for Herb to cut. "Cut 'em thin and win. Cut 'em deep and weep."

"Cut the crap," says Herb. "I hate that damn dealer patter of yours."

But Herb cuts thin anyway.

After an uncomfortable silence during the first few rounds, with everyone appearing to concentrate extra hard on scrutinizing their cards and stacking their chips, the guys eventually fall into their usual routines.

Officer Rich tells about a four-foot alligator that some kids found in the creek and how he had to strap its jaw together with his belt until he could get some duct tape and then drive it to an exotic-pets expert in Cleveland.

Al rants about the cost of graduation—yearbooks, proms, cap and gown, photographs, trips to look at colleges, application fees. Herb complains about how the new variety store at the edge of town is taking away his business and insists they should revitalize the downtown area while they still can, before all the new strip malls and outlet centers kill off Main Street. Mr. Bernard jumps right in on that one. I'd heard him grumbling about that at dinner just the other night. It turns out to be something that Herb and Mr. Bernard have in common. Possibly the *only* thing, at least as far as I can figure it.

I can also tell that Officer Rich and Pastor Costello are concerned about taking Mr. Bernard's money, he being a newcomer and all. But after Mr. Bernard wins a pot with three threes they don't seem to worry anymore. Herb, on the other hand, seems to be extra careful not to lose to Mr. Bernard. He bets more aggressively when it gets down to just the two of them. Meantime good old Al doesn't give a damn whose money he takes, or, though he doesn't necessarily like it, who takes his.

We end the night with me winning about thirty dollars and Mr. Bernard up by ten. I didn't have good cards and couldn't have done much better. On the other hand, I didn't want to piss off Al and Herb by making a killing, because I was afraid they'd blame me for altering the deal. And they'd have a valid point. Bringing in a new person changes the way the cards fall, though theoretically it doesn't raise or lower any individual's probability of getting any one card. But they would have been looking at all the hands where the guy next to them got the card they'd needed and then blamed me.

Herb wins fifty bucks or so, which is actually good, because it makes him friendly. By the end of the evening he's calling Mr. Bernard "Bernie" (and Mr. Bernard isn't correcting him the way he does everyone else) and the two of them are talking about getting a petition together to protest the proposed Grocery Depot, which will divert traffic from both their businesses in town. And though Mr. Bernard doesn't say it, I know that he'll make a point of patronizing Herb's drugstore in the future.

Al drops ninety bucks, but he doesn't bitch about losing or me having shifted the deal by bringing a guest. Because Al knows the truth, as Herb does, that I brought them some easy money in the form of a newcomer, basically a sucker delivered right to their doorstep. I mean, it didn't take long for them to figure out that Mr. Bernard was hunting for tripods and closing up without them. So they should have been able to do something with that knowledge. But at the end of the day you still need the cards.

"See you guys next week," Officer Rich calls to Mr. Bernard and me as we leave. From the look on Mr. Bernard's face I decide that hearing this pleases him more than the ten bucks he managed to win.

On the way home Mr. Bernard insists that we stop at the convenience store for creamsicles in order to celebrate his initiation into the Buildings and Grounds Committee. The last time I saw him this excited was when he found the original papers in the back of a Solomon Stowe mantel clock.

"You know," he says confidently, "with a little practice I could really excel at this pastime. For instance, there were a few hands when I knew that if I'd tried for a straight rather than just three of a kind, I would have made it."

I just nod my head like, *Oh really?*

"And why did you kick me after I played those two pair? If Herb hadn't gotten that spade for his flush I would have won. And what were the chances of *that* happening?"

"The chances of that happening were real good, since all that was left in the deck were seven spades and one heart."

"Oh, well—"

"It's a good thing you didn't win any *more* money, that's all I have to say. Because you'd be impossible to live with."

When we pull into the driveway, the house is dark except for a few table lamps left on downstairs.

"Tell me something—how can you keep track of all those cards?" he asks.

"Same way you keep track of period furniture, I guess. There are only fifty-two cards in the deck. You know the value of a least a hundred different types of clocks and chairs."

"But the cards are thrown down so fast. I barely had time to look at what everyone had showing."

"It's like that auction you took me to—I didn't know what was going on and yet you were bidding on lamps and bureaus and making notes in your book. You knew how much everything was worth and even what the other dealers in the crowd wanted and up to how much they'd pay. It's pretty much the same thing."

"When I had those three threes I should have raised more."

"You would have scared everybody into thinking you had a full house and they all would have folded. Two of them were showing and everyone else had a shitty hand."

"You don't know for sure that's what would have happened," he replies with the unshakable confidence of a first-time player.

" 'Night, *Bernie*," I say.

"Ha, ha," says Mr. Bernard. " 'Night, Hellcat. You think I didn't hear that one?"

"Yeah, well, Hellcat is going to sleep thirty smackers richer."

"Just wait until next week," warns Mr. Bernard.

"You're kidding me, right? You really want to go *back*?"

"Absolutely. Only I believe next time I'll wear jeans with a black T-shirt and loafers. No socks. Much more *dangerous*, don't you think?"

"Yeah, your picture is in the dictionary under 'dangerous.' Right between 'daffodil' and 'delphinium.' "

Climbing the stairs to go to bed, I hear Mr. Bernard laughing to himself in the living room as he switches off the lights.

Against the Odds

★

Early the next morning I head over to the shop with Mr. Bernard because he's paying me to dust everything. While I clean he works on a new window display featuring antique tin toys, oil lamps, watches, and fountain pens. He claims they make good gifts for graduation and Father's Day.

Eventually we return to discussing my recent employment offer in the local gaming industrial complex. Now that Mr. Bernard sees himself as a card-carrying member in what he perceives to be society's romantic under-belly, he's waxing philosophical. Meantime I'm reconsidering my promise to take him to the racetrack this summer for fear that he'll soon be watching *The Godfather* and getting into the carting and hauling business.

"Listen, I'll never beat you at poker and I'll never be able to multiply and divide without a calculator. But forget about what I'm thinking for a moment and concentrate on what I'm saying. Of course I want you to go to college and get a respectable job, I'd be lying if I said otherwise. But if you proceed however you feel is appropriate for *you*, then we won't feel any differently about you. I promise."

"Yeah, well, you've never met Cappy. Much as he jokes about it, he's done hard time. You don't fool around with RICO."

"Who's Rico? A gambler? A hit man?"

"Worse. The laws against racketeering. Betting on the ponies is legit—well, the betting part is at least. What some of the owners and jockeys do is questionable. But making book on sports, oh boy . . ."

"Then you answered your own question. It's enough for me just to keep Mother out of the state pen. I'd much rather visit you at Penn State."

When we arrive home I help Mr. Bernard prepare Ottavio's arrival feast, which features sweet-and-sour pork with dates, pomegranates, and apricots as a main course.

"Tomorrow is Sassanid Arabian night," Mr. Bernard declares as he grinds a mound of fresh almonds onto wax paper. He chooses exotic dinner themes the way my mom chooses a Winnie the Pooh motif for our birthday parties and bedrooms at home.

"Couscous is a staple in Northern Africa and the Middle East," Mr. Bernard duly notes as he hands me a container of couscous that I assume I am supposed to boil.

"That was a good alligator story Officer Rich told last night." I laugh as I picture the slow-cornering Officer Rich trying to rope a gator. "You haven't told me a story from work in a while."

"I thought you'd never ask," Mr. Bernard replies cryptically. "Someone you know stopped in just the other day. However, I'm sworn to secrecy."

This is my cue to continue probing. Ms. Olivia and Mr. Gil have a saying: "Telephone, telegraph, tell-a-Bertie. Which is the fastest?"

"My parents?" I ask hesitantly. Maybe they're offering to buy me back, like at a slave auction. "Or perhaps someone from the administration offices at my old school?"

"I'd never allow that. Anyway, I was surprised not to see you with this visitor."

"Oh-kay. Maybe you happened to run into *Craig* . . ."

"Funny you should mention it! He stopped by the store just this afternoon." Mr. Bernard is still acting as if he's just drawn an inside straight.

"Oh really?" Then it dawns on me. "If this is about the stupid junior-senior prom, then forget it. I'm not going. I told Craig that if he's that desperate to go, then he should take some other girl."

"It's obvious that Craig has no desire to attend the prom with some harridan. He wishes to go with *you*."

"So he went and spoke to *you* about it? I mean, what's that all about? I should be mad at him for that."

Mr. Bernard pours brown sauce into a sizzling wok and his face is momentarily obscured by smoke accompanied by a loud hiss from the stove.

"Apparently the young gentleman is under the impression that I hold some sway over you. Many people are of that mind. I can't help it. It's just my demeanor."

"I'm *not* going to the *stupid* prom. I told him we could do anything else he wanted that night but go to that stupid prom."

"Well, as long as you're going on a date that evening, then why not just attend the *stupid* prom? If this is about the money, then I could certainly—"

"No, it's not the money. It's just so *stupid*. Those stupid ugly dresses and corsages and pictures under a plastic arbor and standing around all night when nobody really knows how to dance together anyway."

"But what if when you're thirty years old you decide it wasn't so ludicrous, excuse me, I mean *stupid*, after all? By then it will be too late—no photos, no tiny pink flowers surrounded by baby's breath neatly pressed into a memory book, no flashbacks of a beautifully decorated gymnasium when you hear the old prom theme song."

No wonder Mr. Bernard is urging me to go—he wants to influence the prom theme. "You just want to use our votes to push through something like a Mongolian night."

"Oh, I love the idea of Mongolian night—some Genghis Khan curried camel, Kublai Khan steamed pork buns, and Marco Polo honey fritters. In any case, I have an incredible idea for a dress. When Gil and I were researching *Suddenly, Last Summer* costumes in Macy's, we saw this *très elegante* full-length black shantung silk dress that Mother could hem to tea length and ixnay the tulle poufs on the sleeves [Mr. Bernard is the only grown-up I know who can successfully work pig Latin into a sentence]. It would be killer *chic* with a single strand of cultured pearls, black high heel open-toe sandals, and a Chanel clutch bag."

"Since when does Ms. Olivia sew? She has me take buttons that need to be sewn back on over to the dry cleaner."

"Mother is an accomplished seamstress. She sewed all the costumes for the school plays when I was a child. Once she made seventy-five leprechaun ensembles by hand and then dyed them emerald green in our washing machine. My underwear was shamrock-colored for a year."

"Mr. Bernard, I don't even know what size dress I wear anymore."

"Don't be ridiculous. You're a perfect size eight." He mixes the sliced pork strips into the wok and another round of spitting and hissing shoots toward the ceiling. "I picked it up just in case you want to try it on."

"Ugh. Just tell me something—did you go to *your* prom?" I figure I've found my way out.

"Most certainly. I was on the committee. It was delightful. We had a French Riviera theme, St. Tropez specifically. Of course, I originally lobbied for a Monte Carlo night so we could invite Princess Grace of Monaco. But the PTA put the kibosh on anything that hinted of wagering."

"You're making all this up," I say.

"It's the God's honest truth. Just ask Mother. In fact, I'll show you my album."

"And did you have a date for this Riviera Night?"

"Of course. Amy Block. But everyone called her *The Block*. She was the goalie for the varsity field hockey team and took the school right to the state finals that year."

"You dated the *goalie* of your women's field hockey team?"

"It made sense. I was the shy and cerebral captain of our TV quiz show team, while she exuded strength and physical vitality. Besides, her girlfriend was a lipstick lesbian and the star of the school's production of *Bye Bye Birdie*. We double-dated with the oboe player in the orchestra, who was handsome in a brooding and pensive sort of way. He reminded me of James Dean in *East of Eden*. If only I could recall his name . . ."

The couscous is about finished, and so I place the saucepot on the back burner to simmer. "You really want me to go to this stupid thing?"

Mr. Bernard places his wok-ful of sweet-and-sour pork on the counter to cool. "I just think you're too young to be cutting yourself off from experiences. So what if you have a lousy time? At least you tried it. No regrets."

"All right already, I'll go. But Craig better not think this is his big chance to go all the way with me."

"Oh dear." Mr. Bernard looks as if he hadn't given any thought to that part of the evening. "How about we have a scrumptious breakfast back here early the next morning and that way you can tell Craig that you have to come home and help me prepare for it?"

Stuffing what appears to be a huge wad of yellow chewing gum into the bread machine, he sets the automatic timer. "Yes . . . we'll fix up the dining room as a buffet area with lovely fresh pink panda fragarias floating in a punch bowl of mimosas and I'll serve strawberry blintzes and sun-dried tomato frittata and . . ."

In the pantry I search for raisins to mix into the couscous. Mr. Bernard baked cinnamon raisin bread the day before, so they could be absolutely anywhere. The fact that he seems so pleased that I've agreed to attend the prom causes me to smile. I consider what would have happened if I'd had this conversation with my mother and how I would have dug in my heels and threatened suicide if I was forced to go anywhere near that high school gymnasium with the red and black crepe paper bunting dangling from the bleachers. And if she had picked out a dress for me I wouldn't have given her the satisfaction of even looking at it.

So why have I let Mr. Bernard talk me into attending the prom so easily? I don't know. Am I glad to be going? I don't know that either. However, it can occasionally be less exhausting to be part of the crowd instead of constantly arguing about everything.

"Now what about a *theme* for the breakfast?" Mr. Bernard calls to me from the kitchen.

"How about Joan of Arc?" I call back jokingly.

"Brilliant!"

Only I don't know if he's kidding or already looking up soufflé recipes.

"We'll make café brulot in my big silver chafing dish and croissants with homemade marmalade, individual coquilles St. Joan omelets, and then an immense flaming orange dessert with Grand Marnier. . . ."

There was my answer.

The Game of Love

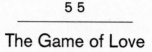

While the Stocktons and Mr. Gil head off to the airport to welcome Ottavio Vespignani, I go over to my old house for lunch. We've reached an unspoken agreement that we won't talk about school or the Stocktons and that my mother won't ask me to stay the night or, worse, when I'm coming home for good.

It's funny, but I don't really mind my parents anymore. There's nothing for them to be annoyed or worried about since they're no longer in charge of monitoring my daily movements. For the most part we just yak about what all my brothers and sisters are up to and the baby that's due in two weeks. The ultrasound showed it's going to be another girl. On the refrigerator my mother has tacked up this grainy photograph of what looks like a jellyfish invertebrate preserved in formaldehyde. Mom wants to call her Grace. But Dad's in favor of Megan.

I'm astonished when they actually ask my opinion on the matter. Though just because we're getting along so well I don't see any reason to lie. I tell them that Grace sounds like the teacher's pet and Megan is too common these days. They both just frown and give me this look like, *You'll never agree with anything we say or do, will you?*

My mother sighs and says, "Well, do *you* have a name in mind?"

I suggest Arabella. Ms. Olivia has been teaching me some Latin while we read Ovid's *Ars Amatoria.* I explain that *Ara* means eagle and *bella* means beautiful. Only I hadn't meant to bring up life at Nuthatch Lane, since I can tell that my mother doesn't appreciate being reminded that, being of sound body and questionable mind, I'd actually chosen to go and live with another family.

Meantime Eric is beating his chest because he's received a full scholarship to Indiana University. My folks are of course pleased as punch about this, and not just for the educational opportunity, but also because he'll apparently have a good shot at playing a lot of football the first year instead of just warming the bench.

I'm pleased for Eric, too. It's a damn lucky thing for me that he's a sports star, because wherever my dad goes—office, grocery store checkout line, gas station—people always compliment Eric and say stuff like "a chip off the old block," as if Dad was a quarterback for the Pittsburgh Steelers before he was drafted into the Ohio civil service.

Eric's scholarship will also act as a big assist to the family finances. In fact, my father is looking at minivans since they'll need room for two car seats, and so he offers me the old station wagon. The discussion gives me chills, since in a way the car issue is what started this whole chain of events in the first place. Although Ms. Olivia says that despite the fact that most significant upheavals can be traced back to a single catalyst, if it hadn't been that particular incident then it would have eventually been something else. For instance, even though the American Revolution was precipitated by the British slapping the colonies with the Intolerable Acts, the pot was already bubbling and it was just going to take one more grievance to make it boil over, which could have been about almost anything.

I thank my father for his generous offer. I truly believe that he wants to give me the car. When I say I don't need it since I can use the Buick whenever I want, he appears disappointed. However, my parents make it clear that if I want to attend college, and they're of course hoping that I will, they'll be more than happy to help out with the tuition.

Usually after returning from my parents' house Mr. Bernard will say something like "So, was the prodigal daughter welcomed home?" But tonight is different. He's too preoccupied with everything being absolutely perfect for Ottavio. The house is alive with music, brimming with laughter, bathed in candlelight, and decorated with overflowing vases of tall exotic-looking orange and purple flowers called birds of paradise. From out of the kitchen wafts the smell of baking bread. However, I happen to know that Mr. Bernard made the bread more for the smell than for toasting. He read in a decorating magazine that a whiff of fresh bread makes a house more inviting.

Ottavio is seated on the couch next to Ms. Olivia drinking tea, and they've just starting nibbling on Mr. Bernard's homemade scones.

"Bernard dear, I'm detecting a hint of chili powder in your scones," Ms. Olivia says and puts hers down on the edge of her saucer.

"Mother, that's cinnamon with a touch of—" But a look of horror suddenly crosses Mr. Bernard's face and he lunges for all the remaining scones, piles them back onto the serving platter, and dashes off to the kitchen. Mr. Gil and Ms. Olivia and I just laugh. After we break the ice, Ottavio happily joins in. Ottavio couldn't possibly look more different from the Judge. For one thing, he's about an inch shorter than me and slightly round, or built close to the ground, you might say. His hair is still dark but thinning on top, though he's not attempting a comb-over. My guess is that he's in his late fifties, but because the few extra pounds serve to smooth out any wrinkles it's difficult to tell exactly. Not that it matters. Mr. Gil says that Ms. Olivia is young for her birth year, which no one seems to know for sure anyway.

At dinner Ottavio appears to enjoy the food and accepts second helpings of everything. He has a friendly smile and his eyes sparkle when he laughs, which is often. Ottavio beams at just about everything. When I ask how his trip was or if he wants another roll, he flashes me that 100-watt smile. Mr. Bernard hovers around the table like an expectant father, frowning and tsking and saying that the pork is overdone and that the sauce is too thin. And so we have to keep insisting how wonderful everything is.

Ottavio's English isn't terrific, but that doesn't stop him from barreling ahead with the conversation and either filling in the blanks with a few hand gestures or a French word that Ms. Olivia then translates into English. He refers to us as Bernardo and Gilberto and somehow I'm Hallonia. But when Ottavio says it, like when he says *Oh-leev-eah*, it sounds pretty, like the name of a star.

It is apparent that Mr. Bernard truly enjoys Ottavio, even if he isn't thrilled with the idea that his mother is entertaining a gentleman caller. At least he now refers to him as her Gentleman Caller as opposed to Casanova or The Individual. He asks Ottavio questions about places I've never heard of, such as Perugia and Portofino. And they talk about making something called tapenade from fresh olives for what seems like an hour.

A few minutes after ten, Ms. Olivia and Ottavio rise from the couch and cheerfully bid us all good night. One at a time we step forward to shake hands and hug Ottavio, and he grins and laughs like Santa Claus and kisses everyone on both cheeks. We keep saying what a pleasure it is to finally meet him, and he keeps agreeing and wagging his head and beaming that high-octane smile. But, of course, all we can think of is whether they're going to retreat upstairs to Ms. Olivia's bedroom and close the door or if Ottavio is expecting us to recommend a nearby hotel.

"How about an after-dinner drink?" Mr. Bernard suggests, an obvious attempt at a delaying tactic. "Perhaps some Amaretto di Saronno or Cointreau?"

"No, thank you, dear," Ms. Olivia answers for both of them.

"Then what about a little more dessert?"

"Oh, I couldn't eat another bite," Ms. Olivia says politely.

Ottavio smiles appreciatively and gently takes Ms. Olivia's arm in his, and together they ascend the staircase. Mr. Bernard, Mr. Gil, Rocky, and I all stand there in stunned silence.

"Good gravy!" Mr. Bernard says when they're out of hearing range. "Get the ammonium carbonate. I'm about to have a spell." He dramatically throws his arms in the air and lets himself fall backward into the down-stuffed couch cushions. Rocky mimics him by dramatically throwing up his arms and falling backward onto the couch right next to Mr. Bernard.

"Oh my *gosh* . . . ," I say, equally alarmed. "Do you think he's just taking her up to bed, or do you think he's actually going to spend the night in there?"

"I think he's taking her to bed, all right," Mr. Bernard replies gravely and closes his eyes again for emphasis. He clutches at his heart with his right hand. "I'm too old to have a sixty-something, sexually active mother."

"I thought children were supposed to give their mothers the heart attacks," I say. "Haven't you got it reversed?"

"Lighten up, will you both?" Mr. Gil says and laughs. "He's a terrific guy. And certainly better than anything creaking around the Cosgrove County golf course in plaid pants and an aqua-and-tangerine-striped polo shirt."

Mr. Bernard's eyes suddenly open and flare with light, and he sits up as if he's just had a brainstorm. "Would it be terribly indelicate if I went into the pantry and listened through the vent that goes up behind her headboard? Perhaps they need an extra blanket and are simply too exhausted to go and fetch it."

"Bertie, don't you dare!" Mr. Gil says sternly, the way you would threaten an eight-year-old not to light matches near a tank of gasoline.

Just then Ottavio appears on the staircase, and Mr. Bernard leaps to his feet as if he doesn't want to miss the opportunity to make up a spare room or drive him to a local bed and breakfast.

"*Un poco* warm latte for Ohleeveeah, *per piacere.*" He gestures to indicate a small amount with his fingers.

"Of course," says Mr. Gil. "*Due* warm lattes coming up. Why don't you go back upstairs and I'll bring up a tray in just a moment."

"Zhank you, Gilberto. Zat is so kind of you. You're just like a zon."

As soon as Ottavio disappears upstairs, Mr. Bernard jumps into action.

"Brilliant!" says Mr. Bernard. "You're a genius, Gil. Go and get a silver breakfast tray and some cookies. I'll put on the coffee. Hallie, you warm up some milk."

But Mr. Gil pushes him back down onto the couch. "No. You're staying right there. *I'm* bringing up the tray." Once again Mr. Bernard leaps up and Mr. Gil pushes him back down, and for a second I think they're going to have a full-blown shoving match.

"Who are you kidding?" Mr. Bernard says. "You can't make a tray. You almost killed me the last time I was in bed with the flu."

"Forget it, Bertie. Besides, you heard what he said. I'm just like a *zon.*"

"Fine, be that way. Only be sure to include those nice marble pinafore cookies and use a doily, for heaven's sake."

Mr. Bernard sinks into the couch cushions and crosses his arms like a petulant student waiting out the last fifteen minutes of detention. "And add a shot or two of brandy. I want him to sleep well. *Very well.*"

By the time Mr. Gil returns with the tray I've managed to distract Mr. Bernard with a few hands of blackjack. Only just as Mr. Gil is about to venture upstairs Mr. Bernard leaps to his feet with alarm and shouts, "Smoke! Something's on fire!"

We all look to the top of the stairwell and see a murky cloud of spinning particles surrounding the bright overhead lamp. Mr. Bernard makes another dash for the stairs, but Mr. Gil effectively blocks him with an outstretched leg and his free hand. "Calm down," says Mr. Gil. "Nothing is on fire. It's just cigarette smoke."

Mr. Gil goes up the stairs, but we gallop up after him and crouch around the corner so that we can observe the door to Ms. Olivia's bedroom. From this position the aroma of cigarettes escaping from under her door is unmistakable, commingled with the distinct but sweet smell of a strong cigar. For a brief moment as Mr. Gil passes in the tray, Mr. Bernard and I spy Ottavio standing in a silvery satin bathrobe and, behind him, a mirage—Ms. Olivia silhouetted by a haze of smoke and the flickering light of a dozen votive candles, lounged across the bed in a filmy scarlet negligee with her head tilted slightly back as she laughs at something that Ottavio must have just said.

As Mr. Gil gently closes the door, from over my shoulder I hear a muttered *en flagrante* quickly followed by the full weight of Mr. Bernard's body as he slumps on top of me and we both sink to the floor with a tremendous thud.

A Done Deal

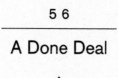

By the middle of June the air is tangy with the aroma of manure spreaders working overtime on the wheat farms off to the west and the sweet but pungent lilac bushes that exploded just three days ago in our own yard. It's now become necessary to start the day with a baseball cap in order to shield my face from an ever-strengthening morning sun.

The garage door mural is finally completed. When my mother arrives to deliver my SAT scores, she asks if the two marionettes that I'd fashioned out of the hundreds of tan wooden spools in the garage are supposed to be Raggedy Ann and Andy.

I say, "No, they're just dancing marionettes. They're being controlled by people you can't see. It's the Marionette Dance. Ms. Olivia told me about it."

"Aren't you going to paint them?" she asks.

"I'm leaving them plain, because I painted the background and I'd rather have that stand out instead." There is a sailing ship and a tropical island with lots of palm fronds and the things I imagine fill most people's dreams. I'd even added a layer of pachysandra at the bottom just for good measure.

My mother scrutinizes the garage door and gives me a look that I've seen before. It's the one that says, *You're either going to be president or you're going to land in jail, and this is one more reason I'm not going to get my hopes up.*

I actually enjoy these little visits from Mom now that she's no longer attempting to bribe, threaten, or kidnap me. And I can tell that she enjoys snooping around the Stockton place. Not that she's really interested in what

Mr. Gil and Mr. Bernard do for a living or what political party they belong to. She's more curious about what they eat, what kind of houseplants we grow, and what kind of soap and towels they put out for guests. Mom somehow changes into a social anthropologist when she visits, poking through stacks of magazines and studying the framed photographs on top of the piano as if they might yield clues to some great mystery of the universe. At least she doesn't do anything embarrassing like wear gloves or refuse to drink out of the glasses.

"Aren't you going to check your SAT scores?" She glances down at the envelope I've been holding on to for the past ten minutes.

"Okay." I tear it open. "Fourteen-ten," I say. "Seven hundred eighty on math and six hundred thirty on verbal."

"Oh," she exclaims. "Eric got twelve hundred and twenty, mostly language points, I think. But then, he arrives home so late from practice or work that I don't know where he finds the time to study in the first place."

"Yeah," I say, "it's an achievement that Eric managed to find the cafeteria where they were giving the test." But fortunately my mother doesn't catch the sarcasm and takes it as another compliment for Eric.

"Have you applied to college?" she asks hopefully.

"The Cleveland Institute of Art has a special program where you can make a portfolio and then apply to the regular four-year-degree program after that. I'm thinking of becoming a graphic artist. But I haven't decided anything for sure yet."

"Of course not. You're not even seventeen. There's plenty of time for all that."

"Maybe I'll take a year off and travel—you know, go to France for a while. Or maybe just work here and save some money."

Before she leaves I give my mother a tour of the gardens, which by now have begun to bloom. Underneath the apple trees there's already a dusting of pale pink and white blossoms that hover and skip in the spring breeze. Mr. Bernard is of course pleased with the warm weather we've been having, because he wants the yard to look nice for the postprom breakfast.

Across from the summerhouse is a lovely new white hexagonal gazebo that Ned the carpenter completed last weekend. To decorate the white lattice overhang Mr. Bernard and I planted smooth green vines dotted with pea-like flowers in purple and blue and white, called vetches. Around the sides we arranged window boxes filled with pink peonies, and leading up the path we put in handsome slender plants called blazing-stars, in both magenta and violet, which lend a feathery and ethereal appearance to that entire corner of the backyard. Miniature red and white roses cascade over the trellis like waterfalls. I've decided that if fairies truly do live in the bottom of gardens, like in that silly old Bea Lillie song that Mr. Bernard is always singing, then it's right here that they'd make their home.

Ms. Olivia is doubly pleased with the gazebo and surrounding flora because Ottavio says it reminds him of his house back in Italy. In the late afternoons after Ms. Olivia finishes my lessons, they've made it a habit to sit in the gazebo or on the white-painted wrought-iron bench near the fountain and read poetry to each other and sip lattes or Campari with club soda. Or sometimes they just talk and hold hands and smile a lot. It's very sweet.

Ms. Olivia also made Mr. Bernard find someone to install a fountain. It isn't very large, but it gurgles pleasantly around a statue of Pan holding his flute and the birds like to land on the edge of the white marble to take a drink, dip their wings, and generally refresh themselves. Mr. Bernard got his merry-go-round out front, too, though he didn't exactly order it. I tell the story to my mother, but I'm not entirely sure she believes me. I'm beginning to sound like Mr. Bernard with his factual but far-fetched narratives.

A week ago Mr. Bernard purchased a lot from an auction house sight unseen because one of his "operatives" called at the last minute to say that a dozen nineteenth-century hand-painted pine rocking horses were being sold in Dayton. He was assured that they were in excellent condition, complete with glass eyes, finely modeled neck muscles, and the original brass-studded leather harnesses. Mr. Bernard has some connection with a toy collector in Vancouver who leases antique rocking horses to Los Angeles filmmakers, so he bought the entire lot. Only when the truck arrived there was also a fiberglass three-horse carousel that plays carnival music when you switch on the power. Ms. Olivia considers the carousel a wonderful addition and immediately named the horses Burns, Joyce, and Kipling. Mr. Bernard decided it was kitschy enough to keep and that we can dress the horses up for the prom so that they'll be in keeping with the theme.

When my mother eventually leaves Ms. Olivia and I begin my lessons. Ms. Olivia has been slightly frantic about my upcoming exams, so in addition to the usual afternoons we've been having review sessions for an hour after dinner every night in her den while Ottavio and Mr. Gil and Mr. Bernard play cards. I'd done so well on the practice tests that the school recommended I sit for the advanced placement exams that are administered three weeks prior to the regular finals.

Aside from the current exam tension and Mr. Bernard's prom breakfast planning frenzy, life is tranquil and Ottavio's cheerful presence has gradually incorporated itself into the daily rhythms of Nuthatch Lane. And Mr. Bernard has relaxed about the fact that Ottavio is officially his mother's beau, in every sense of the word.

That evening, when the bottom of the sun starts to sink behind the orchard, Ms. Olivia and Ottavio sit out in front of the summerhouse smoking while Ottavio patiently works at teaching her Italian. In the air lingers the scent of freshly mown grass and also hyacinth, which are just starting to bloom along the back fence. Off to the side Queen Anne's lace blankets the Druid Circle like a bridal veil.

Mr. Bernard and I are busy in the garden erecting tall green wire cages around the budding tomato plants, and we can occasionally overhear what Ms. Olivia and Ottavio are saying. Every few minutes Ottavio leans over Ms. Olivia and attempts to reshape her mouth with his hand and then has her repeat some Italian phrase such as *selvaggia femmina* or *nel parlare*. And at regular intervals they simultaneously burst into laughter over her mispronunciations.

Eventually Mr. Bernard stands up, stretches his back, glances up at the setting sun, and then contemplates the two of them for a long while. Above us, birds swoop like arrows into the folds of the trees.

"I can't believe what an ass I was," says Mr. Bernard.

"How do you mean?" I ask. Though I think I know how he means it. "Regardless of how you initially felt about Ottavio you were always courteous to him. And he likes you. He tells me all the time how talented you are."

Mr. Bernard smiles at this. "Really? He does?"

I've already said this to Mr. Bernard on several occasions, but he enjoys hearing it, in detail, like a favorite childhood bedtime story. However, this evening he has something more serious on his mind.

"Well, I've learned a lot. You see that . . ." He nods to indicate where Ottavio and Ms. Olivia are sitting in front of the summerhouse in the last square of available sunlight. "I can never be that person to my mother."

"You mean that she has *needs*," I say.

"Yes." He smiles, obviously recalling the last time this subject came up. "And it was selfish and ridiculous of me to imagine that I could ever fill them all." As if on cue, Ottavio laughs his exuberant and infectious laugh at something Ms. Olivia must have said, or not said.

"Well, for starters you'd have to learn Italian," I say.

The phone rings, and Mr. Bernard glances at the offending handset that we've left near the back door in case Mr. Gil calls from his cell phone. I answer it.

"Someone's calling for Buster Stockton," I yell to Mr. Bernard, though loudly enough so that Ms. Olivia can also hear. She and Ottavio rise and pick up their Camparis and stroll over to where Mr. Bernard is still bent over, caging the last tomato plant.

I've never before heard any reference made to a Buster Stockton, and I can no sooner imagine Mr. Bernard allowing such a nickname for himself than he would ask people to call him Zippy or Bubba.

"What do they want?" Mr. Bernard says.

"They're offering Buster a free dental exam and X rays," I reply.

"Tell them that Buster is deceased," Mr. Bernard says nonchalantly. "Pushing up lilies, literally."

"All right, Bernard," Ms. Olivia says. "That will do."

Oh dear. I can't help wondering if Buster was the Judge's nickname. Though it would seem a bit of a leap for someone with the given name of Abelard. I notify the salesperson that Buster has passed away, and he offers condolences and apologizes and says he'll remove Buster from their list.

"Buster hasn't had a call in almost a year," observes Ms. Olivia.

"Remember the lawn service people—offering a golden retriever a consultation on how to improve his grass!" Mr. Bernard recalls.

"A golden retriever?" I ask hesitantly.

"Buster was our dog when we moved into the house," Mr. Bernard explains. "I didn't want people calling at home about the business, and so we requested an unlisted number. But then Gil found out that you could list the phone under any old name, even a fake one, and that way avoid paying the fifty dollars to be unlisted."

"So your number is in the phone book under Buster Stockton?"

"Buster D. Stockton. The *D* was for dog."

"Buster expired at home of natural causes with his family and favorite squeaky toys around him," Ms. Olivia assures me. "He was a centenarian in dog years."

"So did you bury him out here in the yard?" I ask.

"Heavens no," responds Ms. Olivia.

"As a matter of fact," Mr. Bernard pauses and gives his mother a sideways glance, "if I recall correctly, Buster's body was left at the animal hospital in order to study the effects of some arthritis wonder drug he'd been taking."

"That's right," Ms. Olivia chimes in. "All for the greater golden retriever good."

"I should have known that Father was next," says Mr. Bernard. "I sincerely believe that Mother is planning on donating us *all* to science. Hallie, I wouldn't take any catnaps on the living room couch if I were you."

Dressed to the Nines

♣

The following morning is Saturday, and from the top of the stairwell it's possible to hear Mr. Bernard and Ms. Olivia arguing down in the kitchen, their usual battleground. I can only assume that Ms. Olivia has dropped some sort of bomb—such as she's planning to marry Ottavio and decamp to Tuscany. I occasionally wonder if Mr. Bernard isn't so much threatened by Ottavio as he is afraid that Ms. Olivia is going to desert us. And that's why he goes to extra lengths to prepare delicious meals and why he built Ms. Olivia her gazebo and installed her fountain, to keep them both here in Cosgrove.

"Running away from one's troubles never solved anything," I hear Ms. Olivia say.

"You ran away to New York when you were eighteen and then off to Paris," Mr. Bernard counters.

While listening to the voices I quietly descend the stairs. I know I shouldn't stand in the hallway and eavesdrop, but I'm also interested in finding out who ran away or is at least threatening to do so. I remove one of Mr. Bernard's architecture magazines from the pile next to the stairs and pretend to browse through it just in case Mr. Gil or Ottavio should walk past.

"Ah, but I wasn't running *from* anything," Ms. Olivia scoffs. "I was running *to* something. Or rather, after something."

"Just as Hallie is. Or *should* be. She just doesn't know what that something is yet."

"Make sure you're not playing God, Bernard," Ms. Olivia warns him.

"More often than not we operate out of self-interest rather than in the best interests of others, no matter what we may tell ourselves."

The teakettle whistles and I know that Ms. Olivia will be coming through the doorway at any moment. I consider sneaking back upstairs before she sees me.

"Mother, as much as I appreciate your concern for Hallie, the world just *doesn't* work the way you think it does. If it did, all the poor but clever young souls out there would be attending the best colleges and universities."

I replace the magazine and move back toward the bottom of the stairs. And that's when I hear Mr. Bernard deliver a doozy. "And what about when I was thrown out of Ohio State for having a beer keg in my dorm room and you made Father straighten it out with the president, who *just happened* to be his fraternity brother from Kenyon College?"

"That's different. That was absurd."

"Absurd or not, I wouldn't have graduated if Father hadn't pulled some strings."

"Then you would have graduated from somewhere else."

"You win. I'm too exhausted to carry on."

I hear Ms. Olivia's spoon go clinking into the bottom of the stainless-steel sink and assume she'll be heading to her den any second now, so I dash back up the stairs.

After Ms. Olivia retires to her den I come back down the stairs and this time cough to announce my presence before entering the kitchen. Mr. Bernard lifts the hanger holding my reconfigured prom dress from off the top of the pantry door. "Mother finished it last night. Isn't it to die for?" Just as Mr. Bernard had promised, Ms. Olivia could sew like a pro. She'd created a knockout gown out of his Macy's find.

That afternoon Mr. Bernard makes me watch the movie *Funny Face* starring Audrey Hepburn, Fred Astaire, and Kay Thompson. Following that, he has me practice walking in the matching high-heeled sandals until he's convinced I can move properly.

"It's not a balance-beam routine," he keeps repeating. "Put your arms down!" Then he replays part of the movie. "Now observe how Kay Thompson elegantly sweeps into the room at the beginning of the 'Think Pink' number."

After carefully studying Kay sweep, I try again, but Mr. Bernard only groans.

"You would be so statuesque if you'd stop *concentrating* on walking and just let it happen. Stop staring at your feet. Just face forward, look straight ahead, set your shoulders back, and then glide like a swan moving across a placid lake at dawn."

"What if I fall down?"

"You're not going to fall. And don't take such lengthy strides. It's not a relay race. Poise comes from within."

As Mr. Bernard is making me descend the staircase for the umpteenth time, Mr. Gil walks through the front door carrying a bag of groceries and the newspapers.

"I'm surprised he doesn't have a book on your head and 'The Rain in Spain' playing in the background," says Mr. Gil.

"Honestly, you'd think she pushed a lawn mower all year," Mr. Bernard says to Mr. Gil with exaggerated exasperation.

"I *do* push a lawn mower all year," I say.

Ms. Olivia appears from around the corner and locates her mislaid eyeglasses on the coffee table. "Lovely," she says admiringly.

"You did an amazing job!" I say.

"I'd be happy to teach you to sew as long as you promise never to admit that you know how. A modern woman must never confess to being able to sew, cook, or type if she wants to make a real career for herself."

"Something about the darts is bothering me," Mr. Bernard says critically and hikes the dress up at my shoulders. "Mother, fetch me your gay deceivers."

"Gay *what*?" I ask. "Do I look like a lesbian?"

"Décolletage helper," explains an amused Mr. Gil.

"Oh, Bernard, I haven't seen those things for years," Ms. Olivia says dismissively. "Not since our twenty-fifth anniversary party when I had to rent a gown after the dry cleaner ruined mine." No sooner has she said this than Mr. Bernard is detaching the stuffed half-moon–shaped petals from the corners of a rose-shaped pillow on the couch.

"I am *not* going to stuff myself!" I insist. Even I have limits when it comes to playing dress-up. "Besides, it's false advertising."

"Don't be ridiculous," says Mr. Bernard, who literally dives right in by pushing the velvety covered semicircle poofs into my dress, directly behind the darts. "This will be you in another year or so. Just think of it as a spring preview." He takes a step back, clasps his hands together, and finally appears to be entirely satisfied. "Hallie of Troy!"

Mr. Gil nods his approval. After checking my reflection in the front hall mirror, even I have to admit that the dress now looks perfect, as opposed to caving in at the armpits and bunching at the neckline. "Better to be looked over than to be overlooked," Mr. Bernard says in a sultry alto voice.

"Mae West," Mr. Gil interprets.

"Just don't dance near any candles," warns Ms. Olivia. "That polyester filling is highly flammable."

Heads or Tails

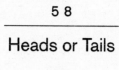

The day of the prom also happens to be the day my reply to the Cleveland School of Art needs to be mailed in if I want to attend the summer program. I'd passed my high school exams, much to the delight of Ms. Olivia and the relief of Mr. Bernard, and so I'll soon have a diploma. Though if I go to college it will mean living on campus and working weekends in the art studios and thus the end of my yard person days. It's a tough choice, no matter how many ways I look at it, and worse, I have to decide by tomorrow!

At about four o'clock in the afternoon I take the information packet, a quarter, and a bottle of Ms. Olivia's apricot cordial out to the summerhouse in order to think about what I should do. Every time I flip the coin and it comes up tails, which means I stay at the Stocktons', I find myself making it into the best out of three. And whenever the best out of three lands me in Cleveland I decide to start over. And whenever I decide to start over, which is often, I take a big swallow of cordial.

However, after an hour of coin tossing all that has been decided is that the floorboards need caulking, as my quarter slipped through the slats, never to be seen again, and the empty cordial bottle is ready for the recycling bin.

By early evening I can hear Ms. Olivia and Ottavio coming out into the yard to enjoy their customary sunset cocktail. Rocky often joins them. He's taken a shine to Ms. Olivia's beau, since Ottavio always hides watermelon candies in his pockets for Rocky to find. I'm quite certain that Ms. Olivia knows my whereabouts, since I asked her if I could have the apricot cordial and she saw me heading out to the backyard.

Mr. Bernard is still in the kitchen, where he's been busy most of the day preparing for the postprom breakfast bash. After much to-ing and fro-ing, he's finally decided on a South of the Border theme. The clincher was the full set of dishes decorated with red chili peppers that he found at a tag sale last weekend, along with two brightly decorated horse blankets that he's planning to employ as table runners. Starting last Monday he's been serving a new Mexican dish every night, experimenting with paella, corn bread, Tijuana chili, and honey-glazed deep-fried dough desserts. Yesterday he even had Ms. Olivia and Ottavio sipping green gazpacho instead of their usual glasses of wine.

"Where's Hallie?" I hear Mr. Bernard call out from the window of the Florida Room. "I want her to sample one of these virgin margaritas."

"I haven't seen her for over an hour," Ms. Olivia says.

"She's not in the house," Mr. Bernard says. "The cars are all in the driveway. I don't think she went anywhere on her bike. She was helping me slice Mexican breadfruit just a few hours ago."

"Perhaps she went for a jog," suggests Ms. Olivia.

"Don't be ludicrous, Mother. Does this have anything to do with the prom being tomorrow night? She's been acting peculiar all day."

I can see Mr. Bernard come out the back door and head toward the summerhouse. Once he's on the trail of something there's no stopping him.

"Why don't you leave her alone, dear?" Ms. Olivia remarks as he makes his final approach. "She's getting sloshed."

"Mother, you're an enabler." Mr. Bernard tries the door handle on the summerhouse, but I've turned the flimsy catch. Though he can obviously see me slouched up against the couch through the screen door.

"Holy jalapeños. Mother's correct, for once. You *are* imbibing."

He makes an eyeshade with his hand and pushes his face right up against the mesh to get a better look at my sad sack self. "It's the ghost of Lars come back to haunt us. Hallie, this is so *unlike* you."

"Sorry," I say. "I'm fine. Just a little tired. I might skip dinner if that's okay."

"Hallie, will you please unlatch this door? Listen, if this is about the prom, I didn't mean to coerce you into attending. Of course, you should do whatever you want . . . I just thought it'd be fun . . ."

"No, it's fine. I'm going to the prom," I reply sloppily. Though I still don't get up to let him in. Quite frankly, I don't think that I can get up. My limbs feel as if they're filled with lead sinkers.

"Oh. Well, then is something else the matter? I mean, you don't normally tie one on before dinner."

"I'm okay, really. It's probably an allergy to pollen. Tomorrow morning I'll set out the glasses and dishes for the party."

Mr. Bernard abandons his post at the door and I can hear him conversing with Ms. Olivia just a few feet away. There's a buckeye tree practically next to me, right outside the open window. And it's erupting with buttery flowers that reek to high heaven and are making me want to puke. I wonder what idiot decided to call Ohio the Buckeye State.

"Is she drinking to forget or to remember?" I hear Ms. Olivia casually inquire.

"I don't *know*." Mr. Bernard raises his voice. "And what *difference* does it make? Will you just please go in there and speak to her?"

"Sinclair Lewis and William Faulkner did some of their best work under the influence. Perhaps she's just in the middle of an enormous artistic inspiration," Ms. Olivia suggests.

"Like Raphael," Ottavio helpfully suggests and smiles at Ms. Olivia. Because whatever Ms. Olivia says is absolutely dazzling as far as he's concerned. The man *ha un grande amore per Ms. Olivia*. Last week he presented her with two baby Angora rabbits, which I have to admit are awfully cute. Ms. Olivia named them Alessandro and Manzoni, after the author of *The Betrothed*, her favorite Italian novel. After A & M mowed down the lettuce, cabbage, and carrots, Mr. Gil and I constructed a spacious hutch for them out of plywood and wire mesh. I assume it's just a matter of time before Mr. Bernard lists them in the phone book.

"I vote we leave her alone," I hear Ms. Olivia say. "Not everyone is a compulsive sharer like you, dear."

"Mother—"

"Why should *I* talk to her?"

"Because I certainly don't know what to say. Besides, that Unitarian church of yours, that debating society for the religiously challenged, has AA meetings at least twice a day. I think she's upset about the prom or graduation or Craig. Or perhaps it's a womanly concern."

"Bertie, I warned you not to interfere. You'll never change. Even as a boy you were always trying to tame wild animals and bringing every abandoned baby muskrat into your bedroom for rehabilitation. Sometimes you just have to let nature take its course."

"Mother, I'm being serious."

"So am I, my darling. Why must you always treat the word *no* as a request for more information?"

"Because if you ask me, a sixteen-year-old having a Dionysian revel on the day before her cotillion is a desperate cry for help. It's not as if she doesn't have a lovely dress and matching shoes to wear."

"Oh . . . all right. Though it's not as dramatic as all that."

"Not as dramatic as all that? Mother, she's drunk off her ass!"

"Well, I haven't the slightest idea what you expect me to say."

I drag myself over to unlatch the door and then watch while Ms. Olivia nimbly treads the few feet to the summerhouse across shattered buckeye flowers. She taps lightly on the wooden frame, even though we can see each other perfectly well through the screen door.

"Are you receiving visitors?"

"It's open," I reply.

"What an enchanting spring evening to be enjoying some liquid refreshment." She alights on a white wicker chair with a green-and-white-striped damask cushion, and I can tell that her careful eye doesn't miss the Cleveland Art Institute catalog lying on the coffee table with the empty bottle of booze resting on top of it like a paperweight.

"You know, Hallie, some people are born in the right place and time and never think anything of it—just lead their lives, often in the same manner as their parents before them and their grandparents before that." She pauses and looks out the window. I'm not sure if I'm supposed to say anything. However I can't help but notice that Ms. Olivia appears radiant. The lines of last winter have disappeared entirely from her forehead, now that they've been filled in again by love.

"And perhaps they're the fortunate ones. Because others can sense that they've been born in the wrong place, maybe out on an onion farm, when inside they're really city folk. Or they were born in Toledo but belong in the Australian Outback. Some people even sense that they were born in the wrong time—that they would have flourished in the nineteenth century or else the 1950s. And many are simply ahead of their time. Galileo was sentenced to life confinement for writing that the earth moves. Hypatia, the head of the Alexandrian Library in A.D. 415, was burned to death for being a scientist."

You can always count on Ms. Olivia to work a woman into her examples.

"Darwin knew he would be persecuted. He purposely held back his findings as long as possible, until a contemporary threatened to 'out' him as an evolutionist. So you see, dear, everyone must experiment to find their own place and time." With that Ms. Olivia rises, smoothes the wrinkles from her skirt, and moves toward the door.

"But how will I *know* if and when I find them?" I ask.

She turns back and with a quizzical look and contemplative tone says, "I'm not sure we ever truly know. Oftentimes we're only aware when we're *not* where we belong. Or occasionally we back into our destiny. Or else come upon it by a process of elimination."

"But how did *you* find it?" I ask.

"By making the biggest mistake of my life," Ms. Olivia replies with an amused glimmer in eyes that shine like forget-me-nots in the kaleidoscope radiance of dusk. "Hasn't Bernard ever told you how I met the Judge?"

I shake my head to indicate that indeed he hasn't. I vaguely recall Herb saying something about a Farmers' Union and picturing a nymphlike Ms. Olivia waving her placard on the steps of a Parisian Court House and catching the eye of the dashing young counselor Abelard Stockton as he confidently marched in to support The Workers.

"The Judge *married* me," she says and smiles mischievously, fully confident of the shock value of this revelation, "to another man! Or at least he interpreted for the Parisian official and so it was really the same thing."

"Excuse me?" Was it Ms. Olivia or the apricot cordial now doing the talking?

"I ran off to Paris to marry Leon, a dashing and talented French watercolorist I met in Cambridge and with whom I fell madly in love. Or so I thought. And the Judge was boarding with *le maire*, who performed the midnight nuptials. It was everlasting love at first sight."

But what happened then? How did she *know* it was Everlasting Love with the Judge? And what about poor Leon? All these questions burst in my mind like firecrackers on the Fourth of July, and yet before I've managed to utter a single word Ms. Olivia has spun on her heel and flitted out the door. Then she briefly pauses in front of the window screen around the side of the summerhouse. "Life is a gamble, isn't it, Hallie?" says the gray mesh silhouette. "If you're the type of person who wants to win big, then sometimes you have to bet big."

Wild Card

★

The day of the junior-senior prom dawns clear and bright, the morning sun an enormous disk of pure gold against the liquid blue sky. At breakfast Mr. Gil refers to it as a "Chamber of Commerce day," perfect in every way, the only reason a person needs to live in Ohio. The hepaticas that we planted last month in the blue garden, or *le jardin bleu*, as Ms. Olivia calls it, appear to have shot up three inches during the night. The house is as aromatic as the Macy's perfume counter in Cleveland. Mr. Bernard says it's the fragrance from the Dutchman's-breeches that are closely knitted together in the bed directly underneath the windows of the Florida Room, their cream-colored flowers with fernlike leaves resembling a delicate lace shawl draped across tall green stems. And the cicadas are calling as if it's already summer.

The day passes in a blur of activity and preparation. Threatening me with a steel-pronged circular hairbrush, Mr. Bernard forces me to blow-dry my mane so it looks "more First Lady and less Cowardly Lion." Then he plunks me down with Ms. Olivia at her vanity table and scowls over our heads, all the while insisting upon "more contour and less shine."

Finally it's early evening, I'm all gussied up, Mr. Gil and the Stocktons have officially declared me "exquisite," and Craig arrives.

"You look totally beautiful!" exclaims Craig, handsome in his black tux, red bow tie, and shiny black shoes, clumsily proffering a lovely corsage of red tea roses. Only he appears more terrified than thrilled by the transformation, as if this must be my twin sister and the real Hallie is out back chained to the shed wearing a tracksuit covered with lawn mower grease.

Now, normally I would say something sarcastic, such as "You sound *surprised*." But wearing a fancy dress with high-heel shoes and seeing my boyfriend in formal wear makes me feel proper all of the sudden, and so I just say, "Thank you very much." And I glance down to make sure the "gay deceivers" aren't launching themselves skyward like two doves in a magic act.

On the way out the door Mr. Bernard executes a sneak attack on the back of my neck with an atomizer of stinky sandalwood perfume. "Finishing touches," he breezily declares while I wave my arms as if killer mosquitoes are circling.

First we stop at my parents' house. Eric is there with his date, Emily, the permanent rebound girlfriend; my little brothers and sisters are dirty from playing outside all day, and my father is yelling at them not to touch us. Mom is carrying baby Lillian in one arm and a plate of cookies in the other. It's hard to believe that she produced a child only eleven days ago, but after all, she's a birthing machine. The twins have already decorated the baby with small purple sunglasses and plastered a haphazard array of dinosaur stickers across her Snugli.

My dad shakes hands with Craig, gives him that *don't you dare sleep with my daughter* tight smile, and then asks what his plans are. Craig responds with the typical spiel that most college-bound teenagers have perfected by the time they're seniors in high school in order to get adults off their backs in a hurry. He's been accepted at the University of Michigan, will try out for the lacrosse team, and major in biology to become a horticulturist or possibly a genetic engineer.

However, my dad knows that Craig was on the football team with Eric and that on its own is enough of a credential for my date to be offered a beer and welcomed into the Palmer Clan. My dad is probably thinking that if Craig and I get married he'll have enough players for regular weekend games of touch football in the backyard.

From the way my mother hastily yanks off her reading glasses I can tell she's startled that I'm wearing a black dress. But then, she's also shocked that I'm going to the prom in the first place, and with a normal-looking boy. She insists on taking a photo; however the balloon caption over her head says that before showing it to anyone she'll find a way to retouch the color of my dress to a more ladylike peach or lavender. And I notice she glances at my slightly enhanced chest the way women scrutinize good hair-coloring jobs, with an expression that says, *Does she or doesn't she?*

Next we drive to Craig's. Stationed on the front lawn is an entire country full of relatives toting camcorders and arranging Minoltas on top of tripods and taking wide-angle disposable cameras out of the plastic wrapping. They're loitering in the shrubbery like a busload of tourists looking for bears at Yellowstone National Park. As we pull up, a column rushes the car and I suddenly know what it's like to be a famous person stalked by what Ottavio calls *paparazzi.*

"What the heck, Craig, I thought it was just going to be your mom and dad showing me baby pictures of you naked in the bathtub. Why didn't you tell me all these *people* were lying in wait for us?"

"I was afraid you wouldn't come. I'm an only child. My life has to be heavily documented. It's the law."

"I'll say."

"And besides, it's a small town. They all want to get a good look at you—the girl who needs to be home-schooled for mental health reasons and shows up on the evening news dressed as if she's a heading off to fight in the Crusades. They want to see for themselves if you're demented or else a religious fanatic. And of course my aunts and uncles are concerned about the genetic makeup of the next generation."

Just then the heel of my left sandal sinks down through the grass and into the mud and I fall to my knees as I step out of the car. Damn, there wasn't anything in *Funny Face* about squishy front lawns—just perfectly manicured country estates, beautiful bridges in Paris, and winding marble staircases. As my hands reach out to break my fall about twenty flashbulbs go off. Good. Maybe they'll decide that's why I have to wear armor, to keep from injuring myself. And I'll be able to tell Mr. Bernard that I managed to make at least one grand entrance.

After the massive photo interrogation it feels as if it should already be time to go home for the night. Not a chance. In fact, as we climb back into the car I catch Craig's cousin giving him a lascivious wink. It's not as if I don't have an older brother. I know what that means.

Upon seeing me enter the gymnasium in a dress and makeup and on the arm of a handsome boy, Gwen pretends to faint and fall backward into her boyfriend's arms while Jane shouts, "Ohmigod! Buy stock in Revlon!"

The prom starts out stupid and boring, and for the first hour everyone stands around not knowing exactly what to do. You can tell the other jock girls by the tan lines left from baseball cap visors, short-sleeved uniforms, and calf-length sweat socks. And also by the way they keep checking their hair to see if it's falling apart, their borrowed jewelry to see if it's falling off, and their nylon slips to see if they're falling down.

A group of tall, gangly girls from the basketball team stands anchored near the far wall, basically afraid to take a step without their sneakers, wrist-bands, and Ace bandages wrapped firmly around their extremities. The cheerleaders and student council girls—no strangers to formal dress—purposefully sashay back and forth across the gymnasium floor, making their breasts bounce and the skirts of their dresses flounce as they work the room and check out what everyone else is wearing.

An assemblage of a dozen guys looking like penguins huddled around a plate of fresh fish crouches in the far corner with dollar bills in their hands playing a marathon game of liar's poker. Another cluster of tuxedoed teens has converted one of the collapsible round dinner tables into a surface for playing penny hockey. They've removed the red polyester tablecloth laid with black place settings and made the commemorative mugs with the date of the prom etched on the front into obstacles while employing their thumbs and pinkies as goalposts. More guys drift over, as they always do when any kind of game is in progress, whether it's dodgeball or duck duck goose.

Trying to work his way into the throng, unsuccessfully, is Brandt, skinny as ever and easily mistaken for a barbershop pole in his white tux, blue shirt, and red satin cummerbund and bow tie. No boutonniere, though. Apparently he hasn't found a date. Poor Brandt. Always on the outside looking in. And now the whole town aware that his mother might be indicted for fraud.

The band is a bunch of middle-aged white guys in light blue tuxedos with wide lapels playing icky ballads that you hear on the soundtracks of romantic comedies. Couples start sneaking out to the parking lot to either get drunk or make out or a little of both. Craig and I wait to get our picture taken in front of a fake-looking white arbor with hanging green plastic ivy that resembles tree snakes.

Gwen and her date Richard stand in line behind us. When Sheryl Shaeffer walks in, absolutely stunning in a shimmery emerald gown, upswept hair, and heavy makeup of Oscar-night caliber, Gwen nudges me. "Pregnant," she loudly whispers.

"No!" Craig and I say in unison.

Gwen points at the man handing her a glass of punch. And this is a *man*. I doubt he ever had a pimple in his life, or if he did have a brush with adolescence, it in no way overlapped with *our* high school careers.

Jane and her on-again, off-again wrestling captain boyfriend, Nolan "Bruno" Murphy, join us in the photo line. "Are you talking about Sheryl?" Jane asks excitedly. "I just wrung it out of Brandt—shotgun wedding right after graduation."

"He's going to *marry* her?" Craig blurts out. I can't tell if it's the idea of marriage in general or the idea of marrying Sheryl that's grossing him out.

"No way!" exclaims Gwen. Gwen had not been trumped in gossip since Miss Heffley, our third-grade teacher, had a nervous breakdown and the principal lied and told us it was a family emergency. However Jane's aunt worked at the sanitarium in Cleveland where they sent Miss Heffley to recover from us and she dutifully reported the true story. Gwen is innately competitive when it comes to defending her gossipmongering tiara, and so she adds, "My father says that Sheryl and Brandt's mother will probably go to jail soon."

"But it was only eight hundred dollars," says Bruno.

"Several of her customers were found to have money missing from their accounts at the brokerage firm," Gwen says quietly, as if from the other side of the room Sheryl might be reading her lips.

All five of them look to me since they assume that I should know the most about the case from having sprung the trap that eventually blew her in. But after that day Officer Rich came to the house he never discussed the case again except to say that it was confidential and that witnesses and a jury were involved. And that I was too young to testify in court, anyway.

"Don't look at me," I say. "Somehow Officer Rich made sure that I got *my* eight hundred bucks back." I tap the front of my gown as if I'm wearing jeans and there's a wad of cash in the pocket. Then it's our turn to be photographed.

After dinner the band finally cranks out some songs that people can rock to, like "Run Around" by Blues Traveler, and of course Craig requests Chumbawamba's "Tubthumping," and so we all run out on the dance floor, even the chaperones. The girls who have batting averages or keep hockey sticks in their lockers kick off their heels and hike up their skirts. The throbbing bass line causes the bleachers to shudder and balloons come unfastened and drift across the dance floor like big bouquets of red and black soap bubbles. *I get knocked down . . . But I get up again . . . You're never gonna keep me down.* The chorus pounds away.

Then the band plays old favorites like Chubby Checker and Michael Jackson's "Thriller" and a Beach Boys medley including "Surfin' USA" and "Help Me, Rhonda."

In the girls' bathroom Jane informs me that Brandt told her that I look more beautiful than the Queen of Naboo.

"Nay-*Who*?" I ask.

"You *know*, in *Star Wars*. It's the highest compliment he can pay to an earthling. You should be *flattered*."

"I think *frightened* is the word we should be looking at." But while joking about poor Brandt I realize it's unfair not to take into account the fact that he offered to turn in his own mother in order to clear my name.

As the keyboard player hammers out the first few bars of Meatloaf's "Bat Out of Hell," Brandt asks me to dance. He confidently leads me to the center of the dance floor, and I'm shocked to discover that he's in possession of some incredibly skillful footwork. At least it's much more elaborate than the rest of ours. A few girls agree to dance with him, especially if they're bored because their boyfriends are out getting stoned in the parking lot and they don't want to stand around or dance with other girls. But most of the time Brandt stays out on the middle of the floor alone, eyes closed, feet tapping time, body swaying to the music, in his own Branch Universe.

Finally, it's the end of the night, and after the King and Queen are crowned the band announces the theme song, "Nothing Ever Changes" by Donna Lewis, and everyone dances with their date, no matter how much they might be hating that person by now. The lights dim and overhead a mirrored globe momentarily transforms the gymnasium into a planetarium, with bursts of flame spangling our hair and faces like shooting stars.

Some of the girls get weepy, more from drinking rum and turning in circles than from nostalgia. Couples that have previously agreed upon post-prom heavy-duty sexual encounters and arranged motel rooms are revving up their engines on the dance floor, seriously sucking each other's faces and running their hands up and down each other's butts in time to the music. Craig and I dance close, and my date also begins some dance-floor foreplay with his hands and mouth.

"I'm not sleeping with you after the prom," I say as we continue to turn at right angles with metronome regularity and flecks of light dapple our eyebrows. "So if that's what you're planning, then you may as well take me home."

"Jeez, Hallie, who said anything about sleeping together?"

"I saw your cousin giving you that wink."

"Well, at least I've got to let him think that I *might* get lucky."

"And you'd better not go around telling your football pals I'm easy, or I'll make up something about you that will be even more embarrassing."

Craig takes my hand, looks directly in my eyes, and says, "Hallie, I really care about you, for one thing. And I know that you didn't want to go to this dumb prom in the first place, and so I really appreciate it. Number three, I'd never try to take advantage of you. And four, I'd never tell anyone anything about us, even if we did sleep together. I mean, if all I cared about was sleeping with someone I would have stayed with Sheryl."

"Then why did she break up with you?" I finally ask.

"I broke up with *her*," says Craig. "She wanted to talk about television shows and movie stars the entire time. And when it rained, all she worried about was getting her hair wet . . . She wasn't much fun."

I consider this significant piece of new information—a veritable hidden joker in the deck.

"Like you are," he adds.

"Oh," I say. "Well, I'm still not going to sleep with you," I quickly remind him.

"That's fine."

"At least not tonight," I say.

"I wasn't planning on it, honest."

The lead singer croons: *Nothing ever changes, nothing ever changes.* And all I can think is, what's the point of going to school for fifteen years if nothing ever changes? What if we all have acne for the next thirty years? And A-cup bras? I imagine that most of the kids in the gym, myself included, are sincerely hoping that *a lot* of things change, and soon.

Final Round

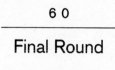

Following the main event Craig and I drive to Cleveland with several other couples. It's a tradition to go club-hopping on the waterfront since most of the bars stay open until three in the morning, and after they close, the alcoholics, insomniacs, and over-served revelers simply drift out of doors and continue partying from the trunks of their cars.

It's a warm dry night, and some kids decide to drive the four hours all the way to Niagara Falls. However, no matter which plan you choose, you have to stick with at least a dozen other promgoers in order to avoid looking incredibly foolish in your formal dress clothes. A lot of people in the bars think we're arriving from a wedding reception and ask who is the bride and groom, and we take turns volunteering and getting free drinks.

We finally arrive back at about six in the morning, after a short stop at the local park to lie on top of the hill and watch the sunrise, another après prom tradition. Dew glazes the grass and the air smells loamy from surrounding farms that stretch toward an endless horizon.

Back at Nuthatch Lane, Mr. Gil is out front directing parking. He has carefully organized several rows of Roman candles to demarcate the driveway and expertly waves two heavy-duty flashlights as cars pull up. In his Day-Glo orange windbreaker and with a strip of silver reflective tape on the back of each pant leg, Mr. Gil looks prepared for a shipwreck. Apparently he isn't taking any chances with the designated-driver thing.

Inside, Mr. Bernard is cuff-link-deep in tamales, guacamole, black bean salsa, breakfast burritos, and his very own Alamo orange juice. A large tan and red woven sombrero sits in the middle of the buffet table, blue and yellow tortilla chips bursting from its brim. In the background a Mexican flute and recorder band plays with psychotic abandon.

Ms. Olivia and Ottavio are merrily overseeing the buffet table while Mr. Bernard buses clean plates and trays of food back and forth to the kitchen. Someone has found a brightly colored poncho for Rocky to wear, and he stands next to Ms. Olivia gaily serving the punch. Above their heads dangle red and green plastic chili pepper lights that Mr. Bernard has strung along the curtain rods.

About fifty kids manage to locate the house, including my brother Eric and his girlfriend, Emily, all looking sleepy and worse for the wear. Cummerbunds and boutonnieres have vanished; even some of the boys' socks and shoes are missing in action. The flat black silken ends of disassembled bow ties dangle from their pockets like the tails of kites.

The girls are no longer wearing silk scarves around their necks or have bobby pins or butterfly clips holding up their hair, or hosiery and high heels on their tired feet. It's all dropped away like the petals on their corsages. Their foundation makeup has slowly worn off or been absorbed by the shoulders of their boyfriends' tuxedos, and traces of mascara and lipstick can be found an inch lower and slightly to the left of where it had been applied twelve hours before. The bonfires of orange zinnias that Mr. Bernard has arranged on tabletops only serve to make faces appear paler and cause tired eyes to squint.

I notice Ms. Olivia whispering to Ottavio and subtly motioning toward the grass stains on the back of Jane's pale yellow gown. That gets the *big* smile from Ottavio, the one he usually reserves for fresh tiramisu and winning at pinochle.

The soon-to-be graduates appear to get a second wind after generous helpings of Mr. Bernard's *huevos rancheros* and *vaya con Dios* spicy tomato juice. He isn't holding back on the Tabasco sauce either, so there's a lot of coughing and sputtering and running to the kitchen for chunks of ice and glasses of cold water.

Also, it hasn't hurt attendance that Mr. Gil made such a detailed map of how to locate the event. In fact, there are about ten or twelve kids who didn't attend the prom, a few of them I don't even recognize from school.

By ten o'clock, the last of the crew has either gone home or fallen asleep in their cars. Craig and I start clearing up, but Mr. Bernard tells us we look so wiped out that we should go and rest before we frighten the paperboy when he arrives to collect.

"You can sleep in my bed with me if you want," I say to Craig.

"Are you sure?" Craig glances toward the kitchen, where Mr. Gil and Mr. Bernard are emptying the ice from the punch bowl and we can hear the cubes crashing into the sink.

"Why not? The Stocktons don't care." Ms. Olivia and Mr. Bernard both have boyfriends bunking with them, so I highly doubt they'll object to me following suit.

"That'd be fun. I mean, I've never gone to sleep with a woman before."

"Okay. But it would just be *sleeping* together, you know, I mean, you'd just better not try anything." Though I realize that with my exams now over I did have a promise to make good on, as per Ms. Olivia's suggestion.

We go upstairs to my room, but it feels funny taking off my clothes in front of Craig, so I grab my T-shirt and go down the hall to the bathroom. When I come back his tuxedo is neatly laid out over the back of Mr. Bernard's antique balloon-back rocking chair and he's already in the bed, on the side closest to the wall. I climb in beside him, and he places his arm around my shoulder and asks, "I can kiss you, can't I?"

"Sure, I mean, we can go to third base, but like, after that, you have to stop. I don't want to end up in a big fight about this."

"Of course. After third base I'll stop. You won't have to say another word."

"You can go take a shower or something if you have to," I suggest.

After we make out for a while Craig pushes up my T-shirt and touches my breasts with his fingertips. Even though we've done this part before, I'm suddenly nervous. It might feel good if I wasn't so worried about what's going to happen next. I can feel his hard cock against my leg, and it makes me wonder why men have to be built so weird. No wonder some women are lesbians—at least they know what they're getting into, or at the very least, where everything is stored.

I keep repeating to myself, *This is supposed to be really fun and exciting,* but the mantra doesn't help to ease my anxieties. In fact, it makes them worse, because now on top of everything else I'm worried about not being able to enjoy something I'm supposed to be enjoying. What if all those years spent pretending to be a stoical Leni-Lenape Indian permanently damaged my emotions?

The kissing part really is terrific. But I've been kissing since seventh grade. I recall how back in middle school I'd been so nervous about just plain kissing—saliva regulation, lip pressure, length of kiss, how to breathe properly. And then in ninth grade how I simultaneously dreaded and dreamed about tongue kissing.

I consider calling for a time-out just to buy a few minutes in order to think things through. But what is there to think about? Either I want to be closer to Craig or I don't. It's not as if I *have* to take Ms. Olivia's advice. However I conclude that I'm just panicky about doing something wrong and embarrassing myself.

Meantime, Craig doesn't seem to be experiencing any apprehensiveness. In fact, it's just the opposite. While he is passionately kissing me, his one hand slides down to caress my stomach. Then he places a knee on each side of my waist and I can feel his heart beating almost on top of mine, like two bombs ticking. In fact, if our heartbeats don't synchronize soon I fear that one may knock the other out.

Craig gently slips his hand down the front of my panties, and I try hard not to notice. But it feels as if some smoke from Mr. Bernard's Cuernavacan *chorizo churros*—aka fireball donuts—is exiting my brain by way of my ears, and I begin to sweat.

"Have you ever done this before?" I ask.

"Yes." His voice is warm and smooth, like melted chocolate.

"What I meant was have you done more than this?"

"Yes."

"Oh."

Craig's tongue softly circles my left breast, and from all the movies I'd seen I imagine that right about now I should have my back arched, head thrown back, hair arranged in a tussled fashion on the pillow, and be writhing with pleasure. Only I'm thinking so hard about what I'm supposed to do next that he may as well be a nurse administering a sponge bath after a tractor-trailer accident.

"Craig?" I whisper.

"What's the matter?" He comes up for air and pulls a chunk of my hair out of his mouth in the process.

It occurs to me that now is the perfect moment to halt everything. To simply say that third base had been an overstatement, when what I actually meant was rounding second. On the other hand, I don't want to stop. I like

Craig. Though I don't know if I *love* him. Because I don't even know what love is. I make a mental note to ask Ms. Olivia what love is. She'll know.

And besides, I *want* to have experiences. I don't want to just sit around my whole life and read about other people's experiences. Craig traces the curves of my body with his fingers while we kiss, and for a brief moment I feel the sea rising up in my heart. I place my hand on the front of his shorts, subtly, as if I didn't do it exactly on purpose, that I may have been reaching for a barrette.

He rubs against me and says, "Umm."

At this point in Ms. Olivia's amorous tales the interested parties tear off each other's bodice and breeches, or they remove their own clothes in a seductive manner—for instance, by doing a veil dance. For us, though, it's more like rushing to get ready for gym inside a crowded locker room. After Craig slips down his dryer-safe Fruit of the Loom underwear they become tangled around his right ankle, and when he finally kicks them off they act as a slingshot, sending the metal tissue box holder flying off my night table and crashing into the closet door.

He places my hand back where it had been, only now it's against his nakedness. I gasp, mostly from shock, but I think Craig confuses it for a passionate sigh, and he slides my hand slowly up and down his cock. Somehow the top sheet becomes snarled between his elbow and my armpit. We can't get it sorted out because the ends are still anchored firmly underneath the mattress. Craig eventually pulls the entire sheet off the bed and hurls it onto the floor, and we both giggle and my heart finally stops racing. Gently I move my hand up and down and then he places his hand around mine and moves it faster until he suddenly stops, squeezes my wrist, and lets out an enormous groan. I feel his semen running down the inside of my thigh.

"I'd better get some tissues." He says this in an efficient tone of voice, like someone who has had prior experience with preventing body fluids from leaking onto linens.

"They're on the floor next to the closet," I say. "Near your underwear."

We both laugh self-consciously. He retrieves the box and wipes the inside of my thigh and then himself. It's sweet how he attends to me first.

"Do you need to take a shower?" I ask.

"I don't think so," he says. "Can I do stuff to you?"

"What kind of stuff?" For some reason I don't think he's talking about a manicure.

"You know, to make you feel good."

"I'm kind of tired. But thanks anyway."

"You're welcome. And thank you."

We sound as if we're exchanging compliments on each other's casseroles at the church potluck supper. But maybe it's customary to thank a person for a sexual encounter. And if one person doesn't have a climax, does he or she still formally express gratitude? So much to learn . . .

Craig curls up behind me so that we're like two teaspoons in a drawer, and by the sound of his steady breathing I can tell that he's fallen asleep. Personally, I don't know if I'll ever be able to sleep again. I keep replaying the movie of everything that has happened. Then I become slightly excited imagining the "stuff" that Craig suggested he could do to make me feel good. Maybe I should have said okay. I decide that next time I will.

His big furry arm hangs over my shoulder, and at first it's cozy and romantic, but then it begins to feel more like a lead weight. I shift underneath him, but after a few minutes I still can't get comfortable. And he's snoring, softly at first, but gathering steam, like a locomotive pulling out of the station. I thought you had to be my father's age to snore. When I attempt to move out from under him he awakens slightly, rolls over, and faces the wall. But he's tall and broad-shouldered, and now our backs press up against each other and my arm dangles off the edge of the bed and starts to go numb.

I turn over to face his back, since this seems to be the best use of space, if you treat the whole business as a geometry problem. But the bed begins heating up like a blast furnace and Craig awakens just long enough to push the blanket off us both. My feet quickly become cold, and I try to rearrange the covers so they're only on my side of the bed. But I still can't fall asleep.

Eventually Craig turns back around and once again we're facing each other. Only now he's fully awake.

"Hallie," he says.

"Yeah."

"Promise you won't be mad?"

Mad? Is he going to break up with me? And here I thought the hand job had gone really well. "Mad about what?"

"I'm not used to sleeping with another person."

"Me neither," I admit.

"Maybe I should go home."

I consider the options. In my heart I don't want Craig to leave just yet.

"Maybe you could sleep downstairs in the Florida Room? Olivia and Ottavio always take a drive on Sunday afternoon, and Mr. Bernard will be off to his garage sales by now."

"Okay."

Together we trudge downstairs and make Craig a bed on the pullout couch, draw the curtains in the sunlit room, and kiss good night, or rather good afternoon. When I glance at him from the doorway he appears to have already fallen back to sleep.

I suddenly wonder if we'll get married and have children. Or if Craig is just my first real boyfriend and someday I'll hardly remember him, the way Mr. Bernard can't recall the name of his first boyfriend.

Luck of the Draw

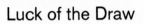

When I next awaken it's dark outside. But the light is on in the hallway and I can smell the rich aroma of lamb chops and rosemary rising from downstairs. It must be around dinnertime. I wonder if Craig is still asleep in the Florida Room. After pulling on my jeans and a sweatshirt, I dig around the dresser for a new ponytail holder. The old one is lost somewhere in my bed.

Descending the staircase, I glance at the grandfather clock in the entrance hall. It's half past seven. Wow. I must have gone into a cayenne pepper coma. From the kitchen I hear the clattering of dishes woven into the agitated voices of Mr. Bernard and Ms. Olivia disagreeing about something, as usual.

In the living room Ottavio and Mr. Gil are sipping cognac and playing chess, as they often do in the evenings while Mr. Bernard reads or plans menus and Ms. Olivia writes.

I slip through the hallway so they don't hear me and quietly pass by the swinging door to the kitchen, which is closed. The Florida Room is dark, and when I switch on the closest table lamp I see that Craig is long gone, the bed has been put back together, and the linens are neatly folded in a pile on the Judge's old armchair.

"If she doesn't want to go, then she shouldn't go," I overhear Ms. Olivia saying. "I didn't force you to attend design school when we both know you should have gone."

"That's exactly my point, Mother. I wish you *had* made me go! If you'd been a little more like Angela Lansbury in *The Manchurian Candidate* and a little less like Angela Lansbury in *Mame*, then perhaps I would have—"

"As you well know, I don't believe in pushing people, young or otherwise. And furthermore, we're not her parents and so we have absolutely no say in the matter."

"Well, then what's she going to do? Mow the lawn here forever, like an episode of *The Twilight Zone*?"

"That's not the point, Bernard. It's *her* decision."

"There's a whole world out there waiting for *her*."

"Let me tell you something, Bertie, the world is an oyster, true enough, only sometimes you get the pearl, sometimes you get a handful of sand, and sometimes you get food poisoning."

"Then why did you give her the application to begin with? *You're* the one who started this whole thing!"

"You don't need to raise your voice, by the way. My hearing happens to be just fine," Ms. Olivia says. "I believe in *presenting* people with choices, not in *making* choices for them."

"You know I'm right," Mr. Bernard angrily announces before exiting the kitchen. He runs smack into me as he storms past the pantry, down the hallway, and into the foyer, grabs his jacket out of the closet, and heads out the front door. I follow him out the door, around the side of the house, and to the backyard. It's a cool spring night, with a bright sliver of a moon hanging just above the orchard treetops. The universe is strung with thousands of tiny lights and the shiny white apple blossoms resting in the tree branches look like stars sewn across a bright blue circus tent.

Mr. Bernard pauses in front of the garden. "Can you smell the lilies?" He stops and takes a deep breath. "I suppose you overheard us."

"Yes."

"And?"

"You think I should go?" I ask hesitantly.

"It may be that it's time to throw in the trowel," he says. "But would you mind finally telling me why you wouldn't attend high school?"

"You really want to know?" I say.

"Yes."

"The bells."

"The what?"

"It was like being a rat in a maze. There's a bell for everything—five minutes to homeroom, start of homeroom, end of homeroom, three minutes till next class, one minute until next class, next class, ten minutes until the end of that class, one minute until the end of that class, and on and on all day long. There's even a late bell that rings exactly sixty seconds after the regular class bell—as if you don't know you're late. I couldn't take it anymore."

"Ha!" Bernard starts to chuckle. Then he laughs even harder. Then he bends over and begins to choke. "The bells?" he wheezes, though he can barely breathe now.

"Yeah. What's so funny? How about I put fifty frigging alarm clocks in your store and you see what it's like?"

"No, I'm sorry. It's just that, Jesus—"

"What?"

"Nothing, I guess. I mean, it just goes to show you . . ."

But I'm serious. "That's not all. They start it all over again at the end of the day. There's a bell to go to your locker and then one to announce that the buses have arrived and then another to signal that the buses are leaving. Then there are after-school bells for detention and the four-twenty buses and the five o'clock buses and the six-ten buses."

"Bells, bells, bells," Mr. Bernard chants, still gasping through his hearty laughter. "It reminds me of that poem by Edgar Allan Poe. And now that I think of it, it's quite maddening to read."

"By the time you settle down and take out whatever supplies you need or change into gym clothes, you only end up doing something for twenty minutes—sketch four lines of a still life in the art room or read five pages of *The Odyssey* in English class or jump on a trampoline eight times—and then the bell rings and you go on to twenty minutes of something else. It's like being in a science experiment."

"I see. This bell system would appear to favor the student with the shorter attention span."

"I suppose so," I say. "As a matter of fact, they aren't even bells but electronic buzzers, timed to go off automatically."

"Like having electroshock therapy all day long," suggests Mr. Bernard.

"Yeah, only you don't feel better afterward. So now can I ask *you* something?"

"My life is an open cookbook," Mr. Bernard states good-naturedly.

"How come you didn't go to design school?"

"Design school, design school . . . ," Mr. Bernard says as if he's rummaging through his long-term memory for exactly why he didn't go to design school, as if he can actually make me believe he's forgotten something like that. But instead of answering right away, he turns his gaze toward the summerhouse. Shadows from a nearby elm tree stoop over us like eavesdroppers.

"Didn't you think you had enough talent?" I persist.

Mr. Bernard seems to ponder this question.

"Were you worried about making a living?" I ask. "I mean, what artist isn't?"

"I was . . . I didn't attend design school because . . . have you ever heard Mother speak of a poet named Rilke?"

"Yeah, only like all the time. Ms. Olivia says that Rilke believed we must rally toward exalted moments and that we must try to love the questions themselves."

"Exactly."

"But I've never understood exactly what all that means," I say, slightly embarrassed. "Unless it's like, you know, live for today."

"He also said that our fears are like dragons guarding our most precious treasures." Mr. Bernard pauses. "You understand *that*, don't you?"

"You were afraid?" I ask tentatively.

"Hesitant . . . irresolute . . . skeptical."

"Uncertain?" I say helpfully.

"Afraid," he says.

"So . . . that's normal. A person could be considered a good artist at his or her high school, or right here in town, but art school is the big leagues. Maybe I'm afraid, too."

"I—I don't think that you are," Mr. Bernard replies slowly. "In fact, I'm envious. Perhaps that's why I want you to go. It wasn't my ability I doubted. I don't possess the courage with which you and Mother seem to have been blessed. It enables you to just throw it all on the line. You know, bet the farm. Cast your fate to the wind."

"But that's not true!" I insist. "Look at the way you handled the police and the school Nazis and my parents, and look at the way you can steal . . . I mean rescue flowers from people's backyards!" I say.

"Hmm." Mr. Bernard seems to contemplate this laundry list of his strengths.

"Hallie, I'm a behind-the-scenes person. I guess I'm more like Father—

well, I suppose most people would never guess that. But I operate close to the boundaries and just nip across the border every once in a while to taste life on the other side, to pluck a stargazer lily, and then quickly sneak back to my place before daybreak."

"But you're so different from anyone else I've ever met," I insist. "I want to be just like you when I grow up."

In the moonlight I watch Mr. Bernard toss his head back and chuckle at this suggestion. "That's awfully sweet," he says affectionately. "I can't imagine that I'm the idol of many girls your age."

"And Ms. Olivia," I add. "I want to be like her, too."

"Aha!" he says accusingly, as if the truth has finally come out.

I smile sheepishly. "Mr. Bernard?"

"Yes?"

"How come Ms. Olivia returned from Europe if all she was going to do once she moved back here is protest the American government the entire time?"

"Three reasons, I suppose. First, she loves this country and that's why she works to improve the bits and pieces she finds unappealing or not well thought out. And then she met Father and he proposed. And his life was here, of course."

"Oh, wow. I can't imagine meeting someone and then having the entire course of my life altered by a single kiss."

"In mother's case it was more like a kiss immediately followed by a glance, though not from the same gentleman. But it was the start of the Kennedy administration . . . Camelot," he says. "Love was in the air."

"You said there were *three* reasons Ms. Olivia left Paris."

"Mother claims that if you stay in any country too long you'll become a victim of American foreign policy, which she wouldn't wish upon anyone."

Mr. Bernard delivers this line to sound so much like Ms. Olivia that I can picture her saying it, and this makes me laugh.

"I have an idea," Mr. Bernard says.

"What's that?" I ask.

"Why don't you venture out and conquer the world and then come back and tell the three of us . . . er, make that the four of us, or rather seven, including the rabbits, all about it?"

I'd always thought that having a place to return to would make it easier to leave. But for some reason it doesn't.

"Can I come home and get my yard person job back if it doesn't work out?"

"Absolutely. And you may come here on weekends and vacations and any other time you want. We're not going anywhere. Except for Mother, of course. She's threatening to rent an atelier in Verona for the winter."

Mr. Bernard and I walk farther into the yard, past the marble fountain, the spiky herb garden, and Ms. Olivia's garden with its ivory-colored roses dotting the dark bushes like cotton balls. The fountain gurgles in the background. Mr. Bernard had placed daisies in the water for the party and they're still floating on top, though now loosened of some of their petals. We stroll all the way back to the orchard, the exact spot where I used to hide my bicycle when I was sleeping in the summerhouse. It seems like such a long time ago. A lifetime. So much has happened.

"Look up at the sky," says Mr. Bernard, and he stands behind me and places his hands on my shoulders.

"There are a lot of stars out tonight," I say. And it's true. It appears as if thousands of fireflies are winking in the sky, way up above our heads, and silvering the grass beneath our feet.

"Choose one," he says.

"A star?"

"Yes, a star. It doesn't have to be anything famous like Polaris or Vega. In fact, it's much better to find an innocuous star, a total unknown—one just waiting to be discovered."

"Okay, I've got one. Now what? Are we going to adopt it through NASA and name it the Chicken Déjà Vu Quasar and send money every month?"

"Something along those lines. That's your lucky star. Now make a wish on it."

"But I don't think I'll ever be able to find it again."

"You don't need to. Just strive as hard as you can, and whenever you feel worried or confused go outside, gaze up at the sky, and know that it's out there somewhere."

"And this works?"

"Most certainly," he says. "So long as you realize that it doesn't matter so much where you live, but to live where you are."

So *this* was the secret behind Mr. Bernard always wanting to make every day special. "What if I try it the first week of college and it doesn't make me feel any better? Then what?"

"Then pick up a phone and call us collect."

"Deal." Cappy always says that there are three horses who never come in first, second, or third and their names are Woulda, Coulda, and Shoulda.

We turn toward each other and shake hands and then stroll back toward the house. Inside Ms. Olivia has put on her favorite Edith Piaf recording and we can hear "Avant Nous" drifting out over the freshly mown grass. An enthusiastic amateur chorus of Cosgrove County crickets accompanies the French chanteuse.

"And don't ever forget what I told you about Ethel Merman," Mr. Bernard says when we reach the back door.

I recite Mr. Bernard's collection of Mermanobilia by rote. "Ethel Merman never had a voice lesson, managed all her own affairs, and answered all of her mail because those weren't just her fans, they were her customers. She saved her money, lived within her means, and cared for her elderly parents."

"And what else?"

I think for a moment. Mr. Bernard had played so many Ethel Merman CDs and videos. "Oh yeah. She'd turn over in her grave if she knew that actors today use body microphones when performing live onstage."

"Exactly!"

Run for the Roses

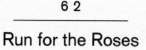

The day after graduation I finally purchase a used car, a green '99 Volkswagen Cabriolet. Only it's not heading for Vegas, as I initially planned, but for college.

I carefully pack up my belongings, including the worn copy of *The Adventures of Huckleberry Finn*, and a book of Shakespeare's sonnets compliments of Ms. Olivia. Inside the front cover she has pressed a small white rose from the garden.

As I take one last look around the room Mr. Bernard enters. "I still haven't found a place for that marble statue," he says as if it's been on his mind the entire time.

"Don't worry," I say. "It makes a good drying rack."

I'll miss my pink bedroom. I go over to the window and stare at the crescent of birch trees with feathery bark that line the driveway. Outside the sunlight is pure and clean as honey. Velvety bees hover around the long-lashed daisies underneath my window. Next to the driveway the merry-go-round stands still.

"There's something I need to tell you," begins Mr. Bernard. Only he's interrupted by the sound of tires crunching across the gravel beneath my window. It's Officer Rich's familiar blue pickup truck.

"Oh no!" I exclaim. "*Now* what?"

"Yes . . . ," Mr. Bernard says hesitantly. "That's what I was meaning to caucus with you about. It's just that . . ."

But I'm not even paying attention to Mr. Bernard. My gaze is fixed on the easily recognizable heft of Officer Rich as he shifts his weight from the cab seat to the gravel and then goes around to the passenger side and swings open the heavy door. I can see the outline of another person, but he or she doesn't jump out.

"It's just that Officer Rich has informed us that Mrs. Shaeffer's trial has become rather complicated," Mr. Bernard continues. "And it's going to move to Cincinnati, where the head office of the brokerage firm is located."

The word "trial" certainly catches my attention.

"And then she'll probably have to serve twelve months, even if all her customers don't press charges, which they probably won't."

Uh-oh. Is that who I think it is? I turn back to the window and watch as Officer Rich finally encourages his passenger to exit the truck. Brandt Shaeffer drops to the ground holding a knapsack in one hand and an orange bowling bag in the other.

"Branch!" I practically shout. "What's *he* doing here?"

"Well, that's what I've been trying to tell you . . . He doesn't have anywhere to go at the moment. To move in with his relatives would mean transferring to a high school in Philadelphia, and he only has one year—"

"You mean Brandt is coming to live *here*!" I interrupt him. I can't tell if I'm shocked, jealous, or just plain horrified. "Are you kidding me? Do you know anything about this geek?"

"Now, Hallie, Officer Rich said he's a nice boy and is just in need of some proper guidance and a good—"

"But he has *ears*!" I yell. And then put a hand to each side of my head as if doing some kind of Mouseketeer call to arms.

"Well, I should hope so," says Mr. Bernard.

"No, I mean big rubber Vulcan ears!"

But Mr. Bernard just smiles as if he's seen kids with worse baggage than a set of rubber Vulcan ears. And I suddenly realize that I showed up with no food, the law on my tail, and God only knows what else. What would have happened if I hadn't met the Stocktons and Mr. Gil when I did?

"Now come downstairs. I've prepared a special luncheon. You're leaving a bit early to have dinner, and besides, it's my poker night." Mr. Bernard says this as if I need reminding that he has become a regular at the Monday night church card game. And lest anyone should try to forget, he regularly works into his conversations such lingo as "ante up" and "niner from Carolina."

Mr. Bernard and Ottavio serve an elaborate farewell meal of chicken Belarus, mashed potatoes, creamed onion cassoulet, and white asparagus. Mr. Gil once told me that Mr. Bernard collects the memories of special meals the way others collect coins.

"Wow, everything is like *really* white," says Brandt, as if he's just discovered a new element to add to the periodic table.

"Yes, it's a White Russian theme," explains Mr. Bernard to his newest culinary acolyte.

"But I thought Russians ate borscht," says Brandt.

"Well, yes, they're certainly known for their borscht and vodka and pickled cabbage, but under Peter the Great cooks were brought in from all over Europe. So you see, a Russian theme is open to interpretation."

"Bertie, not everyone is interested in the color-coding of food," says Ms. Olivia.

"And not everyone thinks that Surf and Turf results from mixing Hamburger Helper with Tuna Helper. Mother has no appreciation of the gastronomic epic," Mr. Bernard says, mostly to Brandt. "For instance, did you know that Russian dressing isn't Russian at all?"

"No, really?" says Brandt, ever the budding chemist.

"It was only given that name because the earliest versions contained mayonnaise, pimento, chives, ketchup, and spices, including a distinctly Russian ingredient. Can you guess what that was?"

Brandt enthusiastically raises his hand as if we are back in school. I could just die with embarrassment for both of us—him for being so weird and myself by prior association to such weirdness.

"Yes, Brandt," Mr. Bernard officially calls on him.

"What is caviar?" states Brandt in perfect *Jeopardy!* format.

"Caviar is the roe of a large fish, usually sturgeon."

Obviously Mr. Bernard thought Brandt was asking *what* is caviar. Perhaps I am going to have to stay after all in order to interpret.

"No, Bertie, the boy knows what caviar is," explains Mr. Gil. "He was just answering in game-show style."

"Oh, yes, of course," says Mr. Bernard.

Ottavio trots around the table, smiling and refilling everyone's glass.

"*Un altro bicchiere de Yoo-Hoo cioccolata?*" He shows me a new bottle of chocolate Yoo-Hoo as if I might be interested in sniffing the plastic lid or inspecting the bright yellow label.

"*Si, per piacere, grazie,*" I say. When Ottavio first arrived I just assumed that his English would get better and better. And he does throw in *some* English. However, Ms. Olivia insisted it would be "less xenophobic" for all of us to learn some Italian.

Mr. Gil suggests that I show Brandt up to my old room while they clear the dishes and lay the table for dessert.

"Of course, it must be redecorated," Mr. Bernard reassures Brandt. "We'll do the space over in a deep russet or possibly indigo."

"Don't be *ridiculous,* Bertie," Ms. Olivia pounces on him. "The poor child will be addicted to antihallucinogens after only one night. A boy's room is either taupe or light blue."

"Della Robbia blue!" exclaims Mr. Bernard.

I lead Brandt up to my old room and show him how he can store shoes and extra clothes under the bed since the closet is still loaded with Mr. Bernard's junk. The big marble statue of the angel catches Brandt's eye and he stares at it for a long time.

"It makes for a good towel rack," I offer. "And the fingers hold belts."

"They're a little weird," says Brandt, his voice thinned by adolescent shakiness.

"Well, you know," I reply, "lots of people say the same thing about you and me."

"Yeah, I guess so." But he says it in a way that suggests being thought of as weird is not an ideal way to go through life.

"They're weird in a good way," I say. "Trust me."

"Then why do you want to leave?" asks Brandt.

I'm not entirely sure myself why I'm leaving. But I know that it's really hard. And yet I'm not about to tell this to Brandt.

"I have to go out and have experiences," I say with a confidence I don't at all feel.

Brandt sits down on the bed. "It's funny that I'm taking your old room. I mean, it's like a sign that, you know, that we're living parallel lives and are destined to be connected in some way, don't you think?"

Now I'm a firm believer in signs. After all, it was through a sign down at the Star-Mart that I met the Stocktons and Mr. Gil. However, under the circumstances, I really hope this isn't one of *those* kinds of signs, that it's more like, say, a stop sign. On the other hand, I wouldn't mind having Brandt as a friend.

Before decamping I store my bike in the back of the garage. It will definitely be safe there. And also, I know that I'll be back. Taking one last look at my mural, I consider the household I'm leaving behind. It is truly amazing—six of us at lunch and only Mr. Bernard and Ms. Olivia are kin. If somebody asked who these people were to me, I wouldn't be able to begin to describe it. We aren't related. Or pledged to one another on paper. And they're much more than friends. Now that I think of it, I don't know that such a word for us even exists in the English language.

Or maybe there is *one*. My mind wanders back to one of the first nights I stayed for dinner at the Stocktons' and we watched *Breakfast at Tiffany's* and Audrey Hepburn sang "Moon River." *We're after the same rainbow's end, waitin' 'round the bend, my Huckleberry friend, Moon River and me.*

And that's when it becomes clear to me. They are my Huckleberry friends. We are not bound together or beholden to one another through accident of birth, legal documents, or vows recited before clergy.

No, it is much *more*. Because a body can so easily turn his back on all that. The magic of the Huckleberry friend arises from the fact that there is no covenant to be broken. Our connectedness endures solely as a result of the stirrings within our own hearts, and continues whether we are near to one another or far apart.

Craig has left work early to come and say good-bye. And my parents and Gwen and Jane also arrive to see me off. When I return from the garage everyone is gathered in the living room talking and laughing as if they've been friends forever, as if the standoff on the front porch just nine months ago never happened and the golf money never went missing.

Mr. Bernard presents me with a microwave cookbook. He tried most of the recipes and then inserted notes and corrections in the margins with a red Flair marker. Next Mr. Gil gives me one of his Rolling Stones CDs along with instructions to blast "Ruby Tuesday" immediately upon my arrival at college to ensure that I make the right kind of friends.

Craig kisses me good-bye and says he's going to come and visit as soon as he gets a day off from his landscaping job. For my dorm room he's been carefully sculpting a bonsai tree in the shape of Just Call Me Dick. In fact, it's already so lifelike that his mom thinks it's supposed to be a mosquito that was sucked into a jet engine. He kisses me one more time, and after he's finished Rocky comes up and mimics Craig by also giving me a big smooch, and this makes everyone laugh.

Finally it's my parents' turn. Dad hands me an envelope containing two thousand dollars. I can tell how much it is just by glancing in the top, because the stack is fifties and it's a quarter of an inch thick.

"It's two thousand dollars," says Dad. "A graduation gift."

"The money we were going to give you toward a car," says Mom.

"Thanks," I say and kiss them both. "It's very kind of you." And I mean it, too.

"Now, don't gamble it away," my father warns, as if there's already a gleam in my eye indicating that I'm going to scare up a game of five-card draw at the first gas station I see.

"And don't talk to strangers," my mother adds, not one to relinquish the final word of parental advice to my father.

Now, under normal circumstances, or perhaps I should say under the old circumstances, I would have started an argument about this. For instance, that every choice one makes in life is actually a gamble, and that every potential new friend is at this moment still a stranger.

However, I don't. When dealt a hand with no obvious merit, it is the immediate inclination of the cardplayer to want to exchange as many cards as possible in the hopes of getting something better. Yet I've learned that sometimes the existing hand doesn't need throwing in so much as careful rearranging in order to transform it into a winner.

"I promise," I say. "No playing cards with strangers. And no talking to gamblers."

My parents appear pleased that I seem to agree with them and are thus satisfied that I have finally come around to their way of thinking. We hug one last time and my mother wipes away her tears. But I'm not as sad as I thought I'd be. Perhaps the past is not what we leave behind, after all, but what we take with us.

"Break a leg!" Mr. Bernard shouts after me as I step over the threshold.

Outside it's a perfect spring afternoon, blue as eternity, with wild geese honking overhead as they travel north for the summer. It's the kind of day that can make you feel lucky, if you believe in luck.

Beginner's Luck

Laura Pedersen

A Reader's Guide

A Conversation with Laura Pedersen

Julie Sciandra and Laura Pedersen have been friends for years and worked together at various times. They recently sat down to talk about life and Laura's book Beginner's Luck *after bowling. (Julie won, but only by a few pins, and there will definitely be a rematch.)*

JS: You shouldn't have asked me to do this. I know too much.

LP: That's the reason I can't get rid of you.

JS: Let's start with the cooking. There's a picture of you in the kitchen with a big red X through it. *You're* the one who blew up the potato because you didn't know enough to poke holes in it!

LP: You should talk, Miss Lipton Cup-a-Soup. Anyway, that's why it's called fiction. I can write about food even if I can't cook it myself. Nothing bad ever happens to a writer. It's all material.

JS: Same with the flowers. You're allergic to almost anything outside.

LP: But I love to look at them. Pictures are best. However, feel free to bring me chocolate anytime. The Irish have a saying: "You can't eat flowers."

JS: I've noticed that all your stories involve these large families and yet you grew up as an only child. Are you stealing from the Pyne family again?

LP: Mostly. They lived behind me and had two parents, nine kids, two dogs, and a cat. I spent a lot of time over there when I was growing up. It was a predominantly Catholic neighborhood, and several families had enough kids for their own football teams.

JS: And what about these Christian families? Your parents divorced when you were a teenager and are so liberal that they probably vote left-handed.

LP: Buffalo, where I grew up, is a melting pot of every ethnicity and religion. When immigrants came to New York from Europe, many headed upstate to work in the grain elevators and steel mills. At my public high school we had everything—Baptist, Jewish, Catholic, Presbyterian, Greek Orthodox. I believe that truth can be found in almost all religions but that no one religion holds all the truth.

JS: But you're Unitarian. Aren't the people at your church going to burn you on a question mark for making fun of them in the book?

LP: They laugh at themselves more than anyone else does. Worst case is that I'll get hit over the head with a clipboard. The real reason they're going to be mad is that the official name is "Unitarian Universalist," and they're sticklers about that. But with ten syllables and twenty-one letters it would take up the entire book.

JS: Two of the main characters, Olivia and Bernard Stockton, are rather eccentric. Are they based on real people?

LP: Not specifically. I've had several terrific teachers and mentors throughout my life. I've also known many type A personalities, gamblers, bohemians, and oddballs, especially having worked on Wall Street in the 1980s and then in journalism and television. And I must confess that for the most part I'm charmed by them all—their terrific energy, idealism, creative vocabulary, and love of life. Also, growing up in the Unitarian Universalist Church exposed me to a large number of protesters, peaceniks, petitioners, and so forth.

JS: What did you steal from yourself? Give me one similarity between you and Hallie and one difference.

LP: I gambled as a kid. I'm an only child. My dad is an only child. His father was an only child. My mom has a brother and sister, but they don't have any children. So it was all these grown-ups and me. They weren't about to start playing Chutes and Ladders and Barrel of Monkeys. When I was five my mom taught me poker, and later I learned to count cards at blackjack. But I can only do math when

Beginner's Luck

I'm betting or there's a dollar sign in front of the numbers. Otherwise I'm a disaster. The major difference between Hallie and me is that I always knew what I wanted to do with my life, and if my parents had any expectations they kept them so well hidden that they haven't surfaced to this day.

JS: So what happens to Hallie after the book ends?

LP: She grows up and one day there's a cousin, niece, nephew, or neighbor's kid who can't talk to his or her parents and so she returns the favor of lending a sympathetic ear. Then they all join hands and sing "Will the Circle Be Unbroken" in a round.

JS: Yeah, sure they do. I can ask you anything and you have to answer, right?

LP: Yes, there are electrodes attached to my fingertips.

JS: What's the one thing you wouldn't want readers to know about you?

LP: As a teenager I didn't exactly volunteer the information that my father was a folksinger. But now I don't mind. I suppose I wouldn't want people to know about the shoes, the pigs, and the Knicks.

JS: I know about the shoes. When no one is around you have some of the worst shoes. The boxes they came in would look better on your feet than the shoes themselves. And I know about the pigs. You took care of the pigs on a farm when you were a kid, became emotionally overinvolved, and now everyone gives you pig paraphernalia (except bacon!). But what's with the New York Knicks? They're the local basketball team.

LP: I wrote a story for *The New York Times* and spelled it "Nicks." Of course, my editor fixed it before we went to print, but it became clear how little I knew about sports.

JS: But you played soccer in high school.

LP: That's why Hallie plays soccer. It's the only game I know how to play. Though she's much better than I was.

JS: I believe your claim to fame is never having scored a goal in four years.

LP: I was a fullback. We're just supposed to stand tall near the goal, more like security guards than athletes. However, I did score once. Though it was for the other team. My heel caught the ball and chucked it into our own goal.

JS: I was curious as to why there wasn't a dog in *Beginner's Luck*. You love dogs.

LP: The Stocktons had a dog named Buster, but he's dead by the time Hallie arrives, though he's still listed in the phone book. I think in the movie version the town will be the setting for a fight between two rival gangs of dogs, corgis and Chihuahuas, and it will be choreographed as a dance sequence like in *West Side Story*.

JS: I've seen you wandering around with scraps of paper falling out of your pockets, which means you're working on another book. Spill the beans.

LP: *Last Call* is a surprising romantic comedy about a somewhat alcoholic dying Scotsman who falls in love with a cloistered nun who also happens to be terminally ill.

JS: It doesn't sound romantic or comedic.

LP: That's the surprise.

Reading Group Questions
and Topics for Discussion

1. Why do you think Hallie's mother is never given a first name throughout the entire story?

2. Officer Rich is an African American in a predominantly white town. Do you think this makes him more empathetic to Hallie's feeling that she doesn't fit in?

3. Is it wrong for Olivia to seek companionship outside of her marriage while her husband is suffering from Alzheimer's disease, even though there's no possibility for his recovery?

4. Craig's parents are able to provide much more by way of material comforts and individual attention for their only child than Hallie's parents can for their seven children. Is this a sword that can cut both ways when it comes to the best interests of a child, or is one scenario better than the other?

5. If Craig is accustomed to a normal home life and has everything—he's a football star, smart, and has money for college and material items like his own car, computer, and TV—why do you think he's attracted to Hallie and the Stocktons?

6. Is there any character in which you see yourself or one of your friends, coworkers, or family members?

7. Do you think Bernard and Olivia enjoy being different, or are they just being true to themselves?

8. From what the guys at the poker game tell Hallie about the Stocktons, it appears that the Judge never knew his son was gay. Do you think the Judge's slow demise would have been any less traumatic for Bernard if his father had known about his sexual orientation?

9. Hallie's parents object to their daughter residing at the Stockton house on the grounds that it's not a Christian home. They object

without really even trying to get to know the Stocktons. Can you think of examples where people may slightly twist their religious beliefs to justify a personal agenda?

10. Olivia's behavior can seem contradictory. One minute she speaks as if she doesn't care what people think, but then she does something to suggest she cares very much. Is this because her heart occasionally takes over for her mind, or because she really does care but just doesn't want to admit it?

11. Gil's family appears to have disowned him for being gay. Hallie has elected to leave her family, at least temporarily. Meanwhile, Olivia and Bernard are constantly disagreeing and bickering. What does all this say about the challenges of being part of a family? Should one always strive to reach understandings, or is it sometimes necessary to break away from family members?

12. Though we are told the Judge's first name, he's never called it or referred to by it. Also, he never speaks. Whether he hears or not is unclear. Is it possible the Judge is symbolic of an entity overseeing the action? Is it significant that he dies at Christmastime?

13. Although Hallie isn't aware of it at the time, her parents sign her guardianship over to Bernard. Is it true, as the adage goes, that if you really love something you should set it free?

14. One night when she can't sleep Hallie reminisces about how things went wrong in the relationship with her mother. Yet she can't come up with one specific moment or incident. Do most young adults arrive at a point where they're going to oppose authority just for the sake of being oppositional? Is this just part of growing up?

15. Hallie's brother Eric and sister Louise appear happy and contented to follow the house rules and engage in the typical routines of teenagers in their school and town. Why is it easier for some people to adhere to "the norm" than others?

16. Is there any one moment or particular incident where you would say Hallie transitions from child to adult, or is this a gradual evolution based on a series of events?

17. Most of us eventually become a version of our parents. Do you think Hallie will turn out to be more like her mom or more like Olivia?

18. Has your own definition of family changed and expanded over the years to include some select friends? What makes a person "like family" to you?

For an exciting preview of Laura Pedersen's new novel

THE BIG SHUFFLE

available in bookstores everywhere
from Ballantine Books, turn the page. . . .

It's a cold and windless January night following a two-day winter storm. All across the campus of the Cleveland Art Institute a blanket of snow sparkles as if encrusted with tiny diamonds. Thick clouds blot out the moonlight and for a moment it feels that all of nature is hushed.

Suzy, Robin, and I walk the half mile to the Theta Chi frat house, a box-shaped building with dark brown vinyl siding that looks like it could be the back part of a church where the priests reside, were it not for the large wooden Greek letters hanging between the second and third floors. Theta Chi is hosting a Welcome Back keg party and all comers are indeed welcome, so long as they can produce an ID, real or otherwise, along with twenty bucks to be paid in cash at the door.

I have to go because my roommate Suzy has a huge crush on the president, and she convinces Robin and me to be her accomplices in the manhunt. But being that it's a new semester, and a brand-new year, I'm certainly open for adventure. When you're eighteen, the possibilities seem endless. At the same time, I'm feeling a bit lonely, since Craig, the guy I really like, attends college in Minnesota. We're eleven hundred miles apart, and he and I both agreed that it's best not to be exclusive with each other, at least for now.

Once inside the front door we pay our cover charge and a guy wearing a multi-colored felt jester hat uses a stamp to emblazon the backs of our hands with big purple beavers. In the strobe-lit entrance hall Billy Joel blares from speakers that seem to be everywhere. The jacked-up bass causes the wooden floorboards to thump so it feels as if there's a heartbeat in each foot. The couches are pushed back against the walls and from the ceiling of the large living room hang dozens of strings of chili pepper lights that cast a crazy quilt of patterns onto the guests. Young people stand around holding big red plastic cups, occasionally leaning in close to yell something at one other. They nod or laugh and over near the fireplace a few dance.

A guy wearing a T-shirt that says, FRESHMEN GIRLS—GET 'EM WHILE THEY'RE SKINNY, rolls a fresh keg past us and catches my eye. He's heading toward a place underneath a mangy bison head where participants in a Chug for Charity contest appear to be making excellent progress.

Oh my gosh—it's Josh! He's a junior in the art department whom I had a crush on the entire first semester of my freshman year, while he didn't even know I was alive.

After dropping off the keg he comes over and hands me a beer. "Do I know you?"

"Hallie Palmer," I reply, trying not to feel devastated that he doesn't remember my name.

We begin a shouted exchange and I remind him of the shared computer graphics class.

"Oh yeah," he says and nods.

Though whether he means that he remembers the class or me is impossible to tell.

Our talk segues to general stuff like movies and families. Only the problem is that now, after so much fantasizing about our nonexistent relationship, and several beers, I'm experiencing difficulty separating the real conversation from all the imaginary ones I had with him last fall. For instance, Josh looks surprised when I talk about having nine brothers and sisters, whereas I'm thinking we covered that *months* ago.

I act interested in everything that Josh says about where he's from and what he's studying even though I already know all of this from looking up his campus profile on the Internet. I may be majoring in graphic arts, but like most college women, I minor in stalking.

Just when I fear we've run out of conversation, he says, "Hey, wanna dance?"

We put down our plastic cups and move to the area in front of the fireplace where throngs of intoxicated students dance to Jason Mraz's "I'll Do Anything." I'm probably reading too much into the situation, as usual, but it's as if every line of the song has a double, or even triple meaning.

When the next song begins Josh appears to be finished with the dancing part of the evening. He stands still while everyone begins jumping around to "Heat Wave." Meantime, Suzy pushes her way toward us through the closely packed gyrating crowd, carefully ducking and maneuvering so as not to disturb any of the headgear with beer cans attached to the top and plastic tubes running into the mouths of thirsty revelers. Her cheeks are flushed. "I found Ross! He's upstairs!"

"This is Josh," I lean in close and say to Suzy.

"Hey Josh," she shouts, barely glancing over at him. "Hallie, they're playing strip poker upstairs and you have to come because I don't know how to play and—" Suzy stops midstream and looks back at Josh. "Is that *Josh*?" she asks me. The emphasis is code for: the guy you were so obsessed with that I thought a counselor was going to have to be brought in for an assist?

"Yes," I bob my head up and down to indicate it's *that* Josh.

Suzy smiles. This translates to: He's really cute and you're going to get lucky tonight!

"You said that you found *Ross*," I remind her.

Suzy grabs both our hands. "Come teach me how to play strip poker."

"Actually I'm not much of a poker player," says Josh, holding his ground.

"Me neither," I lie. I've been playing poker since I was seven, but why appear anxious when Suzy is going to close this deal for me?

"*Please*, you guys." She pulls us in the direction of the wide staircase that empties into the back of the living room. What might soon qualify as a three-alarm blaze is now roaring in the fireplace. The room was already hot and redolent of spilled beer, and now it's becoming filled with thick gray smoke.

Suzy is giddy with excitement, turning back and smiling every few seconds as she directs us to the second floor, and then up a narrow staircase that leads to a refinished attic. Eight kids are lounging around on oversized pillows in a dimly lit room with a lava lamp in the corner and music wailing from a stereo in the corner. Everyone is still fully dressed, and if the loud laughing and joking is anything to go by, no longer fully sober. A guy wearing khaki shorts, a frat house T-shirt, and a cowboy hat shuffles a deck of cards. There's the faint but distinctive aroma of marijuana, though given that the one hexagonal window in the room doesn't open, it's impossible to tell whether the scent is from tonight's group or previous parties.

"Are you outlaws here to play poker or are you delivering the pizza?" says the guy nearest the boom box, whom I recognize as Ross, Suzy's big crush.

Everyone laughs uproariously at this stupid joke. Suzy releases our hands and I come out from behind her. A girl named Jennifer and a guy named Kevin, both of whom I recognize from my freshman dorm, say, "I didn't know I was going to play against Hallie Palmer," and "Now things are really getting exciting."

It's not unknown for me to sit in on a dorm game and clean up a pot or two. Most of the kids aren't exactly strong opponents to begin with; however, they usually drink while playing, giving me an even greater advantage. People who booze while they bet tend not to fold nearly as early or often as they should.

The cowboy-hat guy calls for a game of five-card draw with deuces wild. Ross announces that we all have to start with our shoes and socks on or off.

Jennifer holds up her hand and says, "We didn't decide about underwear."

The four guys yell "*No*" to underwear while the five women shout "*Yes.*" "I'll do odds or evens with one of the girls," states Ross. The girls could argue this but they don't because some secretly want to play down to the nude. Let's face it, a girl doesn't join a game of strip poker unless she likes one of the guy players or she's incredibly drunk.

Suzy volunteers to throw out fingers against Ross, promptly loses the underwear option, and then conveniently remains sitting next to him.

Picking up my cards I find a pair of sixes and a wild two. With the chance to replace two cards, the prospect of four sixes! Though I don't receive another six or wild card, an ace comes my way. Kevin's three sixes made with a wild two have only a queen high and so I'm the winner. The others good-naturedly remove an article of clothing and throw it into the center of the circle. After four more rounds I've lost only my pants, while almost everyone else is down to their underwear, and Jennifer has also lost her bra. The girls nervously alternate puffs on cigarettes with long sips of beer. Between the cloud formed by their cigarettes and the stream of smoke rising from downstairs, the room is becoming more than hazy, and so I don't know how much we'll actually be able to see when people are fully naked.

Mr. Cowboy Hat, whom I've since found out is named Justin, is the first one required to throw in his underwear, but removes his Stetson instead. The girls cry foul.

"You'd better show us more than your side part!" exclaims Christine.

"There's no rule against hats," insists Justin. "You could have worn one."

"If that's the case then my ring and necklace count as articles of clothing," argues a braless Jennifer.

The more those two bicker the more everyone else roars with laughter. Between Josh placing his hand on my knee every few minutes and the good cards that keep coming my way, I decide that this must indeed be my lucky night.

"*Hall-ie . . .* " I hear my name echoing somewhere within the swirl of music, shouts of laughter, and a gauzy but pleasant alcoholic haze.

It can't be. It *cannot* be the voice that boomerangs through the garden at the Stocktons' and calls me in for dinner at the end of the day.

Sure enough, Bernard Stockton, my longtime mentor and summer employer, crawls toward the circle on his hands and knees, panting with exhaustion. Oh no—could there have been another breakup with Gil? They've been so happy since getting back together and adopting the two little Chinese girls. Or worse, maybe something terrible has happened to Olivia and Ottavio on their trip to Italy. A plane crash?

Bernard drops to the floor as if he's been crawling through the desert and finally reached an oasis. Covered in a heavy down parka with a scarf wrapped around his neck and carrying a fleece hat in hand, sweat pours off Bernard's face, his eyes are rimmed with red, and he's gasping for air. But something else is odd. Those aren't his usual gabardine wool winter slacks. They're navy blue silk pajama bottoms! Bernard *never* goes out of the house unless he's immaculately dressed and every salt and pepper hair is in place.

"Hallie!"

"Bernard!" Whatever is *he* doing *here*, right *now*?

"Heaven's to Betsy Bloomingdale." Bernard begins coughing uncontrollably and pounds his hand on the floor while catching his breath. "I'm tipsy and tripping and dying of asphyxiation without having imbibed nor inhaled." Bernard raises his head an inch. "And possibly betrothed—some woman thinks I'm George Clooney and kissed me solidly on the mouth. She has eyes like cherry strudel and appears to be riding high on everything but skates."

"Kimberly," everyone says in unison.

Jennifer grabs a T-shirt off the mound of clothes in the center of the circle and covers her bare chest. Otherwise the group doesn't appear bothered by the adult intrusion, at least after making certain it's no one from the dean's office or else the campus police on the prowl for underage drinkers.

"Hallie, I've been searching absolutely *everywhere* for you. Come on—we have to go!" Bernard doesn't so much as say hello to the rest of the kids, which is totally unlike him. "I don't want you to be alarmed," he says in a voice that suggests I should be very alarmed indeed, "but your father had a heart attack."

Huh? My dad—a heart attack—impossible! He's young and strong and not even forty! I sit there stunned.

With a certain amount of dramatic huffing and puffing Bernard rises to his feet. "We must go to the hospital *now*!" He enunciates the words as if talking to someone who can only lip read.

Not knowing what to say I stand up and walk toward him like an automaton. It's only when I reach the door that Bernard says, "It's rather chilly outside, you might want to consider pants."

Josh has anticipated this and dug my jeans from out of the clothing pile. After handing them to me he retrieves my socks and shoes from the corner of the room.

I quickly dress and we head toward the main floor. The entire house is now chock-full of people partying, swaying to music, and propped up against walls, their outstretched legs blocking the hallways and stairwells. Bernard is *pardonnez-moi*-ing every step of the way through this obstacle course while towing me along behind him. We finally reach the front door, but it takes another moment to push through a crowd of rowdy women who claim to have paid earlier. The heavyset doorman is effectively blocking their entrance and shouting, "Show me your beavers!"

Bernard looks questioningly at me. "Hand stamp," I explain. But it's too loud to hear anything, and so I hold mine up to Bernard's face and he nods in understanding.

Once we're outside Bernard continues to yell as if he's still competing with the music. "Gil is waiting in the car with the girls. I've been to so many different parties I don't even know where I am anymore."

"What did you park in front of?" I holler back, though it's quiet now but for a few shouts coming from a late-night snowball fight across the quad.

"There was a sculpture out front—like a giant toadstool."

"That's the science building," I say. "It's supposed to be a molecule or something."

I hurry Bernard in the correct direction and the fresh air clears my head slightly. "Is it serious?" I ask.

"I'm not sure. Your sister Louise phoned." We've been jogging for a few minutes, and it's not so easy to catch our breath. "You . . . can . . . call . . . her . . . from . . . the . . . car."

I locate the maroon Volvo that Bernard recently traded for his vintage silver Alfa Romeo parked across from the science building with its engine running, the exhaust puffing a cloud of gray smoke into the cold winter air.

The girls are asleep in their car seats in the back and I climb between them while Bernard dives into the passenger side. The moment I pull the door closed Gil shoves a cell phone in my ear and puts the car into gear so that we jump away from the curb.

My sister Louise is frantic on the other end of the line. "Hallie? Is that you?"

"Yeah," I exhale heavily.

"*Thank God* they found you! *Please* go to the hospital right away and find out what's going on. I'm stuck here with the kids. Every time the phone rings I practically faint." Louise sounds as if she's starting to cry, and that it's not for the first time over the past few hours. "I woke up and the paramedics were flying down the stairs with Dad on a stretcher and Mom threw a coat over her nightgown and yelled for me to watch the kids. Reggie's been screaming bloody murder. I finally gave him a bottle of regular milk. It'll probably kill him. Tell Bernard and Gil that I'm sorry to have woken them up, but I didn't know what else to do."

"No, it's fine." I'm suddenly feeling incredibly sober.

"I got hold of Eric about an hour ago," reports Louise. "He's taking a bus from Indiana."

"I'll go to the hospital, find out what's happening, and then call you right back." I click off the phone and let my head tip over backward.

"Don't worry," says Gil. "The new hospital has a terrific cardiac unit—state of the art."

"How old is your dad?" asks Bernard.

"Both my parents are thirty-nine." It's easy to remember because I just have to add nineteen to Eric's age.

"Oh, that's *young*," says Bernard. "He'll be fine. They can do quadruple bypasses and even replace valves with animal parts. We eat too much ham and bacon and then the surgeons give us pig aortas. It's one giant recycling system. If your heart can't be salvaged, then they just throw it away and stitch in a whole new one."

I certainly hope Bernard is right, but I fear that he's just trying to make me feel better.

© Denise Winters

ABOUT THE AUTHOR

♠

Laura Pedersen grew up near Buffalo and now lives in Manhattan, where she contributes to *The New York Times* and volunteers at the Booker T. Washington Learning Center in East Harlem.

Visit her Web site at www.LauraPedersenBooks.com.